# CONQUERED

## *Sleeping Giants II*

### *By*
### *Ally Fleming*

CONQUERED

This is a work of fiction. Characters, names, incidents, organizations and dialogue in this novel are either products of the author's imagination or are used fictitiously.

Cover Artwork Courtesy of Melody A Pond~ Cover Artist
(http://melodyypond.weebly.com)

To loyal fans and new readers. Enjoy the ride...

# PROLOGUE

*Memphis, Tennessee~ The Present*

He was due for a shave. Nathan Alberts studied his reflection in the oval mirror above the porcelain sink in his private washroom. To the naked eye, one couldn't tell that his perfect goatee; tinted dark to match his natural color, could stand a trim.

Nathan prided his appearance at all times...for all occasions. One couldn't afford to look anything other than one's best when one was partner in one of the most powerful organizations in the world.

Amusement had his mouth twitching then despite the situation.

"One of the most powerful organizations in the world," he mused.

Even in the safe barriers of his mind, he wouldn't tell himself that it was the *most* powerful. Hubris was a dangerous thing. Nathan's smile faded. God, he despaired, hadn't they suffered enough from the consequences of pride?

The GAN- Grodins Alberts Network- would never recover from this. That was another thought he'd share nowhere else but inside the barriers of his mind. He and his oldest friend had started the company when they were looking for their next/their *first* big score after leaving their jobs as medical supply salesmen.

Now, their dream was a thing of the past-not quite- but as good as. A feature broadcast weeks earlier had seen to that. Now the country; the world, knew what The GAN was beyond what he and his partner Lorne Grodins always wanted it to be. The *only thing* they'd wanted it to be.

The world would never view The GAN as anything more than a murder-for-hire organization that hid its foul deeds behind a governing board that was as revered as it was perverse.

No, Alberts thought, favoring himself with one last look in the mirror before he left the washroom. There was no coming back from this.

Already there were whispers in the air. It was only a matter of time before the authorities came looking to follow up on the allegations made during the broadcast. There was a time such a broadcast; though rep damaging, wouldn't have the repercussions he now feared. That was, however, when The GAN boasted a governing body that wielded strength enough to quash such allegations. Any inquiries made by authorities would've been silenced the instant they were voiced.

Now, it was The GAN's governing board, The Ten, that had been silenced and by the most unlikely of perpetrators.

Nathan sneered as those memories surfaced. They had done a good job with the cover up, he recalled. They damn well couldn't afford to have the authorities poking around in *that* mess.

But this...The GAN secrets now displayed for the world's consumption...there was no covering or *re*covering from that. After decades of searching for respect alongside power, Nathan Alberts realized he no longer gave a damn.

~~~

"They need to know and if not now, when?" Gerrick Ferguson's clear voice was as flat as his searing hazel gaze.

Daniel Schultz's stare and voice tone was as flat-as unreadable as his colleague's. "Do you have any idea how fast we'd be signing our own death warrants if we go this route?" he asked.

"Would we be signing our death warrants or putting a new spin on the organization?" Gerrick challenged.

Daniel's resulting laughter was short, crisp and without humor. "Do you think one side would get us a different outcome over the other?"

"Our earlier efforts haven't been successful, Dan," Gerrick quietly voiced the reminder. "We can't let this go on- what happened with Van Deer and Zubin is proof of that."

Daniel spared a moment to form a mental picture of Harris Van Deer and Grant Zubin, two GAN soldiers both responsible for a recent string of gruesome murders. Quickly, Daniel Schultz shook away the haunting faces. "Look Gerri, sharing this particular can of worms could have one side working to kill us as fast as the other," he cautioned.

Ferguson was already voicing his disagreement with a slow shake of his head. "Not all the monsters we created are without a sense of decency, Dan."

"And you're willing to take that as fact?"

Gerrick sighed, his gaze never wavering from the scene across the office. "At this point, Dan," he watched Nathan Alberts being lowered from where he'd been found dangling above his desk- a noose around his broken neck.

"At this point," Gerrick continued, "I'm more than willing."

# PART I

*Where we go is not determined by where we want to go*
*Marty Rubin*

# CHAPTER 1

*Las Vegas, Nevada~ 6 years earlier*

"I'll be in the car!" Berrill Clayton stalked toward the curving brick drive outside the spacious town home. The click of her pinprick heels gradually slowed before silencing altogether when she was only halfway to the vehicle.

Only then, did she slip out of the layer of stony confidence she'd been fortifying since the beginning of the nightmare she'd gotten her three friends involved in.

The use of the word 'nightmare' may've been a little presumptuous, she thought, mouth curving on a tremulous smile. She had a feeling that the nightmare aspect was only about to begin. God, why didn't she just tell that bitch to go to hell when she approached her with that envelope full of cash? An envelope full of cash and the method of repayment being by way of the oldest profession.

Berrill closed her eyes and spoke the answer inside her head. *Because you were broke, that's why, Stupid.* Ramen noodles and white bread- dry toasted when they were feeling fancy. That had been their nightly meal for the last 6 weeks. The money they'd taken to leave Virginia was all but a memory now. They'd all managed to secure jobs, but those incomes went pitifully short distances when work had to be scheduled around classes-and not even full loads, at that.

They'd lived comfortably, but frugally for about 3 years before frugal lost its allure and began to nudge against impoverished. They focused on working to keep a roof over their heads and some semblance of food in their stomachs. It had been the way of things for the last 4 years. College dreams had been scrapped long ago. College-Berrill snorted quietly. What a joke. A good intention, but a pipe dream without the dollars to fund it.

Loans were out of the question. Her friend Prin feared the applications would lead to their whereabouts. Why the fuck that mattered, Berrill had no idea...at first. It was a story best saved for another time anyway. There were bigger concerns at hand. Concerns along the lines of what the approaching evening would do to them- the toll it would take not only on their bodies, but on their emotions.

Sex for money. How did crossing that line shape a woman's view of herself? What kind and how many demons did it allow to fester?

"Hey?"

Berrill gave a jolt at the hand on her elbow. Stony confidence back in place, she fixed the man at her side with a smile and hoped it boasted the certainty she sure as hell didn't feel.

"You okay?" Caleb Stein could guess the answer even before the tall, caramel complexioned beauty nodded the affirmation. Her lush, mocha eyes held a cool confidence. Caleb however, had been on hand for enough of such trips to recognize the stricken look of a woman who had run out of options. It was a look he resented- resented the part he played in putting it there.

Still holding onto her arm, Caleb took a step closer. "Listen-" he broke off at the sound of the front door opening to release a tangle of female voices.

Berrill looked to the townhouse and her friends as they left Diversion. The brothel's owner, Dorinda Patterson, stood waving them off like a mother bidding her children a great day as they headed off to school.

Berrill guessed the four of them were in for an education of sorts. The thought made her want to vomit. She watched her friends Etienne Shaw, LuCarolyn Young and Prin Holland heading her way. The

10

chatter they'd shared with Dorinda silenced quickly once the door closed at their backs.

Berrill wondered if they were as terror stricken as she was. Their expressions practically screamed, Yes! She remembered the guy next to her then. Caleb. He'd introduced himself when he and his partner arrived at the brothel. Dorinda had been proud to tell them their 'dates' had sent a car and bodyguards to collect them. She'd said it like they'd earned a prize, Berrill recalled.

Caleb had taken hold of her arm. Now, he squeezed it. Berrill wondered if it was her nerves that had her imagining the sense of urgency she felt behind his touch.

"We're gonna take you there and bring you straight back," Caleb gave the explanation with soft encouragement. He slid a look to his partner Luke Robb who was already escorting the others into the back of the Mercedes Limo that would whisk them into the night.

"We'll take you to the hotel room door and we'll wait outside in the hall until you're...done."

Berrill gave a shaky nod. "Right," she cleared her throat on the ragged sounding word. "So um...do these things usually go smoothly?" Her tremulous smile made another appearance when she caught the truth in Caleb's pale gray eyes before he could mask it.

"It's fine if you want to lie," she said.

"Listen," Caleb's grip firmed on her arm once more as he tugged her a bit closer. "Just do what you have to and get out of there and never look back."

Berrill nodded, the gesture fueled by the same grim determination she heard in Caleb's voice. Never looking back was the only thing motivating her to see the night through.

***

"Berrill? Berrill?! Take this."

Berrill snapped to enough to hear Caleb Stein's voice again. It was later-much later and they were back in the car. Caleb and Luke had told them to stay there before they'd headed back into the hotel. They were back and she was just able to register that Caleb was pushing something into her hands. Discs?

"Put these in the bag," Caleb ordered when Berrill's eyes met his. He could see that the earlier stricken look had inched aside to leave

11

room for blankness-something utterly hollow. Caleb didn't know which rattled him more, the sight of her stricken or hollow.

Berrill made a mediocre attempt to take the discs. Caleb took it upon himself to put them into the bag that was already half filled with the discs they'd taken from the room...where they were being recorded.

It was then that other sounds began to register. Berrill heard her friends-LuCarolyn's breathing came out in shudders. Prin's silence seemed to carry on its own frequency. Etienne-Tee-, seemed to be the only one capable of speech.

"What are those?" Tee asked Caleb.

"From the hotel's main security hub. We needed to wipe all traces of you being there. We at least needed to hide your faces," Caleb said. "You have the discs from the room. There were cameras all over the hotel that could've caught you guys leaving-"

"And us helping you leave," Luke Robb added as he settled in behind the wheel.

'All traces of you being there,' the phrase started a loop inside Berrill's head. She would've loved to have wiped all traces of having been where she'd spent that night.

"The gun," she took Caleb's hand in a death grip. "The gun I gave you-"

"Shh...it's alright, it's alright," Caleb patted her hand until the hold eased. "I took care of it, don't worry. Now let's get you guys out of here."

Though it could've, in no way, been classified as a 'run of the mill' kind of night, the events of that evening had gone beyond anything Berrill had imagined or dreaded. There would be no forgetting any of it.

Her plans to never look back...well that was all shot to hell. Following a hearty round of drinks; she'd been sure would put her in a sublime state and ready for anything the night might bring, the overdone hotel suite had filled with 10 men. They'd arrived ready to receive their money's worth and they'd gotten it.

The evening started with a round of heavy groping, mingled with lurid chatter and demeaning compliments. Berrill thought she'd withstood it admirably. She could've chalked it all up as just an unpleasant experience were that all that was in store. It wasn't.

Hours later, she and her friends had been the party favors and enjoyed over every square inch of that tacky suite. No...there would be no forgetting that and yet...as nauseating as that experience had been, she would've considered herself a lucky woman had they been able to walk away at that point.

How had it all gone so completely off the rails? Berrill would've liked to have said that was all a blur, but that would've been a lie. She remembered everything with crystal clarity. The blood, the knives...there were even a few silenced gunshots. It was the *why* of it, though.

The way it had all started had Bear and, she supposed, her 3 dearest friends in the world, suspended in a state of confusion. Had all the tension and desperation of the last few months-

Ha! *Months*...if only her tension and desperation had merely been a recent occurrence. She'd fought that battle longer than she wanted to remember.

Still, she had to wonder if the evening of depravity had been the catalyst that set her-set them all-off simultaneously? They had just committed murder-multiple murders and left the scene wearing nothing but remnants of blood on their skin and the robes embroidered with the hotel's logo.

As if reading her mind, Prin asked what happened. Her voice was small, brittle even, Berrill thought. Nevertheless, the sound of it was a relief. Prin hadn't spoken since they'd found her being... enjoyed by one of their dates.

Perhaps it was finding Prin's blood on the sheets or the chains on the bed, that had set the spark that had Tee slicing the throat of the man with Prin and leading to the deaths of the others who lay slumbering contently after enthusiastic sex.

"We killed them," Prin said before anyone provided an answer.

Tee; sitting closest to Prin on the back seat, pulled her near. Squeezing Prin closer, Tee brushed a kiss across her temple and then smoothed a hand across her hair- a mane of natural honey wheat blonde. The tone, accentuated by honey brown skin and an unexpected cornflower blue gaze, gave Prin a rare look. In that moment however, it was a 'look' that exuded terror.

"We killed them all, honey," Tee hoped her words would reassure her friend that they were safe.

Prin's expression remained stricken. "Not all," she murmured.

LuCarolyn toyed with a coarse lock of her hair as her light eyes further dimmed under the weight of emotion. "Did we really do that?" she pulled her hand from her hair suddenly as if remembering what had

13

touched it. She studied her blood-stained palms as though she could still see the acts they'd carried out that night. "Why'd we-why'd we do that?"

"Seriously Lu?" Berrill heard herself snap. "Did you see what that muthafucka was doin' to Prin?"

"Bear. Don't." Tee urged, before LuCarolyn could form a retort.

Berrill closed her eyes, remorse immediately pooling. "I'm sorry, sorry," she whispered, tugging Lu close.

Silence carried in the dark, spacious rear section of the long car.

"I'm the one who's sorry. Sorry for tonight," Tee's voice was haunted, weary.

Berrill, Prin and LuCarolyn looked over in unease.

"Now it's *you* who needs to stop." Berrill used the same tone of reprimand Tee had moments earlier. "A lot of people are at fault for tonight. You aren't one of them."

"I don't know why or where it came from," Tee continued to dissect her actions. Shuddering, she raked her nails across the close crop of ebony waves capping her head. They carried a healthy lustre and almost matched her skin, a flawless molasses, for darkness.

"I just...I walked in that room and...saw what that garbage was doing to Prin-"

"Realized you had the strength to stop him and you did."

"Bear...they paid us to be there," Tee argued Berrill's point.

That was a truth Berrill wouldn't allow to weigh on her-she *couldn't* allow it. After all, what did it say about her? They didn't have to be there. So what if there was money to be repaid? They could've told Dorinda and her *ten* to go fuck themselves and hit the road. That she hadn't even suggested it to her friends...

"There were chains on the beds, weapons all over that trashy suite, whips...who knows what those assholes had planned for us when they woke up? They didn't pay us to be there for that," Berrill's words were biting-a testament to how pissed she was with herself. "We did what we did and we're done with it," she sighed.

"We're done with it," LuCarolyn reiterated.

Tee nodded slow, but didn't voice her agreement. Prin was silent as well.

Berrill leaned her head against the seat rest and wondered if she'd ever believe her own words.

***

### *Outside Kenwood, California~ 18 months later*

"Is it just me or is anybody else's head spinning?" To emphasize his despair Slayte Miltiades dragged a hand through the hoard of blue black curls crowning his head.

Grinning, Rutger Eliades' whiskey colored eyes sparkled with sly amusement when he clapped Slayte's shoulder. "You're just ditzy enough for that to be the case, but no, it's not just you. Patch, for the love of all, enough with the percentages already."

Patroclus Kostas gave an exaggerated sigh. "I've never met a group of people less interested in discussing the tons of cash they're about to make on top of the tons of cash they just made."

Rutger reciprocated Patroclus' sigh as though the question were a mystery for the ages. "As the only math prodigy among us, Patch, I'd say you're interested enough for all of us."

A calming rumble of laughter stirred among the 5 men looking out over the expanse of land- an unending sea of rolling green. Moments earlier, they'd all joked about being able to detect the hint of citrus in the air. The spot was located in the upper part of Sonoma Valley considered to be wine country. Therefore, no one argued that the fragrance detected was most likely accurate.

"It's a helluva place, Merc." Patroclus reached out to pat the back of the man who dwarfed his height by well over a foot.

Mercuri Nikolaides spread his hands and gave an exaggerated shrug. "It was Pope's eye for property that's responsible," he deferred to the other man who towered over Patroclus by a similar margin of height.

Pope Apostolou's ultramarine gaze seemed to glint more vibrantly against the late afternoon sunlight when he graced his friends with a satisfied grin. The gesture triggered the single dimple ideally spaced alongside a beautifully sculpted mouth.

"You said you wanted peace and quiet," Pope reminded Mercuri. "If you can't find it here, I'm fresh out of ideas."

Mercuri took another look over the property. "Nah...this is it."

Pope studied the area he'd scouted, though not with as much awe as the prospective buyer. "I don't get it," doubt narrowed his gaze. "All the shit you could buy now and all you want is a house?"

"This from the guy who already has three and in three different countries," Patroclus spoke out while everyone else laughed.

"And counting!" Slayte added.

"Investments." Pope clarified with haste. "For monetary purposes only."

"Well the place I want to put on this land will be for family purposes- a place we can call home wherever we are in the world- in whatever house we're in at the moment." Mercuri sent a playfully agitated look in Pope's direction before his face set into sober lines.

"Wherever we are, we'll know we've always got a place to call home."

Silence held for a full 30 second span before Slayte chuckled. "You're a real sap, you know?"

Mercuri merely shrugged, drew Slayte close. "Every idiot should have a sap for a friend."

Laughter held for a time, but the men all felt the weight of Mercuri's words.

"You're a good man, Merc," Rutger said.

"Damn right he is," Slayte added, "it's because of Mercuri that we're done. Done all the way."

"That's the damn truth," Pope scanned the property again. "If it wasn't for him, none of us would be standing here on five hundred plus acres and talking about putting a house on it."

They were true words that echoed of a chilling past-one they'd escaped (fought their way out of) thanks to Mercuri's planning and commendable strategizing. Not long ago, none of them could see beyond their lots in life- soldiers for hire. Not even for hire, actually.

The GAN never *hired* them. Never *asked* them to join up. They'd been more...indentured (enslaved). Perhaps that phrasing was more accurate. The GAN had practically raised them, trained them- molded them into experts at the most detestable of occupations- murder.

It was Mercuri who had seen a way out when a night like any other had ended in the brutal slayings of The Ten- The GAN's governing body. Such a bold move against a powerful entity like The GAN demanded retaliation.

Ten months after the murders, GAN soldiers descended on the home of the man held responsible. It had been Enrique Roya who often supplied The GAN's demands for diverse entertainment. He had provided the women who'd carried out the deed. Not only had they murdered The Ten, they'd left the scene with discs containing evidence of what had transpired and who had been present. Present, not only at the

16

scene of the crime but at the hotel itself. Such social circles, could have been damning to a great many high-profile careers.

In short, Roya had The GAN by the proverbial balls which made ending his life all the more necessary. They were going to lay waste to all the man held dear. His family at the center of the plan.

When Mercuri told him what he was planning, Pope thought his best friend had lost his mind. Still, Pope had to admit it was the gutsiest thing he'd ever heard of.

Many GAN soldiers felt the same and had Mercuri's back when the mission within the mission commenced. Having forewarned Roya of the impending danger, the man fled long before The GAN's arrival. To show his gratitude, he rewarded Mercuri and his closest friends with a monetary 'thank you'- a substantial 'thank you'.

Now, there they were, Pope thought as a bold, aromatic wind whipped black jaw-length waves about his face. He observed the land drenched beneath a low hanging California sun. They were there and it wasn't just Patroclus who seemed over-the-moon happy.

Mercuri, Slayte, even Rutger's lovably gruff persona seemed to reflect more mellowed shades. They'd all fought their way out of hell and come through better for it on the other side. It was like they were all done with it. Sure, he knew they still had their own personal demons to battle, but that particular demon-their sentence and subsequent escape from The GAN was one demon defeated. End of story. Done.

So why was he still harboring doubts? Because he didn't believe it? That's what all the crazed property buying was really about and that was a thing he'd admit to no one but himself.

He wanted to grab what he could, while he could. He took a closer look at his friends then- the four men he'd give his life for if it would save theirs. No way would he break their spirits with a dose of reality.

No way would he tell them he thought this was all folly- that they weren't 'done'-not even close. This was only a break, an intermission, before the real battle began.

# CHAPTER 2

### *Las Vegas, Nevada~ 6 years earlier*

Christopher Morrow's shamrock green stare glazed over from worry to fury when he saw the two burly men heading his way. Spreading his hands, expectancy wedged in alongside fury.

"Where is it?" He hissed.

"Take it easy," Jake Grodins, the fairer of the two, urged. "It's safe," he promised.

"Where?" Morrow demanded.

"We were just upstairs checking out the area," Brody Alberts, the second of the two, explained. "We left the bag in the suite, the surveillance closet's there."

"Jesus," Morrow looked faint. "That's where they'll be later."

Heirs to The GAN fortune, Brody Alberts and Jake Grodins exchanged grins and knowing smiles.

"Just calm down," Brody insisted. "Upstairs is the safest place for it, trust us."

"Exactly what is this 'leverage' you think will get us what we want?" Jake sneered.

Morrow wasn't offended by the clear disbelief. "Just trust me when I say it's good. You'll know in due time."

"Well trust *us* when we say you don't want something that's supposedly *that* valuable floating around down here," Brody retorted.

Morrow bristled, but didn't argue the point. Besides, Alberts was right he thought, eyeing the hotel lobby with cool disdain. He fixed a glare in the direction the men had just come from. "Is your guy in place?" he asked.

"We're all set," Jake's brown eyes sheened with suspicion. "You sure you wanna go this route? Isn't Tommy Doyle your guy?"

"Thomas Doyle is my employer," Morrow's tone was dry, callously so. "His time has passed."

"If that's the case," Jake posted up on the toes of his boots and seemed to gear up to play devil's advocate. "Won't people see that and vote him out?"

Morrow's smile resembled one a parent might reserve for a child who had amused them. "How lucky you are not to know how democracy really works. Mr. Grodins. Senator Doyle is the incumbent, an incumbent who's held his position for the last eighteen years. A senator's constituents rarely vote him out of office unless he's publicly disgraced which would be bad for us. Terms last six years and we're on the brink of a new election. Unless the fucker dies, he'll be gearing up to be sworn-in for a new term. I'm not waiting another six years."

"What makes you think you'll get his seat?" Brody asked. "You're only an aide, right?"

"I see you two also have no idea about the idiocy of voters," Morrow shook his head. "I'll ride in on the good senator's coattails. In situations like this, I'd be just as good as the incumbent. Everyone knows we're like this," he twisted his middle and index fingers to indicate closeness.

"Many view me as Doyle's apprentice. That, plus sympathy over the man's *hoped for* demise… I'm a shoe-in to take the seat."

"Hope you're right," Jake drawled, still sounding unconvinced.

"Gotta admit, it's risky," Brody added.

"Can you guys think of a better way to get this product marketed? The senator's high moralistic code has cost him a lot of friends over the years."

Jake grinned. "High moralistic code?" He thought of the man he'd seen on more than one occasion with his face in the pretty crotches of countless whores.

Morrow shrugged. "It's the public image that matters, and mostly during election time. We've got a lot of support for this product. With the senator gone, it's only a matter of time before those who followed his lead come over to our side. Just make sure your man's up for the job and not getting lost in the night's entertainment."

Again, Brody and Jake exchanged smiles, those less grim and more relaxed.

"Jake, I think the Senator's aide could stand to lose himself in some of the...night's entertainment," Brody moved to take Morrow's elbow.

"Shouldn't we wait to make sure everything goes smooth?"

"Don't worry, Senator," Jake grinned, seeming to appreciate the man's unease. "It's all good."

~~~

It was most definitely not 'all good'. Morrow stood cursing himself hours later. Awe had rendered his jaw slack, his mouth dry as he studied the scene across the nearly deserted lobby. While the special hotel's varied sex salons were exceptional, they hadn't been mind blowing enough for him to forget the task at hand.

No one had heard a peep from the group in the penthouse suite and Morrow had grown more than a little antsy. This had to go off without a hitch. Doyle had to die if his plan had the slightest chance of working. His plans might be dead in the water anyway if what was transpiring across the lobby, meant what he thought it did.

If he weren't dead sober, Morrow would've sworn he'd been seeing things. He wasn't. There was no mistaking the sight of the four women all garbed in long white robes, leaving the hotel. One carried a distinctive black bag with a chrome bottom.

"Oh Jesus," Morrow moaned.

20

# CHAPTER 3

### *Burlingame, California~ The Present*

Burlingame was about a half hour's drive from San Francisco and the place Berrill Clayton had called home for almost 6 years. When she, Tee, LuCarolyn and Prin left behind the madness of Vegas, they decided to try their luck further west.

Trying their luck was easier given the fact that they'd each left Las Vegas millionaires thrice over. Enrique Roya, Dorinda Patterson's boss; and the go-to man for establishing high class entertainment for high class clientele, had been surprisingly grateful when he'd discovered Berrill and her friends hadn't walked off the job with only the robes on their backs.

Roya had been more than a little interested in the contents of the bag they'd smuggled out with them. What he'd seen on the discs inside, was something he was willing to pay dearly to acquire. The young women in possession of the valuable information weren't so dazed over the night's events that they didn't realize the seriousness of their situation. Given that, they were unwilling to hand over leverage that might very well be their only bargaining chip.

It was a bargaining chip that was valuable not only with the authorities, but with those seeking to avenge the deaths they were responsible for. When the girls arrived in California, they arrived with

21

the discs as well. As Prin nor LuCarolyn wanted to be within a foot of them, the bag and its contents remained in Berrill's and Tee's care. After a while, Berrill became the sole caretaker. It was the sensible move considering the security of the place she called home.

New found wealth, had allowed Tee to start an interior design business. LuCarolyn used her portion to wisely invest, though she made her living in Hollywood- a career path in which she thrived. Prin had taken barely a quarter of her portion which was no big surprise. She'd repaired the relationship with her estranged parents and started collecting on the substantial allowance they provided her.

Berrill wanted space and a business that was something altogether different. Eclipsing pines formed a natural fence around a vast outlay spanning 60,000 acres. Besides an astounding 10,000 sq ft. estate, the property boasted another marvel which made it a perfect place to secure what was most valuable to Bear and her friends.

Bear Arms Gun Ranch provided generous spacing for indoor and outdoor target practice. Defensive firearm use training was popular with law enforcement professionals across the state. Bear Arms had gained its immense popularity however, for its free range shooting packages. Armed with the most advanced weaponry-loaded with paintballs or rubber bullets- participants in groups of four or more set out on missions to take down opposing groups.

Participants were required to complete their missions within a specified timeframe and were limited to no more than 3 missions per week. The shooting soirees were the ranch's most popular ticket. Groups had their run of the entire ranch over the course of a four day weekend. Registration included accommodations at the ranch's exclusive lodge. Missions ran from dawn to dusk. The group with the fewest members hit, won a complimentary ranch weekend and first refusal to take part in the next soiree.

Berrill Clayton was a woman unafraid to toot her own horn. She'd damn well earned the right to. She'd had to demean herself and get bloody to do it, but she'd damn well earned the right.

~~~

"I've damn well earned the right," Bear muttered, silently cursing the fact that she still needed to encourage herself with that phrase after 6 years following a lifetime spanning 31 years.

Though old ghosts had made room for newer ones, the fact had not rendered her a shell. Moreover, she was a capable woman at the helm of a respected business most people believed had been envisioned by men.

Sighing, Bear considered her present attire and wondered whether a respected business was worth the discomfort.

*California Business Magazine* was a big fucking deal and a respected entity that carried undeniable weight. Each year, the publication devoted its glossy, high quality pages to a photo spread featuring the best of the state's entrepreneurs. Bear's shoot was that day. She had been part of the CBMs Best In Business spread many times. Now, she had made the cover.

Hence the attire which; while not actually uncomfortable, was far from Bear's preferred style of dress. The gown was a creation of silk, satin and chiffon in tones of beige and cream. The empire bodice was a twist of fabric that accentuated a generous bustline that appeared more ample given the slender frame it adorned. The folds of the gowns skirt swept the ground in a shimmer of beige beneath a cream chiffon draping that flowed into an elegant train.

It was a killer dress, but Bear would've given anything for a pair of worn jeans and a T-shirt. Still, she was content. Thankfully CBMs head photographer had a playful streak. His concept had called for Bear's 'killer' dress to be offset by a pair of her favorite hiking boots.

~~~

"Mr. Apostolou?" Shaun Oates approached the man who stood just outside the designated area for the photo shoot. He approached with a measure of caution. Shaun wasn't one to scare easily, but his trusty sixth sense warned it would be unwise to sneak up on (to *try* to sneak up on) the man in his sights.

Pope turned, eyes narrowed amid mid-morning sun as a smile curved his mouth. "Mr. Oates," he accepted the man's extended hand for a shake. "Lively morning," he took a look at Oates' dapper tux. "Am I underdressed?" he tugged one cuff of the black shirt he wore with a steel blue suit coat and matching trousers.

Shaun seemed confused for only a half second before glancing at his attire and grinning. "The photographer wants group shots, he's going a little overboard setting the scene."

23

Pope turned back to observe the bustle of people and camera equipment along one side of the property's east end. "Looks like a big deal," he noted.

"Agreed," Shaun's grin spread. "The boss is being featured in the magazine. She's the cover girl."

A smile hinted at Pope's mouth. "She sounds like quite a lady. Guess I should've picked a better day to try meeting with her for a tour."

"Today would've been a perfect day actually," Shaun squinted against the sun while taking in the excitement. "The shoot had to be rescheduled at the last minute, Ms. Clayton had some things going on that she needed to handle."

Pope didn't need to guess at what those 'things' might involve. He knew well enough. The GAN news feature over a month ago; put in place with a little help from his old friend Mercuri Nikolaides, had sent many people into a tailspin.

Though he was equipped with his own share of the details into the matter, Pope could only imagine how the revelations in that news broadcast had affected the woman he'd stood admiring for the last 10 minutes.

10 minutes...Pope felt his jaw tensing over the inaccuracy. Berrill Clayton had been on his mind since they'd met, er-encountered-one another over a month ago at his favorite restaurant. The extraordinary ultramarine of his stare, harbored a more jolting quality as he followed Berrill across the portion of her yard that then resembled a photography studio.

"So what are my chances for at least getting an introduction?"

"Quite good, actually," Shaun included a nod in response. "She loves meeting new clients especially when they come with the kind of business you're offering." He looked down suddenly at the mobile vibrating in his hand and grimaced following a brief check of the screen.

"They need me over there, but this is the last series of shots," Shaun explained. "We've been at this since last night but we should be wrapping in another twenty or so. I should be able to get you in to see her then if you don't mind waiting?"

"No problem. I appreciate it."

Shaun waved toward the patio. "Help yourself to anything there. It's the least crazy place around."

"Got it." Pope accepted another of Shaun's handshakes and then made his way to the covered patio.

The L-shaped structure boasted ceramic tiled roofing and spanned the southern and eastern ends of the stunning house. The area was furnished with wide, cushioned seating that made for a comfortable and breezy, waiting place.

Pope helped himself to one of the beers on tap at the hot and cold beverage bar provided in the patio's kitchenette area. He settled down, content to watch the shoot wind up. Looking on, he returned to Shaun Oates' comment regarding the kind of business he was offering.

Of course the business offered was just a ruse to get closer to the woman occupying his thoughts with unrelenting prowess. He'd done his best to keep his distance after they'd parted ways at The Rascal. After learning who she was connected to, he'd commanded himself to hold back. That was especially true after the broadcast that had spilled many of The GANs darkest secrets.

He was done waiting now. Besides, he knew very well that there was never an absolutely perfect time to do anything. There was always a new challenge, a new battle to fight, a new fire to douse. He saw Berrill Clayton and, God help him, he wanted her.

She was a type he tended to steer clear of. It had nothing to do with her race. He'd lost count of how many times he'd indulged himself in the arms of a black woman. Berrill Clayton, with her skin the tone of dewy caramel, was a treat he very much wanted to sample.

Unfortunately, she was both strong-willed and outspoken. That much he'd gathered from their meeting in The Rascal's lounge area. The qualities, though admirable, were two he tended to avoid when choosing his next bedmate.

For Pope Apostolou, there was never an absolutely perfect time to do anything except fuck. It was a pleasure he'd pretty much denied himself over the last few years. He'd been more interested in acquiring every piece of land he could scope out. Now that he was actually working to draw sex back into his lifestyle, he had no desire to spoil that kind of perfect time with the strong-willed and outspoken.

He'd *had* no desire for such things. Now...well now he didn't know what the hell had changed or why it had.

Bullshit. He knew why it had. The 'why' was sex. The 'why' was usually sex. Hadn't that attraction tugged and powerfully when he'd first seen her lose her temper during the phone call he'd walked in on when they met? Was that all it took? Had it been so long since he'd enjoyed a woman that a loss of temper was all it took to have him wanting to toss her into the nearest bed.

He took a steep swallow from the long-necked bottle, sighing when the brew relieved a measure of the heat inside his chest. She'd probably try to beat the shit out of him if he was just honest with her and told her what he really wanted. She'd have every right to do just that and would he really be honest giving her that line? He wouldn't admit that any of his recent uncertainty questioning his outlook on women, had anything to do with what Mercuri had found with Berrill's best friend Tee.

Etienne Shaw, all 5'2 inches of her, had thrown Mercuri for a loop the moment he'd set eyes on her. They'd been going strong since that moment and Pope was sure Mercuri would be going ring shopping soon, if he hadn't already.

Pope couldn't be happier for his old friend, but such things weren't for him. He didn't have the time for it.

*Mercuri does.* Pope gave a silent snarl for the voice issuing the helpful reminder, to shut up. *He* didn't have time for it. Nor did he have the patience- it wasn't how he was built. He had such a hard time with the strong-willed and outspoken because he was every bit of that. Long ago, he'd convinced himself that no woman could match him there- not in the way that would captivate and make it all worth his time.

Was Berrill Clayton's display of temper all it had taken to have him *this* infatuated? He saw the object of his current desire being positioned for her next shoot and he smiled. She was a gorgeous little thing. He supposed she would be considered tall by most standards. Those standards fell far short when countered by his own 6'8. She was leggy though, slender yet built...Yes, it had to be the sex- the lure of another conquest.

Pope stretched his legs, reclined a bit more in the wide Adirondack chair he'd selected on the patio. Yes, the lure of another conquest was a much easier concept to handle than anything more.

Besides, *anything more* was dangerous. As he'd already noted, there was always a new challenge, a new battle to fight, a new fire to douse.

***

## *Memphis, Tennessee~*

"You and I both know it was Pope and the rest of those bastards behind this. Those sluts wouldn't have known to pull Rand's name out of a hat, let alone reveal the choice bits of info that show leaked." Jake Grodins ranted, referring to Randall Cafrey, GAN Alum and current VP of Programming for the Feature News Network.

Cafrey's award winning news show *In Scope*, had broken the story that had become the latest in a string of publicized scandals.

Brody Alberts hissed a curse and shoved out of the easy chair he occupied behind the big desk in the room. The latest publicized scandal had been his father's suicide two weeks earlier in that very room. The room used to be Nathan Alberts' office.

"Pope and the rest of those jackasses may've set the story in motion," Brody growled, "but those sluts were at the top of things. The exchange, the hit would've gone off without a hitch had they not gone crazy and murdered the room."

"You still buyin' that they murdered them all? All ten?" Jake's expression was as dubious as his tone of voice.

Brody gave a flip shrug. "I don't see how there's any question. Besides, Zoo would've said something, right?"

Jake shrugged that time. "Maybe. Maybe not. Maybe he was cool with ducking for cover and letting them handle it."

Brody looked stunned. "Why didn't you ever ask him about it?"

"Would you?" Jake was incredulous, his mouth curved on an outraged smile. "The man was psychotic. We were there over a month ago, remember? You saw what he did to Roya."

Brody went silent as he dug up the gruesome memory of Grant Zubin slicing Enrique Roya's throat with one of his beloved carving knives. He put the memory into a deeper hole and cleared his throat. "You said he *was* psychotic. Do you think he's dead?"

"No one's heard a peep in over a month from him or Van Deer and those two were thick as thieves."

"What about Caleb or Luke?" Brody argued. "Maybe they-"

"Cale and Luke have been on vacation for the last month. You know as well as I do, that we aren't prone to leaving breadcrumbs when we split for sun and fun. They're dead, Brody." Jake said in a resolved tone. "My brother and his cocksucking friends are totally responsible." He referenced his half brother Rutger Eliades.

27

"They're responsible for whatever happened to Van Deer and Zubin just like they were responsible for putting together what happened at that hotel. We already know Patch was supposed to handle taking out my old man and yours." Jake prowled the office, massaging his neck.

A muscle flexed in Brody's jaw. There was no denying that bit of intel. Patroclus Kostas had admitted as much when they'd tracked him down living the quiet life in New England. They'd seen to it that he was now living the quiet life 6 feet under.

"So what now?" Brody spread his hands, let them fall to his sides in a resounding slap. "We would've had a real shot at taking charge of this place six years ago had it all gone as planned."

"What do you think your old man has in store for you?"

Brody looked ready to laugh off his old friend's question. "I prefer not to think about it. If the S.O.B.was anything it was unpredictable."

"When's the last time you heard from Morrow?"

Brody gave into a grin, but the gesture was hollow. "The senator's finally gotten around to doing what I expected him to do- not returning my calls."

"Son of a bitch," Jake switched his neck massage to one at his temples while reclining on the back of a gleaming brown leather sofa. "What'd he say the last time you talked to him?"

"That he was working on a plan to recover what we lost and it wouldn't do to have a lot of ears involved."

"What the fuck does *that* mean?"

"Beats me, that's all he'd say."

Jake snarled a curse and slammed a fist to palm. "Circumstances are dire. I'd say it's long past time for our old partner in crime to ante up on the details."

Brody gave a full shrug then. "He's not returning my calls, remember?"

"No prob," Jake drawled. "I've always preferred the face to face approach."

***

"Guys don't forget! The tuxes leave when the photographers do!" Bear sang the reminder from her relaxed pose in the cushioned scoop chair where she'd spent the last half hour of the magazine shoot.

"Seriously Boss? After all we did to make you look good out here?"

Bear laughed, but didn't look up from where she worked on her phone. She'd grabbed the wide mobile within 60 seconds of the photographer announcing they were wrapped.

"Thanks Skip!" She called to her lead assault weapons instructor Skipper Autry. "And thanks to the rest of you!" Her voice carried well across the busy yard.

"I appreciate you guys wearing the monkey suits. You looked adorable in them, but your checks will be devastated if they aren't back on the truck in an hour's time!"

"Utter destruction?" Skip, still devoted to his unofficial role as the group's spokesman, set his attractively weather beaten face into a skeptical mask. "Or just slight shock?" He finished the query.

"Total annihilation," Bear looked up from her phone to favor the grinning redhead with a sly smile.

Skip replied with a quick salute. "Tuxes back on the truck in an hour, guys!"

With the soothing rumble of laughter and conversation on the air, Bear returned to her phone. She'd managed to put in 3 minutes worth, before she was interrupted again.

"I'm about to make your day."

"You already have," Bear didn't look up when she heard Shaun Oates' voice overhead. "Just keep standing there and blocking out all that sun," she told the man.

"I can do better than that. There's a guy waiting who wants to book the ranch for a weekend for a friend of his."

"Great," Bear's voice was light with the satisfaction new business always brought. Still, her major focus was the phone.

Brows beginning to knit, Shaun rubbed his nape where his cap of fuzzy auburn curls tapered. He then squatted next to his boss' chair. "He's already put in a deposit- the wire transfer came through this morning."

"Great," a hint of laughter colored Bear's voice then. "Have him talk to booking and make sure we have the dates to accommodate his request."

"Bear," Shaun put his palm over her phone, "his deposit was fifty thousand dollars." Satisfied he had her attention then, Shaun pushed to his feet.

"Fifty K?" Her voice was like stone. "What the hell does he think he's buying?"

Shaun's guileless grin broke free on his round handsome face. "A weekend at the business on the cover of California Business Magazine, that's what."

Bear snorted, hackles rising as they tended to do when she encountered people who squandered sizable portions of their wealth, instead of using it to make statements that mattered.

"I'll tell you what he thinks he's buying," Settling back deeper in the chair, Bear threw her leg over the side. The cut of the dress protected her modesty. "He thinks he's gonna plunk down his wad and come out here for his long weekend to have us jump through all kinds of crazy hoops. Elitist jackass. How many times have we dealt with folks like this?"

"Come on, Bear you're probably as rich as he is."

"Only I wouldn't drop fifty k of my hard earned money for a weekend I don't even know if I can book or not. You know what that says to me? It says he expects us to jump every time he makes some stupid request like letting his grandkids use our rifle collection to play cops and robbers."

"Actually, I was just hoping it'd get me the courtesy of a tour from the owner herself."

Recognizing the voice of the gentleman currently under discussion, Shaun's back went rigid beneath the rented tuxedo that was suddenly sweltering beneath the midday sun. He worked to soften the smile that felt as stiff as his shoulders and then turned to offer the man a nod.

The move gave Shaun the chance to regard the potential client with a mix of admiration and pity. Few had the nerve to interrupt, let alone approach his boss when she was in the midst of a rant. Shaun observed the man who was focused on the woman seated quietly then, but who Shaun guessed had one hell of a tongue lashing in mind. He then felt another element wedge in- amusement.

Shaun was sure to wipe away any trace of it before he turned back to his boss and made the introductions.

"Berrill Clayton, Pope Apostolou."

# CHAPTER 4

"Thank you, Shaun."

Like a man reaching out for a life vest, Shaun accepted Bear's permission for him to excuse himself.

"Shaun," Pope spared an appreciative smile for the man before looking back to his employer. "Got 'em well trained, don't you?" He glanced in the direction Shaun Oates had all but run toward.

Bear maintained her relaxed pose on the chair. "I like a man who knows his place."

"I'm afraid I never learned that trick."

"Obviously," Bear gave herself a moment to study the work of visual excellence before her eyes. God, how tall was he? It wasn't the first time she'd wondered. That day, standing beneath the brilliance of a high California sun, he cast a more formidable presence. She realized that he was patiently waiting on her to complete her assessment and she smoothly, albeit reluctantly, retasked her thoughts to the discussion requiring her participation.

"You seem to have a knack for eavesdropping on my conversations, Mr. …" She winced and snuggled her bottom a little deeper into the chair "Apos-stow or stew? Shaun's got such a way with pronouncing people's names- I'm afraid I might massacre yours."

"Stow-stress is on the third syllable. Apostolou," he supplied without hesitation and waited on her to make the connection. He could all but see the coincidence hitting home and felt the tug of attraction stir same as it had when he'd first met her. The mocha hue of her gaze was so lush, he thought he could drown in it if given the chance.

"Apostolou," Bear nodded during the pronunciation, noting its uniqueness. "Italian?"

"Greek."

"Right...one of my best friends is dating a guy whose Greek-Nikolaides? Mercuri Nikolaides- know him?"

He moved closer then and Bear prided herself on not panting. Her disappointment weighed in over the fact that he'd bound his hair that day. The low ponytail only emphasized the patient craftsmanship of a darkly beautiful face. Still, she'd have enjoyed seeing the jaw length waves of black framing it.

She had to wonder how long a woman lasted in this man's presence before throwing herself at him. Silently, she threatened herself with bodily harm if she so much as swayed in her chair.

"Shipping guy, right?" Pope was saying. "Yeah, I've heard of him. I always follow those who give the rest of us Greeks a good name," he waited, watching her enchanting face closely to see if she'd find it worth her time to question him further on that point. There was an inward sigh of satisfaction for him when she appeared to decide against it. Though remaining mute on just how well he knew the esteemed Mr. Nikolaides didn't sit well with him, Pope decided to worry later about the ethical ramifications of his decisions.

"So are you saying you're a Greek without a good name?" Bear had already moved on to a new topic. She took the time to size him up while he considered her question, easing his hands into his trouser pockets as he sidled closer to her chair.

Christ, he was a big son of a bitch. *No swooning, B*, she heard the silent command languish inside her head.

"Well I already told you I have a hard time staying in my place. Guess that would put me in the category of Greeks who could use someone to make them look good."

Gathering the folds of her gown, Bear pushed elegantly from the suede scoop chair and put it between she and the giant who had so boldly invaded her space. When he smiled, her eyes fixed on his-brilliant sea blue orbs deep set beneath long brows black as pitch. Somehow, she resisted curling her hands over the back of her chair or even fisting them at her sides. She relied on her suspicions to keep her level.

"I don't buy that you came all the way out here just to become a new client, Mr. Apostolou." Bear saw the probing intensity of his gaze give way to something lighter- Surprise? Amusement?

Feeling a bit more at ease then, she folded her arms at her chest and waited patiently for that stunning gaze of his to complete its survey of her breasts elevated a smidge by the move.

"I have lunch in a place I rarely visit-"

"You should," he inserted.

"And you're there."

"It's my favorite place."

"And I find you eavesdropping."

"It was an open space. No door."

"And now here you are. Coincidence? No one drops fifty k for a tour."

"They do when they want it from you." Pope saw some of the confidence eeek out of her expression and immediately regretted his response. What's more, he regretted trying to get her attention by using the business she'd had to demean herself to build.

"I'm not for sale," her glare was as frosty as the brief but meaningful phrase.

"I promise it wasn't my intention to imply that you are," sincerity rang true in his expression and the canyon depths of his voice.

"Oh I believe you, Mr. Apostolou," her smile was tight, knowing. "So why don't we continue on this level of honesty and discuss who really sent you here."

***

*Harve de Grace, Maryland~*

"I appreciate you coming up, Coop."

Senator Edgar Cooper squeezed the younger man's hand in a firm clasp. "No trouble at all, Chris. 'Specially when I'm out for fishing. By the way, I'd like to see you on the next outing, so would a few of our other colleagues."

Senator Christopher Morrow's grin developed traces of curiosity. "Are folks worried about me?"

"Nah, nah, nothing like that," Cooper waved a pair of beefy hands. "Only we've all been there, kid. The first election after the freshman term. We all know how it is to be on edge, wondering if you've got what it takes to do it again- secure the voters' trust and reclaim the seat."

Morrow dropped his gaze, nodded. It was an election year and though his term had been a fairly successful one, he hadn't accomplished half the things he'd wanted to. Not on a personal level anyway.

"I appreciate your concern, Coop," Morrow told the 3-term senator whose hand he shook. "But I have to admit I'd feel a helluva lot better with Doyle here to help me navigate."

Cooper's rotund frame shook when he laughed. "My boy! If Tommy were here you wouldn't need to worry about being navigated!"

Hearty laughter livened the hall.

"On that note, I'll be sayin' goodnight to you." Cooper reached out to shake Morrow's hand again. "Should I call with details on our next trip?"

"I'm actually planning to head back to the home state for a few weeks. Catch up with you when I get back?"

"Sounds good!" Cooper gave Morrow's shoulder an approving clap. "Just don't spend all your time campaigning. The invite you wanted me to wrangle from my friends out there should help with that, eh? Go get some of that California sun- it'll do you good. Might even do some good for that marital status of yours."

"Oh yeah?" Morrow voiced the query in a chuckle.

"You can hold off on that 'til after the election I suppose, but then use the time to find yourself a lady to give a ring to. Hell, at least find somebody to take with you to that shindig," Cooper leaned closer to shrug bushy brows at his younger colleague. "Fancy parties are a sure fired way to get a yes to a marriage proposal."

"Marriage..." Morrow drawled with exaggerated slyness. "That another trick to keeping the seat secured?"

"It was in my time, son." Cooper sounded nostalgic. "That's not so much the case, these days. Folks are still comforted by the idea of voting for a family man, but the allure of the single man is quite the draw. When he's got some cute 'lil thing on his arm, they're even more intrigued."

34

"So long as he doesn't have too many, right Coop?"

The tease stirred the elder Senator's jovial laugh and then he was clutching Morrow's hand in another shake.

"Be seein' ya, kid!"

Morrow saw his colleague to the front door where the man was met by members of his security and escorted to the imposing SUV idling in the brick drive. Following one last wave, Morrow headed back inside the sprawling 2 story he'd called home since acquiring his seat. There, he dropped the facade of the easy going young senator.

"Fat fuck," Morrow hissed when he entered the den.

"Having problems with the Gentleman from Washington State?" teased the man seated in one of the high-backed black leather chairs before the tall windows.

Morrow bounded over to a black chrome bar cart trimmed in gold. "Where's it written that you have to socialize with your co-workers?" He waved an envelope which he dropped to an end table near the bar. "At least all those hints I dropped were worth it."

"The way the game's played," Rich Lehman sighed from the chair where he worked at his tablet.

"It's bullshit," Morrow tossed back the bourbon he'd poured, smiling in approval as the liquid awakened his gullet. "At least the clown will lay off a while. I told him I was headed home- campaign trail and all."

Lehman nodded, his eyes still fixed on the tablet screen. "We're gonna be hitting it hard. I've just been making sure there aren't conflicts with your upcoming events out there."

Morrow refilled the stout glass with another hit of the bourbon and then made his way across the room. Standing before the room's floor to ceiling windows, he absorbed the view of the pier leading across the Susquehanna River from his backyard. Contentment slid through him as it often did when he studied his boat docked there. The spoils of success, he thought. He'd been determined to have far more to show for it than a sailboat by the time it was all over.

"Thanks Rich," he told his event manager before taking another taste of the liquor. He sipped lightly instead of devouring it all in one long gulp. "Jer's gonna make a fine campaign manager once he learns the ropes, but I thank you for having his back until then."

Rich nodded, smiling at the mention of his younger brother Jerome Lehman. He shut down the tablet. "It can be a nightmare keeping the office running smooth. Then there's dealing with the press and staff. It'll be a real load off his shoulders to not have to worry over event schedules and locations," he shrugged. "Besides, this was the part I enjoyed most when I had the job, so it's great to do it fulltime."

"Well I appreciate all of it," Morrow raised his glass in toast. "Your brother damn well has his hands full out there with this Berrill Clayton mess."

Lehman's expression tightened. "Any new developments?"

"Nothing more since what was revealed during the *In Scope* broadcast," Morrow helped himself to more bourbon. "The silence isn't doing anything to boost my confidence though. At least getting chummy with that fat bastard Cooper was worth it." He strode to the end table, reaching for the envelope containing the invite Edgar Cooper had pulled strings to obtain.

"Think she'll honor it?" Lehman asked.

Morrow grimaced, regarding the now empty glass as though he had intentions to hurl it through the window. "I'll worry over Ms. Clayton when the time comes. Right now, it's a matter of principle with her. She wasn't gonna let me set foot there given all the bad blood between us." He set the glass down hard on the end table and moved past it. "Now more than ever, I'm desperate to get some eyes on that place."

"You've done it before," Lehman noted.

"Yeah...the first of my mistakes."

"You couldn't have known it would go down that way."

"But when it did," Morrow stroked his round jaw and bristled. "When it did, I should've kept quiet instead of trying to use what happened to launch a search for what she stole. That definitely didn't put me on her list of favorite people."

"Is it really so important to have it back?" The potent shade of Lehman's gaze lent urgency to his question. "We don't even know if she still has it. Three years is a long time."

"Yeah..." Morrow spent half a minute pondering that aspect before shaking off his doubts. "But I can't walk away from all the work and time it took to get it. Besides...the ones left, still hold the kind of power we need." He gave Lehman a hopeful look. "Do you know what that kind of leverage could be used to accomplish?"

"You could always reacquire it," Lehman's response was tinged with the same kind of hope.

"It took us long enough to get it the first time," Morrow argued. "The people we had to put in place to make it all possible...we aren't going to have it all come together that way again," he smirked, leaning against the window to gaze out at the pier hazy beneath a sky filling with clouds.

"Coop would be easy enough, the babbling shit. All it'd take is joining him on one of his fishing trips to get what I'd need. But the others..." Morrow shook his head again. "After what happened in Vegas, it'd take too much cajoling, reassurances and...fuck...*money* to convince them to put together another batch of that kind of leverage. I've invested too much to walk away from this."

"It could come to that, you know?" Lehman turned on the chair to study his employer. "Berrill Clayton giving you an invite to her soiree is one thing. You being able to get out there- use what Duncan found out about where she keeps that bag...well that's another thing entirely. Not to mention, the bag actually being where Duncan saw it."

Morrow began a slow pace of the den. "The problem is that I've spent too long pussy footing around this. As soon as I have a way set, I'm stopped in my tracks. Bolder moves are needed, Rich," he stopped to aim a finger in the man's direction.

"You need to remember you're in the midst of trying to reclaim a senate seat." Lehman left his chair. "Whatever new plan you come up with, needs to stay on the sidelines of that."

"You're right. You're right, Rich," Morrow worked all ten fingers into his nape as he resumed his pace. "You'd think I'd learned my lesson on that by now. Going there under the assumption that our package is still with her is foolish, but still worth the trip."

At Lehman's blank look, Morrow smiled. "There were cameras all over that tacky hotel, Rich. Ones that caught me doing things I'd as soon as leave in the past. It was dumb of me to leave every damn bit of leverage I had with those idiots."

"You had no other choice. You'd only just gotten the material that night outside the hotel. It would've been unwise to walk around with it in plain view. Sad you had to leave it with those two, but dumb to let too many people see you waving it around." Lehman noted.

"Yeah, dumb..." Morrow sighed. "It was dumb luck my face didn't show on that In Scope broadcast. Berrill Clayton may not have that bag, but she has those discs."

"Or she knows who does," Lehman added.

Morrow's pacing slowed. "Maybe it *is* time to bring the GAN back into this…"

"Chris…"

"Relax Rich," Morrow signaled with a raised index. "I don't need the whole rotten bunch yet, just two of its members." He tapped an index to his chin as though settling on a decision. "Get me a meeting Rich. I need to see Jake Grodins and Brody Alberts."

***

"A senator?" Pope allowed laughter into his response to Bear's allegation.

When she merely stood there, arms still folded beneath what, to him, looked to be a very excellent pair of breasts, he released another quick rasp of laughter.

"Jesus, you really know how to insult a guy."

Bear remained rigid despite the semblance of a roar she heard beneath his words. The element had held his voice at a softly consistent octave, but seemed boosted somewhat then. Bear wondered if it was a tell, signifying when he was pissed. She was curious to know what other circumstances might encourage the gesture.

Pope was too preoccupied over being tagged a senator's lackey, to notice how intently he was being observed. Habit had him raising a hand to take through his hair, but he fisted it remembering that he'd worn it bound that day.

"Do I look like I work for a senator?" His tone was patient with the barest flavor of an edge.

Intrigued by his reaction to her simple query, Bear indulged in a more leisurely perusal of her guest. More than 6'5 that was for certain. Despite the finely crafted jacket and trousers, she could tell that his frame was packed with muscle. He wore his considerable height and weight with the ease of a man familiar with putting it to lethal use, yet pleased when the opportunity to rest, presented itself.

Cool curiosity still on simmer, Bear leaned into the back of the chair. "I'd think a senator could find all kinds of uses for a man like you."

"I'm not a leg breaker, Ms. Clayton."

"Anymore." She tacked on helpfully as though he may've forgotten to add the qualifier.

38

Pope felt his budding agitation throttle back then as though he'd realized she was intentionally goading him. Though she might be suspicious of his connection to this senator she seemed to hate, she seemed more interested in getting a rise out of him than real confirmation to her allegations.

He didn't know if he was amused or unsettled by her ability to unbalance him the way she had. Correction. He didn't know if he was amused, unsettled or pleased by her ability.

"I don't work for your senator, Ms. Clayton."

"My place is exceptional, but fifty thousand is an awful lot to put down for a deposit for a tour of the grounds."

"Would you have taken me seriously otherwise?"

"I take all my clients seriously."

"Enough to give them personal tours?" He countered, the ultramarines narrowed in challenge. "I'm guessing folks don't get on the cover of California Business Magazine without doing a lot of business. You wouldn't get much done granting tours to everyone who came knocking at your front gates."

"Your friend must be pretty special for you to go through all this?" She couldn't help but smile when she saw his grin emerge. The gesture was totally without guile and almost made her regret giving him such a hard time. She wasn't absolutely ready to buy his story, but perhaps he hadn't come to do Morrow's bidding.

"My friend is a huge hunting and gun fanatic- it's like a religion for him," Pope smiled as Rutger came to mind. "He's been hinting around for almost a year that he wants to come here for a weekend. I love him a lot and I wanted to make it special for him," he spread his hands. "I couldn't tell from your website whether you took bookings to reserve the entire ranch. I decided to let my money speak and wound up insulting you by going that route. I apologize. I just really wanted to make this happen for him…" he couldn't decipher her expression and figured his explanation was ample enough.

While this was all just a ruse to get close to Berrill Clayton, he was serious about granting Rutger's wish. Chances were strong she wouldn't give him the time of day-not the kind of time he wanted, anyway. If he could salvage the trip for Rut, that'd be something.

Bear's expression was most definitely set, but with shock being its motivating factor. She'd been on edge ever since questioning his connection to Mercuri Nikolaides. Mercuri's connection to Tee made him the only one, aside from the late Enrique Roya, who had seen the replay of the murderous events 6 years prior. She would've preferred Pope Apostolou being sent to do Morrow's work, to him knowing Mercuri- knowing things that still made her sick inside.

But now...on edge didn't even skim the fringes of what she was feeling. Booking her lodge for the friend he loved a lot? What the hell? How had she missed that? Had there been even the slightest hint of that the first time she'd met him?

She was sure there'd been *some* sexual innuendo at play during the brief conversation they'd shared in The Rascals' lounge. Clearly, she'd read *that* wrong. Just as she'd misjudged him checking out her tits moments ago.

Jeez...grimacing, Bear tapped fingers to her brow in some attempt to soothe the mad scramble inside her brain. There was little that truly stunned her anymore, but this? Accepting that the man before her- this giant, this...*god*, this work of physical perfection was...gay? She swallowed and then decided to clear her throat before attempting to try her voice.

Pope had closed a bit more of the distance between them. "Are you okay?" His wickedly dark features were sharp with concern.

"I..." she nodded. "Yes um, thank you," her tone was weak. "It's uh, it's been a long day."

Pope began to nod. "Yeah, Shaun let it slip that you've been shooting since last night."

"Yeah, but that's not it, I-" her lips twisted on a sour smile. "I'm just feeling a little disgusted with myself right now."

Pope wasn't quite sure how to respond, so he opted for silence.

Bear moved from behind her chair and closed the remaining few feet of space between them. "I'm sorry," she could've laughed over the surprise claiming his face, if she weren't so miserable.

"I value my clients because they trust me and allow me to do what I love," she continued. "Some of them are a bit harder to take than others."

"Ah," Pope flashed his single dimpled grin, "the guy who wanted his grandkids playing cops with your guns."

"He's real," Bear gave a weak smile, weaker nod. "In his defense, he's a pretty dynamic grandfather." She sobered after a moment, returning to the situation at hand.

"In spite of the kinds I come across, I've never treated any of them as disrespectfully as I have you. I apologize for that."

His gaze filtered with more concern. "It's okay, really-"

"No. No it's not," she insisted. "Things have been a little crazy lately, but that's no excuse- not when you're being so sweet."

For a second, Pope was sorely tempted to put a hand to her forehead and check for fever. *Sweet? Him?* He'd done a better job of masking his true motives than he'd realized.

Only a second ago, she seemed to despise him. What had changed?

"It won't take me but a minute to get out of this," she slid her fingers inside the gowns' bodice.

"That um," Pope followed the move helplessly before shaking his head- at first dazedly and then with more rigor. "That's not necessary. Like you said, it's been a long day." He put space between them. "I only wanted an intro, we can do the tour another time."

"I honestly don't mind," she responded with a small, defensive wave. "It's the least I can do after treating you the way I did."

She meant that. She felt like a heel for treating him so callously when he was just trying to do something nice for the man he...loved.

"I promise you haven't upset or offended me," Pope put a hand to his chest to stress the sincerity of his words. More words failed him when she moved closer, curling her fingers trustingly around his.

"That's because you've got a lot more manners than I do."

*Now* he was well mannered? Pope silently marveled. Boy, she had no idea.

"I accused you of having ulterior motives for being here," she squeezed his hand. "I treated your business like it was unappreciated and all the while you were just trying to put together something special for your friend. I feel like crap."

Pope used his free hand to cover hers where it rested on his other. He bent slightly toward her, praying he'd stop before jerking her high as his hormones were demanding.

"Please forget it. I already have. I'll call and arrange the tour some other time. I should get going."

It took Bear a few seconds to realize he was waiting on her to release him. Doing so, she moved back, absently realizing she'd been standing on her toes.

"Walk me out?" he asked.

41

They fell in step once Bear obliged with a smile. As they walked; skirting members of the photography crew packing up, Pope took time to survey the property.

"Quite a place."

"Thanks," her smile widened in appreciation and pride. "I grew up somewhere similar to it. When I saw this...I knew nothing else would do. I wanted it."

His brow quirked. "You always get what you want?"

"Not always," she gave him a lingering sideways glance. "Not always," she repeated with a sigh.

They took the rest of the walk in easy silence and were soon rounding the side of the house.

"This is me," Pope waved toward the wide gravel drive where a muscular navy truck waited. "I'll be seeing you soon about that tour."

"Mmm..." Bear let her hand slip inside the one he'd extended. "Well you've already talked to Shaun so just connect with him and he'll set it up."

"I will," his voice was as steady as his gaze. "Thank you for your time Ms. Clayton."

"Call me Berrill or Bear-mostly everybody calls me Bear."

"Doesn't fit you."

She wouldn't-couldn't let herself read anything into the way his marine blue eyes traveled her frame. Briefly, she closed her eyes to break the spell cast by his.

"I can be pretty grizzly," she warned.

He responded at once with a sly grin. "I haven't forgotten the conversation I walked in on."

"Eavesdropped on." Habit, had her biting her bottom lip when he laughed over her intended tease.

He spent another few seconds studying her. "I'll see you soon, Bear."

She watched, until the massive truck carried him away in a flurry of dust and gravel. Regretfully, she shook her head. "What a goddamn waste," she sighed and headed back the way she'd come.

42

# CHAPTER 5

Bear could be found most mornings somewhere on her property reclining on the hood of her Jeep and taking in an exceptional view. It was the part of her daily routine that she enjoyed most.

Things at the ranch didn't get started 'til around 7am when early bird shooters started their day. At present, they had no clients scheduled for that time, so Bear felt quite secure taking in the sunrise from the Jeep's hood.

She had nothing on tap for that morning-not even the usual meeting with Shaun Oates and his counterpart Mike Hough. Both men served in dual roles as her Operations Managers- necessary posts given the work required to keep a place like Bear Arms running smoothly. At any rate, the morning was hers and she planned to enjoy it.

Low grinding filled the air and she was cursing herself for tempting fate moments later. Her mobile vibrated on the hood. Shaun.

"I'm not coming back, no matter what," she sang upon answering.

"No need," Shaun chuckled. "I only wanted you to know we're sending company your way. Mr. Apostolou. He uh-doesn't seem like the type who'd appreciate being asked to wait any longer," Shaun added the last as if expecting his boss to argue over the intrusion to her morning.

"No-no Shaun it's fine," Bear inched up a bit on the hood. "I told him it'd be fine to come back any morning this week."

"Well we offered to drive him out, but he said he was okay heading out to find you on his own. We told him you were near the rec stop-told him to follow the signs."

"Yeah I uh-I'm actually parked right near the cottage."

Shaun hesitated before continuing. "I figured it was alright since there were no early morning sessions-"

"Shaun? I'm fine. It's okay, you did fine." Bear's tone was reassuring in its softness. "I'll check in with you and Mike later."

"Should we have the kitchen prep lunch for you guys after?"

"No need," the hint of an edge crept into her voice. "I'm sure he won't stay long once we're done looking around."

Shaun disconnected moments later. Bear eased her phone into a back jeans' pocket and spent another minute with her view. The rec stop marked the end of her property and was where clients usually stopped for rest and refreshment especially if their time wasn't done. They would save themselves the exhaustion of heading all the way back to the lodge for a quick drink or a few minutes of downtime.

She and her newest client could just as easily have lunch there as opposed to dining at the house. The rec cottage boasted a full service kitchen and was always well stocked. Sadly, it was as she'd told Shaun, she doubted Mr. Apostolou would spare any more time than necessary once they'd completed his tour.

She could at least delight in the fact that she'd have time to indulge in the provocative image he cast. His was an image far more preferable than the one presently in her midst.

During their chat, Bear didn't think to ask Shaun if there had been any new developments pertaining to her purchase. *Hoped for* purchase of the rec cottage. Though it was an enchanting place with a view of land, sky and trees from virtually any angle, she wanted it for one reason only: to raze it to the ground.

An engine cut through the sound of wind, birdsong and her heated memory. Bear smiled as her tour date approached. The gesture deepened when she saw that he'd arrived alone. She was of course pleased that she wouldn't have to share him with his significant other just yet.

Quietly, Bear berated herself but delighted when pleasure made its next stab as Pope Apostolou left his truck. His hair was loose that day. The wind stirred thick locks of black around a remarkable face.

From the Jeep's hood, Bear watched admiring the unhurried stride as he approached. His manner of dress was far more casual than when they'd seen each other 2 days earlier. Hiking boots that managed to appear rugged as well as casual, showed beneath the cuffs of dark fleece pants. They matched the lightweight hoodie he wore beneath an open denim shirt.

A waste indeed, Bear mourned but managed to cease her inner panting by the time Pope's long strides brought him to the Jeep.

"Ms. Clayton-Bear." He corrected when she gave him a look.

"Mr. Apostolou."

Pope responded with a look of his own. "If I can call you Bear, you can definitely call me Pope."

"Pope." She said and indulged in another scan of his face- the sapphire eyes, broad staggering face comprised of sharp angles and a bone structure that spared him the anguish of being called 'pretty' by scarcely a hair.

"So did your mother have plans for you along those lines?" she probed.

Her query had him turning to scan the horizon and squinting against the sun that climbed higher against a pale sky. Bear instantly regretted the probe. It was easy to see she'd brought unwanted thoughts to mind. He shut down the reaction easily enough, treated her with a look she couldn't quite puzzle out.

"My mother had a lot of plans for me," he shrugged. "I think I did the complete opposite of everything she wanted. My last name is Greek for apostle-messenger," he shrugged again. "Guess she was just making sure the first connected with the last. Maybe she'd predicted I'd need all the help I could get."

He spoke in a way that made her think his mother hadn't played a role in his life in quite a long while. Something in common? Bear supposed she'd never know. Conversations about mothers and the lack were ones she worked hard to steer clear of.

Pope appeared to be done with the topic as well. Once again, he scanned the land. "This place really is somethin' else," he leaned against the Jeep's hood. "You were very lucky to get it, place like this...I can't imagine the former owners letting go of it easily."

"It was a property tax thing," Bear scooted from the hood. "Kept changing hands among the family until they finally decided it was too much of an expense. I came to the rescue-right place, right time."

Pope smiled. "It's the way most deals get closed."

She leaned beside him against the Jeep. "You know a lot about that?"

"Some."

"Any good at it?"

"Some would say I am."

"I wouldn't mind your help acquiring that place." With a sigh, Bear sent a rueful look toward the rec cottage.

"It's not yours?" Pope frowned at the structure.

"My land ends a few yards away from it. *Those* owners don't seem to have money problems-not the kind that have them eager to sell, anyway." She shook her head, fidgeting with a long tendril that curled beneath her chin. "I don't even know that for sure. I've only been in touch with the real estate company. They've been gracious enough to let me rent it."

"Gracious?" Pope turned, propping his elbow on the hood. "Why aren't the owners involved?"

"Beats me," Bear folded her arms over her chest. "The realtors aren't sharing that info. Apparently they aren't obligated to tell me who their clients are. Guess I can understand that, being an entrepreneur myself."

Pope studied her closely, fist clenching on the hood as the need to touch her funnelled up like a twister. The sensation, was unexpected and urgent. "But you want it?" He asked instead.

"I want it," Bear confessed simply. "But..." she couldn't resist another quick scan of him. "I don't always get what I want, remember?" Smiling off her despair, she moved from the Jeep.

"But you didn't come here to listen to my sob story," she went to the driver's side. "If you don't mind, we'll tour the cottage when I bring you back to your truck. That is, if you don't mind me driving?" She knocked on the Jeep's door.

Pope grinned. "So you really can move this thing?"

She slid behind the wheel. "Fasten your seatbelt."

A minute later, they were speeding toward the opposite end of the ranch.

\*\*\*

46

### Memphis, Tennessee~

"Why the hell is he on this list?"

"I think that's pretty clear, don't you Jake?"

Brody and Jake turned to the small, slender man seated on the other side of the modest desk along a quiet corridor of Womack, Mebane and Urnst Attorneys at Law.

Reading the expression on the faces of his larger guests, Cory Sumner stood- hands extended to urge caution. "It's all I know fellas-"

"The hell it is," Jake's voice was a snarl. "Why's Pope's name on that list?"

Cory swallowed after a few attempts, praying he wouldn't get his face smashed in for stating the obvious. "That list names everyone I've been instructed to contact about Mr. Alberts' will reading."

"So he's in the will?" Jake persisted.

Cory took another moment to compose his reply. "These are the people my bosses need to be there. If they're being asked to attend-"

"They're in the will," Brody finished. "Thanks for the heads up, Cory," he pushed a bulging envelope across the man's desk, and then nodded to Jake.

"Gentlemen?" Cory slipped the cash payoff into a drawer, calling out as his associates prepared to leave. "The back exit leads to a rear stairway. Please?"

"Of course," Brody gave a half smile, understanding the need for discretion.

Jake kept his silence until he and Brody were in the private corridor leading to the back of the stately brick building. Then, he loosed a string of curses- the majority were directed at Pope.

"Are you forgetting your father's still alive, man?" Amused incredulity held the question. Brody shook his head. "It's *my* dad who's most likely left me out in the cold."

"If your father betrayed you, I'm sure to be in line for the same treatment," Jake began to pace the small area. "The man's a shell right now," he said of Lorne Grodins.

"He and Daddy were real close," Brody said of his father's partner.

47

"Old fucks," Jake continued the insults as his pacing gained speed. "They'd rather leave the keys to the kingdom to the bastards who conspired to kill them instead of to their own natural blood-"

"Jake!" Brody sliced the air with a fist. "Shut up. We don't know that's what this is about."

"I think we both know it is, Bro. The question now is what to do next."

Brody joined in with the pacing then. Gradually, distress emerged beneath the cool mask he'd managed to keep in place. "We still have the meeting with Morrow-"

"Fuck that!" Jake spat. "Whatever that jackass is dangling don't mean shit if what we have a right to is given away to those two freaks of nature our fathers worshipped." He moved into Brody's pacing path.

"You know what it means if that happens. I'm not interested in working my way up from the bottom, Bro."

Some of Brody's calm had returned. "Do you know why men without power hate men who have it?"

Jake's ill-humored smile prefaced his reply. "Because they don't have it."

Brody appeared satisfied. "I know why you're on edge, J but I'm not so quick to think my dear brother's gonna tear it all down once he has it."

Jake's smiling face turned into a scowl. "Givin' a shitload of credit to one of the S.O.B.s who tried to kill your father. Who *did* kill our cousins. Barely in their thirties and already sentenced to their graves."

"He won't have the power to destroy it, Jake. If Daddy does...leave it to him he-he'll put restrictions in place-"

"Okay, so he won't destroy it. How does him keeping it help us?"

"Everyone who found working for us so reprehensible, high-tailed it out of the GAN when Mercuri came up with his master plan to fuck us over." Brody said.

Jake looked bored. "I'm still waiting for you to tell me why your outlook's suddenly changed? A month ago, you were as ready to put Pope and Rut in their graves as I was."

"If Pope comes back here to keep his inheritance, it's because he'll think he can reform it. I say we hear Morrow out, but hold back until we know what Pope's planning. All I have to do is wait for him to fail, to reclaim what's mine."

"So why wait?" Jake seemed both bored and confused.

"Because you know like I do that there's still some on the inside who sympathize with what Mercuri did. Even after all that's happened, they'd stand behind Pope if he worked to reform it. He won't succeed- the sympathizers will see that and when he's out of the picture, I step in with no argument."

Brody moved closer, hands clasped in an uncharacteristic pleading gesture. "Jake, we can't afford another mess like six years ago. It's taken us *this* long to get back to half our capacity. If we're to keep our outside interests and friendships going, they've got to see us united. With The Ten out of the way, we're gonna need those friendships, if anything else gets revealed from those hotel recordings. This is a game full of uncertainties. I'm just trying to navigate us through it until we know where we stand. Tell me you get that, man?"

Jake's expression was unreadable then. "I get it, Brody, but understand that if this shit doesn't play out the way you expect, that's it," he raised a cautionary finger. "No more waiting- not for you and your united front or Morrow and his secret interests. We tried this once before, waiting...and you see what a mess we wound up with. I'm sick of bowing down to these traitors. If that means pissing away my inheritance, and our connections, so be it."

Jake brushed past Brody with enough force to send him slamming against the wall.

"Jake!" Brody waited for his old friend to give him the courtesy of eye contact. "I'm with you- you've got my word on that. I see this thing flyin' off the rails, that's it. We hit 'em and hard regardless of what they're holding over our heads. Pope, Mercuri, Slayte, Rutger, we get rid of 'em once and for all. Damn the consequences."

Jake regarded Brody with a long look and then bolted down the creaking back stairway.

***

"So? What do you think?"

Pope was already nodding in response to the questions Bear rattled off from behind the wheel of the Jeep. At ease, he let his head rest back on the seat and scanned the outlay of property beyond the windshield.

"This'll do just fine. He'll love it out here."

Bear gave a single, satisfied pump of her fist. "We'll head over to the last stop now," she said.

"Hold up on that," he suddenly straightened on the seat, one hand going to her knee.

Bear realized she was holding her breath while studying the smothering capacity of his hand where it rested.

She'd done a worthy job of keeping her mind off his...size during the tour, but the simple touch- commanding yet gentle, threw her thoughts right back to what she'd already known. Pope Apostolou was a man of considerable power, considerable control, considerable appeal.

"Why don't you tell me about this place and why you hate it?"

She blinked, catching tendrils of her long bangs with her lashes. His words had her shaking her head in denial. "What makes you think I-"

"Forget it," he spurned her attempt.

"You didn't come out here to discuss my property issues," she said.

"I don't do very many things to be polite, Ms. Clayton and I don't ask questions I'm not interested in knowing the answers to."

He'd decided not to tell her that he'd already glimpsed the haunted shadow that held her eyes before they left the site earlier. He was, by no means, a mind reader, but he recognized a haunted soul all too easily when he encountered one. Somehow, he didn't think the tough as nails beauty seated next to him would approve of such an accurate assessment coming from a stranger.

He noticed her gaze fixed on where his hand covered her knee and gave a squeeze. He released her, but not without a great deal of reluctance. He smiled as she mouthed a curse and wondered how hard it was for her to stifle what he'd already witnessed of her dynamic temper.

"You know you could easily Google this story," she said softly and with practiced restraint.

"I'd like to hear it from you." Although he was most intrigued by what put the shadows in her mocha eyes, he was grateful for anything that lengthened the tour that was quickly reaching its end.

He'd hoped she'd start speaking soon and give him the chance to just sit and delight in the flawless texture of her skin. It was like dewy caramel beneath the morning light. She'd gathered up her shoulder length hair in a high ball that left several wispy strands clinging to her nape.

Her breathing was a touch elevated which caused her very excellent breasts to strain against the capped sleeved khaki shirt she wore. With a wince, Pope silently scolded himself for objectifying her when she was about to bare her soul.

"I'm not sure if you noticed we didn't run into any of my female employees during the tour. There aren't any- except inside my home."

"Coincidence?" He asked.

"Necessity. Two of my female employees were raped inside that cottage. One was killed."

A silent scolding didn't seem adequate then. Pope drew a fist that he was sorely tempted to use against himself.

"I'm sorry Bear. I wouldn't have pried if-"

"Don't apologize. It's a matter of public record." She put the Jeep in drive and resumed the trip. "One was approached while she worked at the lodge. She had a friend who worked inside my offices in the training sector...encouraged her to come along."

"I would've rathered getting this by public record than having you remember it." Pope continued to kick himself.

"It's alright," her voice was elevated over the Jeep's engine though sadness claimed it. "I think about it every day," she frowned as the familiar pressure of tears twinged behind her eyes.

"I want to buy the cottage so I can tear it down."

Pope observed the inviting construction coming into view a quarter mile away. "You've put a lot of work into something you want to destroy."

"Well, otherwise it becomes an eyesore- makes the whole situation even more intolerable. The asshole owners sure don't seem to give a shit about it."

"Did they ever catch the guys who did it?"

"You bet your ass they did," a measure of triumph stamped out her sadness. "The place is still there as a reminder, though. I'll rebuild, but I need that one gone."

"I get that. I'm still sorry about asking you to dredge that up." Doubly sorry, he added in silence, considering what an incident like that must've had her remembering.

"Keeps me from getting complacent about what needs to be done," Bear said after a few silent moments of her own.

"How about we skip this part of the tour?" Pope suggested once weighty quiet held the Jeep's cabin for another full minute.

Bear put the Jeep in park as she rolled up to the side of the cottage where Pope had left his truck. Dismay pooled her eyes when she half turned on the seat to face him.

"You've got to see it," she urged. "It really is a great place in spite of what I think of it personally." When he didn't look convinced, she gave a determined smile. "You know, I bet your friend would enjoy using it instead of having to hoof it all the way back to the lodge or the lounges inside the practice halls." She gave a quick shrug of her brows when he gave her a considering look.

"You sure?" Pope asked.

"Absolutely." Without waiting on further discussion, Bear hopped out of the Jeep and headed for the cottage at a fast stride. A stride that seemed more like a shuffle when paired against Pope's.

"Booking the place for the whole weekend, you guys will have the cottage to yourselves but it may still seem pretty cramped if he's as uh…"

Pope's brows lifted as he waited for Bear to continue, intrigued by what she wouldn't say. His expression hinted that he had a good idea.

They were heading inside and Bear was still searching for the most appropriate phrasing. "It could get pretty tight in there if your friend's your...size."

Grinning then, Pope nodded. "I don't think we'd spend much time inside."

"Well he'd still need the downtime. The man can't shoot twenty-four seven."

Pope's grin glided into a chuckle. "You don't know my friend."

"You've at least got to sleep-oh!" Bear snapped her fingers and broke into a light sprint toward the back of the cottage. "You should see the bedroom!" She called over her shoulder.

Pope followed, taking in the cottage with its cozy living area, full service kitchenette and dining nook. He supposed it was...cute, but only for one-maybe. The place might work for Rutger alone, but for the 2 of them or the 4 of them if Mercuri and Slayte joined in...nothin' doin'...

He found Bear at the end of a short hall. With a flourishing wave, she encouraged him to take a look inside.

Pope laughed. "Does it open up into another room?"

"Not exactly," Bear's smile was cheery and unoffended. "It's bigger than it looks and there's a pullout in the livingroom. It's actually the largest space in the cabin, but the beds still aren't as big as the ones

52

in the lodge. If you and your boyfriend want a more private getaway, then the cottage is-"

"Excuse me...what?"

He'd leaned forward and Bear wasn't sure if he was moving to hear better or about to faint.

"What did you just say?" Furrows had formed between Pope's long, jet brows as he appeared to be in heavy concentration.

"You um," Bear pressed her lips together, briefly considering her reply. "You won't have to share the cottage with other guests...so it'd be perfect for-"

"Me and my-my boyfriend?"

"Dammit I-I'm sorry," Bear realized her mistake then. "Is it sig-significant other is-is that...what you uh-use?"

Pope didn't know whether to laugh or swear, both reactions seemed to fit.

Bear watched as he raked a hand back through the ebony waves of silk covering his head. Her fingers ached to test the texture. Another tell, she mused, recalling when she'd riled him a few days prior and he'd reacted in similar fashion. The fact had her regarding the cramped confines of the cottage. The space seemed smaller than a matchbox against 6 feet 8 inches of heating temper.

"Boyfriend."

Hand still tugging at his hair, Pope muttered the word like a curse. He was pissed alright and Bear could feel her skin heating as her own emotions flared. *She* was the one who should be pissed. What woman wouldn't be, faced with the sad reality that she had absolutely no chance of enjoying what was unarguably a walking orgasm.

"Boyfriend..." Pope put a bit more feeling behind the word that time.

"Look, I'm sorry, alright?" Bear latched onto her temper. She fisted her hands at her sides to resist shoving his excellent chest. "How am I supposed to know the proper etiquette? Shit! You walk in here, looking like the fuck of the century and I'm supposed to wrap my head around the fact that you're gay?!" She heard then, what sounded every bit like a roar stirring low in his throat and looked on in fascination as he tousled his hair again.

"Goddammit, Bear," he squeezed his eyes shut before turning on his heel to head for the front door. "Fuck," he hissed and turned again, grabbing her that time. Cuffing her throat in his hand, he used his thumb to tip back her head for his kiss.

Bear decided there was only one thing to do when being kissed by a walking orgasm. Pray brain function would resume so that the moment could be fully appreciated. For the time being, nothing appeared to be working except her mouth...that was just fine, she realized.

The kiss was a force which she met-*tried* to meet with her own brand of fire. She did her best, considering all she wanted to do was savor. The act was tireless and sultry. Pope Apostolou kissed her like he'd been doing it all his life. He knew just how long to rotate his tongue around hers before she shuddered in the midst of consistent moaning. He used just the right pace to time his thrusts as he claimed her mouth.

While he had no way to confirm it, he seemed to know just how deep to drive his tongue to have her panties go damp. More than damp, they were saturated. The sensation was so overpowering, Bear clenched his open denim shirt in hopes of supporting her suddenly useless legs.

His hand at her throat was in no way uncomfortable. Still, it unsettled and in a way she found terribly satisfying. For a woman who made her living being in command, all she wanted then was to relish the quiet possession of his touch.

Pope was praying his manner exhibited the control he sure as hell did not feel. Her soft, steady moans every time he probed her mouth, heightened rather than tempered his need to claim-to conquer. He was sure there were cautionary voices trying to reason with him, but he couldn't hear them- didn't want to hear them. Her mouth was as sweet as the caramel tone of her skin. All he wanted...was more.

Bear felt her feet leaving the floor, but she didn't open her eyes to investigate where she was being taken. The shift in elevation put her at a better height from which to enjoy his kiss. Her moans intermingled with gasps echoing need and she shamelessly suckled his skillful tongue. Sensation radiated from her breasts crushed high against his chest. Hungrily, her fingers tunnelled through his hair and she shuddered over the realization that the mass of glossy onyx was as luxurious as it appeared.

He broke the kiss and Bear felt herself being lowered. Yet, she refused to open her eyes for fear that the fantasy would end. The decadence of the bed beneath her back registered-she kept her eyes closed. Though pleased that the encounter had not yet reached its end, there was something a little *surreal* about being on her back in a bed she'd raved about moments earlier as though she were a salesman relaying the finer points of a product.

She would've never gone on and on about it-never would've led him back there, had she known he wasn't...what she thought.

The sound of snaps popping, tucked her deeper into fantasy and she risked opening her eyes. The man was extraordinary, as it pertained to his looks. The skin, a flawless and sun kissed copper made the ultramarine of his eyes all the more staggering. As was his body. The need to feel him closer, had her achy and anxious.

Arousal stormed her from the simple act of his nose outlining the swell of bosom above her bra cups. Shuddering a curse, Bear moved to unhook the front fastening and found both her wrists shackled by one of his hands before she could complete the act.

Despite the fact that his pitiful reserves of control were almost totally drained, Pope waited- studying Bear's sensational eyes. He watched for any signs of uncertainty or intimidation. She exuded a tough exterior but he'd already glimpsed the softness beneath and prayed he hadn't unsettled her with the restraining move. His bright eyes skimmed her breasts seconds before he closed his mouth over one of the lace clad mounds. He started to suck, which forced gasps from her throat and a long groan from his.

He refused to take her out of her bra, but he refused to deny himself the treat-no matter how brief- of sampling what had him feverishly curious since the first time he'd seen her. She braced against his hold at her wrists, but made no real attempt to free herself.

Pope was glad. If she touched him again, he'd take her there. That much he knew. He couldn't- not there-not after what she'd just told him of the horrors that had occurred in that very place-perhaps in that very room. He'd have her in time. Knowing that, was enough to have him tethering his hormones and stonily refusing to give her more of what she'd begged for with her gaze when he backed off. Gently, he raked the soft curve of her jaw beneath his knuckles.

"Thought I should make myself clear," he said once the storm in her eyes had eased. "I've known my friend since before we could talk. I love him because he's like my brother-*only* my brother." He smiled at the eager nod she gave to convey her understanding.

Pope braced off the bed, but not before skimming his thumb across her covered nipple and enjoying the way arousal sent her lashes fluttering.

"You're right," he leaned closer to speak against her ear. "This is bigger than it looks."

Open mouthed, Bear watched him leave the room. She didn't move- not even when she heard his truck engine ignite to signal his departure.

# CHAPTER 6

*Half Moon Bay, California~*

A long weekend with friends, could be difficult to organize. Especially when those friends were as busy as Berrill Clayton and the three women who were like sisters to her. As a previous attempt at a long getaway had ended with Bear being a no-show, she refused to let anything stop her from attending the outing Prin had put together at one of her favorite escapes.

Half Moon Bay was located 35 minutes south of San Francisco. It was a real find for anyone craving the inviting local flavor and incomparable beauty of a coastal town. It wasn't among the more lavish trips the women had enjoyed, but given the excitement of late, it was just what they needed.

With the chill off the bay harboring a bit more iciness; as the months began a slow roll toward fall, finding 80 degree temps was getting more and more difficult. Prin had booked lodgings at The Bay Shores Inn, that was right on the shore hence the name. The place was an enchanting oasis next to the thriving hum of San Francisco. As a result, the popular and cozy motel was often booked to capacity.

The inn's owner, Staunton Colton was a customer of Holland Furniture and an old friend of Prin's parents Jamus and Samantha Holland. Therefore, Prin was usually able to secure accommodations whenever she called.

The girls left early that Saturday morning with plans not to return until early the following Wednesday. Upon arrival, they were promptly shown to their rooms which all faced the quiet bay drenched in sunlight. The area held a hazy allure given the time of day.

The rooms were spacious and surprisingly luxurious in color schemes of earth tones and pastels. The atmosphere promised relaxation and it delivered. By noon, the women were unpacked and enjoying a light brunch on the terrace outside Prin's room. They had spent the first half hour discussing Bear's upcoming cover appearance for *California Business Magazine*.

LuCarolyn Young, relaxed on her lounge with one hand hovering airily above a bowl of plump, red grapes. "Does anybody else, Tee not included, need this as much as I do?" she asked.

Etienne 'Tee' Shaw, relaxing in similar manner, frowned slightly but didn't open her eyes. "Why am I not included?"

"Don't even try it," LuCarolyn tossed back, not opening her eyes either as she shifted her statuesque frame on the lounge. "There's no such thing as wanting to get away when a woman has something as sexy, gorgeous and...mmm...what's the word I'm looking for ladies?"

"Big." Bear and Prin offered in unison and dissolved into giggles along with LuCarolyn. It wasn't long before Tee joined in as well.

"Alright, alright let's be serious here," LuCarolyn waved her hands over her head. "Tee you can admit it, you know? We know it was torture having to drag yourself away from that man of yours to join us for the weekend."

Tee remained a picture of ease and refused to comment on any difficulties she'd experienced leaving Mercuri Nikolaides, her boyfriend of only 2 months.

LuCarolyn's light, honey colored eyes sparkled devilishly even as she put forth an effort to be sincere. "You know I'm just teasing, right Tee?"

"Mmm...but not really," Bear drawled, reclining on her lounge while savoring one of the plump kiwi slices from a platter that included cheese, peaches and tomato slices. She sent Tee a sly, curious look. "Are you all moved in with Mercuri, yet?" She asked.

LuCarolyn bellowed a laugh. "She may as well be! Whatever he hasn't already moved into his place or put in storage, Tee's leaving for the new tenants."

"What gives, Tee?" Bear's eyes were still on her small friend. "You having trouble letting go of the place?"

"It's not that," Tee replied without hesitating.

"But it's something?" Prin knew.

Tee sighed, her eyes opening to thin, dark slits. "It won't be easy letting go of it. That place...it's seen me at a lot of low moments, dark nights after..."

She didn't need to finish. Her friends knew all too well about the 'low moments and dark nights after...'

"You think you'll need to go back to it?" Prin asked.

Tee was already shaking her head. "It's like a security blanket. I know I don't need it. I just...I still want it."

"You think Mercuri's okay with that?" LuCarolyn queried.

"Seems to be," Tee shrugged halfheartedly. "I know it's got to make him wonder...but everything happened so-so fast with us, I guess he's fine for now...it'd only become an issue for him if..."

"The 'M' word came into the picture," Prin smiled before giving a quick wave. "Not 'Mercuri' the other 'M' word."

"Marriage," LuCarolyn purred.

"Please," Tee gave a tiny snort. "It's way too early to even think about that. *But,*" she stressed before LuCarolyn could pipe up to give her grief. "I won't be holding onto it for long. Things like that broadcast a few weeks ago are putting more and more distance between me and my security blanket."

"You guys think it's over?" Bear asked, her tone hollow. "Could that broadcast mean the end of the line for those creeps? That we'll never have to talk about this anymore or...share any more of what we took?"

No additional clarification was needed then either. 'What we took', served as ample reminder of the visual account of the night of carnage they were responsible for. There had been additional recordings, ones recounting the debased moments they'd all participated in with the perverse members of the GAN board.

"I wish I could say yes, B," Tee's voice held a hollowness similar to Bear's. "But we're only a few weeks out from the broadcast.

Aside from Nathan Alberts' suicide, I don't know if it's the end of the line for them as far as any real...justice is concerned."

"Is that what we want? Expect? Hell, do we even *deserve* justice?" Bear pondered.

"How could you ask if *we* deserve justice?" Prin challenged.

"We were paid to be there, remember?" Bear retorted with the same challenge in her voice, but lost the desire to remain challenging the longer she looked at Prin.

"I'd have told them all to go fuck themselves had I know what we'd really been hired to take part in," challenge left Bear's voice to be replaced by something fierce.

The GANs notorious theme parties were favorites of the organization's board. Bear and her friends had been the unwitting participants in The Ten's master and slave sex fantasy.

"Right or wrong we stopped them from doing it to anyone else," Bear decided.

"The guy who took me from my apartment- Van Deer..." Tee's hollow tone sounded more so in the wake of her quiet, "he told me they made him attend-different themes of course. He did it thinking it'd get him a big seat of command in the organization."

"All it got him was dead," LuCarolyn sighed. "Thank God."

"Your bodyguard who survived the attack, didn't he say there were two? Van Deer had a friend who helped him."

"Vince was my bodyguard. Vince Folksom," Tee told Bear. Mercuri had arranged a 2-man security detail for her when the situation began to escalate. Folksom's partner, Kevin Jonas had been killed. Folksom had survived-barely.

"I don't know if I would've come out of that if Vince hadn't injured Van Deer's partner too badly to follow when he took me." Tee shuddered over the memory. "According to Vince, he was even more psychotic than Van Deer."

"Are they still looking for him?" LuCarolyn probed.

Tee nodded. "But I figure he won't show his face 'til he's ready. Thank God, Vince was able to give a description of the albino jackass."

"Albino," Prin said.

Tee settled deeper into her lounge chair. "Tall, platinum blond with a buzzcut."

Prin settled deeper on her lounge chair as well. She sighed, the gesture coming in unison with LuCarolyn's.

"Could we end this dismal conversation by saying it's a lucky thing Tee met Mercuri?"

"I agree, Lu," Bear sent a playfully chastising look toward Tee. "And you didn't think it'd last a month."

Tee shrugged. "Wasn't for lack of trying on my part."

"We know!" The others chimed in unison.

Tee laughed, hugged herself lightly. "He just wouldn't go anywhere."

"Now *that's* what I'd call lucky," LuCarolyn hugged herself as well. "And blessed," she added.

"Damn right," Bear watched her friends grow quiet as they relaxed under the hazy sun with the wind and gentle roar of the surf all around.

She thought of 'meeting' Pope Apostolou and wondered if that was luck finally working its way into her life. If so, what was in store and did she have what it took to see it through? Did she have what it took to keep a man like that beyond the one night of sex she hoped to experience with him?

At that point, she'd take a good hour of the stuff. The man hadn't drifted two seconds away from her thoughts since the tour a few days earlier. Like that, she was back in the cottage on her back, while he... Bear cleared her throat to mask the moan that shuddered through along with the sudden throb that tantalized her core. Thankfully, LuCarolyn clapped and provided a welcomed interruption into her heated memories.

"Before I forget, just a reminder about my wrap party. Prin- I expect to see you. Tee, bring Mercuri and Bear bring your dancing shoes."

"No way," a slow smile curved Bear's mouth.

"You promised..." LuCarolyn pouted.

"I said I'd *critique* your performance. I never said a thing about joining in with an audience."

LuCarolyn's wrap parties had become events of legend and so had her dance offs. She'd recently promised that a choreographed routine would be on tap for the next event. When her staff demanded she be the featured dancer, it didn't take much prodding for Lu to accept.

"Well I can't do it by myself!" LuCarolyn's horror meshed into cunning. "If you refuse, I'll have to bully Tee."

"Forget it," Eyes closed once more, Tee smiled. "Prin's got my back if you even dare."

Prin made a play of tugging off her earrings in preparation for a coming rumble. "Where's my Vaseline?" She muttered, pretending to launch a fake search for the item every woman needed before entering a physical altercation with an enemy.

The women shared bold laughter and the lazy afternoon rolled on.

\*\*\*

### *Memphis, Tennessee~*

"I'll bring new ones next time, I promise, Den," Brody's somber smile held as he studied one of the miniature model airplanes atop the wide marble tombstone marked with the name Dennis Alberts.

"Sorry I forgot," Brody replaced the airplane atop the stone. "A lot goin' on...Daddy's death and all. Son of a bitch," he hissed, hand fisting on the corner of the white marble marker.

"How could he do it?" Brody didn't mind the pressure of tears behind his eyes. He didn't mind it at all in the midst of his cousin. "He knew what losing you did to me. Don't know why I'm surprised," Brody sniffed, ran the back of his hand beneath nostrils that had not yet started to leak.

"He never gave a fuck about me," he told the corpse beneath the stone. "Guess staying alive while my favorite cousin was goin' into the ground long before his time, was just a 'lil too much to ask. All he ever cared about was his bastard."

Brody reached out again to straighten the row of small planes his cousin had been obsessed with since they were kids. "They invited Pope to the will reading," he smoothed a hand across the cool slab of marble and laughed once, shortly.

"Can you believe that? After what he and his shiteatin' friends did to us- to you? They wanted out and instead of comin' to us like men, they plotted and deceived their way out."

Brody wouldn't confess; not even to his dead cousin, that coming to them like men wouldn't have earned Pope and the others their freedom either. One didn't just decide to resign from The GAN. There was only one way and it led 6 feet under.

"Jake's ready to wipe 'em out now- can't say I blame him," Brody sat in the grass and tugged up a few blades. "I'm not thinkin' too clear right now, Den. I should be tryin' to figure a way around Pope and

Mercuri to those sluts they hired to kill The Ten and air our dirty sheets to the press. Instead, I'm wallowing in Daddy issues because the old fool will probably leave everything to his perfect specimen and not the son who earned it.

Remember how we used to talk about one day being in charge? With Daddy gone, I thought...son of a bitch...Now, all I can hope for is that the crackpot didn't leave the whole kit and kaboodle to that traitor. If he did..." Brody grimaced and reclaimed one of the planes from the stone.

"I'm trying real hard to be positive here, Den. All that bullshit I told Jake about bein' okay with it. Who was I kiddin'...? If that jackass left everything to Pope to do with as he pleases...then it's like I told Jake, I'm all in- GAN be damned. I'll tear it all down before I let Pope have the pleasure. I'll blow this sham right out of the water and the only thing left to destroy will be my dear brother."

*** 

*Pacifica, California~*

"What's wrong? Why didn't you use your key?" Pope's greeting included a frown that Saturday morning when he opened the door to one of his 3 best friends in the world.

"Calm down," Mercuri Nikolaides smiled, the gesture bringing light to the already radiant pools of a stirring amber gaze. "Everything's fine. I guess I just get a little curious whenever you're in state and almost a week passes without me seeing you."

"Nice to know you care," Pope left his front door open for Mercuri to enter.

"Just making sure I'm not about to lose you to the easy life the way I did Rut and Slay."

Pope grinned as the men came to mind. Rutger Eliades and Slayte Miltiades were quite happy in their lives of leisure while their friends dutifully managed their considerable wealth.

"I didn't use my key because I didn't know if you'd been MIA for almost a week because you had company."

The comment got more of a laugh from Pope as he moved through the expansive corridor leading to what looked to be a vast living area. On the way, he gathered his locks into a low ponytail and secured the mass with a small band he'd taken from his wrist. "You know I don't do that out here," he said.

"You don't do much out here as far as I know," Mercuri countered.

It was true. Pope chose to stay with Mercuri whenever he was in town.

Grin refreshed, Pope sent it as well as a sly look toward Mercuri. "I think it's *me* who has to be careful when I visit. You're the one with the company now. Me, Rut and Slay are just waiting for you to ask for your keys back."

The guys had made a practice of exchanging house keys years ago.

"Don't worry about it," Mercuri said. "I told Tee to be on the lookout for weird types visiting. And anyway, she's met you all-can't get much weirder than the three of you."

"Tee adds class to the place," pretend gruffness flavored Pope's tone. "Keep her."

"I plan to."

Pope observed his friend with a raised brow. Folding his arms over the front of a worn Aerosmith T-shirt, he regarded the man with a knowing stare. "Somethin' you wanna spill, Merc?"

"Not yet."

"But soon?"

"I hope so," Mercuri's gaze, though naturally vibrant, dimmed just slightly. "She's... independent. I don't think she's gonna be ready to leave her place for a while. No big- we haven't been together long and...hell... I'm having enough fun trying to convince her."

Nodding slow, Pope seemed pleased. "I'm proud of you, Merc," his manner was sober.

The words tugged a playfully curious frown from Mercuri but he remained silent and waited on Pope to continue.

"I'm glad all the shit we've been through hasn't jaded you the way it has the rest of us."

"I think you're confusing jaded with afraid."

"Afraid."

"I believe you're afraid of what it'd do to you to let one woman get to you the way Tee has to me."

Pope rolled his eyes. "Like I said, it's nice to know you care. Thanks for stopping by, but I'm alright," he went to bury himself at his desk.

Mercuri nodded as he walked the vast living room that was awash in morning light. The house rivaled his for space and location. Perched on a lonely cliff overlooking the Pacific, the place was a work of art on the outside as well as inside. Sadly, it was more like a museum than a home- a place meant to impress instead of rejuvenate. Unless his friend was brooding, Mercuri knew Pope spent precious little time there.

"I guess you heard the news out of Memphis?" Mercuri took a seat on one of the overstuffed midnight blue recliners before the room's bay windows.

Pope tossed aside the papers he'd only pretended to be studying. "I heard. Condolences aren't necessary."

"Didn't think so," Mercuri grinned. "Has anybody else tried to make contact?"

"Not yet..." Pope looked back to the cherrywood desk and contemplated scanning another of the papers lying there. Instead, he hissed a ragged curse and changed his mind.

"Everything okay?"

"Fantastic. And you can cease with the scary observation." Pope turned to fix his friend with a smug look. "My being out here doesn't mean I'm about to have a meltdown. Nathan Alberts was just a sperm donor."

Mercuri laughed, the fullness carrying high into the lofty ceiling. "You don't really believe I think you're out here mourning his death, do you?"

Sighing then, Pope gave Mercuri the full benefit of a frigid glare. "So what's up?"

"We just lost Patch," Mercuri voiced the truth softly as though attempting to jog Pope's memory. "Losing him was bad enough," he continued, "the *way* he died made it worse."

Silence carried as both men reflected on the friend they'd lost to a brutal beating at the hands of their former GAN colleagues.

"The rest of us are always unloading on you with our stuff," Mercuri gave a lazy roll of one massive shoulder. "I know Patch was your go-to guy when you needed to vent. I just wanted you to know I'm here."

"I know that, Merc," Pope came down off some of his frustration, "I'll remember it. I swear I'm okay. Go on home to Tee before she starts to miss you."

"She won't be missing me anytime soon," Mercuri relaxed back on the chair. "She's on a trip with her girlfriends."

Interest flared in the surging blue of Pope's eyes then. "For how long?"

Mercuri sighed, reached for a mini figurine of a hockey puck and stick on an end table. "They should be back by Wednesday afternoon."

"They all go?" Pope tried for nonchalance, sliding his thumb along the edge of the desk as he probed.

"Far as I know," none the wiser, Mercuri tossed the figurine back and forth.

"Bear too?"

"Yeah, she-" Blinking then, Mercuri straightened on the chair and fixed his old friend with a steely look. "Tell me the answer to what I'm thinking, is 'no'."

Pope only shrugged. "What are you thinking?"

Mercuri responded with something quiet and profane as he set down the tiny sculpture.

"What?" Pope felt sparks of his own temper beginning to flare. "Why do you get to enjoy Tee and we can't even get to know her friends?"

"Because I want to *keep on* enjoying Tee," Mercuri's voice matched the steel in his expression.

"For shit's sake, Merc what the hell do you think we'll do to 'em?"

Mercuri winced at Pope's misunderstanding. "That's not it," leaning forward, he braced elbows to knees and raked back his hair. The crop of blue black was close cut, but for the longer locks on top.

"That's not it," he insisted. Meanwhile, thoughts of hotel security discs from a night 6 years ago, flashed through his mind. He knew some of those discs contained material that went well beyond the security footage he'd viewed. It was material that a man couldn't easily forget.

"It's not that," he persisted a third time and looked up at Pope.

"Listen man," Pope's tone held a pleading chord. "Tee's friends are safe with us. I'm sure that even Rut's and Slay's intentions are

66

honorable," he shrugged then, giving Mercuri the treat of a lopsided grin. "Pretty much," he qualified.

"How'd you meet her?"

"Rascals."

Resting back on the chair again, Mercuri indulged in an eyeroll of his own.

"She's so goddamn beautiful, Merc. Hell…" Pope grinned over his phrasing which was highly accurate but not part of his usual vocabulary. He shook his head then. "Helluva temper. Didn't take long for me to discover it was one to be reckoned with especially when *she* discovered I was standing there while she took a phone call and I…Jesus…"

Again, Pope shook his head and appeared truly bewildered. "I was hooked…stupid…"

"I get it, man," it was Mercuri's turn to grin. "I don't think Tee would mind getting you a real introduction."

"I already, I um…I already got one Merc," Pope waited on some type of explosion but Mercuri only shook his head.

"For a minute, I thought you'd lost your edge," Mercuri mused, knowing how sly his friend could be when it came to arranging something to his favor. It was then that he took note of the uncharacteristic unease Pope wore and his suspicion set in.

"What'd you do? Po?" Mercuri called when no explanation was forthcoming.

"I set myself up as a potential client for her gun range, alright?"

Mercuri waited, having known Pope too long not to sense there was more to explain the look he wore.

"I put down a deposit to arrange a weekend for my friend…the one who hunts."

Mercuri grimaced. "I'm assuming no names were exchanged?"

"Only mine. Hers."

Again, Mercuri leaned forward on the chair. That time, he held his head in his hands as though it ached. The dense onyx strands shielded his broad forehead like thick slashes.

"Did you sleep with her?"

"No." Pope seemed proud to give the answer, but was soon appearing edgy. "Almost. She um… she gave me a tour. We wound up at this cottage at the far end of her ranch…" he shifted to spare another look to his desk as he continued. "She showed me to the bedroom and um…"

Mercuri only shook his head in wonder. "I know you're capable of coming up with a better plan than that piece of stupidity?"

"Well," Pope took no offense, cast off the criticism with a wave. "I was thinking with my dick so excuse me if my strategizing was a little off."

Mercuri was back to reclining on the chair, massaging his eyes with the heels of his hands. "Idiot."

"Nothing happened, goddammit!" The natural roaring intensity of Pope's voice came through on a towering wave. "It's not like I had a choice."

"No choice?" Mercuri moved his hands from his face, smirked. "So she forced you? I've seen Bear Clayton. To Tee, she's an Amazon, but really none of her friends are bigger than minutes compared to us. Excuse me, if I find that one hard to believe."

"She didn't force me," Pope seemed to resign himself. "I had no choice because she thought I was gay, alright?"

"Gay?" Mercuri repeated the word behind the hand that had gone to his mouth. Slowly, he exhibited perfect posture on the chair. "How-"

"I went on and on talking about getting the weekend for Rutger," Pope launched a slow pace of the room that appeared to be an ode to blue in the vivid swirls amid black in the carpeting and chairs of navy and metallic blue.

"I told her I wanted to make it special because I loved him a lot and she-" Pope put his back to one of the bay windows framing the room and waited for Mercuri to get a grip on his emotions. The man's laughter filtered the air.

"So glad I could amuse you."

"That's good, because you have!" Mercuri's laughter lingered a few seconds longer and then he was thumbing tears from the corners of his eyes. "This could still work out," he considered. "But you need to tell her the truth about who you really are. She may have a temper, but-"

"A lot of the temper's an act," Pope smiled over the observation. "She's a steel vault wrapped around a marshmallow," his expression tensed. "That doesn't mean she won't try to kick my ass for deceiving her and she'd be right to do it."

"Well then," Mercuri spread his hands, shrugged. "Tell her and let the chips fall."

"But I...I want her, Merc."

68

"By deceit. Trickery. We aren't those guys, Po. You've said so yourself. You even had to remind *me* of it a time or two."

"That was different," Pope murmured. "You and Tee didn't know anything about each other when you met. Clean slate and all that."

"So?"

"So Bear won't want to look at me, much less sleep with me when she finds out we're friends and that I know what she was part of. 'Scuse me for not sharing your optimism, but I can't think of many women who'd want a man they're sleeping with to know she once provided sexual entertainment for ten men."

"You've still got to tell her."

"I know, goddammit! Fuck! I know..." Pope smoothed his hands back over the hair tamed into its low tail. He shoved away from the window, prowling the room with the grace and intensity of a big cat.

"Maybe I would, if that's all I had to tell her."

Mercuri's sigh, was a weary one. "And what the hell does that mean?"

Pope stopped near the desk, bracing both hands to the surface when he hunched over it.

"That cottage of hers? She wants to buy it but she's getting the run around from the folks who own it. In short, she hates their guts."

"And you know who owns it?"

"Very well," Pope turned from the desk. "I do."

# CHAPTER 7

$T$he outdoors held a special allure for Bear, no matter the time of day, but it was the early morning hours that carried the greatest weight. Her favorite mornings were the ones that weren't earmarked for meetings or performance drills before sunrise. Those times, found her up no later than 5:30am.

For Bear, that time of day served for quiet moments of reflection-a time when she gathered her thoughts or ranked them in order of greatest importance. Something about the stillness of the pre-dawn hours that soothed-easing instead of kicking her into the day.

A cup of coffee-tea when she got to enjoy a rare day off-and she was all set to ponder her cares. There were usually at least 2 or 3 matters occupying space at the forefront of her mind. That morning, there was only one.

She'd prepared a deep mug of the rich, Hazelnut blend provided in her room at the inn. Bear threw a robe on over her PJs and; with the ceramic mug in hand, made her way down to the establishment's wraparound porch.

The space was furnished with an ample supply of white oak rockers that swayed consistently against a fragrant sea breeze. Bear tucked into a rocker facing the inn's ocean view. Methodically, she blew across the coffee's surface, sipped and willed the strong invigorating flavor to set her mind to rights. Specifically, she needed her mind freed of Pope Apostolou. *More* specifically, she needed it free of that moment in the cottage.

What had come over her? Talk about unprofessionalism at its best. It was a miracle she hadn't hit anything on her way off the estate yesterday when it was time to meet her friends for their weekend. She was halfway to LuCarolyn's place in Malibu, where they'd agreed to meet, when Bear realized she was running from herself-from what she wanted. Pope Apostolou definitely, but more than that. It was the reminder of what she'd denied herself for the last 6 years and how much she'd missed the sheer wonder of intimacy.

Sadly, intimacy and all it entailed rarely came without a price. It was a price she wasn't ignorant of. As a result, she'd decided to spare herself the aggravation of such an involvement. It was that decision, she believed, that had her up before the sun cast its hazy rays across the water.

Had it really been by way of her own decision that had spared her the unwanted cost of intimacy? Had she really found a way of avoiding that cost or had avoiding been easy because she hadn't encountered a real challenge?

She ran a business where there was no shortage of successful, gorgeous, intelligent men. Men, whose interests in guns often paralleled their interest in wooing the woman who helped to facilitate their past time. Had she remained immune to their interest by her own design? If so, why couldn't she get Pope Apostolou off her mind? Did he pose that much of a challenge? That much of a threat? He was definitely a distraction and that was threat enough.

A shiver kissed her through the robe and Bear was sure it had nothing to do with the chilly air coasting in off the shore. Warming her hands around the walnut brown mug, she sipped and tried to lose herself in the temperature and flavor of the brew. She was halfway through the coffee, when she saw Prin rounding the corner of the porch.

"Done with your beauty rest?" Prin's gaze was alight with teasing flavor.

Bear laughed. "I don't even think I started it."

Prin moved behind Bear's rocker. "I at least expected to find you singing. I'm hoping to get a good Patti rendition before we leave."

"Ha! Don't start," Bear pleaded in response to the jab at her habit for singing aloud when she was alone and in deep thought. Those 'private' performances were often overheard by her friends, amusing and impressing them to no end.

Prin tousled Bear's hair before dropping a kiss to the top of her head. "Lot on your mind?"

"Mmm…" Bear helped herself to more coffee.

Prin didn't press, instead settled to the porch's oak rail, a smooth surface coated in a finish of glossy white. For a time, only the soft roar of waves against the surf filled the air.

"So is that why you were so quiet yesterday?"

"Quiet?" Bear blurted, caught off guard. An instant later, she muttered a curse, recalling Prin's talent for observation. The woman seemed to have a knack for sensing the moods of others, regardless of how well they tried to hide them.

Instead of arguing her friend's suspicions, Bear only shrugged. "Didn't realize I was being quiet."

"Well," Prin rested her head back on the column she leaned against. "When LuCarolyn Young is in the room…"

Hushed giggling commenced. Anyone would seem 'quiet' when propped next to LuCarolyn's outspoken persona. With laughter then working to supplement the coffee's energizing effects, Bear decided a little confiding couldn't hurt.

"I met someone," she shared in an uncharacteristically small voice.

Prin turned her back on the slowly illuminating environment and smiled cautiously. "Met as in…?"

"Met."

The intriguing confirmation had Prin leaving the porch rail to take a seat in the rocker closest to Bear.

"Can we keep quiet about it for now?" Bear frowned towards the active waves. "I don't know where this is going and I don't want to deal with all the questions if…"

Prin was nodding, understanding all too well. The unexpected blue of her gaze added more urgency to the surprise filling them. "So is he uh…"

"Incredible? Yes. Gorgeous? Hell yes."

Prin bit her lip, obviously debating her next question. "Mercuri's caliber?"

"Oh yes," Bear didn't hesitate to confirm.

Prin leaned back against the rocker and sighed. After a moment, she frowned. "So why are you here and not snuggling with him in a bed somewhere?" She shifted on her chair when her question was met with silence.

"Is he married?" Prin whispered.

"No," Bear blurted, but winced. "I don't think so." Silently, she prayed he wasn't as a replay of the cottage scene unfolded inside her mind.

"I don't really know much about him, aside from the fact that he has a soft spot for his friends."

"Oh, how sweet," Prin crooned.

Bear sucked her teeth. "Hell, Prin this is not the beginning of a fairy tale."

"Why not?" Prin bristled at the look Bear gave. "That was six years ago. We can't keep turning our backs on chances to live or...at least stop denying ourselves pleasure."

"It's not that," soft tapping emerged from where Bear clicked her nails against the glazed mug. "I definitely want that- the pleasure part," she sent Prin a sheepish look and then grimaced. "But I'd be lying if I said I didn't want some of what Tee has."

"Oh Bear! That's great-"

"I can't I-" Bear raised a hand, indicating to Prin that she needed a minute. "I'm not willing to put in that kind of...work."

"Meaning?" Prin inclined her head, causing the messy ball atop it to tilt as well.

"I'm just not willing to compromise what I am to make anything...beyond sex- work."

"And just how do you know that sex isn't all he wants?"

Bear's somber look mellowed as she considered the possibility.

Dawning discovery, had Prin's bright eyes narrowing. "So...you weren't just speaking in general... you'd like some of what Tee has with *this* guy? Whoa...he must've made *some* impression."

"Did he ever..." Bear down the rest of her coffee and set the empty mug next to her chair on the porch.

Prin leaned over to squeeze Bear's knee. "It *could* happen, you know? You might not even have to compromise."

"Oh I would." Bear's lips twisted into a wry smile. "They always want you to. Remember what Tee said about Mercuri eventually wanting her to give up her apartment?"

"Aw Hon," Prin squeezed Bear's knee again. "It's compromise, not surrender."

"It's not even surrender, not really. Men want to conquer. Surrender is giving in. If they conquer, you've given up."

"That's bleak."

"It's true." Bear pulled her gaze from the sun that was just beginning to glint off the water. "You know that," she looked to Prin.

Prin kept silent and Bear used the time to reconsider her outlook.

"Maybe you're right," she sighed with a weary shrug. "Maybe I am making too much of this- at this point I don't really care."

"So you're going for it," Prin's face was luminous.

"You know? I thought you'd give me better advice," Bear folded her arms over her chest and regarded her friend curiously. "Tee's all goo-goo over Mercuri and Lu...well...gorgeous guy, sex, what's the problem?"

"Well I'm sticking to my decision. I say, 'go for it'."

"Just like that?" Bear laughed.

"Why not?" Prin clasped her hands to her chest. "Hell, make it clear to him that it's just about the sex. Men do it all the time. Why can't we?"

Bear's expression turned more inquisitive. "And what about you? Would *you* do the same?"

Prin settled back against her rocker and leveled her gaze out across the water for a time. "If a guy tugged at me the way this one's tugging at you..." she shook her head, looked down at her hands clasped in her lap.

"We haven't let anyone touch us in six years, Bear. You've just had a guy awaken you in the nicest possible way. You deserve to enjoy yourself, so long as it's on *your* terms."

"My terms," Bear nodded as though she were being given the answer to a perplexing issue. Closing her eyes, she put the phrase on loop inside her head.

***

By late afternoon on Sunday, Pope was thinking about all he'd been missing out on by not spending more time at his property in

Pacifica. The place may not have exuded the same warmth as Mercuri's home out in wine country, but Pope discovered his place held its own brand of charm.

Quiet for one. Same as at Mercuri's but different in the way the water crashed along the base of the cliffs. The muted sounds of nature seemed to organize his thinking which had been a fragmented mess since he'd first arrived at the house for his extended California stay. He'd spent much of that Friday trying to track down the owner of the Burlingame property only to discover it was himself.

From there, he'd been preoccupied with thoughts of Berrill Clayton until Mercuri had arrived that Saturday morning. Now; with only his thoughts keeping him company again, they were fixed on one topic only-Berrill Clayton.

He'd spent the years following the violent resignation from The GAN, on building his wealth, outside of the investment, he, Rutger and Slayte had made in Mercuri's shipping corporation. It was a move that would keep them financially secure for the rest of their lives. Pope had wanted-needed-more though. He could admit to only a few that he had an obsession with ownership. Misguided? Perhaps, but he believed it put distance between him and a time when he'd felt like nothing more than property.

He had a hard time giving up on people or situations and was fiercely determined when it involved taking care of things that belonged to him. Now, it was just his luck that what he was becoming most possessive over, was a woman with the fiercest independent streak he'd ever seen.

He'd only spent precious little time with her and yet, she'd been a soother for emotions that had grown rawer since Patch's death. Mercuri hadn't been exaggerating when he'd called Patch his go-to guy when he'd needed to vent. Things were still so unsettled for everyone involved, that Pope, as usual, set his agitations and concerns to the emotional backburner.

Bear had made him forget it all from the moment he'd overheard her tough-talking her employees over a month prior. To say he was hooked, was a real understatement. He'd scarcely been able to string together a single cohesive thought involving all the other things requiring his attention. She got in his way every time and all he could summon was an image of her long bangs hitting the thick fringe of lashes framing those rich mocha eyes.

The mink texture of her eyes, the warm silken tone of her caramel doused skin, they were etched in his thoughts. She hadn't seemed to take offense to his actions in the cottage and God what he wouldn't give to return to that moment-to finish what he'd started.

Her physical tug was a potent one, but it wasn't all there was. It broke his heart to discover she was quietly torturing herself for the situation with her deceased employee. He sensed that occurrence had only made it impossible for her to forget the fix she and her friends had found themselves in 6 years ago. He had to find a way to tell her that, not only did he know about that fix, but that he'd once worked for the very men that fateful night had been arranged for.

Would she care that none of it mattered to him? Care that he had no love for The GAN? Probably not and then...the fact that they'd spoken on more than one occasion and he'd still not fully introduced himself...

Deceit-trickery-just as Mercuri had said.

With a quick scowl, Pope pushed back from the wrought iron patio table and walked to the edge of the brick structure to look out over active waves. Nodding, he silently approved of the plan he'd made to tell her everything the minute she got back from her trip.

He couldn't deny that said plan had him quaking in his size fifteens. He tried to embolden himself on the persuasive ability people seemed to think he had. His friends thought he could talk anyone into or out of anything and he supposed it was true enough. Would that talent work on the likes of Berrill Clayton?

To be on the safe side, he'd decided against having that talk at her ranch. Instead, he made arrangements for lunch at a cafe inside an inn he'd found in her town. He'd called the ranch and arranged the meet through her assistant Shaun Oates. Oates had assured him his boss would be there and Pope celebrated the fact that his 50k was still pulling strings for him.

The satisfaction beginning to course his veins, slowed when he felt the insistent vibration of the phone in his pocket. His softly hissed curse was followed by a quick prayer that it not be Oates with a message from his boss who'd discovered she was, in fact, offended by his actions at the cottage and left word for Shaun to tell him to go to hell.

The name on his faceplate, while not Shaun Oates', instilled the same foreboding-perhaps moreso. Sparing time for another hissed curse, Pope activated the call.

"Gerrick."

"Pope." Gerrick Ferguson's voice was firm and hinted of approval. "Thank you for taking my call."

"Not taking it would've just had you calling again, right?"

"Well I won't hold you long. I don't know if you heard-"

"Hell Gerrick, I hope you're not calling to tell me I'm in your prayers during my time of bereavement?"

"I'm not. I know you could care less he's dead."

"And yet here we are talking anyway."

"There're things you need to know, Pope."

"Not if it's about the GAN which, in case you forgot, I don't work for anymore."

"Maybe not, but there's a chance you're about to play a very big role in the GAN's future. I wouldn't be surprised if you get a call soon from Nate's attorneys."

Pope virtually snarled then and could feel the slender mobile creak in his grip when he tightened it. "I don't want anything of his."

"That may be, kid, but there's a strong chance he left it to you anyway."

Enviably long, soot-colored lashes drifted down over Pope's eyes as he scourged himself over the stab of curiosity Gerrick's words invoked.

"Like what?" Pope heard himself ask and winced.

"We should talk in person-"

"Forget it."

"I don't mind coming to California."

"Good for you."

"Pope-"

"Why now? What is it? Some last minute confession the fucker made to you on his deathbed?"

"Not exactly, but it *is* something we didn't dare speak of before now."

"We?"

"If you'd just meet with me-"

"You know I won't agree to that."

"Alright," Gerrick said once silence had hugged the line for several moments. "I know you need to talk with Mercuri and the others first."

"And you know there's even less of a snowball's chance of them going for this than I would."

"What if I told you there was a chance you could revamp the GAN?"

"I'd ask why the hell you think that matters to me? Especially when I helped try to crush it six years ago? No word yet on whether our latest efforts will prove successful."

"What if there's another way?"

"To what? Crush it?"

"Save it."

"You're just not hearin' me, are you Gerrick? *Why* would we want that?"

"I know why you're upset-"

"You don't know a goddamn thing about me." The well-heeded threat in the quiet roar of Pope's voice came through as though amplified.

Gerrick matched the loathing in the younger man's voice, with patience. "I've known your- I've known Nathan Alberts and Lorne Grodins a long time. What the GAN is, isn't what it was supposed to be."

"I don't want to hear this, Gerrick."

"I understand that, but would you at least run it by Mercuri, Slayte and Rutger? See what they have to say?"

Pope answered with silence.

"You're right, son," Gerrick sighed. "I don't know a goddamn thing about you but I believe you're too intelligent not to be curious about what I have to say. Think on it."

Pope studied the darkened screen for long moments after Ferguson disconnected. As he'd done during the conversation, Pope squeezed the mobile so that it creaked under the crushing pressure of his grip. He was sorely tempted to hurl the device across the room, but stopped.

Memories of another phone crashing into a wall, whirled to the surface of his thoughts. Just like that, Bear had resumed her place occupying the king's portion of his focus. Left dimple flashing in response to his smile, Pope recalled the day at The Rascal when he'd collected the remnants of her outburst. Shards of a destroyed phone had been left in her wake.

Instead of smashing his phone, Pope used it to dial out.

"Heller's Inn, Burlingame California." A perky feminine voice greeted.

"Yes, Pope Apostolou. I have a lunch reservation for Thursday."

"Yes, Mr. Apostolou, how can we help you?"

"I was wondering if I could book a room to go along with it?"

\*\*\*

Berrill learned shortly after moving to Burlingame that there was one huge advantage to small town living. People had a sixth sense about strangers in their midst. Especially the dangerous looking ones. She had been highly motivated to decline Pope's meeting request er-confirmation, as it were when Shaun informed her that he'd already accepted the invitation on her behalf. Bear made a mental note to discuss with he and Mike Hough-her other manager- that a 50k deposit didn't give a client free reign to dictate to their boss-dangerous looking or otherwise.

Nevertheless, Bear reconsidered her thoughts on cancelling with Pope. Stupid, considering all she wanted was to see him. Even if it was only for business. During the drive into town, she'd devoted the necessary moments to berating herself for being a weak, sexually frustrated fool. Once she'd arrived at the inn; and was taking the cobblestone walk leading to the establishment's quaint doors, she recalled her chat with Prin.

"My terms," she'd muttered.

She'd arrived almost an hour early for the precise reason of keeping things on her terms. Most importantly, she was looking forward to wiping the natural self confidence from Pope Apostolou's gorgeous face when he arrived to find her already waiting.

A small victory, but she was okay with taking what she could get. The man was far too self-possessed and sure of himself for her tastes. It made him even more distracting and she needed to keep her wits about her if she planned to get through another encounter without winding up on her back. Which, she had to admit, wouldn't exactly be a bad thing...

~~~

After greeting the diner's hostess; who was also the innkeepers oldest daughter, Bear appreciated another benefit to small town living. People were always willing to share information about the strangers their sixth sense warned them of. The dangerous looking ones always got the bulk of the attention. Bear gave, what she'd considered a vague description of the man she was to meet, and watched the hostess transform.

Lila Heller, a usually mild-mannered sort, then exhibited the manner of a woman on the verge of swooning. Following the unexpected display of feminine delight, Bear learned that her lunch companion had already arrived and that he'd secured a room as well.

~~~

Now, she was standing outside Pope Apostolou's door and asking herself just what the fuck she thought she was doing. The 'keeping things on her terms' argument came to mind, but she knew that was bullshit. She could've kept things on her terms just fine at the table he'd reserved for them in the diner downstairs.

But no...she was there outside his door-a door she'd just hit with a rather insistent knock-to make a point to herself. The point being, that this was all about appeasing the ego of the alpha girl bitch persona to which she'd become a willing slave. It had to be all about that and not the fact that a man; whose presence she'd been in all of a day, was slowly breaking down that persona and she was about to prove herself immune.

An admirable feat, if she could pull it off. All she was capable of, in that moment, was feeling a touch apprehensive while second guessing her actions. Pope Apostolou was not the kind of man whose door a woman knocked on to make a point.

Yet, there she was. The tan, casual jumpsuit felt like a furnace under its matching shortwaist blazer while she debated her next move. Irrelevant, once the door opened. The saucy greeting she'd been anxious to utter, idled in the back of her throat along with a quick lusty sound akin to a moan. It accompanied a lump of emotion that seriously affected the ease of her breathing.

She shouldn't have been surprised to find him...indisposed. She was practically an hour early, after all. Still, it was one of the better decisions she'd made in her life.

The man clearly had no qualms about answering his door...half dressed. What man would with a body like the one he possessed? At last; the words that caught in her throat, tumbled forth on a staggered whisper.

"Is-is this a...bad time?"

# CHAPTER 8

Pope would never claim he was immune to being caught off guard.
While his best friends would claim otherwise, Pope would be the first to
argue in his own defense. He'd never claimed to being *immune* to being
caught off guard. The fact that he'd never *been* caught off guard was
another matter entirely.

He stood silently appraising the unexpected guest on the other
side of his door. He could almost feel his initial surprise and uncertainty
at finding her there, make way for pleasure and the barest hint of
amusement. He'd wager that he wasn't half as surprised as she was.

"Bad time?" He returned her query before cocking his head a
fraction. "I wouldn't say that."

Bear felt her muscles seize but she ordered her body not to
betray the reaction. Of course he wouldn't think it was a bad time, damn
him. Still, she couldn't resist swallowing around the lump of emotion
still holding its own in the back of her throat.

Just like that, her 'my terms' and 'making a point' arguments
evaporated like mist. The devastating blue of his gaze harbored

amusement and a noticeable sliver of devilry when he reached out to run the back of his hand down her arm.

"Are you coming in? I'm getting a chill."

Bear heard him talking. The admission should've had sheer mortification scalding her cheeks. At the very least, she should've been able to break her fixed stare from his bare chest and the nipples that were indeed reacting to the breeze from the hall.

She recalled her fleeting assessment of him as he'd collected the shards of her demolished phone at the restaurant where they'd first met. She remembered marveling at his size and realized now, how incomplete her assessment had been. Nothing compared to how...immense he was in nothing but the towel held indifferently at his waist while droplets of water beaded across the flawless copper of his skin. Damp, jet waves glistened and touched the tops of eclipsing shoulders.

Slowly, her eyes drifted higher along the door. His hand curved at the uppermost edge just above where he rested the side of his head. She was roasting inside her suit then and her pumps felt like she was standing on stilts, she quivered that much.

"I should," awkwardly, she pointed in the general direction she'd come. "Should, um-"

"What? Go?"

"I...I don't know you well enough to-to be here.." She heard him make a soft, tsking sound that sent her eyes sliding across his stunning face to the superb mouth where the lone dimple slashed.

"You know I can't let you go, Ms. Clayton. You knew that before I opened the door."

She did know that and was glad he'd saved her from making the decision. She felt totally outside herself, unable to make the simplest choices. Like what to do when he gave the flimsiest of tugs to her jacket sleeve and indicated that he wished for her to move forward.

"I-" Her tone; still whisper soft and needy, managed to carry her words as she put up another valiant attempt at speaking. "I really don't mind waiting down-" she almost whimpered at the sensation his fingers stirred as they stroked the underside of her wrist.

"Downstairs," she forced herself to finish.

"But that's not where you really want to be, is it?"

He had her across the threshold then and with no memory of how or when she'd stumbled over it. He was right. Absolutely right. That wasn't where she wanted to be. As she'd told herself, a woman didn't knock on Pope Apostolou's door to make a point. She knocked for reasons far more basic-far more... carnal.

The door was at her back. Pope rested one hand above her head on the slab of rich red oak. His other, still secured the towel at his lean waist-barely. Even in the killer pumps, the top of her head just reached his jawline. Her eyes were wonderfully aligned with his chest which looked to have been painstakingly carved as though by chisel. She couldn't help but to marvel at the discipline and agony it must take to hone one's body into a work of living art.

Every part of her tingled from uncertainty, arousal, anticipation. His next words to her proved, he'd sensed all three.

"I frighten you, don't I?"

The question pulled her back a fraction from her captivation. "No," she managed.

Pope smiled, enjoying that she fought even while drowning. "Honesty, babe," he said.

The soothing roar of his voice had Bear whimpering then for sure. His resulting laughter should've roused her anger. It didn't.

"Afraid of me," the truth had him vexed enough to brace his weight to his elbow while bringing a hand to his brow in concern. Was the fear about *him* or what he made her feel? He'd tackle that issue later, along with his own plans for honesty. She'd knocked on his door and his only concern then was in giving her what she needed and taking what he wanted.

"Afraid of me," he continued, "but you want me," he trailed his nose across the shell of her ear, the lobe and the silken sensitive skin beneath.

"You can't wait to have me," subtle amusement held his voice.

Bear gave into amusement of her own. "And you're too sure of yourself," her voice trembled and amusement fled as Pope's damp hair trailed her skin.

His head lowered steadily toward her neck until he was suckling her collarbone. Bear had to bite her lip to stifle a moan that time, but the gesture was no help against the next lone whimper to slip past. The slow, seductive glide of his tongue on her skin took her breath and almost robbed her of thought.

"I should go," she made no move to do so.

Pope raised his head, but kept it at a level to hold his radiant stare aligned with her smoky, mocha one. "Why leave when you don't want to?" his eyes narrowed with devilish humor. "Can't stand to have a white guy touch you?"

Bear may've laughed over the absurdity of the statement especially when she noiticed his tempting mouth twitch in amusement. Instead, she smirked with her own devilish look. "Some of my best friends are white."

"Ouch," he winced and indulged in the slightest chuckle before rising to his full height. "Guess it's a good thing I'm not trying to be your friend."

Her amusement took on a dry edge then and she rested her head back on the door. "Anyone ever tell you, you talk too much?"

"All the time."

Before her brain even registered the action, his hand resting near the door was at her wrist and pressing it to her side with the barest hint of restraint.

"I like to make myself clear," he said, "especially when it comes to moments like these."

"Your life's so full of them, I guess?"

His expression betrayed no sense of humor then. "Not for a very long time." Silently, he added that it had also never been in a way where he felt in danger of his own loss of control.

"Consent is important to me, though," he said, "once I have it, I have a hard time letting anyone take it back. Be damn sure you want this."

"I don't scare easy, Mr. Apostolou."

"I'm aware. I only want *you* to be aware. I take my pleasure seriously and I take a lot of it. You may need to work hard to get out of this once I'm in the middle of it. Do you understand me, Bear?"

She felt inept, incapable of forming the response he sought- the one she wanted to give. She managed a pathetic nod.

"Gonna need words to go along with that, Bear." Still, he closed what space there was between them and set his focus on undoing the buttons along the bodice of her suit. Wavy locks, drier then, shielded the sinful allure of his face in a tumble of lustrous black as his head dipped.

"Gonna need that yes, Babe," he murmured the request against her collarbone which he seemed to find irresistible.

Nodding was all Bear seemed capable of what with his middle and index fingers snug inside her suit. He freed the buttons with stealthy confidence, not stopping until the garment opened to expose her to the waist.

"Yes please," he murmured encouragingly at her earlobe. Moments later, his tongue flicked at a small, silver hoop that played peekaboo in her hair worn loose that day.

When he took the hoop and her lobe in his mouth and sucked, Bear was ready to slide down the length of the door. Pope prevented that easy by lifting her high against him.

The move required that he relinquish his hold on the towel at his waist. It hit the floor with a whisper that was repeated when Bear discarded her jacket moments later. She pulled away the suit's thick straps. The bodice dangled past her hips while she maneuvered from her bra. All the while, she inclined her head, determined to keep her ear exposed for his skillful mouth. His lazy tongue there had her lips parted for a moan she was too overwhelmed to give.

"Is this my yes?" he queried.

She didn't hesitate any longer. "Yes, please," her voice was a husky whisper that merged into low laughter when she heard his chuckle.

"I guess that's it for the talking, then," he gave her a soft bounce and squeezed her bottom once she'd settled into his palms.

Her heart thrummed at the base of her throat while her pulse beat in her ears. Overwhelmed, seemed like a poor descriptor for the sensation gliding through her like a fragrant syrup. The tireless way he explored her ear and the way his hands cradled her ass, made her feel both cherished and secure.

Bear had no misconceptions about what this was. They were about to fuck and there was nothing in that certainty that said cherishing would play a role. Whatever the truth, all that mattered was what she felt and she was damn well determined to enjoy it all.

She was naked to the waist and trembled in reaction to her breasts crushed into the brick wall that was his chest. There, his heart beat strong, steady, sure. His tongue trailed the curve of her jaw and down her neck. His head dipped again and she threaded her fingers through the thick, silken strands that brushed her cheek like mink.

Again, Bear felt her back to the door. That time, Pope set her high against it, putting her chest level with his riveting stare. With her back to the door, he secured her on a forearm that was long and densely packed with muscle. Pope used his free hand to cup and squeeze one breast while his lips and tongue launched a hungry assault on its twin.

Her legs were locked around his back and her thighs clenched his lean waist when his perfect teeth grazed her nipple.

Her fingers curled into his hair when he applied more pressure to the nub and gnawed lightly. Her moans hitched on quiet cries of desire-sensation seemed to thrive inside her. She arched, desperate for him to take more of her body into his mouth.

Pope accepted the offer and Bear fisted handfuls of his hair out of desperation and sheer appreciation. Soft, beckoning sucking sounds stirred, joining the sounds of their mingled breathing.

He uttered ragged, savage sounds in sync with the effort he took to pleasure her with the simple treat. It was no hardship. She smelled like heaven- talcum powder with hints of lavender and tasted as sweet as she looked. He was sensitive enough to feel her nipple pebbling on his tongue as arousal had it firming.

"Christ, Bear," he groaned again, switching his attention to her other breast- its nipple already rock hard in response to being handled by his fingers and thumb. He kept the plump mound cupped for his claiming.

"Easy," he soothed when she trembled anew at his touch. He could feel her rolling just a bit on his forearm, faint thrusting moves that proved her excitement. He could take her there against the door, satisfy them both- and quickly. But this...this he wanted to savor. He wagered she'd regret what would happen between them over the course of the many hours he intended to keep her in that room. With that in mind, he intended to give her a lot to regret.

Still feasting on her breasts, he carried her from the door. His strength was an aphrodisiac all its own, Bear decided. Her bottom shelved on his forearm was all the support she needed. She didn't bother to hold on for dear life. Instead, she squeezed, massaged, kneaded the shoulders that were as unyielding as granite and broad enough to captivate as well as intimidate.

Pope dropped her suddenly and her gasp flew just as she hit the middle of the bed. The storm brewing in her eyes, died a quick death when they lowered from his sapphire blues; brimming with playful challenge, to take in the rest of him.

Bear had compared his primed, powerful frame to living art- living weapon was just as apt a descriptor. She swallowed-tried to swallow. There was no getting around the lump lodged there. Unconscious of doing so, she retreated when her observations took her below his waist where she confirmed that every part of his body was properly proportioned.

He was, without question, superbly built. Undoubtedly long, but it was the girth of his sex that had her eyes fixed and her heart rate elevating. She'd never questioned her ability to take a man before. This one had her questioning, even as she anticipated.

Bear discovered she'd never anticipated...taking as much as she did then. Vague panic had her swallowing when he took her ankle and dragged her back from where she'd retreated. Keeping hold, he discarded the pump she wore and followed by tugging her free of a pant leg. He handled the other shoe and the rest of her suit without ceremony until she lay nude but for the scrap of lacy white panties at her waist. Closer to him then, Bear triumphed over her uncertainty and reached out, intending to drag her fingers along the array of defined abdominals and lower...

Before she could manage it, he was joining her on the bed. Bear experienced a sense of deja vu, memories of the encounter at the cottage emerging when he snagged both her wrists and kept them in place above her head.

"This'll be over too soon if you touch me, Bear." His words were a low murmur wrapped in the soft roar of his voice. Her name silenced on his tongue as it swirled an erect nipple that rapidly lowered and elevated as she panted.

"Too soon," he whispered, drawing the licorice dark gem between his lips.

She braced against his hold, averting her face as sensation slammed her mercilessly. Pope abandoned the nipple within seconds of taking possession. He left the bud glistening and air-chilled while taking the other and treating it to a far more ravenous torment.

All sensation for Bear seemed to stem from his mouth working over her chest. Intermittently, he sucked both nipples, feasted at the undersides of the plump mounds and used his tongue to bathe the valley between. His fingers skimmed her thigh, causing her to brace hard against his hold at her wrists.

"Shh..." he mouthed beneath her breasts and firmed his grip. He lay near her side instead of crushing her beneath his considerable weight. The hand skimming her thigh, brushed the lacy side stitching of her panties. His fingers curved along the middle of the garment as if he meant to explore what lay beneath. Instead, he moved higher and spent a few moments simply rotating the back of his fist over her clit.

Bear hid her face in the crook of her elbow to muffle a ragged cry when it stirred. Her fingers flexed restlessly above his clutch and every part of her trembled. Pope resumed his lazy suckle on her earlobe which did nothing to ease her trembling.

"Relax…" he soothed.

Just as Bear was beginning to think she might be able to give 'relaxing' a try, she heard the definitive rip signalling the destruction of her underwear. There was no time to register anger or even agitation over the loss. His middle finger took possession, spearing high and deep, rotating deliberately. Bear gasped her pleasure into the room.

Meanwhile, Pope groaned into the bed's amber comforter and winced as he stroked her. He'd be coming two seconds after he was inside her-another good reason to take his time. He hadn't been wrong about how small she was. Tight-extremely and while the fact pleased him to no end, it meant having to go the extra mile in tethering his baser instincts to claim and conquer for his satisfaction alone. It was then, that he tuned into her voice, small and ragged.

"Wait…"

His response was to give her another finger to ride. Bear arched, sending another tortured gasp into the room.

"Please wait," she said even as her moisture doused his index finger as it had his middle.

"Please…mmm…" she bit down on her lip and writhed on the tangle of covers. "Pope…"

"You'll have to do better than that…"

Bear was torn between laughter and despair. "I…I don't want to come this way, I…I'm too used to this way…" the quiet confession had her averting her face for a whole other reason then.

Pope understood and his heart broke a little more for her even as he watched her in disbelief. Had she locked herself away for 6 years? Was he the first man she'd allowed to touch her in all that time?

"Babe," his fingers had ceased moving inside her, but he didn't withdraw.

Bear kept her face hidden. "I don't want your pity," she said.

"That's not what I'm giving you. Hey?" He waited for her eyes to meet his. "Honey it has to be this way at first. You've seen the way I'm built, right?"

She bristled and; despite the situation, Pope smiled and imagined that the blood was rushing to her cheeks over the memory of what she'd seen-what was currently resting along her thigh.

"I don't want to hurt you."

"I don't care."

Damn, but she was tough! He mused.

"Maybe you don't," he said, "but I do and since I'm the one with the upper hand," he squeezed her wrists in reminder.

"I can get out of this anytime," she braced against his grip which was firm but not crushing.

"Of course you can get out of it anytime," he spoke near her ear, ran his tongue along the petal soft skin behind it. "Something tells me you don't really want to." He rotated his fingers inside her then, smiling wickedly when she trembled.

"Damn you," she moaned.

"You'll thank me." His laughter held the same quiet roar as his voice. "Trust me, okay? Now shut up and let me make it good for you. I'll let you dictate next time."

He freed her wrists and took his 'next time' comment off her mind. Bear kept her arms above her head and indulged in the mink sweep of his hair across her breasts, ribs, and belly as he kissed his way down her body. Anticipating her moves, he cupped her thighs firmly and seconds before his mouth claimed her core.

Bear tried to arch her hips, but could only faintly thrust given how securely he held her. His tongue invaded as his fingers had moments earlier. The locks of wavy black shielded his striking face as he moved his head shifting with every nuance he brought to the intimate taking. She smoothed her hands down her body until she was again winding her fingers through the strands splayed on her belly as he feasted. She opened her mouth, but there was no sound. Everything seemed trapped in her throat while pleasure attacked.

Pope's hold at her thighs; while firm, wasn't painful. His fingertips massaged the toned limbs with every stroke set rhythmically to the sweeping rotations of his tongue. Soon after, he was draping one thigh over his shoulder. The other, he kept almost flat on the bed.

His tongue speared deeper and Pope heard a low rumble of pleasure emerge from his throat when she shuddered his name. She was almost there, he knew. She'd been streaming moisture consistently against his tongue for the last few minutes. Her inner walls clenched

90

gently as he explored the part of her he was beyond feverish to have. He withdrew, smiling at the sound of her disappointed whine. In apology, he planted an open mouthed kiss to her inner thigh and outlined the small beauty mark there with the tip of his tongue.

"Please," she didn't care if she begged and tugged his hair insistently.

Her hand weakened seconds later, when he tongued the seam of her sex, drawing the petals between his lips to suckle gently at first and then with greater demand. Her clit was next to receive the attention when his nose encircled the puckered nub before his tongue repeated the act. Her entire body tensed, both hands fisting in his hair again. She used the grip for purchase as her hips rocked against him.

She exchanged her hold on his hair to drag her fingers through her own shoulder length strands lying in a tousle on the comforter. She clutched her hair in desperation as the missed experience of a true orgasm visited like a welcomed friend. Pope was utterly patient in the pleasure he gave and seemed to strive, not only to take her over the edge, but to drive her deep into what lay on the other side.

Now, it was his thumb at her clit. The touch would've had her bucking off the bed, but with his weight on her she could only grind into the comforter that was damp with her need. His tongue had resumed its erotic exploration.

"Come for me again," his command was soft yet brooked no refusal given the underlying roughness melded into the chords of his voice.

His tongue plunged deeper, unrelenting and he seemed to shatter right along with her when yet another orgasmic wave seized.

Pleasure slammed like an invisible forcefield and Bear; hands weak and seemingly incapable, suddenly fisted as pain seared below her waist. Her sex protested the intrusion of his which came within seconds of her superb climax. Instinct poised her to fight but Pope countered her attack.

Once again, he cuffed her wrists- one in each hand which he pressed to either side of her head. While the need to fight still prevailed, Bear felt another need slowly begin to consume it. The penetration; painful at first, transitioned into something far more addictive. The moan breaking from her throat wavered, crested as her hips arched to meet his.

"That's it," Pope murmured when he saw the discomfort leaving her lovely face. With her hands still closed in his fists, he leaned over to once again lay claim to her breasts. Her ego-stroking gasps and cries stirred his own satisfied groans. Hungrily, he suckled at nipples still puckered from his earlier attention.

He released her wrists and Bear didn't hesitate to sink her fingers into his hair. She wanted to see his face and her heart lurched at the determination she found there. Her body hummed with every advance and retreat of his well built cock. She moaned wantonly, without shame, and replied with a hushed 'yes' when he abandoned her breasts to take her mouth.

He could've enjoyed her that way forever, but his hormones craved more-demanded he give into his more aggressive needs for however long she'd allow it. Hands at her waist then, he flipped her to her stomach and tugged until she raised up slightly on her knees. Returning the favor of her hands in his hair, he clutched a fistful of hers. He used his knee to spread her thighs, readying her to take him. Using his free hand, he held onto her upper arm to keep her anchored while he took her from behind.

Her cries carried on a sharp, stunned wave of sound. She could've muffled them in the pillows scattered across the bed, but his hand in her hair and the other at her arm, kept her right where he wanted her. Bear bit hard on her bottom lip in order to quiet herself. After a while, Pope traded his grip in her hair for one at her hip. His hand on her arm kept her raised off the bed and positioned for the plundering strokes he pumped into her.

"Fuck," he whispered, dropping her arm then to take both her hips in a smothering grip. He used it to set their pace-rapid and savage when he sought to brand her with his thrusts-slow and sultry when he worked to tamp down the need to come hard inside her.

Bear's unwavering cries of delight and approval never diminished, so Pope happily assumed she didn't find his actions overtly selfish. He savored the opportunity to take the lead. More than that, he savored the moment that had so sublimely come his way. Few things in a man's life could compare to the pleasure of a strong, confident woman coming apart in his arms.

Bear's steady, pleasure-rich breaths sounded closer to hiccups then. When her sex locked around his shaft like a vice, Pope was the one coming apart. He leaned closer to bathe her dewy skin with ragged strokes of his tongue as he erupted inside her. Bear melted onto the rumpled covers and purred over the hot spray of his semen coating her walls. The tell-tale slurping sounds of bodies at sex, filtered in amidst their heightened breaths.

Pope panted harshly as his release was spent. The need to feel Bear against him had him sheltering her beneath him as exhaustion wafted. He didn't mind them taking time to rest. They'd need it to endure all that was to come that night.

# CHAPTER 9

Though the moment hadn't exactly happened as he'd planned it, Pope wasn't about to argue the outcome. His time with Berrill Clayton over the last 20 hours had been surprisingly uninterrupted. She'd knocked on his door around noon the day before. It was close to 10am then and he'd spent the greater portion of that time inside that sleek body of hers.

Dressed now, he was seated on the edge of the very well-used bed and watching her sleep. Chances were strong that she'd be out for several more hours yet. He would arrange for her not to be disturbed when he checked out. The dimple slashed along his mouth as he smiled in approval of the way she rested on her stomach, forearms hidden beneath a pillow. Her soft, deep breaths were a testament to how heavily she slumbered.

*You can't keep her.* The voice he'd dreaded hearing- the message he'd dreaded even more-surged in from the recesses of his mind. In an effort to silence it, he let the back of his hand cruise the line of her spine. Why the fuck couldn't he keep her? She wasn't attached, hadn't let a man touch her in 6 years…

What they'd done together in that room, he'd all but branded her as his.

"Idiot," he murmured.

Such a concept wouldn't go over well at all with someone as fiercely independent as she was. That independence would prove a volatile mix against someone as possessive as *he* was.

Bear shifted and Pope took his hand from her back where her skin began to riddle with gooseflesh. Silently, he told himself to go before he climbed back into bed with her. Resolved, he gathered the sheets tucked at her waist and was drawing them up when she shifted again and turned to her back.

Just like that, his hunger returned to transform the vibrant ultramarine of his eyes into a fathomless midnight blue. With a sigh, Pope accepted that it'd be a little longer before he was heading down to check out. Just a little longer, he promised himself. Probability was high that she wouldn't want to see him again-not this way. That would be a problem, since he was quite simply infatuated with her. Their hours together had done the exact opposite of curbing his desire for her. The need was stronger than it had ever been.

The way she reacted to his touch, the sounds she made when he stroked her, the way she squeezed his dick when he was inside her...she would affect him for a long time to come. The least he could do was enjoy what little time he had left with her.

He let one hand hover above a slowly rising breast. Gently, her nipple bumped his palm until he cupped the mound and worked the flat bud beneath his thumb. Half a second later, he was using his tongue instead. Surprise welded in response to the moan he uttered when the nipple began to pucker in response. His steady breathing turned labored and he raked a hand through his hair when he looked up to see if she'd awakened.

Bear wasn't fully lucid, but Pope could see that his fondling was intruding on her subconscious. Her full lips were parted and the slightest furrows were appearing between her long, arched brows. Pope was content to make the most of the time before she woke and he returned to enjoy suckling her breasts. He sensed when her breathing changed to exhibit sighs and slight panting. He raised his head that time to find himself peering into her sleep-sexy gaze. Once again, his dick was aching to be back where it had spent the night and most of the previous day.

"Why are you dressed?" her words were slurred, yet her grip was firm where it held the material of the dark olive shirt he wore outside charcoal brown trousers.

She tugged and Pope needed no further encouragement to take her mouth in a sultry kiss that had them both moaning. Pope kept one hand fisted in the pillow near her head. His other drifted along the top sheet until he was cupping her sex beneath it. Through the sheet, his thumb circled her clit while his middle finger worked her folds. When she shuddered his name, he felt her moisture seep through the material and told himself it was time to pull back.

"I should go, Bear."

"Why?" Her eyes were questioning, innocently expectant and with a hint of despair.

Pope resisted her tug, but silently acknowledged that the moment would be one of the few times he'd be immune to it.

"It's almost time to check out, Hon," he told her, straightening the sheet where it bunched at her thighs. "I'll arrange for you to stay as long as you need to."

"Can't you stay with me?"

"Babe…" he brushed a kiss to her temple.

She wasn't fully awake, he realized. Yet, she was very high off the electricity firing between them. Pope felt similarly affected, but he knew if he climbed into bed with her, he might never leave. What's more, he'd find a way to never tell her the truth he was still very reluctant to share. He'd find a way to tell her. Regardless of what it would or wouldn't mean for them-he'd find a way. He had taken the most supreme pleasure from her body, the least he could give her was his honesty.

"I really should go, Babe. But we uh-we need to talk."

His words seemed to sober Bear somewhat. Slowly, she pushed up just a smidge higher against the pillows lining the headboard. She gave a slow nod before her words filled the room soft and earnestly.

"I'm…I'm on the pill if…that's what you're curious about," she said, "I'm tested twice-twice a year."

His radiant stare widening slightly, Pope arched a sleek brow in a show of being impressed. "Not quite up to your standards yet- I'm only tested once a year."

Her smiled spread easily. "That's good too."

96

"I had condoms," he offered an uneasy shrug. "I'm sorry I didn't use them. I...had every intention to."

"You came prepared," her smile remained even as her heart performed a small, yet dynamic flip in response to his adorably sheepish grin as his gaze swept the room.

"I'd planned to bring you here after lunch-after we'd talked."

"I see," her smile thinned over the explanation.

Pope knew she had no idea what he meant. Sadly, he felt the time had once again passed for him to breach the subject.

"I want to see you again," he blurted and immediately detected the uncertainty launching in the warm pools of her stare.

"You don't have to, I-" she inserted a sigh. "I don't expect anything."

"Maybe I do." Again, he shrugged. "Will you just tell me you'll let me see you?"

Bear watched him with curious eyes even as she gave an obedient nod.

Pope decided to leave on that note, but not before he helped himself to another kiss.

He studied her so intently afterward, that Bear could feel shivers wisp across her skin. He pushed from the bed, headed for the door and left her without a look back.

***

### Golden, British Columbia~

Located in Southeastern British Columbia, the town of Golden bordered natural wonders and blessed it with amazing views; the likes of which, had the power to leave its visitors both awestruck and humbled.

Homes boasted wondrous mountain views and spent lukewarm summers beneath the shade of heavy firs, pines and oaks. In addition to its awesome beauty, Golden catered to those who hungered for activities that went far beyond the simple pleasures of sightseeing. It was a place that epitomized all there was to love about rugged, outdoor living. From freshwater fishing to mountain biking, there were few activities that could not be experienced.

For Rutger Eliades, hunting was the only outdoor activity that mattered-that deserved to be worshipped. Rutger rarely spent time indoors unless it was time to sleep or eat. Hunting was his religion and there was little that had the power to draw his focus away from it.

At least, that had been the case before he met LuCarolyn Young. They hadn't actually met, though. It was more accurate to say he'd invaded her personal space while she'd been minding her own business.

Whatever the case, he'd seen her, talked to her and now he couldn't get her out of his head. That had been over a month ago and the situation hadn't changed. It hadn't improved either which played heavily into why he was inside on a day when he should've been out shooting something.

Instead, he was settled into his favorite recliner and going through the dossier his security chief Ben Weiss had provided on the distracting Ms. Young. Rutger had asked Ben to keep his digging light-knowing the man could uncover relatively all there was to know about anyone.

Inside the thin file, he found what he'd expected. She was a force in her field and had earned a respected name as an up and coming film producer. The conversation he'd caught the tail end of when they'd first met, had told him as much.

She made her home in Malibu-alone. Good. Of course, that didn't mean she wasn't attached. Women like her usually were. Exactly what type of woman was she?

From their brief encounter, he'd deduced enough. LuCarolyn Young and Golden would probably clash-and why the fuck was he thinking of her being in the midst of his oasis? Had she made *that* stirring of an impression? The answer was most definitely yes and Rutger believed the real reason was because he was thinking with his dick.

With a heavy sigh, he left the tan leather recliner and prowled his den like the big game that was most likely prowling his back yard. He needed a distraction that was the complete opposite of the LuCarolyn Young variety. Mouthing a curse, he retrieved one of the 8x10 glossies from the photo array Ben had tucked into the file.

LuCarolyn Young was a goddamn beauty and he wanted to fuck her. It was as simple as that. His mouth curved then into a wolfish grin that mirrored the idea coming to mind. It appeared that another trip to California was necessary. Satisfaction had him stroking his jaw where whiskers, the color of crude oil, were tamed into a permanent 5 o'clock shadow.

The quiet chime of his mobile surging into the room, gave him pause. Satisfaction elevated upon viewing the name on the screen.

"I was just about to call you."

"Seriously?" Pope's response to Rutger's greeting was met with clear skepticism.

"Yeah," Rutger gave the confirmation over a quiet laugh. "I thought I might come down and hang out for a while."

"Well...um...that-that's good."

Rutger relished a swell of satisfaction then. It wasn't often one surprised the likes of Pope Apostolou.

"So um...I was calling to ask if you'd come with me to Memphis."

Satisfaction ebbing, Rutger's inky black brows merged over a beckoning whiskey brown stare. "What I want isn't in Memphis," his flat tone put a more menacing slant to the canyon depths of his voice.

"Same here," Pope sighed. "But I may need you there with me, man."

Setting aside flaring agitation, Rutger turned his back on the view beyond the den windows and began to prowl the room again. "Everything okay?" he asked.

"Did you hear about Alberts?"

"Ah," Rutger nodded while running his fingers across the crop of curls tapered at his nape. "Ben mentioned it, um..." he intentionally dragged out the question as a quick, sly smile tugged his mouth. "Should I be offering condolences?" He laughed full and honest when the low roar that hugged Pope's voice sounded through the line.

"You do and I'll have to beat you to death."

Again, Rutger's laughter filled the room at the threat. "You'll try," he taunted but sobered soon after. "What do you need, man?"

"I don't know, yet," Pope's response came fast but it was genuine. "I've been dodging some calls from a law firm there, but they haven't left any messages so...it may be nothing."

"But you don't buy that?"

"I might if I hadn't gotten a call from Gerrick Ferguson."

"Ferguson? What'd *he* want?" Rutger listened while Pope gave a quick recap of his conversation with The GAN's Chief Medical Officer. "What do you think it means?" He asked once Pope had finished.

Pope initially replied with another one of his patented rough-voiced gestures. "Bastard was vague on purpose," he finally said.

"That's a doctor for you," Rutger laughed. "Have you talked to Merc and Slay?" he asked.

"Yes to Merc. No to Slay. Merc thinks I should hear him out."

"Well I'm here for whatever you decide."

"I appreciate it, Rut. I um...I know it's not easy for you to be around all that either. I'll make it up to you."

"Make sure you make it up good."

"Working on something as we speak."

"Oh yeah?" Rutger mused, fantasizing that the 'something' was around 5'10 of curves and attitude.

"That's all the info you get," Pope chuckled. "I'll be in touch and Rut? Thanks, man."

Rutger's tone was then as somber as his friend's. "Anytime," he said.

***

Bear relaxed in bed at the inn a full hour and a half after Pope's departure. She didn't use all that time for sleeping, but decided it couldn't hurt to wait for the lunch crowd to arrive in full force before she tried to drift out inconspicuously among them.

There was no shame fueling her actions. She was simply in no mood for questions or curious looks for that matter. The thought made her smile. No, she felt not an ounce of shame even though she'd spent almost 24 hours alone with a man she hardly knew, doing things she only got to see when she found time to dive into her extensive adult film collection.

Leaving the inn was as quick and painless an event as she'd hoped it'd be. Still, she knew there was no way she'd leave without taking some aspects of her time there with her.

Sore muscles were one thing. She was halfway to the ranch when those aches and pains began to make themselves known. Her mind flooded with images of her soaking tub ready to be used and with memories of a day and night well spent. The achy muscles she'd suffered had been well worth the discomfort.

The state of Bear's muscles however, were nothing compared to the headache that began to bloom. It emerged during the call that came through as she drove past the opening gates of her home.

"So you guys still can't make it?" Bear's sad smile was a perfect match to her tone of voice.

"Afraid not, B," the woman sighed over the phone line and sounded equally saddened. "Cal's really sorry. He was so looking forward to being there. It's been a helluva time, politically speaking."

"Isn't it always?" Wearily, Bear rested her head against the seat.

Audrey Dupont laughed her agreement. Audrey's husband Callum Dupont headed the Governor's security team and was one of Bear's best clients.

"I get it, Audrey, seriously and it's no problem," Bear's smile remained saddened by the anguish she heard in the woman's tone. "We'll set up a private weekend for Cal when things calm down for him on the job. How's that?"

"Oh Bear, that'd be terrific-only um...I'm afraid that's not the only reason I'm calling."

"Okay..." Bear pulled into the slot along the side of her home that led to a private entrance. She shut off the Jeep's engine, but waited for more details.

Audrey Dupont gave into another sigh. "Cal should be the one explaining this, but he's playing the gender card figuring you won't kick my ass as fast as you would his."

Bear smiled, envisioning all 6'5 of the 240lb man. "It's alright, Aud-tell me."

Yet another sigh expelled from Audrey and then, "It's about Chris Morrow."

Bear felt the first stab of dull pain at the back of her neck.

Audrey took the silence as her cue to continue. "So um, Cal's folks are friends with a senator out of Washington State, Edgar Cooper. He knows how much Cal enjoys your soirees and he contacted him about wrangling an invite. Cal explained there were only a certain amount of spots available, but when he was sure he couldn't go, he passed his invite along to Cooper.

The man's a big talker," Audrey went on, "but he's known to be a generous contributor to good causes. Cal figured he'd make a fine addition to the event and he isn't Morrow so..."

"But he's involved?" Bear rubbed at the pain beginning to work its way up the back of her skull.

"Cooper called to thank Cal for the invite, told him a fellow senator from California would be tickled since he's been trying to get on the guest list for years. It didn't take much for Cal to put it together but he confirmed the name just to be sure."

101

Bear was massaging the middle of her forehead then. Her silence spoke volumes.

"I'm so sorry, B. Cal and I are just crushed about this. We know how much you didn't want him there."

It was true. Christopher Morrow had pulled out all the stops to wrangle an invite to the soiree in the past. So far, Bear had thwarted every move. She could thwart this one too-it took more than showing up for the weekend with an invite. The invite would grant him access to the opening mixer, but full security scans were required before anyone was given a rifle. Still, she had to give the man props for creativity.

"It's fine, Aud. You and Cal aren't in the doghouse."

Audrey heaved yet another sigh, that one of the relieved variety. "So um...what are you gonna do?"

"Who knows?" Bear made her way from the Jeep. "It's a battle I don't mind saving 'til another day." Her words echoed a powerful truth. She was too worn and depleted to tackle anything more than running a bath.

"Thanks for the update, Aud. I'll let you know how everything works out, alright?"

The women spoke for a while longer before the call ended. Depleted or not, it didn't stop Bear from kicking at one of the Jeep's tires on her way past.

"Son of a bitch!" She snarled, storming toward an unassuming steel door that opened only by palm scan. The device beeped for her admittance and she bolted inside the small, brick enclosure that sheltered a private stairwell leading the way to her home office and bedroom wing.

The side entrance gave her the chance to bypass the lengthy route through the expansive 10,000sq ft home. In spite of the short cut, her head was all but pounding between her ears by the time she made it past the locked outer door leading to the living suite.

35 minutes later, she was settling neck deep into the hot, frothy water filling a square drop in tub. The headache that had started to nag on her way inside the house, was already beginning to ebb. Satisfaction cresting, Bear sighed and wiggled her toes amid the fragrant bubbles. It didn't take long for the hot water to infuse her skin, massaging away the annoying aches.

If only there was something to massage away the annoying Senator Morrow. She thought of the man who'd been a thorn in her side since...hell...Bear kept her eyes closed while she grimaced. The man had been a pain almost from the day she'd opened Bear Arms.

With those memories, came thoughts of Cynda Duncan. Her trials with Morrow had come on the heels of that tragedy. Bear remembered him vividly, an angry new senator trying to make a name for himself by using the 2nd Amendment as his platform. She never really knew if the man had any interest in what had happened to Cynda Duncan. He seemed more interested in touting the evils of guns- especially guns in the hands of those too ill-equipped and immature to understand their awesome power.

If he hadn't tried to turn her ranch into a police state, Bear could've almost admired him. She too had a vested interest in keeping guns away from the immature and ill-equipped. Unfortunately, her attempts to engage the man in conversations about working together to change the fatal status quo, met with a closed mind and closed wallet.

It became clear to her that Morrow was only interested in media hype and his own self-image one that confirmed his misogynistic nature. Bear didn't much care if he had problems with women- black or otherwise- running a business like hers. What mattered was that he'd used a woman's fate to drive an agenda he had no real concern for.

Cynda Duncan's fate had gotten lost beneath a lot of rhetoric and shallow campaign promises. Morrow had spoken of the woman fleetingly as though she were a non-entity and that alone was enough to have Bear despising him.

"Let him come..." she sighed the words while smoothing a handful of bubbles into her skin.

Once she publicly accused him of being a fake and cheapskate, he'd only have 2 choices: put his money where his mouth was or slink away in shame. Either outcome worked for her.

With that settled, Bear treaded water to the side of the tub. A bottle of wine had been left to breathe along the fixture's enclosure. The base of black granite had been finished to a dull gleam. At each corner, square indentations supported wide, turquoise plates that carried fat candles of varying heights and aromas. The space hummed with simple elegance and femininity. It was Bear's escape when a hard day had beaten her into a useless lump. Today had definitely been such a day, she decided, smiling contently while pouring a glass of a robust red.

She enjoyed a few sips before setting the goblet back to its glass coaster. Settling back into the tub, she studied the gas fireplace that was built into a wall between the bathroom and bedroom. For a while, she let the energetic flames lull her into oblivion.

She'd reached a decision on her plan to handle Morrow. Now, if only she could find a way to handle the other infuriating man in her life.

To be fair, infuriating wasn't the word to describe Pope Apostolou. It wasn't the *only* word. He was something completely beyond infuriating-something completely...more. That he'd drawn her in so effortlessly was disturbing enough. That she had no desire to escape what he'd drawn her into...ventured into a realm of thought she was reluctant to explore.

Almost 20 hours of nonstop...since she was alone, she didn't hold back the appreciative sigh that climbed up the back of her throat. The things he'd done to her-things she let him do, wanted him to do-wanted him to *still* be doing...

He wanted to see her again. What the hell did that mean? He'd mentioned talking-what about? They'd already settled the issue of him booking a weekend for his friend at the ranch. What more was there to discuss? Sex? The possibility had her bruised core clenching beneath the heated water.

A relationship that was about gratification only, held tremendous appeal for her. What did that say about her? Did she care? She downed the rest of her wine as memories of a night 6 years ago tried to edge in. That wasn't who she was, but if the past 20 hours had proved anything, it had proven that she missed sex very much.

Besides, Pope Apostolou would never know about that night. There would never be any need to worry he might think she was a slut at heart, instead of a hardworking businesswoman who just hadn't had her sexual needs met in a while. A shiver kissed her skin and Bear knew it had nothing to do with the water temp decreasing by a few degrees.

What Pope Apostolou had done to her in that room went so far beyond meeting needs. Sex, for the sake of sex was...nice. Mixed with patience, intensity-aggression...it was phenomenal. Pope had shown that he was a master of all those elements. If he deigned to share those skills again, there was no question that she'd be willing. *Her* terms of course.

She had no reason to believe that would be a problem. Pope certainly wasn't looking for anything meaningful. If it turned out that he was, she'd end it. Simple as that. If that had to happen...she prayed it'd wait until she'd had her sexual fill of him.

Bear reached for the wine bottle and filled her goblet to its gold-toned brim. Drinking deeply, she closed her eyes in hopes of dismissing the voice that warned her that having her 'sexual fill' of Pope Apostolou, would be impossible.

# CHAPTER 10

"I don't mind waiting in her office, you know?"

"It's no problem, Mr. Apostolou. She takes the occasional meet with clients here when we're all in conference. It'll be fine."

Pope didn't bother to tell Mike he'd be unloading all blame on him, should his boss see the situation differently. He hadn't bothered to call ahead-had only just made the decision to drive out to see her after tossing his half eaten breakfast down the disposal.

He'd met the second of Bear's managers, Mike Hough, on his way to the training hall where her main offices were located. After introducing himself, Mike had thanked Pope for his generous business with the ranch. He went on to share that Bear worked from three different offices on the property. That morning, they were working from her private living suite.

"That's convenient," Pope said, watching as Mike shook his head.

"Tell me about it," Mike tacked on, smoothing a hand over his dark shaved head. "We've been burning candles at *all* ends getting ready

106

for the soiree. That, along with the shoot for CBM, everybody's pretty beat. The boss especially."

Pope nodded, but wasn't quite sure how he felt about Bear meeting with her two male employees so close to where she slept. That he felt *any* way about it at all, sent a soft growl tossing restlessly in his throat.

*Turn around now-* reason's voice warned and that time he strongly considered listening. If he didn't leave now, he wouldn't want to let her go when the time came. The time would come, he knew that. As soon as he told her the truth about who his best friend was, she'd most likely spit in his face and tell him to get the hell out of her sight.

They were approaching the side entrance of Bear's home. Mike had urged Pope to leave his truck where he'd parked in the lot near the training area. With Mike behind the wheel of one of the ranch Jeeps, they took a winding dirt path to the main house.

During the drive, Pope had time to appreciate the stunning landscape and the architecture adorning it. No one could help but to be impressed by all she'd accomplished. The gun range portion of the property, was liberally spaced. In addition to skeet shooting and the in-season hunting parties, Bear Arms offered defensive firearm use training. The package was popular with law enforcement professionals across the state. When they arrived at the main house, Mike led the way to a brick enclosure that seemed out of place on the astounding piece of Spanish styled architecture. When Pope said as much, Mike grinned.

"The boss wanted easier access to her wing on the nights when she pulls a late one," he explained.

Pope watched Mike rest his palm on a scanner and eyed the tall steel door when it slid open once the locks disengaged. It was impressive security that he could understand being in place given the culture of the ranch. Still, he had to wonder how logical it was to have the locale of the owner's-the female owner's-private wing so conspicuously displayed.

The enclosure housed a stairway that carried them up a couple of flights and opened into a hall that smelled freshly of pine and lemon. Their steps intermittently fell silent as shoe soles were transferred between glossy golden hardwoods and rows of identical Persian rugs that featured inspiring designs. Images in beige, hunter green and black enhanced the rugs, complementing the soothing butter cream tone of the walls.

Mike moved down the corridor toward its only set of doors. Beyond them, waited a roomy split level lounge area finished in a marble flooring that was stained a dusky gray. The space was both functional and welcoming with an assortment of vases and figurines.

Thin, yet comfortably cushioned sofas dotted the room and showcased an assortment of black and rose blush accent pillows that enhanced the wine colored cushions. A wide round, work table occupied the middle of the room. Same finish as the flooring, the table was cluttered with files, catalogs and other miscellaneous papers.

Spotlights and cylinder hanging pendants were set to dim and doused the room in quiet illumination. Mid-morning sunlight filtered the area more abundantly. The rays touched every spot including the well-equipped eating nook tucked in the corner. High backed stools; same color as the sofa, skirted a bar while a freestanding staircase angled up to the sleeping quarters.

Shaun Oates was leaving the nook, carrying a tall glass of what looked to be OJ. He was in route to the main area, frowning over the papers he studied and did a doubletake upon seeing his co-worker with their unexpected guest.

"Mr. Apostolou," Shaun raised his glass in smooth invitation even as surprise laced his voice.

"Hey Shaun," Pope returned the greeting and then listened while Mike explained how the two of them ran into each other and how it just made sense for Pope to join them there.

"We're finishing up anyway," Mike closed out.

"Okay," was Shaun's quiet response.

Pope bowed his head to hide a smile. It was clear to him that Shaun had made a similar decision to hang Mike out to dry if their boss didn't share his opinion.

"Can we get you anything, Mr. Apostolou?" Shaun raised his glass again. "We've got all kinds of juice, coffee or beer if you want something stronger?"

"Thanks, I'll take you up on that, but let me," Pope urged with a wave when Shaun turned to head back into the nook.

Shaun smiled, raised his glass yet again and set off to join Mike at the big work table.

"So how are you liking the place so far, Mr. Apostolou?"

"Your boss should be proud," Pope said in response to Shaun's question. "She told me she wants to tear down the cottage, though."

"Yeah," a crestfallen look came to Shaun's round face.

"Bad business out there a few years back," Mike added.

"Yeah, that's what she said. You guys should consider outfitting it as a security hub- you could still use it as a rec house but a small modification like that could make all the difference," Pope turned for the tall chrome refrigerator in the far corner.

"Guests could still enjoy it, but with a more concrete reminder that there's law and order out that way beyond the patrols going by every thirty minutes," he continued.

Shaun and Mike nodded as though the idea had serious merit.

"I'll let you guys be the ones to run it by your boss," Pope called over his shoulder and the room filled with rumbling male laughter.

While the guys settled in to work, Pope checked the offerings in the fridge. He was smiling over the discovery of his favorite beer chilling in one of two 6 pack cartons on the bottom shelf, when Bear's distinctive smoky tone carried on the air.

"I thought we settled this?...So why am I getting calls from caterers?...Bidding war?...Hold on- who told you to call them instead?"

"Ah shit," Mike smoothed a hand over his head.

Shaun dragged a hand through his auburn curls and continued to scour his papers. "At least we can't be blamed for this one," he said.

Pope, pleased by the chance to overhear another of Berrill Clayton's boss to employee discussions, removed the cap from his beer. He took a long swallow and leaned against the nook's counter to listen.

"...So because Jameson is friends with a dozen or so of my clients, you figured they should get the job?..." Bear's voice elevated as though she were nearing the lounge's lower level.

"...Well Sawyer is a friend of mine, so that beats it all. Understood?" Heavy footsteps accompanied Bear's voice as they beat the stairs when she plodded down.

"Unbelievable!" She declared to Mike and Shaun when she stopped on the fourth step from the bottom.

"Who was that, Boss?" Mike asked.

"Joel's snobby behind," Bear shoved her mobile into a side pocket on the hooded sweater she wore over a worn *Peanuts'* tee. "Going over my head to hire Jameson instead of Sawyer whose handled every cocktail party we've had out here for the last three years. All because Jameson rubs ass cheeks with the society circle."

"Well Boss," Shaun sighed. "It makes sense for Joel. He's always looking at the marketing angle and Jameson's name looks good on paper."

"Paper my ass," Bear muttered. "What looks good are those 'feed the town' events Sawyer throws for the homeless in San Francisco. Funds it out of his own pocket. All Jameson does is wedding parties for big shots and who the hell talked me into having a fucking four course dinner for these people, anyway?"

"Joel."

Shaun and Mike spoke in unison and Bear couldn't resist laughing. "Our usual opening mixer would've been just fine, you know? A heavy buffet, shooting, simplicity. That's all these folks want."

"Come on, Boss, it's year four," Mike drawled. "Folks might expect you to put on a little flash."

"Flash, my-"

Mike interrupted Bear's retort with a soft clearing of his throat. It was then that she took note of the animated looks he and Shaun kept sending to the other side of the room.

Pope had already waved to the men to indicate they not interrupt Bear's tirade to acknowledge his presence. Mike and Shaun knew there'd be hell to pay if they let their boss go on much longer without letting on they had company.

Bear frowned curiously while descending two more steps and glanced absently in the direction they kept looking. "What's wrong with you guy-" Her heart jackknifed to her throat at the sight of Pope Apostolou's imposing frame filling her dining nook. She considered him for a lingering moment and then turned to her managers who were in the process of standing and hastily gathering their belongings.

"Mike ran into Mr. Apostolou," Shaun explained when he caught Bear's eye. "He didn't think it'd be a problem to bring him along."

Grimacing over the update, Mike kept his gaze downcast. "Thanks, man."

"No um," Bear appeared a little too dazed to spark the tongue lashing her employees clearly expected. "No, it's alright," she managed.

The reply sent looks of unadulterated shock passing between the two men. Belongings in hand, they began making their way to the door.

"We'll just catch you later, Bear." Shaun called.

"No guys um," Bear's voice was still uncharacteristically light, "it's fine we-we're done for the day."

110

Working not to let excitement beam too brightly on their handsome faces, Mike and Shaun bid Pope a good day and quietly exited.

Pope maintained his leaning stance against the counter. "They in trouble?" he used his bottle to gesture toward the door then swigged down a little more of the brew.

Bear eased both hands into her sweater pockets. "They're not in trouble."

"Am I?"

"You said you'd call." Slight anxiety had her fidgeting. She took her phone from her pocket and set it on one of the small square platforms marking the end of the bannisters.

"No...I said I wanted to see you."

"Pope-"

"Are you okay?"

The quiet expectancy in his rich tone, struck Bear momentarily, endearing him to her in a way that gave her pause. When the moment passed, she realized he was standing right in front of her.

"I'm fine," she smiled, enjoying the sensation stirred by the back of his hand roaming her arm. She winced when he cupped her bicep and added the slightest pressure.

"Really?" His arresting eyes were next to stroke the length of her arm as though checking for additional injuries.

"I didn't mean to hurt you," his eyes moved to her face.

"I know. It's okay."

"Not for me, it isn't." The response was more abrupt than he'd intended. He enjoyed sex very much, but always made a point to hold back-to never put his all into the act.

Of course, he made sure the women he took to his bed were always supremely satisfied. It was an easy enough trick, given that he allowed no woman to affect him enough to strip away the controlled veneer he cloaked himself in. Bear Clayton was proving herself impervious to that veneer.

It was more than that, Pope knew. The controlled veneer was about more than safeguarding his emotions. Strength was...seductive. The kind he and his friends had been blessed with, could be lethal if mixed with doses of domination and aggression. Those doses, mixed with sexual desire, made the control a necessity. She was watching him with those deep, hypnotic mocha eyes and he felt yet another layer of the necessary veneer melt away.

"Leaving marks on you, isn't okay for me." His tone was less abrupt that time. He added a slow smile. "Being a leg breaker and all."

"Former," Bear clarified, proving she recalled their earlier conversation.

Pope brushed his thumb across the spot where he'd located the bruise. "I am sorry, Bear."

"Don't be," her voice was a whisper as she took the last step down to curve her fingers into the front of the black V-neck T-shirt he wore outside his jeans.

"I wanted it," she went to her toes to murmur the words against his jaw.

"Bear," Pope's mind warred with his body, waging a battle between resistance and indulgence. "Honey we need to talk."

"Okay," she consented seconds before taking his mouth with her kiss.

To prove to himself that he hadn't yet lost the battle, Pope kept his hands at the ends of the stairway bannisters. She was on her toes and treating his mouth to lazy rotations from her tongue. The soft moans that accompanied the sultry kiss and slow massaging strokes she applied to his scalp, made gripping the bannisters as much about control as it was about supporting his weakening legs.

Once he'd convinced himself that he could touch her without taking her, Pope clutched her biceps again. He took care to keep his hold loose in the event of injuries he'd yet to root out.

"There're things I need to say to you, Babe."

She nodded as if his words were appealing to her sense of fairplay. "Well," she backed away, taking two steps up the staircase. "I'm going to my room," she tugged off her sweater, let it drop. "And I don't like to talk in there."

Pope was silently ordering himself to retain focus. "This is important, Bear."

"I'm sure it is," she grabbed her T-shirt's hem, tugged it over her head and down to join the sweater. Her smile was wickedness personified when he appeared to resign himself. She watched his lashes; ones any woman would kill to have, settle over his ultramarine stare.

With an elbow braced on the bannister, Pope tapped a few fingers to his brow. "You're killing me," he watched her take a few more steps up the case.

"Well that would definitely ruin all my plans," her voice held playful worry. She pulled out of her bra and let it, along with her denim capris fall to her feet.

Abandoning her clothes, she took another step up and then turned. Challenge lurked in her gaze when she leaned against the bannister.

For Pope, defeat settled in slow and resiliently. His hormones were wooed by the sight of her nude but for the wisp of emerald green lace barely covering her ample bottom. Undone, he massaged the bridge of his nose. "Damn you, Bear."

"Fuck me, Pope."

He gave into a grin over the order, but internally his ease was harder to come by. One more time, he decided. One more time and then he'd tell her. It was stupid; he knew, but as he'd once admitted, he didn't think so well when his dick was calling the shots.

Bear looked on and tried not to let her sense of triumph beam overmuch in her expression. Was there anything nicer than the sight of a powerful man being brought to his knees by the sheer weight of his desire? She wondered. For a woman who directed more than 100 men, this was a nice change of pace. Those men, she paid. This one...this one had no reason to let her do the dictating and yet... there he was.

She saw when the decision clicked into place for him; watched as he took the steps up two at a time, tramping her clothes beneath his boots. He reached for her and she evaded with a slow shake of her head.

"Let's do something about that shirt."

Pope obliged, whipping the garment over his head and tossing it somewhere across his shoulder. He took Bear off her feet by snaking one arm about her waist.

Their mouths collided in a furious hunt for release. Bear kept a frantic grip on Pope's shoulders as she met the savage drives of his tongue. She reciprocated the same heat as Pope took the rest of the stairs. He found his way to her bedroom almost too easily and was descending the case leading into the suite when she suddenly broke the kiss.

"Wait," she panted.

"Bear..." his tone was a blatant warning that stopping would be difficult for him.

113

"The chair," she said, "my-my terms."

Grinning slyly, Pope followed her instructions. "As you wish," the words came seconds before his tongue resumed possession of her mouth.

Their path veered toward a chaise lounge set in an alcove near a high, small window that supplied much of the room's lighting during that time of day. Even with the sun pouring down from the window, the area still held a soft-lit allure.

Pope hesitated before settling to the lounge. He was the one who broke the kiss that time. When Bear felt his fist nudging her tummy, she realized he was freeing the belt and fastening of his jeans. Next, she heard the distinctive sound that signalled the destruction of her underwear.

Pope was ravaging the silken flesh beneath her jaw by then. "That's two pair I owe you," he admitted while gnawing the spot he favored.

Bear couldn't respond, not when he lifted her effortlessly and put her down on an impressive erection. He lowered her slowly and she pressed her forehead to his while faint wavering cries lilted from her throat.

The sensation was like no other. He was superbly built, enabling him to stretch her inner muscles to the point that she felt orgasmic before she was even fully seated. He kept a firm hold on her ass, spreading the plump cheeks ever so slightly to ease penetration and triple their pleasure.

Bear threw back her head and let her cries fill the intimate alcove. With his grip steady on her bottom, Pope guided her to his satisfaction up and down the length of his wide shaft. His free hand cupped her breast for his mouth. He nibbled and sucked eagerly, tirelessly until her inner walls squeezed his dick in a manner that had him cursing as he erupted inside her.

"Mmm...bed please," she sighed upon milking the last of his release and easing off his semi-hard sex.

Pope hungered for her again at once and had no issue with obeying her next demand. In one impressive move, he took her up from the lounge and had her moaning over his ability.

His strength was truly an aphrodisiac. Their journey was a brief one from the alcove to the back of the room where a California King sat on a round platform. Pope set her to the middle of the satin, rose blush comforter but when he attempted to follow her down, Bear shook her head and inched up to her knees.

"Uh-uh, on *your* back, Mr. Apostolou."

He didn't argue, simply stood and shed the rest of his clothes. He lay on his back to study her with a hooded but no less scintillating stare as she crawled over to straddle him. Their kiss re-engaged and Pope sank his fingers into the tumble of her hair as it curtained their faces.

When he took her bottom in an effort to sheathe her over a new erection, Bear responded by catching his wrist and pressing it to the bed. She mimicked the action with his other wrist, trapping him beneath her. She smiled over the sound of his breathless and adorable laughter stirring as they kissed.

She took him once both his hands rested above his head. "Be still," she ordered.

He shuddered her name when she moved back to sweep his length in her palm and apply a few torturously slow strokes before guiding him inside her core.

Bear took her time and had to slap his wrists back into place when he would've taken her hips to hasten the movement. "Be still, I said," the command was more of a breathy slur as she continued to work her way onto his erection, squeezing and stroking the organ as she moved.

Pope broke the rules then only to drag his fingers through his hair once she started to ride him vigorously as she claimed her pleasure. He dug the heels of his hands into his eyes to resist taking possession of her hips and directing movement. The quiet roughness that hugged his voice was easy to decipher amid the curses that confirmed his immense satisfaction.

Hours later, Pope was cursing for a completely different reason. One, that was in no way as enjoyable as what sparked his previous rant. He'd come over that day, determined-obsessively so- to talk to her-to lay it all out on the table. Instead…

He gave a quiet sigh, looked down to where she lay resting after their long afternoon together. He'd gotten dressed while she slept and then sat on the edge of the bed to debate. He'd procrastinated long enough.

"Bear," he coasted his knuckles down her back, loving how the rich brown of her skin contrasted against the copper tone of his. He

115

shook his head, refusing to let her lure him back into what he most wanted- to be in bed, beside her.

"Babe," he cupped her side and shook her slightly.

Insistent vibrations radiated from his back pocket and he reached for his mobile. His gaze went cold as blue ice when he read the screen, recognizing the number for Womack, Mebane and Urnst Attorneys at Law. Interest diminished, Pope ignored the call and shoved the phone back into his pocket.

He returned to look at Bear, the malice softening in his eyes as he studied her face. She'd turned to her side, affording him the opportunity to observe her features relaxed in sleep. Enchanted, he reached out to skim his thumb along her brow and temple.

What purpose would it serve to tell her, anyway? Sure, he could pat himself on the back for being honest...finally. She'd still come out hurt regardless. That wasn't just procrastination talking-it was truth. She'd walk away from him; that was a given. Unfortunately, she wouldn't be able to walk away from the fact that he knew what was perhaps her darkest secret. A secret any woman-any*one*- would do almost anything to keep hidden.

Another buzz from his pocket had him growling low in his throat and ready to roast the poor soul on the other end of his phoneline. It wasn't a call; he realized when he checked the screen, but a voice mail notification. He left the bed while activating the message from Claude Mebane, Esq.

*"...Mr. Apostolou, we've been trying to reach you for several days. We apologize for being insistent, Sir but it's urgent that you contact us right away. It's concerning your father..."*

The last, sent an array of muscles clenching along Pope's jaw. Somehow, he resisted the urge to crush the phone in his grip once the message ended. Slipping the device back into his pocket, he returned to the bed. He didn't sit, merely bent to peer down into Bear's relaxed face as though he were attempting to memorize its captivating power.

Gently, he brushed a lingering kiss to her forehead. Then, he was charting a quick and relentless path out the door.

# CHAPTER 11

Her room was almost completely bathed in black but for the beams of silvery moonlight glinting through the alcove's high window. Bear lay in bed for a while after she woke, just staring into the dark.

She'd wondered how long it had been since he'd left. She hadn't exactly paid attention to the time once things had...gotten started between them. She rested silently for about 15 minutes and then made her way downstairs for a bite to eat and to see who'd been trying to reach her while she'd been MIA.

Her phone was just where she'd left it at the end of the bannister. There were a few missed calls, but nothing major. There was nothing from Pope either and Bear wished he'd awakened her before he'd left.

Did she really? Bear turned the question over in her mind while absently stirring the mug of Peppermint tea she'd brewed. A pot of veggie beef soup left on slow simmer, filled the lower level with soothing aromas. Her thoughts however, were far from soothed.

Pope had been insistent about talking, but he'd forgotten that soon enough. Now, alone with her thoughts, she couldn't help but wonder what it was she wouldn't give him the chance to say. Whatever it was, it had to be serious. Men were rarely so persistent about having conversations, she mused, thinking of the men she employed.

They'd already had the sexual protection chat. While there were things he could've held back, she didn't think that was it.

The lid on the soup pot began a soft clatter against the pressure of the steam. Bear quelled her thoughts while setting her mug to the counter and turning off the stove burner. Six minutes later, she was heading for the lounge's main area with the mug and a deep bowl of the soup. Concerns about what Pope Apostolou hadn't said, resumed the spot at the front of her mind by the time she'd curled onto the nearest sofa.

He had to be married. That had to be it. She'd wondered before and; though she'd been off about the significant other, perhaps she wasn't off about the relationship. Men lied about such things all the time.

The soup's aroma beckoned to her and she downed a few hearty spoonfuls that sent contentment surging through her veins.

She would give him the chance to say what he needed to. She'd hear him out and then she'd walk away. Simple. Final. Besides, she couldn't handle anything more anyway.

Bear spooned down more of the soup to help herself believe her own decisions. Her phone sat on the worktable. After a second's debate, she was putting down the bowl and reaching for the mobile.

The ranch was doing a great deal of business. So much so, it became feasible to open a 24 hour call center. It didn't take long for the boss to reach booking and acquire information on any client she desired. In moments, Bear had what she needed and was placing a call. She wasn't sure if she'd reach his home or cell, prayed she wouldn't hear the missus answer and closed her eyes in relief when she got voicemail.

"Pope. Bear. We need to iron out some details about your business here at the ranch, so I'll be out to see you tomorrow evening around six...see you then." She clicked off without a goodbye and exhaled a relieved sigh.

"Idiot," she murmured next and then newly exhausted, flopped back against the sofa.

***

### *Harve de Grace, Maryland~*

Jake Grodins whistled as he and Brody Alberts strolled the walkway down to Christopher Morrow's dock. The man of the house

118

was there, seated in one of the cushioned black framed chairs that dotted an impressive deck.

"Didn't know you had a place on the lake, Senator. Nice," Jake complemented.

"I think it's a requirement of all Senators," Morrow left his chair grinning as he came to exchange handshakes with his guests.

"More privacy than on Capitol Hill too, huh Senator?" Brody scanned the serene river.

"Which is fortunate, since privacy is what we need for this discussion," Morrow said.

"And may we assume this 'discussion' will be more revealing than the others we've had?" Jake probed.

Morrow sobered, nodded. "I understand your frustration, but if all had gone as planned we'd be living off the fruits of our success by now."

"Instead, we're living not knowing when the rug'll be pulled out from under us."

Morrow nodded in further agreement with Jake's outlook and then he was looking to Brody. "I was sorry to hear about your father."

Brody grunted his disgust. "You're sorrier than I am. The bastard died and cut me off at the knees before he did it."

Morrow noted Brody's agitation with a raised brow. "Sounds like we could all use a drink," he gestured toward a small friggie inside the grilling nook at the back of the deck.

"I'll handle it, Bro," Jake offered, already in route to the fridge.

"There's a chance my father disinherited me," Brody went on explaining to Morrow. "I'll be damned if I go down without a fight. You said this plan of yours was life changing. Now's the time for full disclosure, Senator. We've sure as hell waited long enough for it. I'd prefer to know what we're working with before going back to reinvent the wheel."

"Agreed," Jake returned with three beers. He had even taken the liberty of removing the caps from the long-necked bottles.

For a time, the men swigged down the cool, rich brews and enjoyed nature's serenity from where they stood.

"Your fathers made a lot of enemies when they refused to sell their invention," Morrow began. "They had bigger dreams, dreams that not only the military took issue with."

"Damn right," Jake smirked nastily while regarding his bottle.

"Playing God was alright as long as they were willing to do it within the confines of the military," Morrow continued, "Outside the military, well... that had the potential to bring them too much power."

"Good thing they ran a diverse business," Brody chimed in, "one that didn't depend on the success of one product."

"That product would've been their crown jewel," Morrow regarded his bottle then as well. "A lot of folks would've benefitted from its success."

Brody snorted that time. "Too bad none of these folks had the kind of pull to get it past the powers that be."

"That's because they didn't know how to think outside the box."

"And you did?" Brody flashed Morrow a condescending grin.

Morrow sipped his beer and looked to be a man savoring a delicious secret as he slowly strode his deck. "The idea came to me while I was sitting in one of Doyle's boring staff meetings," he laughed softly over the memory.

"I swear the man only held those meetings because it was the only time he could get people to sit still long enough to hear him out. He was passionate about not allowing that product on the market when it became the topic on everyone's lips. It was the price that gave it away, you see?" Morrow smiled while Brody and Jake bristled.

"In one of those meetings, Doyle said he wouldn't let it through even if they put a gun to his head and I thought 'old man you're sealing your fate', but another thought occurred to me- killing everyone who's against this, would be bad for business."

"You said that bag contained...elements of persuasion," Brody closed some of the distance between himself and the senator. "We took a chance, Senator. Deal was, we'd hold onto that bag of yours as payment for services rendered. We staked everything on a bag filled with nothing but a bunch of plastic tubes."

"Exactly."

"We're talkin' blackmail here, right?" Jake queried.

"We are."

Morrow's response and demeanor, caused Brody to chuckle suddenly, but the effort was hollow and humorless. "You'll have to excuse me and Jake here Senator, for not being as diabolical as you are. Could you please speak plain and get to the fuckin' point?"

Morrow took no offense to the order. "Blackmail isn't always about what a person *has* done, but what they're suspected of doing. If, say...a man is suspected of a brutal murder and he leaves behind traces of his own blood or saliva..."

"My God..." Discovery bloomed for Brody.

Morrow's glee brightened his slender, attractive face. "Think of what such evidence could be used for- to seek justice or...various types of support."

"So somehow you managed to get their...DNA?" Jake caught up then. "Your plan is to commit a crime and frame them for it?"

"A frame they could break if they're willing to play the game."

"But that was over six years ago!" Incredulous laughter flooded Jake's words.

Morrow shrugged, his green eyes glinting smugly. "I've been assured that it's still viable. So are its owners-all still very active, respected and powerful."

"How the hell did you manage to pull this off?" Brody sneered. "You were little more than a senator's aide then."

"A lot of people wanted to see your fathers' product on the market, remember? All it took was approaching some of those people, laying out my plan and requesting their help in facilitating it."

"Viable or not, it's been six years," Brody argued. "The odds of us seeing it again are nil. Why not ask these supporters to cook up another batch of his blackmail DNA?"

Morrow's fair features began to darken with signs of annoyance then, but he kept the emotion from his voice. "This wasn't done for free. They're in it for a sizable cut of the profits. I was told that seconds could be acquired to the tune of a quarter billion dollars."

Morrow turned to observe his view from the deck. "Don't let the lake house fool you, gentlemen. I don't have that kind of money. What was it you said, Alberts? About not wanting to reinvent the wheel? I'm pretty sure none of us are in any position to shell out such an amount-not for something that could still be laying around somewhere."

"Like this ranch you mentioned? The owner? Berrill Clayton? Why the fuck would she keep it?"

"She kept the discs!" Morrow snapped to Brody.

"That's different," Brody grinned, approving of the edge beginning to fray the man's cool demeanor.

Morrow pulled himself together. "It's not. Those discs represent a night she and her friends would just as soon cut out of their memories, but they're smart enough to know it's what kept them alive this long."

"But how do we know-"

"It was seen. Three years ago. Sorry gents, but that's too brief a window for me not to confirm its existence."

"Have you seen it?" Jake asked.

"A young woman I put in place," Morrow grimaced, running a hand through his blond locks while moving toward the deck rail. "She was a maid at the ranch. I paid her to keep a close eye on the lovely Ms. Clayton and to report when she saw what I was looking for. She saw it."

"And where's this maid, now?" Brody asked.

"She won't be a problem," Morrow understood the context of the question. "I made sure of it and got myself on Bear Clayton's shit list in the process. She's all but banned me from her property," he turned from the rail.

"I've laid low long enough, gentlemen. The broadcast of that disc a month ago proves we can't afford to wait any longer for them to pick another disc out of the hat," *One that could ruin me,* Morrow tacked on in silence.

"So you're saying it's finally time to pay a visit and do what you've been dancing around? Give this Ms. Clayton a little of what you gave her maid?"

"No, Mr. Grodins," Morrow answered a bit sharper than he'd intended. He could see that his guests were men on the edge-desperate maybe. Desperate men made mistakes- mistakes that could shine unwanted light on his involvement.

"She has a big deal soiree out there every year. I've managed an invite and there's a dinner party in a few weeks. We need eyes out there before we just converge. Bear Arms isn't a place you just go into unprepared. There will be security checks before the main event, but this dinner party is more of a mixer, fundraiser thing. Guests are encouraged to bring a plus one to drum up money for charity and interest for the next event. One of you needs to decide who goes with me."

"This had better be worth our motherfucking time, Morrow." Jake's voice was a virtual growl. "For all we know, that bag could be with Mercuri Nikolaides."

"What's the plan once we're there?" Brody asked.

"If we're lucky, we could get the lady of the house alone and persuade her to open the safe- that's where the maid said she saw it."

"And if we're unlucky?" Brody chided.

122

Morrow sighed. "We get eyes on the set up and you guys coordinate your next visit."

Jake shook his head when he looked to Brody. Silently, they agreed Morrow's plan was bullshit. As they were in a fix that was sure to get worse, it was all they had to go on for the time being.

"Well gentlemen? Are we in agreement?"

Following another moment's hesitation, Brody and Jake raised their bottles in silent confirmation.

***

### San Francisco, California~

"Doc says he plans on kickin' your fat ass out of here by next Wednesday," James O'Hara joined in when the big man in the hospital bed began to laugh.

"Thank God!" Vince Folksom's wide, tanned face was animated with humor and relief that the gesture no longer stirred pain from the life threatening injuries he'd suffered little over a month ago. "I don't know how much more of this pitiful food I can take. Say man, you're the head of Merc's security team. Don't you have pull to get the poor bastards recovering here something decent to eat?"

"Well hell, man aren't the top surgeons we're providing, enough?" Jay's laughter vibrated with greater intensity that shook the rangy, length of his body.

Vince waved his big hands in mock defense. "Don't get me wrong. We appreciate the lifesavers, but hell...give us a reason to live."

"I'll see what I can do." Jay promised once another round of vibrant laughter had topped out. "I'm sure steak for every meal is a small price to pay for the man who saved the life of the boss's lady."

"Just doin' my job," Vince's humor began to ebb. "Me and...Kev."

Vince Folksom and his partner Kevin Jonas were former GAN members, now employed with Mercuri Nikolaides' security crew. Vince and Kevin had been tapped by James O'Hara to serve as security detail for Tee Shaw when the vengeful Harris Van Deer was still a threat. Mercuri had put similar detail in place for the rest of Tee's friends as well.

Jay watched the sorrow cloud Vince's face. "Kev was a good man. Went down in the line of fire the way he would've wanted."

"Yeah, I know," Vince managed a lopsided grin. "Doesn't mean I'm not gonna miss the crazy idiot."

Jay leaned forward and brought a hand down on Vince's leg. "You and me both," he said.

Jay and Vince were interrupted by a quick knock to Vince's room door. A man, the same build as Vince edged in. His brown hair fell past powerful shoulders and was bound in a long braid. He greeted the men, who each referred to him as Andy.

"You in the mood for another visitor?" Andrew Shepard asked Vince.

"Have a seat, man," Vince waved toward the empty chair next to Jay.

Andy shook his head. "Not me, man. Trust me, you'll probably enjoy this visit a lot more than any you've gotten so far."

"Thanks," Jay gave a playful sneer.

Shepard waved a hand then. "You'll agree when you see her."

Interest peaked in Vince's deep set eyes. "Her?"

"Me and Vargas are on her security detail," Shepard explained. "She's one of Ms. Shaw's friends. She's as much a sweetheart as she is a beauty, so be on your best behavior."

Vince nodded, watching Shepard head out. Jay pushed from his chair.

"Sounds like my cue to leave," Jay leaned over to envelope Vince's hand in a hearty shake. "Be well," he said.

Alone, Vince stared off across the room at the furnishings and walls of warm, earth tones. Less than a minute later, his door was opening again. An extraordinary brown beauty with uncommon eyes, even more uncommon hair and a hesitant smile, entered slowly.

"Mr. Folksom? I'm Prin Holland," she quietly introduced. "I'm a friend of Tee's-uh, Etienne Shaw."

"Yes, Ms. Holland, Andy explained," Vince gave a welcoming smile. "Please call me Vince."

"Thank you for seeing me and thank you even more for saving my friend," Prin squeezed her hands and watched the man with an earnest expression.

"You're welcome, ma'am, but the nod for that really goes to Mercuri. He ended the psycho who had your friend."

"If it hadn't been for you and your partner, he may've been outnumbered."

124

"What can I do for you Ms. Holland?"

"The man who killed your partner-wounded you-who is he?"

"Grant Zubin?" Vince blurted before he realized.

"Zubin. Tell me about him."

Vince shifted uncomfortably. "Ms. Holland-"

"He's still out there, isn't he?"

"Ms. Holland, you and your friends are safe. You can trust in that."

"I believe you," Prin took a tentative step closer to the bed. "I guess I'm just curious about who had me and my friends in his crosshairs. I promise you won't frighten me or have me running away in terror."

"No," Vince smiled, shook his head as he regarded the woman in his midst. "No, I don't think I will."

"Please."

Vince hesitated again, but briefly. "To put it simply, Ms. Holland, he's a monster. We've got plenty of those in my world, but Zoo...he's one of a kind." Vince cleared his throat, as though he'd suddenly drifted in from a daze. "You'll have to forgive me, Ms. Holland if I don't say any more. Mercuri would have my ass."

"Will you at least tell me what he looks like? That way I'll know him if I ever see him?" Prin tacked on, at the curious look she received.

Vince sighed, "The food here is nightmare enough, but it's got nothing on Zoo," he chuckled but soon lost his humor.

"Dead eyes," he said. "Blue-not...not warm like yours," he smiled as Prin reciprocated.

"Cold eyes, pale, pale skin and hair-practically white," Vince continued. "You'd know him if you saw him, but don't worry Ms. Holland. He's long gone."

"Yeah," Prin nodded. In silence, she added. *That's what I'm afraid of.*

***

Pope studied the phone after replaying the message. It was rare for the landline to ring-rarer still for anyone to leave a message. But Bear had. Trouble was, he had no idea what it meant.

Coming out to discuss the weekend he'd booked, made no sense. He wouldn't try to decipher it now. She'd called and that was enough.

125

He'd left her the night before, assuming that he wouldn't see her unless he was the one reaching out. He hadn't even planned on returning to the house that night. His plan had been to unplug up at Rutger's place, before deciding on whether he'd make the trip to Memphis.

He knew it wouldn't be possible to avoid it for long. Between Gerrick Ferguson's call and the asshats at Womack, Mebane and Urnst clogging up his voicemail, his past was about to come colliding with his present. He'd only come back to Pacifica because he'd decided to crash there and head to Rutger's in the morning.

After listening to Bear's message, he stashed his duffle in a coat closet. A quick sweep of the house showed nothing out of sorts. There was a lot to be said for never staying at home. It was always ready to receive company. For this visit, he'd be ready, resistent to her charms and talkative.

He'd given her message a third listen, then went to ponder it further from the sheltered expanse of his front porch. The early evening breeze had escalated a few knots. Overhead, the skies appeared restless-a mix of gray clouds mingling with a darker blue. He prayed the storm would hold, at least until Bear arrived- or after she left. There was sure to be storm enough once their conversation began.

It was just past 6 when he noticed the distant headlights on the road winding its way to the house. He straightened from the tall columns, one of several dotting the porch and took the row of long steps leading down to the dirt drive.

Bear cursed softly, when she saw him. No turning back now, she guessed. It had taken all of a second for her to regret the call and all the seconds leading up to the visit for her to fortify the courage to go through with it.

Parking the Jeep, she made a quick exit and her heart made its usual leap when he approached. Promptly, she stifled the usual jabs of arousal he evoked. In a simple white tee and dark cargo pants, he could've pulled off the image of a man at rest. Instead, he looked even more formidable and it was hell on her hormones.

Pope leaned in to take her elbow and Bear let him feel her stiffen. The wind held a moderate strength and chill. Bear felt it was a perfect accompaniment to her mood, which was downright unsteady. Though nerves had rendered her stiff as a board, she appreciated the

126

support of his hold. Nerves would've made it hard to clear the row of wide steps without stumbling.

The front door was ajar, yet she took her time crossing the threshold when he pushed it open for her to precede him. Bear wasn't one to skirt confrontation, but this was one she wouldn't have minded avoiding. The door closed, filling the entryway with a definitive sound that rose almost as quietly as it eased.

Pope maintained his spot by the door. "Are you alright?" he asked.

"Are you married?" she countered and didn't know if it was relief or despair she felt at the surprise she saw register in his electric gaze.

"Bear-"

"Please? I know you have something to tell me. Just say it."

"Babe," closing his eyes then, Pope gave a quiet smile while raking at the hair that tumbled into his face when he tilted his head.

"No, I'm not married. I thought we covered that?"

"We covered that you're not gay."

"Well add, not married to it. No relationship of any kind. As for marriage I um...never thought I'd find the right woman." He added the last quietly. Bear was already massaging her temples and missed the helpless fascination in his eyes as they followed her.

"I'm not married," he said once more when she turned to glare at him.

"Then what the hell is it?! What's the topic of this big fucking talk we need to have?!" She muttered yet another curse and turned away to slam herself for the outburst.

Instead of answering, Pope left the entryway. Bear followed him through to an expansive living room that was so dimly lit, the moon's illumination was visible on the walls as was the wild sway of palm leaves against the wind.

Pope went to a long, maplewood desk that occupied a far wall and sat on a raised platform of the same gleaming wood. Bear waited near a bay of long sofas and eyed the room's high ceilings and large potted palms enhancing its corners.

"What's this?" She said when he returned and handed her a plain white envelope.

"Open it," Pope waited, giving her time to scan the top page. "You couldn't find out who owned the cottage, because that's the way I

127

wanted it. When you own as much property as I do, it helps to have others handling all the inquiries you tend to get about it. They know that inquiries about selling are to be refused. I have a hard time giving up things that belong to me, Bear."

"I want to buy it."

"No need. I'm giving it to you."

The news didn't elicit her appreciation. "Because I've earned it?"

"Because I want to," he ignored her implication.

She shook her head. "I need a price."

"Alright. Dinner."

"Pope-"

"You didn't say it had to be monetary."

"Son of a bitch," she muttered.

"Is that a yes?"

She gave her nod with tangible reluctance and turned away. Pope smiled in appreciation of her answer and the scent of lavender and talc wafting when she moved, teasing his nostrils.

"You're a crafty bastard," she hissed. "I'll bet that seriously cuts down on the number of friends you have."

Pope lost whatever satisfaction he'd found over the secured dinner date. "You get used to people you've known all your life," his voice was quiet. "But there are times when the relationships get strained."

"Yeah," Bear set the envelope to a glass end table she passed on her way to a window wall overlooking the cliffs. The strains on the relationships with her dearest friends were front and center on her mind.

"Friendships are hard," she said.

"Especially when you break certain rules," Pope added.

Curiosity stirred, but Bear waited. She could feel her mood returning to its unsteady state when she spotted the dark emotion straining his remarkable face.

"Mercuri Nikolaides is more to me than a guy I know. We've been friends all our lives. I know pretty much all there is to know about him, including the fact that he's in love with your best friend Tee."

The silence that followed seemed somehow amplified over the active wind. Bear's hand had gone to her mouth halfway through his explanation. She could feel her head spin and was glad for the dim room.

Brighter lighting would've most likely seared her corneas which felt like they were on fire.

She sat, not much caring whether there was a chair waiting to catch her. Pope knelt, his heart thundering in his ears. It was a sensation he never experienced unless he was charging head first into one of the savage situations that had marked so many days of his past life.

The sensation stirred whenever anticipation and fear roiled together in a noxious and violent brew. He'd never experienced the feeling at any other time and realized that standing on the edge of losing her frightened him more than any of the hundreds of bloody missions he'd ever set out on.

What the fuck was wrong with him? He'd expected this to happen-planned on it. Lied to himself that he could handle it, was what he'd done.

"Bear?" He whispered, squeezing her beneath the denim molding her thigh. He shoved aside an almost violent surge of fear and whispered to her again.

"Bear?"

She said nothing, but Pope was sensitive enough to feel her tremble under his hand. "Honey talk to me," he nuzzled his cheek against hers.

That time, she shook her head as fierce and determined as a stubborn child.

Pope heard the phone ring and-what the fuck? He'd owned the place for years and hadn't gotten as many calls on the landline as he had in the last 2 days. He had no plans to answer it until she; her voice, hollow and pained, pleaded for him to.

As the caller was showing no signs of giving up and the machine had yet to engage, Pope decided they could both use a break. The man on the other end of the line, registered surprise in his greeting when he received an answered phone.

"Uh yes, Pope Apos-Apostolou?"

"Speaking."

"Yes, yes Sir, Mr. Apostolou. This is Cory Sumner I'm an associate with Womack, Mebane and Urnst- Attorneys at Law. I'm calling to inform you that your attendance is requested for the reading of the Last Will and Testament for Nathan Cameron Alberts..."

Sumner was giving Pope a list of possible dates and times to coordinate with his schedule, when Pope saw Bear leave the sofa and sprint for his front door.

*Let her go*. That damned voice of reason again. He clenched the receiver and heard the creak of hard plastic.

*Let her go,* the voice repeated. That time, he decided to listen.

"Mr. Apostolou?"

Faintly, Pope tuned into the attorney's query. "I'll be there," he dropped the receiver to its cradle not caring whether the answer sufficed.

Meanwhile, the sound of a car engine grew faint in the distance.

# PART II

*Most of the evil in this world is done by people*
*with good intentions*
*T.S. Eliot*

# CHAPTER 12

*One Week Later~*

Activity usually surged in heightened bursts among the 17 member staff of eShaw Designs and their boss Etienne 'Tee' Shaw. eShaw specialized in interior design on both the corporate and residential levels.

Tee had crafted a respected name for herself among high powered executives and homeowners alike. However, there were those rare occasions between jobs when eShaw offices experienced refreshing bouts of quiet. During those times, Tee gave her staff the option of taking personal time without penalty. On Fridays, the firm resembled a ghost town, but for the presence of one hardworking soul.

Lunchtime found Tee curled in a blanket on a sofa in her office living area where she was reading through a stack of folders. A quick knock, had her dark eyes shifting to the door, smiling when she saw Bear leaning on the frame.

"Well hey!" Tee scooted up on the sofa, her lovely molasses dark face beaming as she began to gather the folders and make room for Bear to sit. "This is a surprise!" She raved.

Bear winced, jingled her keys. "Sorry for just dropping by. I let myself in."

"You know that's fine," Tee moved a stack of folders to the floor.

Bear knew as much. For years, she and her friends had kept keys to one another's homes and offices.

Tee looked up to launch another smile at Bear, but frowned instead as awareness flooded her expression. "What's wrong?"

Bear shoved off the doorframe. "Am I *that* easy to read?"

"Today? Yes. Lu's the open book of the group, remember?"

Bear nodded, an affectionate smile curving her mouth.

"So?" Tee rested an elbow to the sofa cushions and idly raked her nails across the onyx waves capping her head. "You gonna tell me what's up? Or we gonna spend twenty minutes making small talk?"

Bear sat on the arm of the sofa, then changed her mind and took a seat on one of the chairs flanking it.

Concern layered Tee's awareness. "Bear-"

"Does Mercuri have a friend named Pope?"

Tee's concern mellowed and she eased back onto the sofa. "He does. I assume you've met?" She added when Bear only nodded and seemed content doing so.

"Hmph, yes," Bear confirmed along with a breathy amused laugh.

"Impressive, huh?"

"Very," Bear's tone was still a breathy one.

"Well then," Delighted, Tee tucked in the edges of the walnut brown fleece blanket, "since you once questioned me so intently about Mercuri, I think it's only fair I get to do the same with you now about Pope. Are you impressed enough to want to get to know him?" Tee watched the woman across from her, break into an almost hysterical fit of laughter.

Bear left the chair, swiping laugh-tears from her eyes. "Now *that* should've been the first thing I did!"

A different kind of awareness had Tee shifting beneath the blanket. "You slept with him."

Keeping her back turned, Bear only ticked an index finger to confirm Tee's guess. In seconds, another amused laugh escaped her. "To be totally truthful-*now anyway*-we haven't exactly *slept* together, unless you count the naps we've taken between our marathon fucking sessions."

"I see," Tee's voice was a tad faint.

"No, you don't," Bear turned then. "We went for nearly twenty hours the first time."

"Yeah I-" Tee's nod came slow as she cleared her throat. "I'm familiar with the uh-stamina." Thoughts of Mercuri's skill pooled her mind.

Bear let out a weary moan while resting a hip on the edge of Tee's desk across the room.

Playfulness stirred in Tee's dark eyes then. In hopes of lightening the mood and encouraging Bear to share whatever it was that had her looking so woeful, she posed her question. "So is it safe to say he's as good as he looks?"

"Fucking A, he is," Bear blurted without hesitation but her woeful demeanor held.

"B?" Tee's concern made a swift return. "Sweetie, what is it? What's wrong?"

"You mean, besides the fact that I slept with the guy a few days after I met him?"

Tee laughed. "Are you forgetting that I didn't exactly wait a...proper amount of time before I had sex with Mercuri?"

"That's different."

"How?"

"Because he didn't know what you-what you did." Bear left the desk and prowled the office. Absently, she picked up framed pictures and other trinkets lining the bookshelves and end tables.

"The things I did with him...they made that night with The Ten look G-rated."

"That doesn't sound so bad to me, B. With Pope...well you-you wanted it."

"Yes Tee...yes, I wanted it and he *expected* me to want it. What else would he expect, given the way I whored myself for ten men-"

"B-"

"And don't sit there and tell me he doesn't know! Why keep it from me that he's Mercuri's friend? Hell, what we did that night helped them move forward with their plan. A raid on the pimp who sent his girls to murder their board."

"But you know that's not true. So does Pope."

134

"But it doesn't change the fact that we were there, does it?" Bear joined Tee on the sofa and fixed her with a level gaze that dared her to argue.

"It doesn't change the fact that we were there and there for one thing."

Tee scooted forward on the sofa. "Honey, Pope doesn't care about that."

"Every man cares about that," Bear insisted with a raised hand when she saw the argument blooming in Tee's eyes. "If he tells you he doesn't, then he's full of shit. I don't expect you to believe that about Mercuri, when you met him he didn't know what you were-" Bear covered her mouth the instant the words left her tongue.

"God Tee, I'm sorry," her apology was muffled behind her hand.

"Do you believe that?" Tee's voice was as soft as the look in her eyes. "Do you believe that night defined us? That it's who we are at the heart of this?"

"It doesn't matter!" Heat was ablaze in Bear's eyes again. She tried to leave the sofa, but stopped at Tee's hand over her wrist.

"Is it?" Tee demanded.

"No," the denial was quiet but firm and genuine. "No Tee, I don't. I don't but he-he does. He has to."

"Honey," Tee's heart ached for her friend and she exchanged her hand at Bear's wrist to squeeze her thigh. "Have you talked to him?"

Again, Bear shoved to her feet. "I can't even look at him, so forget about talking to him."

"So when do you plan-"

"Never. It's over."

"Does *he* know this?"

"He's an idiot if he doesn't."

"And you really think he'll let you go that easy?"

"Oh I expect it'll be hard for him." Bear crossed her arms over her chest. "Men usually like to hold onto the sure things-"

"Alright Bear, just stop!" Tee unfolded her small frame from the sofa and stood. "What's with all this self pity crap? It doesn't play well on you at all."

Crumpling then, Bear dragged her fingers through her hair and dropped her butt to the edge of the desk. "You're right, Tee and that's why I'm glad this is over. I don't need the drama-don't need to be second guessing myself at every turn and worrying over what he does or doesn't think. That kind of bullshit goes places I don't care to find myself."

"Like where, B? Companionship? Intimacy?"

"This is nothing like what you and Mercuri have, Tee," Bear's expression was blank. "I gave Pope Apostolou exactly what he was looking for and it was *not* companionship."

"Wow…" Tee began to pace the room, tapping a nail to her chin and appearing to be in deep thought. "What was that you said a while back? That word you kept calling me? Oh yeah! Idiot."

"Tee-"

"Shut it."

Bear bristled, but she obeyed.

"So you left right after Pope told you he and Mercuri are friends. *Left,*" Tee stressed when Bear prepared to elaborate, "without giving him the chance to say anything beyond that. You've got no idea what he's thinking because you didn't stick around to hear anything else he had to say."

"But what if he does, Tee? What if he does think that?"

Bear's uncharacteristic despair, continued to weigh heavily on Tee. With a quiet sigh, she settled beside her on the desk.

"So you're okay with letting fear of a 'what if' keep you from finding out 'what is'?"

"I don't think I have a choice, Tee."

"Honey...there's always a choice."

"Not for me," Bear huffed out a decisive breath. "Not with him. He's dangerous, Tee."

The words gave Tee pause, but only for an instant. "You're right. He is. Pope and his friends have done things that would chill anyone's spine, but there are also a ton of good points- the way he came to see me, worried sick over Mercuri when things started to go south for us. He'd never hurt you-physically, I mean.

"No Tee," Bear was already shaking her head. "No, I know that. That-that's not what I mean. I...Tee, I've let him see parts of me I...things that…"

She couldn't finish and Tee didn't need her to.

"So...he's seen past the alpha girl bitch, huh?"

"And I'll be damned if I know how." Bear left the desk. "He just…" silently, she recalled the way she melted for him seconds after the scathing call with one of her employees.

"Nobody gets to see that side, Tee. Shit, I barely let you, Lu and Prin see it. No." Bear shook her head like a stubborn child. "I let him see that half a minute after I blasted some poor guy on my staff and he...acted like he didn't even notice. Like that part of me didn't matter to him, didn't..."

"Make him run like all the rest? Run the way you expect them to-secretly want them to?"

"He's not for me, Tee." Bear exhaled the phrase as though she were sold on a fact.

Tee pursed her lips and shook her head. "You're not just an idiot, you're a stubborn one to boot. How can you be so-"

"Because I know what happens when a woman is so far gone over a man that she can't even think for herself. He could do that and I- it's taken too long to find a way to make it through my days without being crushed by the weight of six years ago and all the other weights I've collected in my life. I can't think around him, Tee." Arms folded over her chest again, Bear commenced a new path to pace across the office.

"When he's there, I can't think about another goddamn thing but him and us...together- and that's just about sex." Deep down, Bear heard the voice calling her a liar. She ignored it.

"It's just about sex. Anything more and I-I'd be useless."

"Honey-"

"No Tee, I- thank you. I shouldn't have come here and laid all this on you."

"It's okay. I'm here anytime, you know?"

"I know." With a fast nod, Bear rushed to Tee for a hug and cheek kiss. "I know," she said again before she all but sprinted from the office.

***

## Memphis, Tennessee~

Daniel Schultz held a bourbon tumbler to his lips, but didn't sip. "So it's confirmed?" he asked instead.

Gerrick Ferguson chose to respond after downing his hit of bourbon. "It's as good as. They've already set the date for the reading."

"Any word on whether Pope's coming alone?"

137

"None yet," Gerrick raised two fingers toward the server who had been tending to he and Dan since their arrival at the pub.

"Will you talk to him beforehand?"

"I'll try…"

Gerrick's airy reply, had Dan Schultz looking on with uncertainty. "Is it just me or are you much calmer about this than you should be?"

"Now don't get me wrong," Gerrick chuckled. "I'm not looking forward to sharing this particular dirty company secret, but I'd rather tell it to Pope than any other."

"Don't underestimate that kid, Gerri. I've seen Pope Apostolou take men apart with his bare hands."

"So have I," Gerrick shut off those images coming to mind.

The server returned with fresh drinks. Long minutes passed while the two men savored the refills in silence.

"In spite of what Pope is capable of physically, he's a smart son of a bitch-one of the smartest I've ever seen. Given that, Nathan's suicide could be the best thing that's happened for the GAN."

"True, but that's only if he leaves everything to the kid," Daniel cautioned.

"Dan, my friend," Gerrick raised his glass in toast, "that's the only part of this entire mess that I *am* sure of."

\*\*\*

### Mykonos, Greece~

For the first time during the sublime period that he'd spent soaking in the sun, cuisine and unadulterated vices to be found and plundered; on the exquisite island where he resided, Slayte Miltiades wished he were elsewhere. California, to be precise.

He hadn't grown disillusioned with his prime piece of real estate- a snow white villa with an incomparable view of the Aegean. He wasn't bored by the ancient, breathtaking town he now called home. Nor was he bored with the playboy lifestyle he'd painstakingly cultivated.

A ghost of a smile held the subtle curve of Slayte's mouth. His violet gaze scanned the colorful late evening skies and winding limestone streets that were beginning to teem with those eager to explore the lush island-a work of architectural brilliance.

No...he hadn't grown bored with the vibrant town. The playboy lifestyle on the other hand...

Slayte bowed his head and dragged a few fingers through wild blue black curls being tossed by the nighttime breeze. The playboy lifestyle had worn thin a long time ago and it had nothing to do with the blonde he'd met over a month earlier- a woman he'd yet to do so much as speak to.

Well...it didn't have *everything* to do with her or the fact that he hadn't been able to get her out of his mind since. That uncommon shade of blonde paired with the cool, honey brown of her skin...

Hissing a curse, Slayte pushed back from the terrace-preferring the refuge of his greatroom. No, the extraordinary Princess Holland did not have *everything* to do with his desire to return to the States- only a great deal of it.

Still, there was more. Older business that begged to be handled. Grant Zubin wasn't dead. Slayte knew that without question. No one had seen hide nor hair of him since his shootout with the detail Mercuri had placed on Tee. But Slayte knew. The man was just laying low.

He had no clue as to the extent of Zubin's injuries, but he knew the man-the beast. He'd known the beast for too long, had once been part of his depraved team. If the psycho was dead, Slayte believed he would've just known it.

That time wasn't far off, though. He'd see it done. He'd see Grant Zubin in the ground where he should've been years ago. Only then, would he be free of his own private ghosts- ones he couldn't even bring himself to discuss with his best friends in the world. Only then, would he be free to focus on the tempting beauty he'd already become more than a little infatuated with.

*** 

"We'll probably have an appetite later, Kimmie," Rutger told the smiling brunette and watched as she worked to maintain her smile and the cool professionalism that went along with it.

"Well just let me know if you need anything," the flight attendant told Rutger, but her moss green eyes were fixed on Pope.

"Promise you'll be the first one we call," Rutger pretended not to notice the woman biting her lip while she spared additional seconds to gaze longingly at his friend. He allowed his grin to spread, once Kimmie had sequestered herself in a rear staff compartment.

"I think you hurt her feelings," casually, Rutger smoothed his fingers across the close cut whiskers shading his jaw and feigned interest in the passing sky beyond his oval window. His voice maintained its usual quiet depth but carried just fine to the other side of the cabin.

Pope smiled, but his gaze remained fixed past his cabin window too. "Why don't you go cheer her up?" his smile defined when he heard his friend's chuckle.

"You're her favorite, remember?"

"I remember," Pope allowed a varied, yet memorable array of thoughts to flash- all featuring… moments with the lovely attendants who staffed the Mercuri Fleets jets.

Rutger spared a look to the other side of the cabin and took note of Pope's set expression. "Well hell, man is it *that* bad?"

Pope didn't hesitate to respond. "It is, actually."

"Wanna talk?"

"Not really."

"Do you realize how many times you've given me that answer over the last week?"

It was true, Pope mused. He'd spent the time at Rutger's following the revealing visit from Bear. He'd kept to himself for most of the stay, which worked fine then. Within the confines of the jet's cabin, it appeared Rutger had had his fill of being kept out of the loop.

"You know I'll nag until you tell me," Rutger saw Pope smile over the threat, but he could tell the man's heart wasn't in it.

"Listen Po, I know I don't have the listening gift or the advice gene like Patch, but I'll damn well try. You're gonna need your wits about you where we're headed."

More truth, Pope agreed with an inward sigh. Succinctly, and in a soft manner that belied his frustration, he recapped the entire situation with Bear. By the time he'd shared the scene in his living room from a week earlier, frustration had slipped past the control he was working to sustain.

"What are you gonna do?" Rutger put a hand to his chest. "Have a heart and tell me, will you? Maybe I won't screw up so royally when my time comes."

"Leaving her alone is what I *should* do."

"But?...Right." Rutger smirked at the look Pope sent him. "Be careful, Po. You don't need me to tell you this is a totally different situation from any we know."

140

"No, you don't need to tell me that," Pope leaned forward to scrub his palms over his face and then looked to Rutger and grinned. "I appreciate the reminder anyway, though."

"So what will you do if she won't see you?"

"She'll see me, alright. She didn't take the deed to the cottage when she left."

"Maybe she meant to leave it behind."

"No way. Besides, I'm giving it to her, remember?"

"How could I forget?!" Rutger laughed. "*You* giving property away?"

"She wants it too much to walk away from it, even if it means taking it from me."

"For free."

Pope shifted Rutger a sharp look. "You think that was a mistake too? Bear didn't seem to appreciate the gesture either," he noted.

"Well think about it, man. Your selfless gesture could've been perceived as...payment for services rendered."

"Shit," Pope grumbled the curse and left the long sofa he'd occupied. "That wasn't it," he bit out the words, while storming to the bar cart in the cabin.

"Well hell, Po, *I* know that," Rutger supplied a lazy shrug. "Bear probably does too, but it might be hard for her to look at it that way right now. Give her some time."

Pope looked as though the suggestion were a foreign concept. "How much time?"

"Fuck man, do you think *I* know?"

Pope only waved and set about removing the cap from the beer he'd found in the bar fridge. He took one to Rutger and they enjoyed the brews in silence.

"This is a new one," Rutger noted, his tone oddly pensive. "I thought she was only about sex for you."

"So did I," the quiet roar was alive in Pope's voice and then he seemed to shudder. "Don't tell Merc I said that," he joined in when Rutger grinned.

"So what'll you do if she's done?"

Pope swigged down more beer. "Maybe I'll know by the time we get back."

Rutger frowned as memory served. "How long does a will reading last?"

"Can't be long." Pope shook his head. "It's what happens *after* the reading that brings the real headache."

"Have you heard anymore from Gerrick?"

"He wants to meet up while we're there."

"Well, well," Rutger's grin came through in his words. "Sounds like he wants to have a chat with the new top dog."

"Jesus, Rut," Pope worked the bridge of his nose between his fingers. "Please don't say that."

"Could be true," Rutger swigged down more beer and regarded the bottle. "And you know that would put you right in Brody's crosshairs."

Pope replied with enthusiastic laughter. "At least I'll be in familiar territory-I've spent half my life in that asshole's crosshairs." A sly element took hold of Pope's features then when he looked to Rutger.

"You shouldn't look so content either. Jake's gonna hold you just as responsible."

Rutger shrugged. "What was that you said about familiar territory? Maybe Gerrick has some magic remedy to help us all get along."

"Doubtful." Pope left his bottle on the bar and returned to the sofa. "I can't even predict what he wants to talk about. I just hope we can get it over and done with fast."

Rutger waved off the concern. "Don't sweat it- it'll all work itself out."

"Right." Pope leaned back against the sofa, again massaging his nose. His thoughts returned to Bear and then he was fixing Rutger with another sly look.

"What was it you said about needing to know what to do when your time came? I'm assuming you're referring to LuCarolyn Young?" He smiled when Rutger bristled.

"Damn your intuition, Po."

Pope's smile became a chuckle. "Like I've said, you guys aren't that hard to read." He sobered then. "No deceptions, Rut. Tell her everything. Who you are. How you know Merc and what you know about that night with The Ten."

"And if she walks away?"

Pope closed his eyes. "Then, at least she'll be out of your life before she has the chance to work her way into your system-before you reach a point where you can't let her go."

142

# CHAPTER 13

Womack, Mebane and Urnst had someone to call Pope and let him know they had taken the liberty of securing suites at The Marshall Club. The Alberts family had been members since the earliest days of the revered establishment. The Marshall was an oasis for men who represented the upper echelons of Memphis society.

Pope politely declined the accommodations-as did Rutger. The Grodins family held membership as well. By birthright, Pope and Rutger were honorary members. Their refusal to patronize the club's suites, didn't carry over to its restaurants however. The Marshall was known to have some of the best steaks in Tennessee.

Once they were settled in rooms across town, Pope and Rutger headed off to make their lunch appointment with Gerrick Ferguson. Joining The GANs Chief Medical Officer, was his lead assistant over the last 40 odd years Daniel Schultz, along with GAN chemists Edmund 'Ned' McCaffrey and Hoyt Ingram. The men were just taking their seats when Pope and Rutger were shown to the table. Once handshakes had been exchanged and drinks were on order, everyone looked to Ferguson to begin.

Gerrick Ferguson, was a striking man whose features; framed by a full mane of silver gray, only seemed to grow more striking with age. "Thank you both for coming," he said to Pope and Rutger. "I know I was pretty vague with my reasons for wanting you here."

"Why are you reaching out to my friend about your reasons, Doc?" Rutger's expression seemed to confirm he'd already reached his own conclusion.

Gerrick Ferguson seemed to recognize that and smiled. "We all know your friend is about to become a very powerful man in the GAN."

"We also know your former employer was a sadistic prick who, just for the fuck of it, could be naming me as sole owner of his stamp collection in this will you're all making this fuss over. He's got another son, remember?" Pope noted as he accepted the chilled mug of beer he'd ordered.

"Nate would've never trusted Brody with something this complex," Daniel Schultz argued quietly.

"He killed himself after that broadcast outed everything The GAN really stands for," Pope countered. "Clearly, he thought it beyond saving. Maybe he had a crisis of conscience and decided it didn't need to be and Brody's bumbling efforts would've been just the thing to finish it off."

"You can't possibly believe that's true?" Dan Schultz looked incredulous.

"But it *is* possible." Pope persisted.

"For the purposes of this discussion, let's work from the assumption that you're about to be the sole 'owner' of one half of the Grodins Alberts Network," Gerric suggested.

"Sole owner, huh?" Pope took a long swallow of his beer before continuing. "An owner who happens to be...damn...now how did 'ol Nate once put it? The bastard child of his favorite whore."

"Pope," Hoyt Ingram cleared his throat. "He couldn't let it be known back then that you meant anything more to him."

Pope's only response was to indulge in another long swallow of his beer.

144

"Gentlemen," Gerrick Ferguson appeared to have accepted the role as the group's moderator. "Let's not let the past dictate the tone of the meeting."

"Then Doc, maybe we should get to the point," Rutger jerked his head toward Pope. "Or this man is gonna be leaving soon as he's done with his beer."

Gerrick nodded, looking to Pope. "I already told you your fath-that Nathan," he clarified, when Pope's fingers flexed on his mug, "didn't like what the GAN had become. It wasn't what he or Lorne intended," he looked to Rutger.

"You also said there were things he didn't want anyone to know while he was alive," Pope noted.

Gerrick nodded. "Right."

"Something that'd make the whole mess worth saving," Pope continued.

"Exactly," Gerrick's tone held trace amounts of relief- one a teacher might express in the face of a student who was finally getting the lesson.

"Lorne and Nathan started their careers as salesmen in the medical supply field," Gerrick continued. "Both had tours in 'Nam prior to that. Lorne had one- Nate, two. They met during Nate's second. Ned and I were there too," he looked to the slender balding man across the table. "It's where we all met," Gerrick added.

"You think you've seen carnage," Ned McCaffrey's haunted expression proved he was looking into his past. "You haven't," he focused on the younger men at the table.

"There're things in life that define a man," Gerrick went on, "they set him on his path-solidify his passions. The things Lor and Nate saw there...being part of the medical field in some way, was because of that. It was a way out for all of us," Gerrick's hazel eyes held their own haunted hue. "After we got back to The World, we found our way to med school. That's where Ned and I met Dan and Hoyt. We lost track the way folks tend to do after graduation, but Hoyt and Ned reached out when they thought they'd...found something."

"We didn't know what it was at first," Hoyt said. "But anytime you're working on things that touch on genetics it's cause for...attention."

Pope and Rutger exchanged bland looks.

145

"I kept in touch with Dan," Ned shared. "But Hoyt and I were part of the same scientific circles so we ran into each other a little more often. Hoyt told me what he thought he had, figured it was crap but a good scientist leaves no theory untested."

"Trouble was, he had no place to test it," Dan said.

"So enter the old men," Pope nodded, "Medical supply salesmen and all-able to get exactly what you needed."

"They set Hoyt and Ned up with a place to research," Gerrick explained. "They were able to produce this...discovery of theirs and test it on the cells of diseased rodents. The um...discovery not only repaired the damaged cells, but it...regenerated the animals in some way."

"Some grew two, sometimes three times as large, with enhanced brain development, motor skills," Dan supplied, "Reflexes, eyesight, hearing-everything was off the charts. Even their coats were glossier."

"So the old men had dreams of saving the world with a super species of rats," Rutger drily noted.

"Thanks for not making me say it," Pope whispered with a quiet smile.

The older men at the table weren't so amused.

"We didn't know what we had until the rodents mated and passed the *improvements* to their offspring." Hoyt said. "Perfect specimens that grew at an astonishing rate, as did their abilities."

"So?" Pope spread his hands inquiringly. "What was the problem?"

Hoyt, Dan and Ned looked to Gerrick.

"Problem was that a percentage-small at first-showed signs of brain trauma." Gerrick took on the task of explaining. "They began to act out violently-even raged against themselves when there wasn't another to attack. Mind you, it didn't happen on a massive scale. Not at first, but just one with that kind of power mixed with that kind of rage..."

"Not a great selling point," Rutger sighed.

Gerrick lifted his glass in toast.

"But the old men loved it," Pope guessed, watching the others nod.

"They were salesmen at heart," Ned's slender shoulders rose in a mystified shrug. "Already had contacts in the military curious and everything."

"Curious about how well it worked on humans, you mean?" Rutger's guess encouraged another round of nods.

"On pregnant ones," Pope added.

The nodding slowed.

"What did you fucks do?" The soft, telling roar underlined Pope's query.

Gerrick bristled. "Like we said, the military was curious, and they paid well to help ease their curiosity. Nate and Lor...hell *all* of us were eager to help. We've seen what war does, fellas. We've seen carnage and trust me when I say carnage isn't the exclusive realm of the dead. The living carnage haunts you more than the dead ever could. Kids ravaged while still inside their mothers' wombs because those women merely took a breath of toxic air..."

"Our studies showed that whatever outside factors the parents were exposed to, the effects never harmed the fetus," Hoyt added.

Dan was next to chime in. "Imagine babies never having to be born with birth defects because their mothers decided to drink or smoke or do drugs, even. It's like being born wearing a bulletproof vest."

"Only the thing that could kill you is already inside your head." Rutger noted, watching the nods resume.

"But no one cared about that," Pope reiterated.

"The military paid well to start the human trials," Gerrick shared. "They never asked questions about how we planned to move forward."

"So you used the taxpayers' money to buy prostitutes," Rutger sneered, gestured to the server for a refill on his Scotch.

Dan and Gerrick shifted uncomfortably in their seats. Rutger had hit a still raw nerve.

"Most of the encounters resulted in pregnancies," Gerrick confirmed. "We kept the women separated and they lived all over the country. They were very well provided for."

"Thoughtful of you," Pope said.

Ned's uneasiness was reflected in his brown gaze. "It looked as if the human trials would show no cause for concern. The abhorrent brain activity showed within the first year during the animal trials. There was nothing like that during the human trials.

"Not until the eighth or ninth year," Hoyt said, unease just as vivid in his blue gaze while he smoothed a hand over his balding head. "The frontal lobe issues were quite noticeable," he said. "At first we tried to label it as a growth stage, acting out, testing limits. We thought it might be confusion over what was happening to them. I'm sure they didn't see many eight year olds pushing five-four."

147

"But it wasn't that," Pope watched Gerrick produce a tight smile.

Hoyt shook his head. "The percentages of brain related issues were nearly double than what we'd seen during the animal trials. Outwardly, they were perfect but the defects were on the inside and far more deadly when they impacted the brain."

"Some of the mothers developed late stage cancers and died," Dan's beefy hands curved into loose fists. "We took those kids, which allowed us to more closely observe them."

"The mothers' illnesses were formulaic," Ned shared. "Something we should've anticipated. After all, we were basically playing around in the lab when we stumbled across this. It was all a result of mixing a concoction containing elements harmful to humans when mixed with others...Dan's right, the kids were our responsibility."

"In more ways than one," Pope muttered.

Dan piped up. "We took the kids whose mothers had died-"

"They really are thoughtful guys," Rutger directed the comment to Pope.

"Fellas please," Gerrick held his hands palm up on the table. "We aren't here to justify what we've done. Don't think that. We took those kids because they were our responsibility *and* because taking them allowed us closer observation."

"And the chance to get them combat ready."

"Not all." Dan said to Pope's assumption. "Some were too far gone to-" He grimaced, unable to go on for a moment. "There were those who learned to mask their insanity so...yes they wound up being readied."

"There were many success stories," Ned waved a hand to Pope and Rutger.

"Hear that, Rut?" Pope sneered. "We're success stories. Got rewarded for that by being taken away from our mothers at ten instead of eight."

"It's how your fathers wanted it," Gerrick's voice was like stone.

"Where are they? Our mothers?" Rutger's tone was harder than any at the table; more so, in the wake of rising temper.

Gerrick treaded carefully, knowing he was on dangerous ground. "We had eyes on them for the first few years after you all were taken. Then...then they just-just vanished. We don't know if they ran or-"

"Whether our fathers decided they were too much of a liability to keep alive."

"Pope-"

"What the hell do you snakes want from us? Forgiveness? Forget it."

"Not forgiveness, Pope. Just a chance to make it right- to make The GAN what it could've been if we hadn't lost our way." Again, Gerrick splayed his palms up on the table in a beseeching fashion. "Please know this isn't what we wanted. Believe us when we say we came from a place with the best intentions."

Pope shook his head, unmoved. "And you must know, Gerrick, what they say about folks with the best intentions?"

*\*\*\**

Jake resisted the strong desire for another drink. It would be his third of the morning which; in his opinion, meant he was far from over served. By noon, he was usually on his fifth drink.

Brody and his goddamn suave approach! All that patience bullshit. Fuck that! Patience was one of the many things they had no time for. Not when Pope Apostolou just arrived and the threat of his taking half The GAN was even closer than ever. And Brody wanted them to be patient- following along behind that pompous sap Morrow. Patience...

*He* wanted action. It had been over 6 years. Granted, they'd had little to go on in that time, but now...Dammit, *now* they knew them- knew who'd thrown the unforeseen monkey wrench into their plans.

Mercuri, Pope, Slayte and Rutger had played their part in the betrayal, but those girls... he couldn't have cared less about them murdering The Ten, but they-he and Brody-answered to more than The Ten and that group wouldn't take kindly to knowing about what they'd cooked up back then with the Senator.

Berrill Clayton and her friends had proof of that plan and had already released one disc documenting that fateful night. He and Brody couldn't afford for one to show up that caught the chat they'd had with that nutcase Zubin.

What they needed was leverage and he was all for snatching one of those sluts to make the others cooperate. He and his guys could have a fine time with the lucky girl while her friends made up their minds.

"Yeah, Patsy?" Jake called out to his assistant when her familiar quiet knock hit the door.

Patsy Grovesman wedged her stout frame just inside the office. "Heading off to lunch Mr. Grodins but there's a gentleman waiting in the lobby for you. He's not on your book-would you like him to come on up or should I make a proper appointment for him?"

"Have you got a name on him, Pats?"

"Keppard. Leonce Keppard?"

"Doesn't ring a bell," Jake waved a hand. "Send him on up, Patsy."

"Should I stay?"

Again, Jake waved. "Nah, you go on and have your lunch."

With 'lunch' on his mind as well, Jake indulged in another drink once Patsy left. Five minutes later, a tall, olive-skinned man was at the door applying the same light knocking Patsy Grovesman had used moments earlier.

Jake observed his guest, but made no effort to greet him. He left that to the man who ventured forth to offer an outstretched hand and his name.

"Do we know each other?" Jake queried.

"We've never met, Sir, but I've worked for your family for quite a while. I was sorry to hear about Mr. Alberts."

Jake finished his drink. "Yeah we're all still reeling from it. It's good of you to come by, Keppard. I'll be sure to tell Brody about your visit."

"Thank you, Sir, uh-I'm not just here to offer my sympathies."

Jake's light eyes sharpened with sudden suspicion. "I don't like guessing games Keppard."

"And I'm not here to waste your time, Mr. Grodins. I have something I think you need. A recording," he hastily added when Jake's expression went from suspicious to downright threatening.

"I'm not a man you want to blackmail, Keppard."

"Not my intentions, Sir, but your appreciation for this information would be more than enough."

"Appreciation for what?" Jake's voice maintained some of its clipped tone, though a strong current of curiosity streamed in. He stiffened, instinctively bracing when Keppard reached inside a trouser pocket.

"For the good stuff, Sir."

Jake relaxed visibly at the sight of the thumb drive the man held.

"The lady's well known," Keppard said, "built like a centerfold, performing like a porn star and one of the four women who conspired to kill our people."

150

\*\*\*

"It's not a bad product," Ned's voice was slightly muffled behind the napkin he dabbed at his mouth.

The men had continued their discussion over a hearty meal of market fresh steak and seafood.

"Had the potential for real change. We saw it," Ned continued.

"Trouble was, others saw it too," Gerrick intervened. "They also saw the nightmare side of it, but that part got hidden behind the profit to be made."

"And Lorne and Nate went right along with it," Dan chimed in with a slow shake of his head.

"And that's the ironic part," Gerrick's smile was tight. "Their greed saved this from being an even bigger shit storm."

"How do you figure?" Rutger interrupted his massacre of a massive T-Bone to pose the question.

"It kept them from selling the formula to the military," Gerrick said.

Dan gestured with his fork. "But that was only because they saw a bigger payday out in front. The open market."

"Ah yes," Pope tapped his fork prongs to the edge of the ribeye platter he'd ordered. "The pharmaceuticals field does pay well, doesn't it?"

"Damn right it does," Gerrick grimaced. "But they weren't trying to market it as a prescription drug-more like a dietary supplement."

Rutger shrugged. "What difference does that make?"

"One means the pesky presence of oversight. One doesn't."

"Right." Pope met Hoyt's explanation with a roll of his eyes. "A drug means approval-not so for dietary supplements. Keeps the formula in-house, right?"

Gerrick passed looks with his colleagues as they all nodded in agreement and approval of the younger man's knowledge.

"The formula could be kept in-house, so long as there were no concerns that its designation as a supplement warranted reconsideration," Gerrick explained.

Dan nodded. "That would've definitely happened unless we'd had an oversight committee of our own."

"The Ten," Rutger gave his absent guess, still more interested in cleaning his plate.

"They promised to keep the questions non-existent and were rewarded very generously." Dan went on. "By the time The Ten came along, we were already in business with the military, staffing the ranks of its most specialized teams with the results of our specialized product."

Gerrick picked up the explanation. "That partnership allowed the GAN to expand into areas that gave us a respected, revered name."

"And allowed you to provide the respected and revered with whatever their perverted hearts desired." Pope pushed aside his platter, leaving the ribeye half finished.

"The Ten allowed us to flourish," Gerrick nodded, "but they turned The GANs bribe into extortion with *promises* to calm those calling for the product's testing. Sadly, that didn't happen, but they've been very useful in getting us every other thing we've asked for so...it's a tenuous relationship at best. We've been in one kind of stalemate or another for years over this product."

"What happened... that night, would've happened sooner or later," Hoyt said.

"There was something being planned to take them out?" Rutger asked. His stomach satisfied he was once again fully vested in the discussion.

Gerrick nodded. "We didn't know anything about it, but then...there was a lot we didn't know about the missions until it was time to bring in the doctors."

"There were whispers, though." Dan said. "Many were sick of The Ten and those sadistic theme parties of theirs. There was talk of new friends inside D.C. who could get us what The Ten could only promise, but we couldn't get rid of The Ten without-"

"Risking them sharing all your dirty secrets. Because, let's face it, The GANs got way more dirt than this *product* you were trying to push on pregnant women."

"It's a good product, Pope," Gerrick said to the younger man's accusation. "It just needs additional work before more testing happens of any kind. We're asking you to give us a chance here by keeping The GAN a viable organization. Help us make it what it should've been-not the abomination the world now thinks it is."

"Stocks are tanking in several of the...legitimate holdings," Ned interjected, lacing his thin fingers atop the table. "Confidence is low and that'll continue until something happens to steady the boat."

"Something like Pope taking over," Rutger noted.

"Exactly," Gerrick clenched a fist. "Not everyone is interested in seeing The GAN remain what it's been, but they're scared. They won't step up to do what's right until they've got reason to believe there's about to be a change of guard. With Nate gone, they're even more hesitant as it looks like Brody could be in charge of things."

Pope began the rhythmic tapping of his fork to the platter again. "Better the devil you know," he said.

"Take your place, Kid," Hoyt urged. "Give the folks trying to change things, hope that doing so, won't result in reprisals."

"And what's to stop those who are, from turning this into a bloodbath?" Pope sent a black look toward Rutger and then back to the men they dined with. "My friends and I have had enough of those," he said.

"What'll stop them is you." Dan insisted.

"What's needed is a firm hand, Pope," Gerrick added. "One that's feared, but ethical. Don't be so quick to throw back whatever tomorrow brings you." Gerrick nodded firmly and stood. His associates followed as did Rutger and Pope.

Following handshakes, Pope and Rutger reclaimed their seats. The server advanced with two busboys to assist in clearing the table. At Rutger's wave for them to hold off, the men smoothly changed directions.

"What are you thinking?"

Pope rubbed his eyes, hesitating a moment before tackling Rutger's question. "I'm thinking how much I'd like to get the hell out of here."

"You're not at all interested in that will?"

"I never was interested. I only wanted to know what Gerrick was keeping."

"And now that you do?"

"Fuck 'em," Pope said after another moment of thought. "What the hell did they ever do for us?"

"It's not about us though, is it? Not anymore." Rutger stood. "It's about a woman somewhere. Alone. Pregnant with a kid who could not only be seriously screwed in the head, but also taken from her.

Forever. If we could stop at least one of those things from happening, we should." Clapping Pope's back, Rutger left him at the table.

# CHAPTER 14

*"Damn, she's good..."*

*"They all are..."*

*"Roya really came through this time..."*

*"Ha! You can say that again. I think we all* came through *very well..."*

*Laughter-low and perverse.*

*"Hey man? You should try some of this..."*

*Bear forced her eyes open, watching as Pope came into view-*

"No!" She bolted up in her bed. She was alone, but for the fading images of the memory-the dream. Pope hadn't been there.

Listening as he told her of his friendship with Mercuri though...it put him right there in the middle of her worst nightmare.

She wanted a drink, but one of those would simply numb her brain. Tempting, but she needed to think. Think about what, exactly? The silent, challenging query had her kicking back the covers and inching to the edge of the bed.

Yes...think about what, exactly? Where were they supposed to go from there? Where *could* they go? She'd never be able to look at him after this. Knowing that he knew...knew *that*. It was almost as bad as having him right there in that overdone hotel room and watching while she-

Bear shook her head quickly and violently as if to clear it. There was no changing this- no changing what he knew- what he must think of her. Why should she even want to change it? She'd already decided to end it.

Somewhat resolved, she pushed off the bed and trudged over to the alcove where she'd been working for much of the day. That wasn't so out of the ordinary. She sometimes stowed away there when certain tasks required her to set aside time to review an array of the documents that always seemed to multiply during soiree time.

"Dammit," she muttered when she sat on one of the lounge chairs that was littered with the said documents. They made her recall the one she'd left behind when she'd fled Pope's place days ago.

The cottage. Nothing had changed there. She still had to have it and it was finally hers for the taking. For free. That reality had shaken her more than once. Why would he give it to her freely?

She remembered his request for dinner and bristled. She'd have to see him again, unless she sent another in her place. She already knew such an attempt would not play well.

Another violent headshake had her bracing to leave the chair. Her phone began to vibrate against the table, sending the grinding noises radiating into the small space. Bear chose to let the call from the ranch's chief mechanic go to voicemail and noticed she'd missed another call during the 5 hours since she'd last picked up her phone.

Pope. Her heart thudded to the back of her throat when she saw he'd left a message. She hesitated to activate the playback, then called herself a coward and started the replay. Absently, she wondered how the hell he'd gotten her number. They hadn't exactly gotten around to exchanging contact information over the course of their last few meetings. Her curiosity didn't last long. He made a point of explaining within moments of his message.

*"Bear...um, it-it's Pope. I figured programming my cell into yours wouldn't put me any higher on your shit list than I already am so...I did it when I was out there while you were sleeping after we... Anyway, I'm out of town for a while, but I wanted to call and um...*

*Babe I'm sorry. For all of it-hurting you was never my plan. I had every intention of telling you, but then I...I let what I wanted get in the way of what was right. I can't say I wouldn't do it again. You're not out of my system and I doubt that'll be the case for some time.*

*You're wrong if you believe that has anything to do with what you think I see you as. I hope you're not thinking of backing out of the dinner you promised me. I think you know it's the only way you'll get your hands on that deed again. Next time I call, answer."*

The phone silenced. Bear pressed it to her forehead and waited for her heart to stop beating in her ears.

***

### Kenwood, California~

Approval, awe and desire measured in equal quantities over Mercuri's expression as he studied Tee from the doorway. He watched her move around the mini parlor he'd organized for her just down from their bedroom. She was so very good for whatever ailed him, even when she was just simply enjoying a little quiet time perched on the edge of her desk.

Unfortunately, she didn't look as though she was enjoying her quiet time overmuch. Mercuri hesitated before going to investigate. He hesitated all of half a second. A few strides had him crossing into the parlor and turning Tee to face him. The worry he spied on her lovely dark face, cleared instantly by the smile replacing it.

Mercuri wasn't easily appeased. "What's wrong?" he asked.

Her smile remained. "I'm fine."

He took the spot she'd occupied on the desk, drawing her close until she was flush against his chest. His steady glare soon had her fidgeting beneath the feline intensity of his tawny eyes.

"I'm just a little worried about Bear. She came to see me a few days ago-wasn't in a good way. I-" Tee shrugged. "I'm trying to give her space, but it's not easy."

"What's wrong with her?" Mercuri gave Tee a slight squeeze when she hedged over the answer.

"Just guy trouble."

The answer had Mercuri's eyes changing with a look that was more malicious. "Goddammit, Pope," he muttered.

Tee's dark eyes turned a tad more intense. "You know about Pope?"

"I know we're about to throw him a funeral," Mercuri calmed himself by stroking her back. "I told him I'd kill him if he put me in the doghouse with you."

"Ha! No need for that!" Tee laughed. "You're not in the doghouse."

"But you're upset about Bear?"

Tee didn't try to hide the truth from her face. "It's no surprise, is it? None of us wants anyone to know about that night and now...It's not easy for her having him know. She's pretty devastated."

"Damn you, Pope."

"Hey? Don't do that," Tee grazed her fingers along the square angle of his jaw. "Bear has herself convinced that he must be disgusted by her. She won't even talk to him-find out what he's really thinking. She's telling herself it's all for the best since she was gonna cut it off anyway."

"I told him that trying to deceive her would seriously endanger his face." Mercuri grinned. "Bear's a tough one."

Tee smirked. "If she was as tough as she's convinced herself she is, I wouldn't be half as worried about her as I am. That toughness isn't all it seems."

Mercuri smirked a little then too. "Pope said she's a steel vault around a marshmallow."

"I like that!" Tee laughed again. "He's really getting to know her."

"Yeah, he is."

Something in his tone had Tee inclining her head. "You don't approve?"

"I do, actually. I think he could use a woman in his life to match that know it all way of his," Mercuri smoothed his hands around Tee's waist to play with the tassels at the string-front bodice of her dress.

"Pope doesn't do so well with losing things," he said, "If he tries to hold her when she doesn't want to be held...he isn't all that good with giving people time to figure things out for themselves either. He pulls it with us all the time and we let him. It could be quite a battle when he discovers Bear's not as easy to bully as the rest of us."

"I'd pay good money to see Pope trying to bully any of you."

"Oh yeah?" Mercuri cocked a sleek brow. "I could show you bullying if you're interested."

"You don't think I could handle it?" She taunted.

"I know you can handle it. Still makes it fun to see how much you can take."

"I see," Tee linked her arms around his neck, then moved to brush her fingers across the locks that had fallen across his broad forehead to soften the harsh beauty of his face with boyish appeal. "Haven't I already shown you how much I can take?" Her voice went whisper soft.

Dipping his head, Mercuri brushed his mouth along her temple. "I could always use a reminder."

"Hey?!" She laughed. "Aren't we supposed to be discussing our friends?"

"I didn't forget," Mercuri stood, took Tee with him and headed for the door. "This helps me think. Promise."

Tee's laughter continued as they headed for the bedroom.

\*\*\*

Pope was considering a raid on the stately bar inside the cherry panelled conference room at the offices of Womack, Mebane and Urnst. All he could think of was a similar trip he'd made months earlier to see to the final business of another who had passed away unexpectedly.

This was leagues away from that, he knew. Nathan Alberts had been an ugly reality, Patch had been a treasured friend. Making the trip out to discuss Patch's murder had been agony he didn't think he'd recover from.

*I could sure use you now, man,* Pope silently noted, studying the contents of the juice glass he had a strong desire to adulterate with gin.

Patch would've surely told him to give Bear her space-to give her time. It would've basically been the same advice Mercuri, Rutger and Slayte would've given, but Patch had a way of making him listen.

Smiling then, Pope downed a healthy swallow of the OJ. He wondered what Patch would've had to say about him leaving that lengthy message on Bear's phone and his smile waned. He didn't need Patch or anyone else to tell him what a boneheaded move that was. Then, to top it all off, he goes and leaves the none too subtle threat for her to keep their dinner date or risk losing her shot at the cottage. Nice.

"Fuck," he regarded the juice with distaste sparking in the vibrant depths of his gaze.

By the time his company had arrived in the conference room, Pope was behind the bar and waking up what remained of the juice with a generous amount of the gin.

The firm's partners Claude Mebane, Walter Urnst and Irwin Womack, arrived with the air of three who knew and reveled in the power they wielded. Following the partners, were a trio of suited types. Pope took them to be firm associates or assistants there to take notes on the proceedings.

Rounding out the crowd were the rest of the invitees. There was Alberts' only *legitimate* son Brody. The new widow and Alberts' third wife, Ruth and a few others Pope didn't recognize. He watched Lorne Grodins enter the room and a small well of hope bloomed somewhere deep. This was something he should've anticipated. Perhaps dear old dad had left the bulk of his estate to his old friend and partner in crime.

He couldn't imagine Alberts naming Grodins in his will only to humiliate his buddy by leaving him an inheritance of his best socks. The idea brought a genuine smile to Pope's mouth-one he was still wearing when Brody approached.

"Looking smug, Pope."

"That's good to know, 'specially since I'm feeling quite murderous."

Brody's hard chin lifted. "We'll fight you," he promised.

Pope's brow quirked. "Your father was a lot of things, but even I have to admit I don't think he was stupid enough to leave behind anything other than an iron-clad will."

Brody moved closer and Pope silently willed the man to do what his stony expression threatened. Irwin Womack was clearing his throat before anything more could transpire.

"Gentlemen and ladies," Womack favored the gentler sex with a soft smile. "Shall we?" he waved one fleshy hand toward the long table near the farthest wall.

"Gentlemen?" Womack called to Pope and Brody who were still facing off near the bar.

Pope finished his drink, set down his glass with a resounding clink and went to take a place at the long table. He opted for the lone seat at the opposing end.

160

The lawyers and their crew opted for seats along both sides of the middle while the rest of the invitees gathered at the other end. Brody refused to sit and instead prowled the wide room, yet kept his distance from Pope's end.

Womack exchanged troubled looks with his partners before sizing up the angry young man pacing in the distance. Womack chose to address the cooler young man to his far right.

"Are we going to have a problem?"

Pope spread his hands and favored the round, balding man with an easy smile. "No problem from me. I can't speak for my brother."

Brody seethed, but did a fine job of maintaining his temper when he spoke to the senior partner. "Just get on with it."

~~~

"I don't see how it could go on much longer with all the yelling coming out of there," Rutger said into the phone, "I can't tell who's talking exactly, but chances are strong that the lawyers would want to break to give Brody and Pope a chance to visit their corners. Hold on, something's happening," Rutger broke from Mercuri and peered in the direction of the conference room.

"They're comin' out, Merc. I'll call you back." Rutger disconnected and waited. He held his spot along the quiet corridor outside the conference office where the group had been enclosed for more than an hour.

Rutger noted the faces of the attendees- not many happy expressions, he surmised. He'd expected at least a few satisfied grins from the healthy group that had made its way into the room for the reading. Nathan Alberts' wealth was vast. There was more than enough to go around in hefty portions.

The real question was whether Alberts had been kind enough to share his wealth...equally. The crowd streaming out had begun to thin and Rutger moved from the shadows to await Pope. His friend emerged from the double doors and was surrounded by the firm's partners. The men were talking almost non-stop to Pope who didn't seem at all interested. Rutger grinned when his friend caught his eye and winked.

"If it's alright with you, we'd like to finish up before you leave the building," Walter Urnst requested.

"That's fine, but I'll need a few minutes," Pope said.

"Certainly, certainly," Claude Mebane traded eager nods with his partners.

"Could we have anyone bring you anything?"

"Not necessary," Pope waved off Irwin Womack's offer. "I'll just be a few minutes."

"We'll have someone sent over to show you to the office when you're ready," Mebane said.

"That won't be necessary, either."

"Oh, it's no problem," the men chined in with a jumble of voices.

Pope moved on past them to where Rutger stood. The partners took no offence to being disregarded and headed off in the opposite direction discussing what was next on the agenda.

"So the windbags decided to give you a break?" Rutger grinned.

Pope returned the gesture. "They need me to go back in and sign some papers, though." He clapped Rutger's shoulder. "Thanks for hanging around, but you can split if you want."

"Are you shittin' me?" Rutger's grin broadened, "You know damn well the trouble I'll get into on my own so I'll just hang if it's all the same to you."

"I appreciate it," Pope's expression remained serene for a while before it shadowed. "I'm damn glad that's over."

"So when are you guys reconvening?" Rutger asked.

"Oh that part's done," Pope slid a quick glare toward the conference room door. "I only need to sign these papers and then we can hit the road."

"What about the others?"

"What about 'em?"

"Well aren't they coming back?"

"What the hell for?" Laughter underscored Pope's question.

"What the hell happened in there, Po?"

Pope appeared mystified for half a second. "The son of a bitch left me everything he owned in the world."

"Bullshit." Rutger frowned at the totally unamused look Pope sent him. "You guys were in there for over an hour," he said.

"Yeah," a sliver of Pope's amusement returned then. "It took almost thirty minutes for that pompous fuck Womack to read off all the shit I inherited in detail. Rest of the time was devoted to the uh... Q and A portion of the meeting."

"Q and A!" Rutger's bellowing laughter emerged. "It sounded like all out war in there!"

Pope sighed. "You say tomato…"

The two were still laughing when Brody walked up to insert himself into the moment with a violent shove to Pope's back. Pope turned while Rutger retreated to give the men a wide berth. Few had the nerve to approach Pope Apostolou in such a fashion without earning far more brutal injury as a result.

"Enjoying the moment, eh Pope?" Brody snarled.

"I'm about to be," Pope's cool was almost tangible. His vivid gaze wandered Brody's face as though he were seeking the spot he intended to pummel.

Brody's own gaze flared slightly as though he sensed the imminent threat. Still, he refused to give Pope the satisfaction of knowing he'd been shook.

"You never accepted so much as a handshake from your father," Brody forged on. "But he dies and you accept the inheritance without so much as a 'Gee, I really shouldn't,'" he followed up the accusation with another shove, that one to Pope's chest.

"You'll be wanting to keep your hands off me," Pope's voice was as quiet and as deadly as his expression.

Brody was undaunted. "Or what?" He added another chest shove. "There's nothing you can threaten me with. I haven't got a damn thing left to lose."

"You sure about that?" Pope repeated his speculative look across Brody's face. "I can think of quite a few things."

"We'll fight you." Brody promised, radiating anger as he posted up on the toes of his steel-toed boots and clenched his fists. "We'll tie this will up in court so long, you'll forget about what you think you own. So you can just trash any ideas you have about taking The GAN apart."

Pope gave Brody the benefit of an entirely bewildered expression. "Why would I want to do that?"

"Cut the shit, Pope. It's what you've wanted ever since you found out your mother was my father's whore and you were the result," Brody moved closer. "Do you think all this new money is gonna clean off the stink of that shame?"

Pope's cool remained unrattled. "Are you talking about today's new money or the new money I came into six years ago when I tried to send our father to hell?"

The words destroyed whatever control Brody fought to hold onto. He reacted instantly, snagging handfuls of Pope's jacket lapels to yank him closer. Instead of moving in, Pope held his ground and responded with a backhand fist that sent Brody to the floor writhing and cupping both hands to his jaw.

"You! You moth-fur!" Brody's try for insult only emerged in a mix of grunts and howls.

From his position outside the line of fire, Rutger's whiskey-colored eyes sparkled as wildly as the grin he sported. "What was that, Bro?" He leaned in a bit to inquire, "I'm gonna have to remember that one."

Pope stepped over the writhing man. "I'm going to handle this paperwork so we can get the fuck out of here," he told Rutger.

"You fuckr!" Brody had managed to recup some of his 'verbal skills'. "You broke my jaw!"

"I pulled that punch and you know it." Pope strode further down the hall. Reconsidering, he turned back to Brody and squatted close. "You wouldn't be able to open your mouth otherwise. You're weak, Brody. Is it any wonder your father forgot you in that shitty will of his?" Expression like stone, Pope's voice was an even quieter roar when he next spoke.

"Don't make me kill you, Brody. In spite of everything, I don't want that." Standing then, Pope continued on his way down the hall.

"Did you mean that?" Rutger asked when he caught up to his friend.

"It won't come to that." Quiet certainty held Pope's voice. "Brody'll stay out of my way. He's known me long enough to know a threat like that is good as gold if he calls me on it."

"'Course he does, but that's not what I mean. You asked Brody why you'd do that when he mentioned you trashing The GAN." He put a hand to Pope's forearm, stopping him just after they'd taken the corridor to the elevator bay.

"What gives, Pope? Have you changed your mind?"

"I hadn't." Pope smoothed a hand over his hair drawn into a low ponytail. "Not before I talked to Gerrick."

"So he did get to you?"

Pope nodded. "He did."

"So what?" Rutger shrugged. "Doing the right thing here doesn't mean falling back in line with The GAN again. Or are you saying you want to partner up with Grodins now? Run this monstrosity by his side?"

"Hell no." The soft roar came through like crystal in Pope's voice even as a lethal grin widened his mouth. "I don't know what I want, Rut, but it sure as shit ain't that." He squeezed Rutger's shoulder then.

"Don't worry. Whatever I come up with, I'll make damn sure it's something the current establishment will have a helluva hard time swallowing."

# CHAPTER 15

Bear didn't realize she'd had an horrendous crick in her neck until she moved to put her hair up in a messy ponytail. She'd been bent over the coffee table in the living area of her office at the training hall going through the latest requisitions.

Judging from the cramp, she wouldn't have argued that she'd most likely been camped out there for over 2 hours. She was yanking the tail into place when a quick knock fell on her door. Mike.

"Got a call," he said.

"Got a name?" Bear sighed the words while digging fingertips into her nape.

"Caleb Stein."

Bear kept up the somewhat soothing massage and frowned. "Doesn't ring a bell."

"He said it probably wouldn't- said you guys haven't talked in about six years."

The massage slowed and Bear left her seat. "I got it. Shut the door, okay?"

If Mike was curious, he gave no indication and left Bear in silence. She studied the blinking light that indicated the call, and then forced a smile into her voice.

"Caleb? It's been a long time."

"Yeah-yeah, it has it- it's good to hear your voice Bear. I uh-I hope my call hasn't sparked too many bad memories."

Bear took the cordless back to her chair. Reclining there, her smile felt easier with the pleasure stirring that Caleb's voice hadn't sparked any urges to panic. "I could turn on the news these days and be reminded easy," she said.

"Yeah," Caleb inserted a rapid laugh. "That's true enough, I uh-I saw the piece. In Scope? The Programming VP is a former...former colleague. Guess the rumors are true that Mercuri Nikolaides' hand was in this. I assume you know him since he's seeing your best friend."

Bear closed her eyes, forced them open. "Your rumor mill's pretty accurate."

"Well good news tends to travel. Over the last several years, it's all tended to come from Mercuri. It's sort of why I'm calling."

Bear shifted on her chair. "Is that right?"

"Yeah, me and Luke-my partner Luke Robb-we were on vacation when it all went down with Van Deer." Caleb explained. "We've been debating over whether to call-just wanted to know if you guys were alright-whether you came through everything okay."

"Yeah. Yeah Caleb we're good." Bear understood his underlying concern. "Mercuri got to Tee before Van Deer...before he did any of what he threatened."

"Good." Caleb's relief surged through on a strong wave. "I really called to tell you-I um, I'm sorry Bear."

The approval Bear felt over Caleb's relief transitioned to confusion and she frowned. "Sorry?"

"We should've done more."

"Caleb you-"

"No Bear. Luke-Luke and me we...we shouldn't have let you guys go that night. We should've taken you anyplace but there."

"Caleb? You had a job to do. So did we. What happened, happened the way it was supposed to."

"No Bear. No, it didn't."

"Caleb?" She called when he said nothing further.

167

"Listen Bear, I'm gonna be in California for a few weeks. I'll call again before I head out, alright?"

"I'd like that," she smiled, meaning it.

Caleb disconnected a second later.

***

He'd meant to join his father for the will reading. Jake slammed a fist to the steering wheel and then favored the parking attendant in the private lot with a dismissing wave.

That damn recording. He'd been like a horny teenager since Leonce Keppard had left it in his possession. He'd already watched it at least a dozen times.

The man had been right, Jake mused. If LuCarolyn Young hadn't decided to make her living in Hollywood behind the scenes, she could've had one helluva career in front of the cameras. She'd clearly had one helluva time that night 6 years ago.

He knew it! He'd known it all along. They were all sluts- pure and simple. To hell with the businesswoman personas they perpetrated now. Frauds.

While he'd yet to determine whether they had any prior experience as the killers they'd aptly portrayed, it was clear they'd come with a great deal of experience pleasuring men. If LuCarolyn Young's performance was any example, it was experience they'd enjoyed honing.

The question now was what to do with what he had. One thing was certain- actually more than one. Brody would almost certainly insist they wait-not rush. Though his old friend worked his nerves when trying to maintain a level head, Jake appreciated it. Some things deserved to be savored, especially when the road to discovering them had suddenly become much sweeter.

The LuCarolyn Young recording sizzled to life in his mind once more and oh yes...satisfaction stirred in his belly. The journey to finding out what Berrill Clayton was keeping in her ranch safe had suddenly become a whole lot easier.

~~~

Rutger hadn't regretted his decision to wait around for Pope until he saw Lorne Grodins walking into the firm's lounge. The rather interesting day, turned sour. He even lost the taste for the bourbon he'd

<center>168</center>

just poured at the lounge's bar. Regardless, he tossed it back, stood and was about to take his leave when Grodins sought to block his escape.

"Son, don't you suppose we could find a way to fix our issues now that Pope is-"

"Pope is nothing to you." Rutger interrupted.

"He's half owner in this organization."

"Which doesn't change the fact that he hates it."

"Well we uh…" Grodins swallowed visibly. "We're all hoping he won't do anything rash."

"I see and is that what this little father son chat is for?"

"It's not, Son. It's about me losing my best friend in the world and thinking about all the things he left undone. The most important being his relationship with his son."

"Lorne," Rutger smiled when the man bristled over the familiarity as opposed to 'dad' which he would've preferred. "The fact that you're so impressed by me, is flattering but understand this, I'll never be the son that you wish Jake was."

"But you are that." Grodins' sternly attractive face hardened with determination. "You've been that since the day your mother told me she was pregnant with you."

"I'm sure that was a great moment for you. It doesn't mean shit to me," Rutger moved to leave the lounge.

"Rutger please," Grodins moved in the younger man's path again. "What can we do to change that? I don't want things to end for me like they did with my partner. Nate wanted to reach out to Pope but he let pride and social standing get in the way and then it- it was too late. By then, the only way he could *reach out* was in a will."

Rutger gave a playful wink. "Gotta give the man points for style."

"Son please, I don't want that for us. Of course, everything I have is yours but-"

"Hold on, Lorne, forget it. I'm not interested."

"And I want more between us than a will. I'd like for you to believe that. A lot has happened- a lot of negative. I don't think it has to stay that way. I mean that and trying to meet you halfway. What will it take for you to go the other half, Son?"

Rutger regarded the man with more consideration before he made a slow return further into the lounge. "You're serious, here? You'd really like to know?"

"I really would, Son."

Rutger shrugged, but kept his expression callous. "I can't promise that Pope's plans for The GAN won't be *rash*, but against my better judgement, they don't involve him tearing it out at the root either."

Lorne Grodins couldn't mask his relief.

Rutger despised the look, as he did the man. "I don't trust you, Grodins and I never will. As for me running into your arms and crying, 'dad I love you,' forget it. The best you can hope for is me not hating you anymore than I already do. So when Pope comes to you for help with...whatever he decides, give it to him." Rutger gave a faint nod and then left the lounge.

Grodins followed shortly after, his head bowed. Neither he nor Rutger had noticed Jake taking in the scene where he'd entered at the back of the room.

~~~

"Sorry for catching you at a bad time. Rut said he'd call back, but he hasn't."

"It's okay, Merc." Pope grinned, pleased to hear from his friend. "I'm on the way to meet him now."

"So how'd it go?"

Pope's steps slowed as he traveled the long corridor. "He left me everything."

Silence carried both ends of the phone line for a while before Mercuri spoke.

"Are congrats in order?"

"Hmph, Brody didn't think so."

"Rut said he thought he heard you guys goin' at it during the reading. Thought the lawyers might have to call for a break to give you time to cool off."

Pope's grin emerged as he took the hall leading to the elevators. "I was the only one in the room *not* talking."

"Surprising," A grin came through in Mercuri's voice then too. "So how does it feel to be in charge of something you came into as a slave?"

"Ask me when I wake up."

"You're in the driver's seat now. What's your plan?"

"No friggin' clue, but none of this is gonna make people happy if my dear older brother's any example." Pope punched an elevator button

170

when he entered the long bay. "We got into it in the hall after everybody else cleared out."

"Ah...got you to lose your temper-not easy to do."

"Easy for some," Pope rested a shoulder against the wall. "He didn't care for me keeping my inheritance. I think he hoped I'd refuse it the way I've refused everything else Alberts' related." A more savory smile curved his mouth then. "I think I even surprised Rut."

"Any reason for the change of heart?" Mercuri asked, chuckling. "Aside from the obvious financial gain?"

"Somethin' Gerrick said, I guess."

"So you talked to him?"

"Mmm..."

"And?"

The car arrived and Pope rested back flush against the panelling once he was inside. "It's a long, ugly story Merc, best saved for when we're not on the phone."

"Got it."

Pope sighed, eager to change the topic. "So how's Tee doin'?"

"She's good," Mercuri's voice was decidedly lighter then as well. "I think she's talked to Bear a few times."

"Did I ask?"

"You didn't have to."

"I thought *I* was supposed to be the know it all?"

"Oh your title's still secure, trust me."

"How is she? She uh-she's not speaking to me right now."

Mercuri hesitated on his response then. "Yeah, I know that too."

"I did try, Merc-fuck," Pope took a moment to silently criticise himself. "I didn't try hard enough."

"I hear you, Po," Mercuri decided not to give the man a hard time. Nothing could top the hard time Pope was undoubtedly giving himself. "Tee told me Bear didn't stick around long enough to hear what you had to say after you told her we know each other."

The elevator doors opened with a quiet whoosh. Pope left the car, but remained in the quiet bay, heading over to walk the small alcove where a lone window overlooked the firm's rear lawn and manmade stream. "I can't blame her under the circumstances. How is she, Merc?"

"Tee says she's acting spacey-a little too devastated to talk, I guess. She's hurt Po, but this'll all work out," Mercuri added when he heard his friend's groan through the line.

"I appreciate what you're tryin to do, Merc but the situation with Bear and me is different."

"I know that," Mercuri insisted. "Pope?" He called when there was no response.

Pope however had taken himself out of the conversation and into his own thoughts. His own worries. Hurt. She was hurt. Her being angry-wanting to kick his ass for lying to her, *that* he could handle. Anger was a weak emotion-easy to fight-easy to conquer. Hurt, devastation, shame...those emotions went deeper-hit harder and were trickier to navigate.

"Pope?" Mercuri called when the silence swayed closer to the minute mark.

"Sorry Merc I uh-I need to go find Rut so we can get the hell out of here. Listen um, thanks for telling me what was going on. I'll tell you about the will when I see you."

"Pope wait-"

"Nah, Merc, I-"

"What are you gonna do about Bear?"

The question stopped him cold. "I'm actually out of ideas." Uncharacteristic uncertainty etched deep in the reply.

"So you're just gonna wimp out? Not do anything to make this right?" Mercuri didn't like the despair in Pope's voice and decided that a hard time might be just what the man needed.

Pope took the bait. "Didn't you just hear what I said? She's not talking to me." He went to pull a hand through his hair, realized he'd bound it and drew a fist instead. Frustration had him tugging off the leather strap half a second later.

"Listen Mercuri, she's not talking to me, alright?" Some of Pope's ingrained control returned. "I don't think she'll even stay in the same place long enough to let *me* talk for a while."

"Well can *I* talk now?"

"I'm not in the mood for bullshit, Merc."

"Are you in the mood for an idea?"

"For?"

"For keeping her in one place so you can talk?"

Pope stopped his pacing in the alcove. "Go on." He said.

# CHAPTER 16

It should've come as no surprise to Pope that Mercuri's idea was pure gold. Though he wasn't looking forward to a second dramatic conversation with Bear on the heels of their last, Pope thought Mercuri's plan alone was worth the heartache.

Still, he could easily imagine Bear not appreciating further secrecy especially when he hadn't given her so much as an apology. One in person, that is.

He hadn't come to the ranch that day for the purpose of apologizing, though. That fact was the only thing that kept him advancing his truck toward the ranch security gate. The apology was for later. *This* pitiful attempt was about getting her riled enough to be blindsided and too off kilter to refuse what he'd come to offer...demand.

Security directed him on through, following a cursory scan of his ID.

"Are you guys sure I'm on the guest list?" Despite his eagerness to see the woman in charge, Pope couldn't resist the question.

The guards; two middle-aged Asian men, tall and stout with muscle, both chuckled.

"You're in, Sir," one of the guards said. "Mr. Oates and Mr. Hough have you on the main list."

Pope nodded. "Right," he had to offer a faint chuckle then as well. If it had been left to the boss, security would've most likely been instructed to shoot out his tires the second he took the road to the ranch.

~~~

"Kadi? Kadi? Now you said it yourself, Hon. He's a hands-on idiot. You and I both know he's got everything he needs to take more time off. He just won't give his staff the freedom-especially not during soiree time. I'll talk to him. Hey? I'll *order* him to take the time. How's that?"

Pope arrived at Bear's open office door in time to catch the tail end of the conversation. From the sound of it, she seemed to be trying to talk down an agitated wife. The smile that curved his mouth then, was a welcomed change from the grim line it'd held since he'd arrived in the immense training hall to discover she was working there all alone.

Though Pope was certain that help was just a phone call away, he didn't care for her on her own in such a remote place. With a sigh, he told himself to get a grip. To the order, he added that if he valued his teeth, he'd keep his opinions to himself.

Bear was ending her talk with the harried wife. Instead of hanging up, she dialed another number and was starting another conversation in less than 20 seconds. The second call was far less cordial than the first.

"Felix, I swear the next time Kadi calls out here to complain about you not taking enough time off, I'm gonna have you start paying *me* to work here."

Bear fell into silence, listening as Felix Hambry launched his usual spiel about his work ethic.

"She appreciates all the nice stuff my work buys her, I'll tell you that." Felix argued.

Bear sighed. "That's admirable, but I'm betting she'd really appreciate having her husband in bed at night too. And what's the problem, anyway? All the heavy planning is done for the soiree. We've still got weeks before the event. That's plenty of time to get away beforehand."

174

There was more silence from Bear's end. No doubt, Felix was launching more arguments, Pope thought. He watched her ease onto the corner of the desk-her back to the door.

"Felix? Felix? This is an order now. If you won't take a break beforehand, then at least take Kadi out for something she'll really appreciate-give her the *entire* night. Then bring her to the soiree dinner, she'll see what all your tireless hours are for and then after that you can take the girl off on an extended trip while thanking your stars that someone actually wants to spend time with your goofy ass."

Bear was silent for a few seconds more and then she began to laugh.

"Felix! If I have to sit here and tell you where to take your wife-" She paused for more listening.

"Alright-alright, listen-Felix? I'll make arrangements for you guys to have a long weekend somewhere. I'll be in touch with the details, but Felix if I have to tell you what to do with her when you get there, I'm callin' Kadi back and advising her to file for divorce right now!"

Bear was still laughing as she ended the call. The smoky, infectious gesture ended abruptly when she saw Pope in the doorway. It was often a jolt to discover big men who moved with such eerie grace and silence. Her reaction to Pope wasn't just jolting, it was downright erotic. She tamped it down with a quickness.

"Thought you said you'd be gone a while?"

Her pointed query to blatantly indicate she hadn't missed him, brought a genuine smile to Pope's face. He began to hope that her anger was closer to the surface than expected.

"So you got my message, after all?" He saw what existed of her anger, drain to reveal the more delicate layers beneath, exposed by his gentle reminder.

He wouldn't let himself be swayed by it. He hadn't come there to apologize. Not yet. They needed to be on territory that could pass for more common ground-for him, anyway. The only way he'd get her there was to first remind her that it wouldn't be in her best interest to refuse him.

"I decided not to wait around to see if you'd take my next call like I asked you to."

"Told me to," Bear muttered while outlining a logo stenciled on a page atop her desk.

Pope managed to hide his smile over the dig. "I just wanted you to know I'd pick you up at seven."

Her head snapped up. "What for?"

"Dinner. Remember? You promised," he was innocence personified.

Bear felt her cheeks burn over the reminder, but somehow resisted the strong desire to bow her head again. "I can drive myself," she said with a calm she in no way felt.

"That won't work for me."

"Wait a minute! You can't just-"

"Part of my price for that lovely cottage if you still want it? I gotta be honest here," he sighed, folding his arms over his chest, "I'm not too sure I want to sell. It might be nice to have a place that's so...accessible to you."

"So seven, then?"

Her retort came so fast, he almost laughed. Anger had her lush mouth tightening in tandem with a clenched fist. Pope knew then why he so adored the emotion on her. Her outrage made all her other attributes more enchanting.

"Can't I just meet you there?"

"No can do, beautiful. It's the chauvinist in me." He straightened in the doorway. "Seven, Bear. Don't make me wait."

~~~

"Mr. Apostolou?"

Pope was on the way to his truck when he ran into Shaun Oates. "Bear's working out of-"

"It's alright, Shaun. I already talked to her," Pope tracked a discerning look across the property awash in late afternoon sun. "Kind of isolated out here when nothing's scheduled. She work out here a lot on her own?"

"Often enough, but she's safe." Shaun insisted with his own measuring look across the property. "Besides having a ton of guns in that office of hers, wireless cameras feed to the security camp. No one's laying a hand on her without us all knowing about it," he snorted then. "She'd kill us if she knew we had patrols going by here every fifteen minutes when we're on light staff and know she's out here on her own."

Pope nodded, pleased by the report. "What about that enclosure to her bedroom?" Given Shaun's candor, Pope decided to probe further. "Is it such a good idea to let everyone know where that is?"

Shaun's smirk became a full blown grin. "Not sure if you noticed all the protocol Mike used when you visited before? The door in the stairwell and the one in the corridor leading to her rooms open by keys that are only in our possession when she's called a meeting there. Otherwise, they're kept in another location. Then, there're the palm scans and the main door to her room carries a double bolt she only unlocks when we meet."

"I appreciate that Shaun," relief and gratitude exuded in equal measure on Pope's face.

Shaun nodded. "Mike and I can't help but notice how you feel about our boss, Sir."

Pope wasn't sure how he felt about being so transparent but knew there wasn't much he could do to change it. He accepted Shaun's shake and the two of them parted ways soon after.

***

"So that's all he said?"

"Jeez man, isn't that enough?!" Jake ceased his pacing to snap out the response.

Brody reclined on a sofa, a compress against his jaw. "What do you think it means?" he asked.

Jake grunted. "Nothing good. Fuck," he smoothed both hands over his close cut hair. "We should've killed them a long time ago," he rolled his eyes when he passed the sofa. "And would you stop babying your jaw? Makes you look soft."

Brody shrugged and continued to favor his bruised jaw. "In the privacy of my own home, I don't mind a little babying. As for your earlier words, killing them would've only brought down the entire force of the newly freed. We would've had people we don't even know coming out of the woodwork to take us down, all to avenge the killing of the ones who gave them their new lives." He shuddered. "Then we would've had to deal with the old men."

Jake spat another obscenity. "Thought I'd go into a diabetic coma listening to him with Rutger. Bastard tried to kill him and there he was, still tryin' to shove the keys to the kingdom in his goddamn hands."

177

"What do you think Rutger meant about Pope calling on your dad to do a favor?"

"Who the hell knows?" Again, Jake smoothed hands over his head while pacing Brody's livingroom. "Right now, I'm in no mood to speculate. I think it's safe to say whatever it is won't be good for us."

"Well," Brody settled in deeper on his sofa. "Least we've got this deal with Morrow-see where that leads before-"

"Seriously? You're really putting stock in that?"

"Only because I don't have another concrete plan just now," Brody's eyes narrowed knowingly. "Something tells me you do, though? Am I right?"

Jake wasn't quite ready to share all details. "While Morrow's set on some covert mission to uncover what those sluts took, I think I've just found a much easier way."

***

"You're kidding me."

The bland tone of her acknowledgement, had Pope grinning and satisfied that he'd made the right choice for dinner that night.

His first plan had been to take her to Pacifica, lock the doors and apologize to her until he was blue in the face. He'd quickly decided against the plan, not sure how long her angry exterior would withstand a private talk. Still, he wanted time with her before they had to dive into all the heavy stuff.

Given her reaction when he'd mentioned his phoned-in apology, they'd have to plunge into the heavy far too soon for his liking. Reminding himself that this wasn't about his feelings but hers, had little effect. Knowing that he'd hurt her, was killing him. It made it damn hard to look into her beautiful eyes which didn't seem to be much of an issue, he noted. She seemed to be having just as hard a time looking at him. He was going to need the night to build his courage at any rate.

Pope kept his hand at Bear's waist and didn't mind the hope that stirred when she didn't inch away from his touch. Somehow, he resisted the urge to cup her hip and tug her into him.

The sheer fabric of her off shoulder green and navy sarong dress was as distracting as what he knew lay beneath it. The agony Pope experienced over the decision to let his hand stay put, didn't last long as they were soon being met by one of the restaurant hosts.

The Rascal was one of San Francisco's most popular eateries. The establishment was usually packed as its dining selections were to die for, as was its location making it the go-to spot for every crowd from finance geeks to film execs.

For Pope, anywhere he could get a good steak, made his list of eating destinations. When the steak was market fresh morning, noon or night, the destination went to the top of the list.

"This place is a madhouse," Bear noted, forbidding herself to settle against Pope when he leaned close to hear her speak.

"It's a madhouse because it's the best," he said just as the host approached.

Bear didn't know about The Rascal being 'the best'. She hadn't eaten there enough times to make a firm decision. Still, there was a lot to be said for a packed restaurant where one only had to wait five minutes before being seated. She was sure the five minute wait time only pertained to those The Rascal deemed its best customers.

The host greeted Pope by name and was all smiles as he led them past a trio of podiums where two other hosts waited to assist diners.

Bear didn't need to see every other man in the room to know that Pope was responsible for the majority of the dazed looks and slack jaws from the women they passed. The son of a bitch knew it too, she surmised while working to keep her expression free of disdain.

"So let me guess," she said once the host provided them with menus, informed them of their server's name and bid them a good evening. "You brought me here to be in the midst of people who love and adore you?"

"No Bear," Pope studied his menu while answering, "I brought you here because it's my favorite place and I wanted to share it with you."

*Well hell*, she gave the retort silently but allowed her disdain to roam freely. How the hell could she justify acting pissed when he was being all syrupy sweet?

"I should've realized we wouldn't get around to business when you didn't leave the car with a shred of paper," she leaned back, tilting her head while eying him provocatively. "Unless you've got my deed tucked away in that five thousand dollar suit?"

Pope's radiant blues narrowed with approval. "Complimenting me, Bear? If so, then I should return the favor by thanking you for not wearing business attire."

"What's the point of that?" Her smile was cool. "You already know what's beneath this."

Nodding slow, Pope let his eyes drift over the dress' bodice. They held on a bare, caramel brown shoulder that he could all too clearly recall biting into as he came inside her.

She gave a meaningful shift in her seat which drew his gaze back to her stony face.

"Will I have to rely on memory from here on out?" he asked her.

"Where's my deed, Pope?"

"Close," he studied his fingers tapping the tablecloth. "But I've got some concerns."

"Concerns."

"Your security."

"What-"

"Hear me out." Pope waited 'til Bear gave her consent with a nod. "I only want to be sure I'm leaving the place in good hands."

"It's a gun ranch," her tone was dry. "Security's everywhere. You can't miss it."

"You're right, Bear. But I have to wonder at the intelligence of a security force that would allow its boss- its *female* boss," he stressed just to see her bristle, "to have her bedroom wing so overtly displayed?"

"What the hell?" Bear straightened.

"That enclosure sticks out like a sore thumb," Pope dismissed her outburst. "It'd have anyone curious about what it's protecting."

"And what the hell does that-"

"Good evening, folks. My name is Steve and I'll be your server tonight."

Pope's genuine amusement for his dining partner, fueled the smile he sent to the waiter. Bear made an attempt to quell her frustration before she too smiled up at the stocky, young man.

Steve left with drink as well as food orders. Pope made the selections. Bear didn't mind, livid as she was over having the layout of her home criticized.

"What the hell does my bedroom have to do with you signing over that deed to me?" She finished hissing out the query once Steve left with Pope's request for a T-Bone and Bear's filet mignon and shrimp.

Though the dig at her security was mainly to see her adorably riled, Pope figured it was as good a time as any to clue Bear into a few realities she may've been overlooking.

180

"Harris Van Deer going after Tee wasn't just about getting back at Mercuri," he began. "The GAN wants back what you took from that hotel that night. Thanks to that news broadcast, they know you've got those discs. They know all too well what's on them and they'll do anything to ensure nothing additional is revealed."

"They'd have a helluva nerve to come fuck with me on that ranch."

Pope smirked then, not out of agitation, but due to the image she cast. Outraged, bold, provocative... he wanted her then in the most basic way and prayed they'd at least make it through the first course before he lost the ability to restrain himself.

"You're right, Bear," he focused in harder on completing his warning. "Unfortunately, they don't give a damn about who you are or that arsenal you've got. They don't even give a damn about who you were six years ago."

Pope grimaced that time in response to the physical blow he could tell she'd absorbed from the reminder.

"They only want what's theirs, Bear," his voice was softly urgent. "They'll use any means to get it and I need you to be careful-even in a place as secure as your ranch. I need you to be careful until this mess is completely over."

Steve returned with drinks then. When he'd gone, Bear only studied her wine glass instead of sipping from it. "You seem to know these people pretty well," she noted.

"I should," Pope leaned forward to run a hand over his forehead. "I spent over half my life working for them, connected to them-some by blood."

Bear frowned over the last.

"Nathan Alberts was my father."

Bear did a rapid, mental recap. "Alberts...but he's...he's dead-suicide, oh Pope I-I'm sorry."

Pope was already waving off the sentiment. "I'm the last person you should be apologizing to."

The reminder had Bear bristling and once again looking everywhere except Pope's face. Silence carried for countless moments, until Steve returned with entrees. His guests couldn't have been happier.

~~~

Bear had to admit The Rascal prepared a good steak. She was halfway through her filet mignon when she noticed Pope had almost completely devoured his massive T-Bone.

"I'm gonna go out on a limb here and guess that you eat too much red meat," she spoke in the bland tone of voice she'd harbored for much of the night.

Pope's laughter was little more than a grunt. "It's a symptom," his tone was equally bland.

The comment made her smile. "Of?" she inquired.

Unfairly long brows drawing close over his eyes, Pope realized he'd spoken aloud and shrugged "Of being raised around so much testosterone," he spoke lightly as if to tease. "If you think *I'm* addicted to the stuff, you should see Mercuri and don't get me started on our friends Rutger and Slayte."

Bear's smile turned breezy. "Big appetites," she sighed.

"Big appetites for everything,"

The clarification had her sigh floating into a gasp. She was taken right back to the varied ways he'd shown that 'big appetite' during their time together.

Grip firmed on her utensils, Bear focused on finishing her meal. "Sounds like you guys are pretty close."

"They're my family." *All I ever thought I'd need*, he added silently.

"Nice to know what that's like," Bear said while she chewed thoughtfully.

"Did you and your friends grow up together?" Pope asked.

"We met during summer jobs we had working for Prin's parents in VA. Her folks are big in the furniture industry,"

Pope nodded, downed a swig of his beer. "Yeah Merc told me. Holland Furniture, right? They're big clients of his."

"Yeah well, back then we were just a bunch of silly girls with big dreams-hopes..." Bear looked determinedly at her food again. "That was before we got a dose of what the world was really like."

When her utensils hovered over her food a bit too long for his liking, Pope reached out to brush his fingers across her wrist. The utensils hit the platter with a clang.

"Jesus this is all my fault," she hissed, holding her head in her hands.

"No," Pope squeezed her wrist then. "No, honey it's not."

182

"It is," she shook her head incessantly. Sleek locks bumped into a wrapped style swung into her face. "It is, I was-I was just sitting there eating that pitiful pack of crackers I-I'd scrounged up enough change to buy from one of the vending machines."

Her laughter ripped out, fast and brutal. "Do you know how depressing it feels to be in a mall food court and eating from a vending machine?"

"Don't do this to yourself, babe," Pope squeezed her wrist again and believed he could actually feel his heart aching for her. "It's over now, love."

"But it's not," she shook her head again. "*I'm* the one Dorinda's lackey approached. Lu came later, but it was me she approached. I'm the one who took that money. Money my friends had to repay on their backs. We were just trying to repay the money we-we weren't hookers, Pope."

"I know that, honey. I know it," his whisper was as stern as the look he bore into her eyes. "It's over now."

"They've got memories in their heads they'll never get rid of, so how could it ever be over? We became murderers that night."

"Bear-"

"No Pope. I can still remember it-still remember hearing the gunshots...I don't even remember firing the gun I had. It was...just there in one of the rooms, I took it, but I used the knife... God..." She tried to reach for her water glass, but her hand shook too badly to hold on.

Pope drew her hand into his, brought it to his mouth and put a kiss to her palm. "How 'bout I get you home?" He smiled when she responded with a grateful nod.

~~~

The return drive to the ranch was long and void of conversation. Pope didn't bother with the radio. Instead, he kept the window partly down to admit the sounds of the air and wildlife into the cabin.

The breeze was a chilly one, but Bear didn't mind. The crisp wind helped to clear her head, something she desperately needed. How the hell had he managed to make her lose it so easily? The question had plagued her since they'd left the high energy of The Rascal. Discussing six years ago was a thing she only did with her friends-her girls.

Pope was the first, the only man she'd been so...open with on the subject. Why? He hadn't even asked her to talk about it for Christ's sake!

Yet she'd gone right ahead blabbing about her regrets and sharing details of one of the most down trodden periods of her life.

It was dangerous to so easily drop one's guard. So dangerous and yet...such a relief. Defenses were so often necessary and far more often stifling. Lowering them, refreshed and rejuvenated and made the effort well worth it. Therein however...therein lay the danger.

"Bear?"

She blinked, realizing that Pope was calling to her. Not only that, they were sitting right outside her front door. He'd already opened the passenger side of the truck and had even unhooked her seatbelt. Her plan had been to thank him for the evening and to scurry out before he had time to shut off the ignition and try to escort her inside. As the idea was a moot point then, she took the hand he offered and let him help her down from the high cab.

Pope's whistle echoed moments after Bear unlocked her front door and waved him inside. Earlier, he hadn't trusted himself to want to leave once he was there with her. He'd simply texted that he was out front and waited on her to join him.

He had already marveled over the outdoor appeal of the craftsmanship of the Spanish-styled estate. The atrium was proof of true architectural artistry. The space opened into an immense portrait-lined corridor of white brick. Supported by stone columns,the corridor led the way to a sunken living room, golden lit by tall lamps on wide bases.

The area smelled lightly, invitingly of coffee and Pope noticed the pine paneled coffee and wet bar across the room. By the time he was done observing the elegant homey space, he saw that Bear had already taken her place on the edge of one of the chaise sectionals of a long L-shaped sofa. The furnishing accounted for much of the room's seating and was accented by an array of burgundy and tanned pillows.

When he came to kneel before her at the chaise, Bear started to push up from the chair.

"I'll get you something-"

"No Bear, wait I um- I'm gonna need to get going," he squeezed her hands then drew them up along her arms and back down across her thighs, calves until he was taking her foot.

His hair was loose that night and shielded his features when he bowed his head to focus on removing the strappy heels she'd worn that evening. Once he'd taken her from the other shoe, he sat running his fingers across the tops of her toes.

When he smiled and shook his head, Bear leaned over to see what was so funny about her French pedicure.

"Bear," he murmured as if to himself, "that doesn't suit you-not all the way. I think 'Cub' fits just as well."

She tried to tug her foot free and he shushed her.

"I'm not trying to offend you," he said.

"I know I-" she closed her eyes for a moment. "My grandfather used to call me Cub." She laughed quietly then, quickly. "He um...he was very old school. Women had their place and it was far from the level where men ruled. We loved each other alot, but I always thought he called me that because he saw weakness when he saw me. Weakness pretending to be strong."

Pope looked down, running his fingers across the tops of her toes again. "I can't tell you what your grandfather saw, but I sure as hell don't think it was weakness. I think he saw strength in the adorable package of his granddaughter."

Bear rolled her eyes, but couldn't hide her smile.

"I think I'd have to tweak that a little, though. I see strength in an irresistible package."

His admission had Bear tugging to free her foot again and experiencing a little disappointment when he released her. She tried to stand again, but he caught her hips to keep her still on the chair.

"Pope-"

"Let me talk a minute, alright?" He put his forehead to hers for only a second before pulling back.

"I'm sorry Bear. Like I said when I called, hurting you was never my plan. Taking advantage of the situation like I did was about wanting you- a tough beauty with a heart to match and my...my curiosity took over. I wondered what it'd be like to have a woman like you in my bed. I pushed for dinner tonight, because you deserved to hear me say 'I'm sorry' in person. Not over the phone.

I hope you'll forgive me, because I meant what I said. I don't expect you'll be out of my system for a long time. It's gonna take a lot for you to get rid of me, Cub."

With that, he stood, put a kiss to her forehead. He left her looking after him as he walked out.

# CHAPTER 17

*Pedregal, Mexico~ 3 Days Later*

An elite oasis, Pedregal occupied the southern tip of Mexico's Baja California Peninsula. There, the Pacific met the Sea of Cortez. Overlooking the brilliant display of ethereal splendor was a cliffside villa of tanned stone and gleaming glass that reflected the incomparable Mexican sun.

"Is that it?" Bear used one hand to point while the other shielded her gaze against the sun that possessed blinding intensity when it bounced off rich turquoise waves.

From a heavily cushioned lounge on the deck of the boat they occupied, Tee used a hand to visor her brow and looked in the direction Bear pointed. "It is," she sang the confirmation.

"Jesus…" Bear murmured.

Tee laughed. "It's even more unbelievable on the inside."

Anticipating what sights lay inside the breathtaking structure, Bear closed her eyes and turned her face up to the sun. Then, she turned and joined Tee on the lounge.

"Thanks Tee," Bear leaned over to squeeze her friend's ankle. "This was just what I needed."

Tee waved her hands, and then let them hit her thighs when the breeze ruffled the gauzy fabric of the hot pink cover up she wore over a snow white bikini. "I'm not the one to thank. This was all Mercuri's doing," she said.

"I'm not surprised," Bear smiled, shook her head. "He's quite a guy. You were lucky to find him. Like I once said, 'he's a keeper'."

"I think so too," Tee hugged herself.

Sharing the lounge, the women enjoyed the view of unending sky dotted with puffy white clouds the yacht couldn't seem to outrun.

Tee didn't have to try very hard to get Bear to join in when she approached her about the trip a few days earlier. Given that most of the planning was complete in terms of the soiree, Bear decided to take her own advice and hit the road for a little rest and relaxation.

They flew by private jet from San Francisco to Baja California and then cruised the remaining distance to Pedregal in Cabo San Lucas. Bear wouldn't give any credibility to any thoughts that she was running. She hadn't seen or spoken to Pope since he'd taken her home after their dinner at The Rascal.

She'd thought plenty about that night, though. What he'd said- what she'd told him- it was all too much. Especially since what he said sounded a lot like he was telling her he wanted more than what they'd enjoyed. It was as though he wanted more than she was ready to give- than she *could* give. That she was even running herself foolish with thoughts over anything *more*, was a waste of time anyway.

After all, she wasn't the type men fell in love with. That was something else she'd once said. And why the hell did she have the L word on the brain?

The question had her pushing from the lounge and taking several deep refreshing breaths as she crossed the deck. Men couldn't handle what she was. Hell, half the time *she* didn't even know what she was. A voice crept in with reminders of how well Pope Apostolou seemed to handle what she was. The reminder was met with a strong desire by Bear to grab fistfuls of her hair and tug.

"Ladies?"

Bear and Tee looked to the crew person who had joined them on the deck.

187

"We'll be docking soon," the young woman said, "would you two like fresh drinks to take along once we make port?"

"That'd be nice," Tee said.

Bear shrugged. "I'm game."

"Thank you ladies, be just a minute."

"So what are you wearing from the boat?" Bear asked Tee when they were alone.

Tee skimmed a hand across the daring cover up. "I doubt we'll need any real clothes while we're here," she said.

"I like the way you think," Bear turned to enjoy more of the view. "So what's next on the itinerary?"

"No idea," Tee drawled, eyes closed. "Mercuri put this all in place. I've got no idea what he's planned."

Bear strode back to the lounge, a teasing light in her brown eyes. "So what's it like to have a man who can put together a girls' weekend for you and your friends and owns a jet and yacht to get you to all the fun?"

Tee gave an overly exaggerated stretch. "It's very nice to have a man who can put together a girls' weekend. As for knowing what it's like to have a man with a jet and a yacht...I wouldn't know. Ask me what it's like to have a man with *some* jets and *some* yachts."

Wild laughter exploded split seconds following the playful boast.

~~~

"Did you believe it?" Mercuri stood with a beer bottle poised for drinking. The story Pope had just shared, left him barely capable of supporting the bottle in his grasp.

Pope, meanwhile, prowled the semicircular media room. His face wore a scowl despite the beauty of his surroundings. "Gerrick isn't one to play fast and loose with the truth," he said, "especially when it comes to his life's work."

Mercuri studied the bottle he held as though he had no idea how it had gotten there in his hand. "It'd explain a lot-this drug-why we were taken, why our mothers were so special to them, beyond what they did for a living and then there's the madness factor..." He followed that with a long swallow from the bottle.

"That's why I believe it," the quiet roar underscored Pope's words.

188

"And Gerrick expects you to let them go on merrily creating this stuff?" Faint laughter held Mercuri's question.

"He says they can fix what's wrong," Pope smoothed palm over fist and slowed his pacing. "No body else seems to care about fixing what's wrong, they only want the shit on the market and making a profit."

"And he's looking to you for protection?"

"More like a deterrent."

"To everyone on Brody's and Jake's sides," Mercuri guessed.

Pope shrugged. "Somethin' like that."

"And you're still not interested?"

Pope returned to his full on pacing. "To be interested means I have to be there and it's the last place I want to be- the last thing I was to be overseeing. Hell Merc," the rough intensity of his voice surged in heavier. "We came this close to blowing away the entire fucking mess," he snapped his fingers for emphasis. "We did damage enough-don't get me wrong but the thing about damage is there's always more of it to go around."

Mercuri let the opinion hang while swigging down more of his beer. "So what is it you really want?" he asked finally. "Gerrick seems to have made an impression."

Pope snarled a curse then. "Don't start that shit, Merc."

"What?!" Mercuri laughed, shrugged. "You know? I kind of like this. I see why you enjoy playing the know it all so much."

Pope's glare should've sent blue daggers slicing the air in its wake.

Mercuri only grinned, raised a hand in defense. "I only want to know what else has you hesitating."

"Gerrick says their studies with this...drug showed whatever the parents were exposed to never harmed the fetus," Pope leaned back on the glass wall he stood closest to. "They had some real successes with it, Merc. Not everyone came out crazy or-"

"Gigantic," Mercuri supplied along with another wicked grin before finishing off the rest of his beer.

Pope reciprocated the gesture, added a nod. "He says the genius rate even surpassed that of the psychotic. Not every batch produced monsters."

Mercuri knew what his friend was getting at. For a while, quiet lingered as the men thought of Patch and his math proficiency.

189

"So you're not interested in being the lord commander of the GAN, how are you gonna give Gerrick what he needs to do his work in peace?"

Pope finally sat, taking one of the linen cushioned bamboo chairs that faced the glass wall. Fragrant sea air drifted in and he indulged in the rejuvenating aroma as a few more seconds passed in silence.

"I've got a plan," he said.

"Would I be a know it all if I said I sensed a problem?"

"Oh the recipe's sound...it's the ingredients I can't quite master."

"What's the trouble?"

Pope let loose a bewildered chuckle. "I don't exactly know where to find them."

~~~

The villa where Tee and Bear were destined to spend their glorious getaway was a magnificent 4 bedroom work of art with one purpose: to pamper. Each 'bedroom' was in actuality a mini apartment occupying two spaces on opposite ends of the wings along either side of the dwelling's common areas- living room, kitchen and dining area.

The house also boasted a library, theater and sauna. It was an open, airy creation with stunning views at every turn. Bear was envisioning the onset of evening when a chilly breeze rolled in from the water. She couldn't wait to settle into one of the low, ice-blue cushioned chairs surrounding the firepit in the alfresco lounge area. She imagined the bikini she'd wear for the occasion and could almost taste the creamy Pina Colada she planned to enjoy. She was still smiling over the plan when she followed Tee into the living room and discovered their 'girls getaway' included two unexpected guests.

"Surprise," Tee whispered, bypassing Bear on her way to Mercuri who waited on the other side of the big room. He scooped her up and into a demonstrative kiss.

"Hey Pope!" Tee called once Mercuri let her down for air.

"Thanks for sharing the place, guys," Pope said before looking to Bear who was staring at the polished hardwoods.

Her feet; partly hidden by the hem of her sundress, suddenly felt as though they'd been attached to 50lb weights. She looked up only when she felt Mercuri's imposing presence nearby and managed to lean into the kiss he put to her temple.

"It was my idea," he murmured where his lips touched her skin.

"I'm sure you had lots of support for it," Bear kept her tone soft as well. "Sorry Mercuri, could you-could you all excuse me?" Quickly she pivoted and bolted from the room.

Tee followed seconds later with Mercuri and Pope following seconds after that.

As Bear had no idea where she was going in the palace-sized villa, her stormy exit took her about as far as the dining room off from the kitchen.

"Bear-"

"I don't wanna hear it, Tee," Bear turned to her friend, her gaze stony. "How could you do that?"

Cool, Tee only raised a brow. "I had nothing to do with it."

"Bull."

"Alright," That time, Tee only raised a shoulder. "Well you can spend your time pouting or enjoying-looks like you've got quite a bit to enjoy."

"So unfair," Bear muttered, curving her fingers into the top of her head. "Weren't you listening when I told you what happened?"

"I listened. Now it's time for *you* to listen." Tee moved closer to where Bear stood shifting her weight in agitation. "He only wants to apologize, B."

"He already has. Twice. This isn't about that."

"So tell him that, Hon."

"And then I can go?" Hope pooled in Bear's lush stare.

"No." Tee was unmoved. "We're here for the duration. You wanted rest and relaxation-you got it. You'll enjoy this even if it kills you." Straightening to her full 5'2, she half turned for the door. "We're meeting for drinks in the lounge area. You've got an hour."

"Tee-"

"That's it."

Bear balled her fists and bristled. In the end, she merely stomped her foot as her tiny friend breezed from the room.

From their position outside the dining room, Mercuri and Pope watched the exchange.

"How'd she do that?" Pope's voice was hushed, awed by Tee's control.

Mercuri smiled. "A gift."

"I'll say."

"So you wanted her on common ground. You've got her." Mercuri clapped a hand to Pope's back. "Make it count."

It took Pope almost a full minute after Mercuri left to brace himself for confrontation. During that time, he watched Bear, enjoying the graceful sway of the long sundress she wore. The mosaic print emphasized the dewy brown of her skin as did the daring halter bodice that left her bare to the small of her back. Her hair was loose, lilting fiercely against the breeze that captured it.

Bowing his head, Pope worked to resist letting his thoughts wander and then he moved into the room. He cleared his throat, knowing she wouldn't detect his presence otherwise. He saw when she bristled in response and smiled.

"I'm sorry this felt like an ambush," he said once they stood side by side and were watching two speed boats race in a distant bay.

"At least I know what your apology was about. Smoothing the way so you could get laid."

The accusation didn't rile Pope, rather brought a sly grin to his mouth. "Do you think I'd need to go to this kind of trouble if that's what I wanted?"

"Fishing for compliments Mr. Apostolou?"

"Truth would suffice."

"Ah, truth," Bear let her head fall back and missed the helpless fascination in Pope's ultramarine stare as he followed the movement.

"That's right," she sighed. "Truth is what we're all about. Then it makes perfect sense I guess. After all, sluts are sure things, aren't we? You sure wouldn't have to apologize to get me in the-"

He grabbed her then, causing her to shriek at the suddenness of it. Even in the midst of his frustration though, his hold was gentle.

"Don't ever say that about yourself in front of me again. Am I understood?"

Bear gave a half-hearted nod, felt his hold intensify a fraction. "Yes," she hissed out. "Why are you doing this?" Misery carried her tone. "You already apologized twice."

"Yes, but you haven't accepted them, have you?"

"Why does that matter? Look Pope, what happened, happened. We both wanted it. I...I needed it. That's that."

"Cub…" Pope cupped her jaw, shook his head in playful sorrow. "Baby that's so *not* that. You're afraid of something. I don't think it's

192

me, thank God but I'm apt to say it's a fear of being conquered." He smiled when she bristled again.

"But it's even more than that, isn't it?" He let the question hang, dragged his thumb across her chin and down her neck to linger at the base of her throat. Then he left her.

~~~

"Am I late?" Bear's soft query carried on the early evening air when she arrived in the lounge just over an hour later.

From his spot along the stone ledge of the balcony, Pope shook his head. "Our hosts ditched us."

Bear smiled as though she'd expected nothing less. Hand perched to her hip, where a gold bikini wrap skirt was knotted, she crossed the stone flooring to observe the brilliant display of lights radiating from Pedregal. The nightlife was already gearing up to be spectacular.

"Get you something from the bar?" Pope offered when Bear found him appraising her attire so intently he'd tilted his head to obtain a more inclusive view.

"I'll help myself," she decided.

He didn't argue, appreciating the view she gave from behind. Still, conversation was the priority for the weekend and he took it upon himself to get things started.

"Don't blame Mercuri and Tee. They were only trying to help."

"Oh I know that," Bear's voice flowed in lightly from the beverage nook. "Tee was only doing what I hinted around for anyway."

"Oh yeah?" Intrigued, Pope turned to face her from the ledge.

Bear was at work preparing a cranberry juice and gin. "I told her I wouldn't mind a set up with a friend of Mercuri's."

"Is that right?"

"That's right," she sang and then raised her glass to emphasize. Enjoying a few sips of the drink, she smiled in approval of the taste before setting aside the glass.

Pope watched her smile wane. He drank deeply of his beer and waited on her to continue.

"It was only supposed to be about sex," she fixed him with a level stare. "Tee knows better than anyone, that's all I'd be willing to handle." She shrugged. "So you see, there's no reason to beat yourself up

193

over not telling me about knowing Mercuri. It was a surprise," she tacked on airily before taking another casual sip of her drink.

"I guess that's what had me running out of your house like an idiot," she enjoyed another quick sip of drink, "but please just know that I'm over it. I accept your apology-all of them. There's no need for you to think on it any further."

Pope nodded and eventually returned to taking in the view while he finished his drink. Bear did the same and then joined Pope at the balcony. Relief was washing over her as she finished her drink and decided on a refill. She gestured to Pope's empty bottle.

"Can I get you another-"

"Please tell me it didn't take you an hour to come up with that bullshit?"

The accusation made her smile. "It's the truth."

"Oh? Which part? That me knowing Mercuri was just a surprise? That you were just in it for the sex?"

"It can't be about anything else, Pope."

"But it is, isn't it?"

Acknowledgement, sent an annoying heat along her neckline. It was worth a try, she thought, while observing him and appreciating the artwork on the Bon Jovi T-shirt he sported with loose fitting camo shorts.

Though he'd all but told her he wasn't looking for a way out, she'd hoped...he'd already glimpsed enough...Maybe he would cut his losses, walk away and she could spare herself the trouble of having to watch him do it once she'd fallen in love with him- a thing she wasn't so sure hadn't happened already.

"I can't do it." She shook her head.

"Do what, Bear?" He pushed from the ledge, taking her arm when she would've turned away. "Admit there might be something more between us than some pretty dynamic sex? Or be honest enough to at least admit it to yourself? Are you afraid if I get too close, I'll see what you're trying to hide under that tough exterior?"

"There's nothing under the tough exterior," she eased her arm free of his hold. "That soft, swooning, moaning sweething I turn into when we're together- that's not who I am Pope. That's sex. Dynamic sex, like you said. The bitch that runs my ranch, she's not an act. I know you think that, but you'd be wrong. You think you can strip away those layers to what you're really after, but all you'd do is strip me down to nothing."

194

"Is that what you're afraid of, Babe?"

Bear retreated then. Pope advanced.

Yes, that was it, he decided, watching as she returned to study the scenery beyond the ledge. Something told him that her fear of him stripping her down to nothing was only one of her concerns though. There was something larger at work, but that discovery could wait. Christ, he thought, was there anything sexier than a complex woman?

Bear flinched when the back of his hand skimmed her arm. Pope felt her breath quicken when he moved in close behind and cupped her breast.

She didn't try to free herself and Pope didn't care to ponder her reasons for not resisting. He felt he'd earned a reward for breaking through one of the many layers he suspected she had. He started to lift the hem of her skirt.

"Don't," she managed and went as far as to hold his wrist.

Her hold was loose, useless and seconds later, Pope's fingers were skimming the fabric of her bikini.

"Stop."

"Make me," he spoke against her nape once her head sloped forward.

For several moments after, he tormented her with slow strokes where the material covered her mound. Bear let her head rest back against the granite wall of his chest. Her own chest heaved as anticipation surged high and strong.

Still, Pope did nothing more than to torment her with the lingering strokes. Bear wasn't above begging and was opening her mouth to do just that, when his hand delved inside the shimmery beige bikini bottom. His middle finger descended on her clit and she discovered she'd yet to experience real torment.

Pope kept the strokes light, with only the barest hint of a rotation across the bundle of nerves that sent lances of pleasure slicing through her. Instinct made Bear want to squeeze his wrist but her grip slackened when his other hand squeezed her breast most insistently. His middle finger was again the tormenter and slipped beneath the fabric of her top to have its way with a rigid nipple.

Her resulting cry was a sharp gasp swallowed by the sounds of their environment- both natural and manmade. Pope molested the nub relentlessly and kept her anchored to him with his hand snug at her core. His thumb replaced his middle finger to massage her achy clit.

195

When he bowed his head to suckle her earlobe, he was close enough for her to bury her hand in the glossy waves of onyx tumbling into his face. Her gasps were closer to shudders then. Bear arched her chest, pushed more of her breast into the delicious rubs and pinches he subjected her nipple to.

Her mouth was a perfect O, allowing the shameless sounds of pleasure free reign across the lounge area. Sensation engulfed when the fingers that had simply teased through her swimwear, suddenly assumed full possession. Pope flexed his hold around her breast when she bucked in response to his fingers taking claim.

With her upper body secure against him, he took her with deep, rigorously thrusting fingers- a move that soon coated his skin in a creamy smattering of her need. Bear rolled her head tirelessly against his chest as her hips arched to meet the persistent invasion that stretched and filled her.

His fingers were long, thick orgasm-inducing digits. They sent moisture streaming slow and steady down her thigh when they lunged, rotated, retreated and then repeated the act. Too soon, her inner muscles were squeezing vice tight as a powerful climax shook her. If he eased his hold in any way, Bear knew she'd slide to the floor. His hold was true however, and she felt utterly secure in his arms. She wouldn't let herself consider the underlying truth in those words, but it was truth just the same.

Rhythmic, throaty sounds confirmed her pleasure and Pope was sure no sound had ever stroked his ego with such unrelenting prowess. That she was so undone by his touch, was stimulating in itself. That she allowed him such complete and familiar reign over her stunning body, was a slice of perfection all its own.

It was a reign he planned to treasure for a long time to come. No way was she ready to hear that now-certainly not the entire truth of what that entailed. She didn't quite trust that he wasn't out to change her. Besides, there was so much more he had to learn about her-that they had to learn about each other.

Her shudders were tapering off. The climax was easing its fierce clutch. She slumped like a rag doll against him, her hair damp from her exertions and hanging limp with her head bowed while she tried to steady her breathing. Pope rested his chin to her shoulder and waited.

"Pope-"

"Shh…"

The gesture assured her there was nothing more that needed to be said then. Of course, she tried only to be interrupted by a low surprised moan- her own.

Pope had simply resumed his thrusts, satisfaction curving his mouth into a smile when he felt renewed streams of moisture dousing his skin.

She pleaded in earnest and he understood that she pleaded not for him to stop, but to let her out of her clothes-what there was of them. He covered her hand with his to stop the tugs she gave to the rounded cups of her top.

"You need your rest, Hon. It's been a long day."

"No," Bear gave the whiny protest and fought to turn in his arms. "No," she insisted when he allowed the move.

"Don't worry. I'll finish what I start," he promised.

Bear's mouth went dry as she watched him suck her need from his finger. A second passed and then she was flush against him and kissing her body from his tongue.

Pope lost whatever ability he'd latched onto to ease back in the first place. The woman was murder on his willpower and he'd need every bit of it in order to barter what he wanted for what she seemed dead set against giving- her truth.

He set her away from him then- keeping her at arm's length. His breathing was just as labored as hers.

"Pope-"

"That 'sweething' you think you just *turn into*?" He countered, "I've seen her when we're not in bed- when I'm not inside you. She's a big part of the so-called bitch who runs your ranch. I'm not trying to tear one down to have the other, Bear. I want you both. I tend to get what I go after."

He straightened. "I think Tee said, breakfast was out here at nine. Goodnight, Bear."

197

# CHAPTER 18

Bear decided to arrive early for breakfast. Once again, she attempted to snag the upper hand during an encounter with Pope. She figured being first on scene, might at least keep the moment from tipping into high drama straight away. She could hope.

It was no hardship getting up early. She hadn't slept worth a damn the night before. The climax he'd sent her into only whet her appetite for the added bliss she knew he was capable of providing. Bliss seemed intent on withholding for some reason.

It wasn't because he wanted her to beg. She'd done that. *Boy* had she done that. Squeezing her eyes shut for a moment, she fought to push back the memories of her sex-starved behavior.

Dressed in a simple gray tee and matching sleep pants, she slipper-scuffed her way down to the airy lounge where breakfast was to be set. The buffet waited as promised, but her attempts to be the early bird were thwarted. Still, a measure of relief bloomed and was evident in the sigh she gave at finding Mercuri there in the lounge with Pope.

"There she is," Mercuri's sigh was as welcoming as his smile and the light in his exotic amber gaze. He stood from the teakwood dining table and drew Bear close as he approached.

They shared a friendly side hug while Bear kept her eyes on the table. Pope didn't bother to stand which made it somewhat easier for her to disregard his presence. Somewhat. His eyes held a searing intensity akin to an electric current. There was no disregarding it.

Bear frowned when her scan of the dining table revealed something familiar, but totally unexpected. That time, she gasped and turned her curious frown to Mercuri before she scuffed to the table. Tentatively, she reached for the small, velvet box sitting on the placemat in front of Mercuri's chair. It was already open and she turned it to study the wide octagonal diamond displayed on a gleaming platinum band.

"Mercuri..." she breathed, stroking the black cushiony bed supporting the ring.

Above her head, the guys shared knowing smiles.

Bear turned from the table, cradling the box in her hands. "Is this a going steady ring?" she asked.

Mercuri's grin epitomized satisfaction with an adorable sliver of boyish guile. "This is an 'I want your friend to be my wife' ring."

Bear was silent for a second longer before she gave a girlish squeal and launched into an even more girlish bouncing turn that had Mercuri and Pope laughing.

Still bouncing, Bear threw herself against Mercuri. She balanced on her toes until he took her off her feet and into a tight embrace.

"Think I'll get the same reaction from Tee?" Mercuri asked once he set Bear to her feet.

"If you don't, I'm gonna punch her like I've been wanting to do since we got in this house," Bear decided.

"You don't think it's too soon?"

"No way! And I speak for everyone who matters. Lu and Prin are gonna lose their minds! When will you ask her?"

"I don't know," a trace of boyish uncertainty joined the guile. "I um...I keep losing my nerve."

"Find it," Bear ordered, placing the ring box in his hand and squeezing tight.

"Thanks B," Mercuri put a lingering kiss to her forehead and then made his way back into the villa.

Bear watched him go and then continued her path to the buffet of breakfast treats displayed on a pine rectangular table. She grabbed a plate and silverware but then her efforts fizzled. She stood there looking down at the fragrant array of food without seeing any of it.

Instead, she registered on an off-white blur in her line of sight. Blinking, she studied the oversized tri-folded document resting on the plate she held. Another moment passed before she was looking to Pope with the same bewilderment she had when asking Mercuri about the ring.

Pope tilted his head toward the plate. "Not as dazzling as jewelry, but I thought it was time you had it."

He gave no further insight, so Bear set the plate down in order to study the page. The deed to the cottage. Still bewildered, she looked up. "Why?"

"I was never *not* going to give it to you, Cub." He shrugged. "I only wanted to give you a hard time about it."

Bear pretended to bristle over the confession. "Pretty shitty on your part," she said.

"Guy's gotta have *some* fun," again, he shrugged. "So what are you getting into today?"

"Absolutely nothing. The way it should be."

Pope grinned. "Agreed. Do you um...do you think you could make time during all the 'nothing' to go out with me later? There's a jet ski race at one of the beaches down here. There's no swimming allowed with the waters being so treacherous but for the folks who love it, that's no discouragement at all."

He frowned while clearing his throat then. "If jet skis aren't your thing, it's still pretty amazing to watch. I've seen a few races the times I've gone down with Merc and the guys..." he cleared his throat once more and shifted his devastating gaze toward the buffet.

Bear realized the man was experiencing a bit of trouble with his self confidence. This, from a man who could turn a dining room full of women into a stuttering bunch of slack jawed idiots when they saw him.

*I'll be damned*, she noted in silence, her mocha stare filtering with awe and amusement. She watched him drag a hand through his wavy locks and noted the habit wasn't just a sign of frustration, but uncertainty. She'd managed to school her expression by the time he looked to her in expectation of a response.

"I'd love to go," she accepted in a quiet demure manner and witnessed the naturally self-assured layer of his persona slide back into place.

Pope gave the barest hint of a nod as though he'd expected nothing else. "So we can meet in the living room around four if that's good for you? The races usually take place close to sunset."

"I'll be ready, but aren't you eating?" She cast a quick look to the buffet when he turned to leave.

"Already did with Merc."

Bear wondered when in the world the men found time to sleep.

Pope was on his way out, but his steps slowed. "Tee and Merc. Pretty nice, huh?"

"Very nice. Tee's lucky. Mercuri's a great guy. She deserves this."

"So does Merc." Pope smiled. "Tee's phenomenal. I know he thought he'd never find anyone like her, let alone deserve her. Given the rest of us hope." He looked at her then. "I'll see you at four."

"Yeah," she nodded, her tone quiet. Alone, she studied the deed she held.

***

Divorce Beach was one of the most unique destinations in Cabo. Despite its pessimistic name, Divorce Beach was actually thought of as a more romantic destination than its counterpart. Lover's Beach was located within a walking distance of about a few hundred feet.

People made a point of taking in one of Divorce Beach's spectacular sunsets. Additionally, they ventured there for the sheer joy of boasting that they'd visited one of the few beaches on the planet where two different bodies of water connected. Divorce Beach presented the Pacific to one side and the Sea of Cortez on the other.

Some often traveled the distance from the mainland by glass-bottomed boat. Others took cruises that allowed participants to view the beach from afar. Many preferred water taxis and dinner cruise options as the beach was a notoriously hot locale. Moreover, there were no restroom facilities to speak of.

Nevertheless, Divorce Beach held an even more riveting draw than its sunsets. The water.

Alas, Divorce was definitely *not* the place to visit for a leisurely dip. Beach signs cautioned against swimming. There wasn't even an on duty lifeguard. Still, the water was an irresistible draw to the most extreme adventure seekers. The waves were...active, to say the least, complete with powerful rip currents and a massive undertow that beckoned the most courageous adrenaline junkies.

Given that the area was only accessible by sea, Pope drove he and Bear the short distance from the villa to the marina. There, he'd arranged to have them transported by private boat. The vessel remained on standby until they were ready to leave.

It was a more luxurious as well as logical idea given the lack of beach facilities. Also logical; as there were no vendors or restaurants nearby, was the eating nook Bear found set up when they arrived.

"Convenient," she noted when her date led her the brief distance from the boat to a rather remote spot behind one of the imposing granite formations that dotted the area.

Pope's sigh was playfully weary. "A guy should be prepared," he said. "Besides, this spot gets the best shade."

Bear laughed. The sun would be setting soon, but it'd still be very hot in the meantime. "Smart," she commended.

"Selfish." He corrected, his vivid blues charting a slow suggestive course down the length of her. "Can't have you burning. That'd spoil all the fun things I want to do with you later."

Bear felt her stomach muscles quake just as a telling throb targeted someplace unmentionable. In an attempt to mask her reaction, she turned her focus to the canvas tote she'd brought along.

"No chance of burning," she called and waved a bottle of sunscreen she'd pulled from the depths of the coral colored bag,

She'd smeared some of the fragrant lotion to her face and was settling to one of the chairs to apply more to the rest of her, when Pope took hold. He'd eased into one of the big chairs on either side of a short table of glossy beige wood. Hand on her wrist, he freed her of the scant wrap skirt she sported and then put her on his lap instead.

"Let me."

"Pope, you don't have to-"

"But I should, since you can't get to the most important places."

The arm chair's wide build, accommodated them both quite comfortably. Pope positioned Bear in the vee of his thighs. With subtle expertise, he tugged loose the halter straps of her top.

Surprised by the move, Bear instinctively clutched at the bikini's cups before they fell.

"Easy," he soothed.

She swallowed with effort then. "I don't think you need to get every spot."

"See that's where you're wrong," his voice had grown softer, deeper. "I'd never forgive myself if I let anything bad happen to such nice skin," his voice was as whisper soft as the graze of his knuckles up her spine.

Bear pressed her lips together in hopes of stifling a responsive moan. It didn't matter when the rapid heaves of her breasts proved how affected she'd become by his touch.

"Relax," he murmured, a clear indicator that he was aware of her elevated breathing.

Bear's hand shook between her breasts but she didn't dare ease her grip on the top. Much of her caution had to do with their surroundings. Unlike the water, that teemed with boats and other vehicles, the beach was sparsely populated. Due in no small part to the time of day, she suspected. While the towering rock formations provided ample shade and privacy, it was still the outdoors. Given her reaction to Pope Apostolou's touch, she wouldn't have put it past herself to indulge in whatever her hormones demanded.

She was already highly sensitized to every part of him that touched her. He wore a dark blue bandana, but she could still feel a few tendrils of his hair brushing her skin as he continued the light grazes along her spine. His head was bowed as he was no doubt following the path of his fingers with those amazing eyes of his, she thought.

Bear only registered she was still holding onto the sunscreen when she felt him tugging the bottle free of her death clutch.

"You okay?" he asked.

"Peachy," she snapped in response to his polite tone. She rolled her eyes while he chuckled.

The lotion soothed like a cool balm when it hit her skin. Combined with the skillful hands applying it however, arousal pulsed and was far from soothing. Pope worked in the sunscreen, using slow massages that began at her neck and shoulders. His thumbs worked the tense muscles at her nape and Bear couldn't stifle her moan then. Her lips parted to emit the sound as her head rested back against his shoulder that was still covered by the dark T-shirt he'd worn that day.

Everything melted away, including the glorious beach. That is, until his big hands circled her waist in order to apply the lotion to her midriff. In the process, he made a point of using his thumbs to stroke the sides of her breasts.

"Pope-"

"Quiet. Gotta do this right and you'll screw with my concentration if you talk."

"It's not rocket science," her tone was breathy, amused.

No, Pope thought, it wasn't. It was something far more important. It was him treasuring the woman he was falling in love with.

Rattled a little by the unexpected truth, Pope finished up with putting lotion to Bear's thighs. He took a bit more time along her inner thighs, but didn't linger. In a sudden and seamless move, he stood scooped Bear up and moved her to the big lounge chair on the other side of the squat square table.

While he diligently applied the lotion to her calves and feet, Bear gave a more intense study to their surroundings. "Lots of boats in the water already," she noted.

"Mmm hmm," Pope sent a fleeting glance over his shoulder but was more fixed on his task. "People come here all day for the crazy waves out there," he shared. "They race jet skis near sunset it's somethin' to see," he added.

"I don't doubt it," Bear was already looking on with interest toward the choppy water alive with the sights and sounds of thrill seekers. "What happens after the race?" She asked.

"Things start to clear out. Most people head back to the mainland and hit the clubs and stuff- a few hang around out here for a while. You can see the fireworks displays at other beaches from here." He shrugged. "Some just enjoy the water," his strokes were slowing on her legs. The long shapely limbs in their irresistible caramel hue, held him almost mesmerized.

"Some come out here and go all night..." he trailed off.

Bear felt her tummy complete a strange flip. It accompanied the strange feeling she had that he was referring to activities completely unrelated to the race.

~~~

Pope would be the first to agree that life had dealt him some pretty shitty hands during his 32 years. They hadn't been easy hands to play, but he'd done alright. Better than alright, in some cases.

Perhaps that was why he could recognize the moments when life seemed to be cutting him a break. Well...he could recognize those moments *sometimes*. Times like these...life was pretty goddamn good.

He didn't bother to open his eyes behind the shades he wore when he heard Bear cry out in a tone of affectionate anguish from her stance atop the wooden table. From that vantage point, she viewed the 3rd race in a series of nine qualifying jet ski events. They would lead up to the 10th and final showdown of the evening.

He'd ordered her atop the table when she refused to leave the comfort of their spot near the immense granite wall that umbrellaed them beneath a generous dousing of shade. He didn't need to see the action in the water, he had all he wanted there in hand.

Although the table was pretty much secure in its space between the chairs, he maintained a steady hold at her calf. At times, he indulged in letting his hand roam the leg he held and the way the strong sea wind seemed to whip in approval.

Yes, Pope thought, there were times when life was definitely good. He wasn't so certain that unravelling Bear's mysteries would be especially good, but there was no avoiding that. Hell, the journey to figuring her out at least partly- would without a doubt-be a novel experience for him. He was usually the one that was the mystery, never the woman who struck his interest.

Berrill Clayton was indeed a puzzle, but Pope knew that fact hadn't fueled the deeper emotions that were now funnelling in. They were emotions he wanted to embrace instead of ignore. She was right when she'd said he wanted the sweething she turned into. Getting her to admit that the aspect of her persona was more than an infrequent phenomena, would be a task all its own. It'd also be a task getting her to believe he wanted all that came with it.

The adorably brittle hardass she'd been when he'd come throwing his money around at her ranch. The sweething she'd *turned into* when he discovered he was doing something nice for a friend. The care and concern she'd shown for a workaholic employee and his wife. Not to mention her outrage upon discovering a high society caterer was on tap to steal a job from a colleague who donated his time and talents for those less fortunate. He wanted all of her. Nothing else would do.

"This is amazing," Bear's voice entwined with laughter when she jumped down from the table to reclaim her chair. "Hard to believe people live like this everyday," she added.

"It's not so hard. You just do it."

She laughed again. "Says the man who can run his business from anywhere in the world."

"But I don't really have a business, though. Just a series of very good investments."

"And you just gave one up." Bear reminded him. "Got the deed in my suitcase to prove it." She sent him a measuring look. "Hope that didn't sting too much."

Pope removed his sunglasses and watched Bear do the same.

"Didn't sting at all," he said. "I don't think I ever enjoyed giving up something so much."

She could tell he meant it and yet a skeptical light held her gaze when his bright eyes harbored an intensity she hadn't expected from a simple tease.

"What's wrong?" She gave a curious shake of her head.

Pope reached across the small table to ease the back of his hand down her cheek.

"Not a goddamn thing," he soothed.

Bear felt the sense of deja vu take hold. For the second time that afternoon, she got the feeling that his simple words held a much deeper meaning.

~~~

Evening emerged, the night gently blotting out the luminescent day. Pope and Bear enjoyed a filling supper served by the small crew aboard the boat that had been chartered for their convenience.

Once the high intensity races had ended, a few stragglers remained. Some adventure junkies were still out braving the thrashing waves. A few had carved out their own private nooks where they engaged in more illicit activities.

Pope and Bear were sharing her lounge chair. Pope relaxed against it with Bear tucked close to his side. A comfortable silence surrounded them while they lay enjoying the environment. Bear shivered and Pope smoothed a hand along her bare arm, the other across her back.

"Cold?" He asked. "Ready to head back?"

"Mmm mmm," Bear quickly shook her head. "I'm good. You're very warm."

"Hmph, runs in the family." Pope managed to keep his voice light despite his furrowing brow.

"Runs in the family…"

Her words had him frowning for another reason. "What?" He prodded.

Bear shook her head.

"Talk or be tickled," he threatened and smiled when she laughed.

"It's nothing, really I just…when I have the chance to enjoy the sky at night like this it makes me think of home."

"I see," Pope studied the sky again, the darkened expanse was smattered with stars. "Still got work on the brain, huh? I'm pretty sure the ranch is holdin' its own."

"Funny. But I'm not talking about the ranch. My grandparents. They had a place-a farm, nothing over the top like the ranch but that sky…" she closed her eyes as though envisioning it.

"That sky could put you in your place fast. It was nothing for us to just leave the house and have dinner right outside in the middle of the land."

"You loved them a lot." Again, Pope smoothed his hands across her back and arm.

"They were all I had 'til I met Tee, Lu and Prin."

"What about your parents?" He felt her head shake against the crook of his neck.

"Never knew my father. I don't think my mother did either. I lived with my grandparents for as long as I could remember-*they* were my parents." She blew out a laugh.

"School stuff, doctor's appointments, choir rehearsals…it all went through them. I doubt my mother knew or even care I was the best in my singing troupe."

Pope put a kiss to her forehead, kept his cheek pressed there.

"She went out one night with some guy…never came back. We didn't think anything bad had happened to her- we were all expecting her to go for good one day. I think my grandparents hoped she would. I know I did. We were happier when she left…for a while, anyway."

She quieted, shivered and Pope got the feeling he'd have to wait to learn what was on the other side of her thought.

"I lost my mother a long time ago too," he shared quietly. "GAN took us when we were about nine or ten. They said it was time we learned to be men and they had people take us to some kind of military school…we never saw our mothers again."

Bear was watching Pope as he spoke. She'd heard some of the story from Tee who had gotten it from Mercuri. She'd had the feeling Tee hadn't told her everything then. Like her, Bear guessed Pope wasn't in much of a mood to share his complete tale of woe either. When he was quiet for a while, she gave him a nudge.

"Life can be pretty crummy, huh?"

Her words made him laugh. "Yes, it can, Cub." He turned the tables then and suddenly shifted Bear to her back.

"But there are times," he spoke the words against the rise of her breasts when his head dipped. "Times when it can be pretty, fucking alright."

Times like that very moment, Bear decided when Pope nuzzled aside the rounded bikini cups. She bit down on her lower lip when he outlined her flat nipples with his nose and then his tongue until they were erect and wet amidst the night air.

She snuggled her head into the chair's linen cased cushions, pushing the bandana from his head in the process. Waves of dark silk pampered her chest when his hair spilled from its confines. The pitch locks, teased the undersides of her breasts as he dragged his kiss down her body. His hands were covering her hips, the long thick fingers curving inside the bikini bottom when Bear remembered where they were.

"Pope," she put her hands over his. "We're outside."

A sliver of the potent moonlight doused his face, fixing a spotlight upon the wicked smile he sent her. "Shy about being outside at night, huh?"

"No," her drawl held a trace of indignance. "Only shy about being outside at night naked."

"Ah," he pretended to be duly clued in and reached up to tug her top back into place. "Better?"

Bear could only laugh, a laugh that transformed into a choked cry when his mouth was rooted against the bikini's crotch to give her a harsh suckle. Pleasure ricocheted like lightning bolts. His bandana slid from her weak hand while she arched from the cushions.

Pope settled a forearm across her middle- a most effective restraint. Returning to his task, perfect teeth sank into the softness beneath the bikini. When another choked cry, resulted and louder than the last, he shushed her. Bear could feel his breath on the bikini's wet fabric where it stuck to her sex, chilling it.

He started to work his tongue there mimicking thrusts against the barrier of the material. Bear rose to meet the sensation-*tried* to rise, anyway. His forearm was like steel and made free movement a chore. Not that free movement was her top priority, just then. Absorbing the influx of sensation pummeling her was enough to focus on.

Pope had moved on down the lounge chair and taken her along with him. Kneeling in the sand, he levered her hips high so he wouldn't have to bend so low. Bear's shapely calves dangled over his shoulders, once he'd freed her of the bottoms.

"Pope," caution held her voice again.

"Shh…" he urged again, sinking his teeth into the lush flesh of her upper thigh as a form of punishment.

Bear squirmed while he rubbed his nose along the moist seams of her sex.

"Quiet, alright?" he gave her one last warning and then plunged his tongue deep.

Bear tried to mute her responses and failed miserably. Luckily, the beach was alive with the sounds of the active waves and a late evening fireworks show at a distance beach.

No one heard her cries that mounted when he worked his thumb over her clit. The move synced to his rotations inside her. She gasped his name, sensing the distinctive pressure building at her center. His name was a plea, rolling off her tongue as she tried to relay to him that she was incapable of controlling her responses.

"I got it, babe," he murmured in the midst of suckling her folds.

"Damn you," she gasped and heard his low laugh in response.

Pope's words weren't just a boast, they were fact. He could feel her need streaming robustly, coating     his tongue and he wanted nothing more than to take her with something thicker, wider and a damn sight longer than his tongue.

He resisted-had *been* resisting-because the trip was about more than getting her away to smooth the waters following all the difficult revelations. It was about cherishing her, showing her that she meant something to him beyond the exquisite pleasure she gave him. He couldn't resist touching her though, hence the small pockets of intimacy he'd indulged in with her since the previous night.

She was trembling then and Pope knew it had nothing to do with her being chilled by the night air. His hands flexed where they'd molded to her hips in an effort to maintain his own restraint.

As he'd already acknowledged, she was murder on his willpower. Her infectious shudders, the way she sobbed his name, caused his erection to tighten and swell to an almost painful state. Her inner walls squeezed his tongue and she cried out for him to 'do more'. Pope was sorely tempted to oblige.

Still, he resisted. A fine decision as it turned out. Seconds later, her cries reached their highest peak of the night. Pope followed her down until he had her resting flat on the lounge again.

She came powerfully that time, a reaction stoked by the assault he carried out upon her sex. His tongue speared impossibly deeper even as she pleaded for him to stop. She couldn't take much more. He relented only when she went limp, depleted from the exhaustive climax. He kissed her cheek, got an indecipherable response in turn and knew she was spent. He dressed her, gathered her close and spent a little longer soaking in the environment to give his own hormones time to settle. Later, he carried her to the boat for their return trip to the villa. Bear never stirred.

# CHAPTER 19

She woke up in bed naked, but alone. Her bikini, wrap and tote bag from the day before lay in a chair near the decadent king size. Bear didn't have long to ponder her time with Pope-time that had been intimacy at its best.

It hadn't escaped her that they'd done a lot more than enjoy adrenaline filled races and other carnal delights during their day at the beach. They'd ventured into new territory, shared more, learned more about one another. Those weren't the actions of people who were trying to end things.

She was trying to end things, wasn't she?

The answer, if there was one, was put on hold. Tee came knocking within 15 minutes of her waking. They had made plans to spend part of the day together and breakfast awaited at one of the beachfront restaurants.

Pope and Mercuri would be leaving the next day, giving the girls a couple more days to enjoy the villa. The guys had already set off for their own adventure by the time Tee and Bear met to take a water taxi that would carry them into Pedregal.

Even at 7am, the small city was already bustling with the sights and sounds of locals and tourists. Fresh market vendors haggled enthusiastically with potential customers. Laughter stirred just as enthusiastically and was underscored by the crash of the surf and song from the array of colorful birds dotting the sky.

Bear and Tee spent a while amidst the frenzy. They haggled eagerly with vendors during the shopping spree where they collected gifts for their friends and valued associates. They missed their breakfast reservation by 20 minutes. There were no worries as the little bistro served breakfast all day. Mercuri had arranged for the ladies to have a table on standby when they were ready. Bear and Tee were settling to the table with their wares by 8:30am.

~~~

The server took their orders for coffee and tea and left the ladies with menus. A more intriguing conversation ensued before the dining choices were browsed however.

"So...sex on the beach, huh? Nice." Tee's dark eyes sparkled with devilish intrigue.

"Hmph," Bear only shook her head while flipping through the menu. "Not exactly."

Tee settled back to her chair as though the wind had been let out of her sails. "Not exactly nice?"

"Not exactly sex."

Tee's expression all but screamed, details were required. Bear set down her menu and turned to take in the view beyond the terrace where they dined.

"We didn't have...sex...exactly," she removed her sunglasses as though that were helping her to choose her words. "He uh...he," her lashes fluttered when she glanced past her waist.

Tee smiled, began to nod. "I get it."

"Do you? Well I wish you'd explain it to me. Gorgeous woman, all but panting for it..." Bear rolled her eyes. "Come to think of it, I think I *did* pant for it and he didn't take full advantage? What the hell?"

Tee shrugged as though the answer were obvious. "He cares about what you need over what he wants? Bear, just because we haven't seen much in the way of romance, doesn't mean we shouldn't recognize when a man is being thoughtful."

"Says the woman who didn't think she and Mercuri would last a month-did a ton to ensure that they wouldn't."

Tee waved off the reminder. "Luckily, I've got a group of nosey, hardheaded friends who didn't mind telling me what an idiot I was being."

"I think the term used was fool and if I may say again, my situation with Pope is totally different."

A waitress arrived and the discussion halted, so the friends could place orders for breakfast potatoes, omelets and fresh muffins.

"You're not your grandmother, Hon." Tee said after long moments of relative quiet.

Stunned, best described Bear's expression. "Well where the hell did *that* come from?"

"From someone who knows how much you idolized what your grandparents had and how you think it worked against them."

"Me and Pope are a *long* way from having what my grandparents did." Bear slammed her shades to the table and reached for her coffee.

"But you want it," Tee challenged, shrugging when Bear pinned her with another exasperated look. "I could see it that day you came to my office."

"I was devastated."

"Because you were already falling for him then. I'm guessing you've already fallen now and hard."

Bear seemed to lose her taste for the coffee and set the cup to its saucer with more than a light clatter. She wanted to change the subject, but her mind had completely blanked of topics. She couldn't even latch onto light-hearted girl chatter concerning engagement proposals. A look to Tee's ring finger didn't show her wearing Mercuri's rock, so there was no diving into that bit of happiness.

"I want you and Mercuri at the soiree dinner party in two weeks," she blurted, desperate for small talk.

Tee sipped her tea. "Don't change the subject."

"I need friendly faces," Bear retorted. "Given that I haven't done an event like this before, I'll be uptight as hell unless I have some help keeping my mind off it."

"You know the best person for that job is Pope."

"Like you said, I'm not my grandmother."

"You know what I meant, B."

"And *you* know what *I* mean. I'm not looking for a relationship-true love."

"Few are." Tee countered. "And then it happens and...there you are."

"Exactly. There you are-blinded by it. So much, that you don't want to be the one to do anything to ruin it. Then things go unsaid and-"

"Honey?" Tee leaned over, squeezing Bear's hand and stopping the budding tirade. "You can say these things to Pope."

"I've already told him way too much. Things I only share with you, Lu and Prin."

"And how do you feel about that?"

"I don't know how to feel about it." Bear curved her fingers into her temples as if in panic. "I don't even know I'm doing it 'til it's done. How can that be?" Misery and confusion welled in her eyes. "I'm stronger than this, Tee."

"Hon, it's not about being strong or weak."

"For me, it is. It's...it's also about being afraid."

"Bear..." Tee squeezed Bear's wrist then. "Afraid? Of Pope?"

"Of...of what he'll think if he ever...knew-*saw* what we-what *I* did that night."

The admission caused Tee to still. "Are you thinking of telling him? Showing him?"

The server returned with orders then. Alone again, the quiet held over Bear's and Tee's table for another extended moment.

"I've been thinking about how I reacted when you said you needed to tell Mercuri. Trust and all..."

Tee looked a tad uneasy then. "Bear you know a lot of that was about me maybe...wanting to sabotage things a little-out of my *own* fears. I don't know...But, in spite of what you think, there's nothing wrong with fear unless you let it rule you."

"I know what you're saying **Tee**, but you keep forgetting that Mercuri had the chance to know you before he knew *that*. It's all Pope knows of me and when I hear the words love and relationship, I freeze because if I ever got there with him and he realized he'd made a mistake...just thinking about it frightens me. Think of what a nutcase I'd be if it ever really happened."

"And you think running from whatever's happening between you and Pope is what it'll take for you to conquer that fear?"

"I think I prefer the alternative."

214

Tee put away the rest of her argument then. Bear obviously had enough on her mind already, Most likely because she'd already come to many of the same conclusions Tee would use to persuade her.

Content that her friend would find her way eventually, Tee focused on the inviting breakfast when it arrived and the equally inviting view. The meal passed in thoughtful silence.

\*\*\*

Early evening found Bear and Tee back at the villa. They'd gone up to change into lounging clothes and met back out at the lounge where Tee headed to the adjourning bar area to mix a batch of drinks. The plan was to wile away the rest of the night in intoxicated bliss with her girlfriend.

Meanwhile, Bear took up residence on one of the chaise lounges closest to the firepit. Supplied with her preferred Ipod and headphones, she'd already gotten a jumpstart on the bliss.

Tee was pulling a step ladder to the counter in order to reach the blender some thoughtful soul had placed on an uppermost shelf. She'd taken the second step, when hands caught her waist and set her back to the floor.

"Got it," Pope effortlessly retrieved the device.

"Show off," Tee accused.

"What's on the menu?" Pope asked with a grin.

"Daiquiris. Want in?" Tee glanced back as if expecting to find Mercuri appearing.

Pope was about to answer, when the singing caught his ears.

Tee smiled, watching as the man headed slowly across the bar area to peer around the corner into the outdoor lounge.

Bear was in her element, belting out an impressive rendering of Sunshine Anderson's "Heard It All Before".

Pope smiled, his stirring eyes alight with surprise and approval of Bear's talent. He winced as the tune's potent message began to penetrate.

"Are guys allowed at your drinking session, Tee?"

"It's nothing personal," laughter carried Tee's words. "She always picks...robust songs with a lot of attitude when she's got a lot on her mind. Says they help her think."

Pope turned back to the lounge, where Bear was launching into Fantasia's "Doin' Me". His smile returned as he listened to the accapella

215

performance. "She's got some voice on her." His voice held surprised awe.

Tee smiled, browsing the selection of flavor packs for the daiquiris. "She thinks we make fun of her for singing out loud that way, but we're really very impressed."

Pope listened in a while longer. "How is it she hasn't been snapped up by one of the thousands of guys that must visit that ranch every month, Tee?"

"Our friend's a paradox," Tee added a fruit pouch to the blender. "Tough and soft. Trouble is...there hasn't been a guy who seems to be able to handle both. Not that she's gone out of her way to encourage that." She shook her head. "None of us have, actually...or *had,*" she gave Pope a shrug in spite of herself.

"Anyway, they can't handle or get by her tough shell and she's not about to give it up. You're the first one who seems to welcome both."

"She doesn't trust me," Pope was leaning against the bar, his striking blues a million miles away.

Tee rested along the counter to face Pope. "It's herself she doesn't trust. Herself she's afraid of. She thought she was okay as far as men and relationships are concerned. Hell, I thought *I* was okay, until I realized I was really...hiding."

"So what do you think I should do?"

"I think you already know that," Tee's laugh was softer then. "You're good for her. Don't give up."

It was Pope who seemed to be on the verge of laughter. "Ms. Shaw," sighing, he smoothed both hands across his hair waved back into a ponytail. "I'm afraid the ship that would've allowed me to do that, sailed a long time ago. If it was ever there to begin with."

~~~

The intended trip into intoxicated bliss, was in reality, a lightly buzzed trek. Bear and Tee enjoyed only one round of the strawberry banana daiquiris before deciding to call it a night.

The day had been an exhausting one, yet Bear found that sleep had decided against paying her a visit for the moment. She lay there, letting her mind wander and hoping to encounter drowsiness along the way. Instead, her thoughts drifted back to the night before and soon need was flaring persistently.

She clenched the bed covers, forbidding herself to do what her hormones craved. Pleasuring herself wouldn't do the job anyway, not when what she craved was just a few feet down the hall. The debate halted when a knock fell on her room door. Pope's voice followed.

"Cub?"

Her heart was in her throat when she sat up and flipped the bedside lamp to its lowest setting. Pushing back the covers, she scrambled from the bed but stopped short to slow her breathing.

She went to pull open the door, absently tugging at the hem of her T-shirt and recalling she wore nothing beneath it.

"Everything okay?" her tone was hushed at the sight of him dressed only in a gauzy pair of PJ bottoms.

"Yeah I uh," Pope's gaze drifted when he noticed her tug on the hem of the excuse for a T-shirt she wore. "I'm um...I'm leaving tomorrow," he managed.

"Yeah Tee-Tee said you and Mercuri were heading out."

Pope nodded, then tilted his head to look into the room. "What were you up to in here?"

Bear glanced back into the room as well. "Just trying to put myself to sleep."

"Is that right?" He advanced slowly, smiling wolfishly when she retreated. "Do you think I could help?"

"I'm sure you could."

"Would you like my help?"

"Please."

With that said, Pope jerked her up against him while kicking the door shut at his back. Bear's T-shirt rode up to her waist. Pope rested his head to her shoulder when he cradled her bare ass in his palms. Muttering an approving curse, he slammed her against the wall as his tongue filled her mouth.

Bear moaned her approval instead of emitting it through curse. She welcomed the ferocity underscoring the kiss. His tongue bruised hers, raggedly thrusting and knocking her head against the wall with every lunge. He'd eased his hold on her bottom to take possession of her thighs, parting them wide for his frame.

Bear made quick work of whipping the T-shirt above her head. She tugged Pope's hair free of its leather strap and then returned to let her hands roam the excellent breadth of his bronzed shoulders, chest and back. He covered the distance to the bed in record time and dumped her to the center.

Pope was about to follow Bear down, but she put her foot to the center of his chest. "If I can do without my clothes, so can you."

Pope took her foot, sank his teeth into her arch and sucked which sent her into a haze of erotic oblivion. Then, he was obliging her request.

His sleep pants fell without so much as a whisper. Bear pushed up on the bed, supporting her weight on one hand while the other reached to touch what she was feening for. She got her hand slapped away for the effort. Mouth curving into a soft pout, she fell back to the bed with plans to at least see to her own needs.

That plan was foiled by a slapped hand as well. Before she could launch any complaints, his thumb invaded her sex and delight throbbed slow and thick as the richest syrup. Greedily, her walls constricted to squeeze the thumb and use it to find her release. She was so determined, that she kept both hands clasped around his wrist, in case he had any plans to deprive her of the skilled finger.

Pope didn't deprive her, only added another finger. Bear moaned when he outlined her mouth with the pad of his other thumb, before thrusting it past her lips. Immediately, she sucked hard on the digit. Pope massaged her tongue whenever she eased the pressure. He worked her harder with the thumb at her core, until she was on the verge of climax. He selected that moment to deprive her of the much appreciated stimuli. There were no complaints. There wasn't much time between his thumb withdrawing and his dick invading. Moreover, it was hard to complain when she still so eagerly bathed his tongue inside her mouth.

The room filled with unmistakeable sounds of male and female pleasure at its height. Bear's were somewhat muffled give her current task. Pope's were a bit louder, but not much more. One of Bear's legs languished over his shoulder, allowing him to favor the supple flesh behind her knee with a ragged tongue kiss.

He felt her muscles contract in a manner that signaled orgasm and slowed his thrusts. Abandoning her knee, he lowered over her until she was caged beneath his rangy, muscle packed frame. He gave her his tongue to suck and intermittently urged her to take him and stay with him. He loved her with slow, long thrusts. The strokes were smooth and direct at times, smooth and rotating at others. Either way, they forced shameless and purely feminine cries of blooming delight past her lips.

Bear sucked his thumb with feverish need when his erection plunged her deep and deeper still. The feverish suckling seemed to heighten in intensity when he commended her skill.

"That's it," he shuddered, his face nestled between her breasts and hidden by the waves of silk covering his head.

Pope luxuriated in the mounds, taking enjoyment in their ampleness. The rich, caramel tone of her skin was enhanced by the lamp's quiet glow.

"That's it, love. That's it…" his words were labored, inspired by Bear's eager sucking on his finger and the eager squeeze of her inner muscles clutching his erection. He gathered fistfuls of the satin comforter while willing himself to hold out just a little longer. He wanted more time to savor the treat of his shaft sheathed by her sex. Again, he commended her skill.

"That's it, that's it-fuck…"

Bear lost her ability to suck with any fervor. She was gasping almost painfully when he began to pump with faster strokes that actually put pressure on her womb. His name was wrapped inside a pleasure over pained gasp. Then, she was apologizing-apologizing for coming hard. She could feel the heavy moisture oozing beneath her to soak the sheets.

"I'm sorry," she moaned never realizing how sweetly she endeared herself to the man claiming her.

For Pope, holding out to enjoy more of her body was a useless endeavor. He erupted hard and unapologetically-dousing her center with thick splashes of his release.

Bear whimpered. She was almost totally depleted by the pleasure she happily labored under. Lightly, Pope entwined his tongue around hers which had her whimpering again, He followed her helplessly, deeper into an erotic abyss.

~~~

They slipped into a coma like sleep soon after and remained there until the morning's wee hours. Bear began to fidget. She left the bed so she wouldn't wake Pope who had only slumbered in his coma for about 90 minutes.

He'd spent his time cradling Bear against him and enjoying the way she felt there. When she wiggled free and left the bed, he watched as she made her way to the sliding doors off the balcony. She took one of the scoop chairs there and spent a while staring off into the dark which

219

was still faintly alive with distant conversation of the night owl visitors to the alluring city. When over 40 minutes had passed, he went to her.

Bear didn't give a start when he cupped the back of her neck and gave a light squeeze. He tilted back her head in silent request for a kiss she willingly gave.

"Talk to me," he said when a breath of space existed between their mouths.

"It's hard to know you know *that* about me," she admitted without further prodding. "The one thing I wouldn't even tell the people I love most in the world had they not been right there with me."

"Me knowing doesn't change anything for me, Bear." He'd knelt to look right at her and then his mouth tightened as he fixed her with a resigned look.

"But that doesn't matter if you won't believe it," he said. "We won't have a shot if you can't believe it."

"I believe it when we-when we're there," she looked askance at the bed. "I can forget when we're there. I love the way you can make me forget it." The smile she fought to keep, wavered.

"And then later, afterwards...I wonder...what you must think of my...eagerness and if I was so eager...that night. Shit," she made a fist, knocked it to her thigh.

"I don't want to be messed up by this, Pope but it's hard."

He understood and, for a moment, considered telling her that the only thing he thought of her 'eagerness' was how goddamn lucky he was to be on the receiving end of it. "I can give you time if you think you need it," he told her instead. "But Bear, don't expect me to back off. Like I said, I have a hard time letting go of what's mine," he smirked when she gave him a look.

"Don't act like you didn't know I felt that way. It doesn't take long for me to get possessive over things that call to me."

"And what happens when things change?"

"Dammit Bear! Why the fuck do you keep expecting them to?"

"I'm, I-"

"You don't have anything to apologize for," he gave her a small shake for emphasis. "This is just...hell, what's that word you used? A crummy situation."

The phrasing made Bear smile and Pope took that as his cue to leave. He was about to cross from the balcony into the bedroom, but slowed his steps.

"I'll give you time, Bear but you should know I've been infatuated with wanting to know you since the first time I saw you at The Rascal on the phone with the poor bastard you were telling off. I didn't know who you were, didn't give a damn about what you did in the past or on that very day even. All I knew was if I didn't get out of there, I might do something that'd get my face slapped or you out of your clothes if you were game. Don't keep me waiting too long, Cub. I don't play too fair when it comes to getting things I already feel possessive over. Have a safe flight back, okay?"

He didn't wait for her to return the sentiment. Bear found herself alone in the room soon after.

# CHAPTER 20

$F$our days passed and Pope decided he'd given Bear long enough to come to grips with what was happening between them. Selfish? Yes. Pushy? Definitely. What could he say? This was new territory for him.

He had never really wooed a woman-never really had to. Women had always given him what he wanted. Minimal fuss-no effort. Then again, when the aim was sex, minimal fuss and effort was very often nothing out of the ordinary.

When the aim was the stuff worth fighting for, worth sacrificing for, he supposed all bets were off.

He woke that morning with the realization that not giving Bear time to 'deal' was quite simply about him not wanting her to face anymore of her nightmare alone. That line of thought had motivated him. He drove out to the ranch that afternoon with plans not to leave until they were in a better place than they'd been when they parted ways in Mexico.

At least, that had been in his plan. The actual unfolding of events had taken a far more hectic path. Given the time of day, he figured he'd find Bear at work in her office along the training hall so he started there.

What he found was a meeting in progress a few doors down from the office he knew to be hers. There was no need to worry over intruding, it seemed his presence was appreciated.

"Well, well, isn't this fortuitous?" Bear welcomed Pope with undeniable sarcasm from her seat at a wide, round table in the middle of the room.

"If it isn't my most generous client, slash ranch designer, slash security consultant. Please come in," she waved.

Pope did as requested and noted the others joining Bear in the sparse but warmly furnished room. Among the group of stone-faced men, he recognized Shaun Oates, Mike Hough and a few others. Judging from their expressions, he strongly suspected he was about to learn how it felt to be on the receiving end of one of Bear Clayton's tongue lashings.

"The rest of you are welcomed to stay," she was saying. "But seeing as how I've already heard your excuses-mmm-excuse me, *reasons*, I'm good with talking to Mr. Apostolou alone."

The conference room cleared in record time. The group had witnessed their boss take on some pretty formidable opponents but none quite so intimidating as the man she was about to square off with.

Pope made himself comfortable while the others hustled out. Bear didn't sit in the living area as her guest did, but opted for a leaning stance against the curve of the wide table.

Pope's expression went from cool curiosity to heightened expectancy when silence carried for over half a minute. "It might help if you start," he said.

Bear pushed off the table. "I plan to," she approached Pope where he sat looking subtly authoritative and she slammed something down on the low table before the sofa he enjoyed.

Pope peered over the table, leaned back. "Blueprints?"

"Don't be so modest. You're the reason those prints exist."

Pope sent another look toward the table, offered a scant shrug. "I don't recall drawing up any plans lately."

"I'm sure such a thing is beneath you- easier to suggest the job to someone else, right?"

Tiring of the inquiry, Pope shook his head once quickly. "This isn't what I came to see you about."

"Oh I'm sure," she dropped a spiteful look toward the low table. "Those are prelim sketches to transform the cottage into a brand new security rec house. The guys said you suggested it, thought it'd be good

223

to put folks in place to facilitate it during the soiree-kind of a trial run before any real construction begins."

"Oh yeah...so I did," Pope's approving smile turned inquisitive. "Please don't tell me you've got a problem with the idea, Cub? It's one of my finer ones if I do say so myself."

"I told you I wanted to tear it down."

"So you did, but it's not what you really want is it?"

"Don't you ever get sick of being such a know it all?" She added a nasty smirk to the question.

Pope took no offense. "I find it to be a useful quality."

Bear finally took a chair, choosing one that flanked the sofa. "Tell me how you came to your conclusions?"

"I'm just very good at reading people, Bear. Please don't hold it against me."

Bear spread her hands. "Then, by all means, share your report."

Pope was despising the task before he began. She didn't like being seen so clearly, he knew. Especially by him.

"I could tell how much you loved the place when you took me through it. When you talked about tearing it down, I could see your anger wasn't directed at the place so much as the situation. I think you would've come up with that idea on your own," he glanced toward the plans. "If it hadn't occurred to you already.

I suggested it to the guys, hoping they'd bring it to you. I'm sorry if they had to go a few rounds with the boss because of it."

"I see," Bear's smile was a knowing one. "Sorry for putting my guys in a bad spot-not sorry for going behind my back to them in the first place."

"That's right. I just don't feel comfortable apologizing for that part. Sorry."

Bear couldn't help it. She laughed.

Pope grinned, not so much out of amusement as he was out of sheer delight over her mood.

"What am I gonna do with you?" She threw back her head to laugh.

He raised a hand. "About fifty things just popped into my mind. If you'd care to hear them."

The conference room phone rang, but Bear took her time getting up. "I'm sure they're things that'll keep me very busy."

"Damn right they will." Looking every bit the scoundrel, Pope rested his head back on the sofa. "Busy, exhausted, satisfied...the list goes on."

Shaking her head, yet still smiling, Bear went to the phone on the credenza near the wide table.

Pope, still reclining on the sofa, indulged in the treat of watching her from afar. He enjoyed the way her breasts stretched out the word 'Boss' against the T-shirt that read 'Boss Here', not to mention the way her round bottom filled out the seat of the faded jeans she wore with black riding boots.

Gradually, he tuned into her conversation.

"He is?"

Pope noticed her demeanor change. He straightened on the sofa to watch her smooth at flyaway tendrils slipping from her low ponytail. The gesture had him smoothing a hand over his own hair worn in similar fashion that day.

"Send him on back," she said to the person she spoke with.

Pope watched her go to the front of the room. It took him some time to recognize the man who appeared in the doorway, but not much. Bear greeted Caleb Stein with a warm smile and open arms.

Caleb chuckled while taking Bear off her feet and swinging her a bit as he held her close.

"You said you'd call," her tone was breathless.

"Thought it'd be nice to surprise you."

"It was!" she laughed. Taking his hand, she pulled him into the room.

They'd taken no more than five steps when Bear felt Caleb's hand leave hers. She turned in time to see him crashing into the conference table.

"What the fuck?! Pope!" Bear was running toward the demolished table where Caleb lay on his stomach amid slashes of splintered wood.

As quickly as she ran, she was no match for Pope who caught Caleb around the scruff of his neck and hoisted him to his feet. Pope caught the other man in a choke hold that had his adversary beating his fist to Pope's forearm.

Caleb countered the move with an elbow to Pope's gut and earned his release. Pope nearly got a fist to the temple for his trouble. Instead, he punished Caleb's jaw with a blow that sent the man to his knees. Again, jerking Caleb up by his shirt collar, Pope neatly redeposited him into the table debris.

"Dammit Pope! Stop!" Fists clenched and beating the air, Bear's gaze would've spewed hot mocha if it were possible.

Pope listened, blinking as he turned to face her. He wore a look which hinted that his anger had made him lose track of where he was. The look of outrage on Bear's lovely dark face, was reminder enough.

"What the hell?!" She cried, rushing to Caleb and helping him to sit.

"You know him?" Pope inhaled deeply, slowly regaining his calm.

"I did greet him with a hug. That tends to indicate familiarity." Bear tried to keep Caleb elevated.

"I'm fine, Bear," Caleb winced a little as he moved. "Just a little roughhousing," he tried for a little laughter. "Right, Po? Unless you lost that killer left of yours? That was a pulled punch if I ever felt one."

"You know me so well." The quiet rage was alive in Pope's voice.

Caleb slanted a wink to Bear. "See? I'm fine, Hon."

Bear didn't miss Pope's guttural sound charging the air over Caleb's endearment.

"How do you know him, Bear?" Pope sensed his anger hadn't vanished, merely simmered ready-eager for the chance to boil again.

Bear didn't answer, instead she helped Caleb to his feet. Her hand to Pope's abdomen, was all she needed to have him move out of her way.

"Sit down, Pope," she ordered while getting Caleb settled in one of the arm chairs.

Pope did as he was told, all but snarling as he returned to the sofa. He gritted his teeth over the sound of Caleb sweetly thanking Bear for her help. He accepted the man's cunning wink when their gazes met, but ordered himself to stay put. Pope reciprocated the cunning wink when Bear left Caleb to join him on the sofa.

Bear sat for a moment shaking her head at Pope as though she were a teacher at her wits end with a difficult student. "I know Caleb. I've known Caleb longer than I've known you."

"Hmph."

"Caleb," Bear scolded the man for the gesture and gave him a dose of the same head shaking. "He and his partner drove us that night...to the hotel."

"Something I'll regret forever," Caleb added when Pope sent a malicious dark glare his way.

"I couldn't go any longer without saying that to your face, Berrill. I owe you at least that," Caleb went on.

"It was a long time ago and it wasn't your fault," Bear huffed out a breath and looked to Pope. "If it wasn't for Caleb and his partner...?"

"Luke," Caleb supplied.

"We wouldn't have gotten those security discs as a parting gift." Again, Bear turned to Caleb. "Those discs helped me and my friends get on our feet in a totally screwed way but that's life for you."

"Yeah," Caleb looked stressed. "I heard the story."

"Then you know you don't owe me anything."

"Except the truth, Bear. I at least owe you the truth about that night."

~~~

"That's bullshit," Pope snapped some twenty minutes into Caleb's story. "Secrets last about as long in the GAN as a bottle of rum passed around after a mission. No way could something like that have been kept quiet."

"It could if it were kept between a select few-or two." Caleb countered.

"My dear half brother and his bestie," Pope needed only a second to puzzle out the riddle.

"The revelations from that disc stirred a lot of unrest," Caleb continued. "Unrest breeds nerves- nerves inspire talking. Lots of it. Maybe you got a whiff of that, Po when you were back there a few weeks ago? Should I offer condolences?"

"Only if you'd like to leave here on your back." Pope's light threat was punctuated by a slight smile.

Caleb returned the smile with a chuckle.

Bear was taking no chances on taking the good natured ribbing at face value. "So what does all this mean?" She asked to put the discussion back on track. "Are you saying those men would've died whether we'd been there or not?"

227

"It's only a rumor-a very quiet one." Caleb leaned over to scrub his face with his hands. "Some say Brody and Jake were plotting a coup-unhappy because of the way their dads were running the show. I can confirm that part's true. They were supremely pissed that Harris and Zubin got the higher rank when the old men sent them to track down the bag."

"Bag?" Pope queried.

"Bag with the discs," Bear supplied.

"Having to answer to Harris and Zoo really chapped their entitled, overfed asses especially having to answer to the likes of those two."

"What's so special about them?" Bear asked, reading nothing into the quick look Caleb sent Pope.

"They had issue with guys who came up in the military ranks of the GAN." Caleb finished, following Pope's quick head shake in response to his questioning look.

Bear was too busy working to puzzle out another riddle. "Why would they go after The Ten? I mean, wouldn't they need them after they became the new bosses? Why not go after their dads instead?"

"Brody and Jake weren't so sure they'd *be* the bosses." Caleb shared. "Turns out they had reason to be wary."

Caleb's pointed look to Pope didn't go unnoticed that time.

"What?" Bear shifted her gaze between both men.

Pope answered. "Nathan Alberts left me everything he valued in the world. Including his partnership in the GAN."

"Nice." Bear drawled, and then looked back to Caleb. "So... taking out The Ten was their strong arm tactic? Pretty weak."

"You're not the first to think so."

"You don't think it was about strong-arming the old men." Pope's voice surged with knowing.

Caleb shook his head. "Like Bear said, it's weak. It's going around quietly that taking out The Ten was over something else. When they were killed by...other means," he looked to Bear. "The crew rallied for a common purpose."

"Revenge on Roya and the recovery of those discs," Pope guessed.

"But that was later," Bear recalled. "If the plan was to take out your board, when did the plan change? We were there for...for hours," she lost some of her enthusiasm for the conversation and left the sofa.

"Maybe they acted before anyone else could," Caleb theorized.

"You and Luke were on post that night." Pope shrugged. "Did anyone come snooping around the suite trying to get in?"

"Well no, I-" Caleb gave a quick frown. "Brody, Jake, a few of their guys were in and out early, while things were...just getting started," he cleared his throat. "Later it-it was quiet enough to hear a pin drop up there-for a while anyway."

Caleb sent another look to Pope along with a nod that said it was best he go. Pope watched while Caleb went to where Bear stood looking down at her wrecked table. The set look on her face was a clear indicator that she wasn't really seeing what she looked at.

Caleb put a light massage to Bear's shoulders, "Send me a bill for the table, alright?"

"I wouldn't think of it," Bear gave a playfully dignified sniff. "The bill's going to your colleague back there."

Caleb's laughter was soft. "Hope I didn't make things worse by telling you about those rumors."

"It's okay. I guess with a group that vile, me and my friends wouldn't be the only ones who'd want them dead."

"I never meant to upset you with this, Bear. I remember how devastated you and your friends were that night."

Her smile was quietly somber. "There were a lot of devastating moments that night. The smoke never clears when you're dealing with the memory of killing ten men."

"Yeah," Caleb's lashes began to bat incessantly as he worked to ease a frown.

"What is it?"

"Just um..." He covered Bear's hand where she squeezed his wrist. "I'm so sorry, Bear. We-me and Luke we've taken so many girls on nights out with The Ten. Something about you and your friends though...you guys got to us- Luke...I think he's a little in love with your friend. The blonde."

"Prin." Bear smiled. "She thought you were both good guys. She doesn't give those kinds of compliments easy."

Caleb grinned. "I'll be sure to tell Luke. Listen, I um, I'll get out of your hair now."

"I'll walk you out, Cale," Pope offered, having watched Caleb and Bear exchange hugs and cheek kisses across the room.

"Pope."

229

He waved off Bear's warning call and nodded. "I promise to be good."

"So...you and Bear, huh?" Caleb chuckled when he and Pope left the room. "If I'd taken her for coffee the way I wanted to, instead of that freak show...who knows? So? How serious is it?"

"Serious enough for me to break your hands if you ever touch her again." Lethal certainty held Pope's promise. "Now why don't we cut the shit and you tell me what you wouldn't say to her."

Caleb bristled but couldn't withhold his smile. "Nothing gets by the apostle," he referenced Pope's well-known and well-placed nickname inside the GAN.

"Let's have it, Cale. What is it you wouldn't say when she pressed?"

Caleb wasted barely another second. "I held back because I wasn't going to make her relive that shit by giving me a detailed account of what happened that night. I didn't think asking what weapons they used to kill those shits would've been the most sensitive course of action, do you?"

"Why would you need to know that?"

"How close did you follow the coverage once the board members were found and...in the various places they were planted?" Caleb asked.

"Not close at all," Pope's manner was resigned. "But then again, I really didn't give a fuck."

"Few inside the GAN did, but *if* you had, you'd have most likely heard that four of them had a combination of knife and bullet wounds."

"So?"

"So there was no gun found at the scene. The only one there was the one Bear gave me that night after the mess was over. She'd carried it out in the pocket of the robe she was wearing. Thing had a full clip, Po and it had no traces of being fired."

Discovery dawned for Pope. "Jesus."

"Yeah," Caleb's manner was grim. "Somebody else was in that room with them. Somebody with orders of their own."

"How do we know it wasn't you?" The malicious tint returned to Pope's face. "We all know you and Luke were part of Brody's and Jake's crew, a crew that also included Harris and that psychopath Zubin. You two were there when they killed Patch. Tell me why I shouldn't finish what I started in there?" He cocked his head toward the conference room door.

"We wanted to be on that crew. Me and Luke," Caleb worked a hand over his nape. "We're sorry about Patroclus but we couldn't do anything to jeopardize our plan. It was the only way we could keep tabs on who might've been coming after those girls. Didn't seem like anyone would ever catch a trace of 'em and then Zoo killed Roya out of the blue and he and Harris were on a mission to find them."

"Roya's son told us his dad had sources inside the GAN." Pope's gaze narrowed to emit slices of blue flame. "It was you and Luke, right?"

Caleb smiled to confirm. "But after Roya's death, Harris and Zubin cut the rest of us out of the loop-including Brody and Jake. It was like they'd said to hell with it. I mean, it'd already been six years so what the hell? But someone else was definitely in that room, Po and no one knows who or why. Those discs can tell us, though. I sure as hell can't see Brody and Jake backing off this again especially now with you claiming half the front seat."

"No," Grimness eased in next to the maliciousness of Pope's expression. "Me either."

"Anyway," Caleb sighed. "Since the discs in question are the ones from inside that room, my guess is we'll never know. I can't see any woman being okay with having something like that reviewed-no matter the reason."

"I can't either."

"I really am sorry about Patch, man. He was a good guy."

Pope agreed with a slow nod. He accepted Caleb's hand when he offered and considered the new revelations as Caleb headed off.

~~~

Pope returned to the conference room where Bear was curled on the sofa and looking toward the mess in the back of the room.

"How much do I owe you?" He asked.

"Not sure yet. You can be sure I'll look for the most expensive table I can find, though."

"I'd expect nothing less." Grinning, Pope took the easy chair nearest the end of the sofa Bear occupied. "I apologize for taking liberties with the cottage."

"Too late. Apologizing now won't make me look for a cheaper table."

"Like I said, I'd expect nothing less." He'd reached for the foot she'd propped on the low coffee table, pulled it into his lap and tugged off the riding boot.

For a time, they sat in quiet. Pope reclined on the chair, eyes closed. Bear sighed appreciatively of his massage.

"What do you think it was that Caleb wouldn't say?"

"What do you mean?" Pope continued the massage.

"So you didn't notice how he hustled to get out of my question before he left?"

"I thought *I* was supposed to be the know it all?" He gave her the benefit of his dazzling stare.

Bear shrugged. "Guess I'm learning from the best."

"Caleb thinks someone else was in the room that night besides you, your friends and The Ten." Pope wasn't surprised when she gawked.

"How is that possible?" She breathed and then listened to him explain about the four bodies they found with the bullet wounds.

"I thought I was crazy," she said once he'd finished.

"Crazy?"

Bear rested back on the sofa, shook her head against it. "I told Caleb I thought I heard gunshots that night I-later, I thought I just imagined it. I found a gun in one of the rooms, thought maybe I'd fired it."

"Caleb says you didn't. He also says the only way to know for sure is maybe to see the discs." Pope's gaze wavered slightly. "The ones from inside the room," he added, feeling her foot stiffen in his grasp as he'd expected it to. When she tried to tug it free, his grip firmed.

"Nothin' to be afraid of, babe."

She only shook her head as if she hadn't heard him. "I knew this would happen. Knew we wouldn't be able to skip this part. Tee was right, there's no escaping the truth."

Pope left the chair, sat on the coffee table instead, he put his hands to her thighs and squeezed. "Do you remember what I told you in Mexico? Me knowing doesn't change a thing."

"It's not just you knowing, Pope. It-it's you...*seeing*. It's like you're there watching while they-while I..."

Pope felt his earlier rage return to slow simmer, spurned by what she couldn't say.

"I need some time with this, Pope."

"Take all the time you need."

She shuddered out a laugh. "If I do that, you'll never see them."

She tried to keep her tone light, but Pope could tell the effort cost her.

"Nothing changes, Bear."

*Except the man I'm falling for is about to wind up hating me.* She kept her response silent, but the thought caused her to cringe visibly.

Pope pulled her close then, tucking her tight into him. "Forget what I said. We'll find another way."

"There *is* no other way," she pushed free of his embrace. "There is no other way, Pope. Don't worry. I'll get my act together. You'll have the discs soon." There was a chime she recognized as her phone. Frowning, she read the screen.

"Need to take it?" Pope stood.

She shook her head. "It can wait."

Pope pulled her close again. "Nothing changes, Cub. I mean that."

"Damn right it doesn't," she managed a watery laugh. "You still owe me for that table." Managing another weak laugh, she put an absent pat to his chest. "Can you show yourself out?"

Pope held on, propped her chin to his fist. "How 'bout together?" Leaning closer, he put a sweet kiss to her mouth.

Bear nodded, her smile a little less sad. Pope tugged her hand over the bend of his elbow and escorted her from the conference room.

# CHAPTER 21

"At the risk of repeating myself I have to ask, do you believe him?"

"Huh?" Pope redirected his frown from the juice glass he nursed to Mercuri instead.

Smiling, Mercuri added another helping of eggs to the platter he'd already scraped clean. "I asked you this same question almost two weeks ago when you came to me with that story of Gerrick's."

Pope gave an eyeroll and downed the rest of the juice. "Unlike Gerrick's story, Caleb's isn't totally unbelievable."

"So you decided to ask Bear to let you see the discs?"

"I already have."

Mercuri sat back from the table. Pope had called about getting together for breakfast that morning. They met in the cafeteria of Mercuri Fleets' San Francisco offices. Mercuri however, had been the only one to partake of breakfast.

"What'd she say?" Mercuri forgot about his eggs.

"Told me she needed to think about it. That was yesterday. This morning she um...texted me. Said she'd bring them over tonight."

"And your first reaction was to call me for breakfast."

234

"It's not the day for teasing me, Merc." Pope left his chair with such force, he caused it to do a three-legged teeter.

"Alright," Mercuri seamlessly recaptured his serious persona. "Why the fuck did you ask her to see that?"

"Seriously, Merc? There's no other way to know who was in there with them."

"So? Forget it. Who cares about who put those asswipes in their graves? What you need to know is what Brody and Jake are up to."

"Maybe the mystery person on those discs could tell us."

"If there is one." Mercuri threw back. "Think Po. Do you honestly believe all this? Do you really think Brody and Jake haven't taken care of whoever could implicate them?"

Pope was silent, considering the valid queries.

"Trust me, Po. You don't want the shit on those discs inside your head."

Pope studied his friend more closely then. "You've seen them, haven't you?"

Mercuri pushed back from the table. His appetite had totally deserted him. "I've seen the security footage from the main entrance-it's what me and Rand used for the In Scope feature. But there's a lot more. The entire place was wired-so was the hotel suite and each room where they kept the girls. They've each got their own...customized videolog of that night."

"You saw Tee's?"

"Totally by accident the way it happened, but she uh...she wanted me to see it. Felt like she was being dishonest somehow by not offering it up. Can you believe that?"

Pope watched his usually unshakeable friend show signs of being precisely that. He was glad he'd snagged one of the small, private dining rooms for their meal.

"What happened, Merc?"

The quietly presented question seemed to ease the tension fueling Mercuri's grim expression.

"Trashed my office," he admitted with a lethal grin. "Think I had my limit of stiff drinks. Couldn't let myself go too far, though. She was there and I couldn't let her see me that way."

"Did it cause trouble for you guys?"

"Not the way you mean. I was good once I trashed my office and got a little juiced. Except for wishing like hell I had at least one of those fucks' necks to snap, I handled it okay."

"And Tee? Right." Pope answered his own question after a few beats of silence from Mercuri. "Is she getting better about you knowing?"

"As 'better' as any woman could be with any man knowing that about her."

"That why you're proposing?"

Any lingering grimness fled Mercuri's expression. "I'm proposing because I love her and want her to know how serious I am when I tell her she's mine and I'm hers."

"Yeah," Pope spoke almost to himself as he began to walk the room.

"But this may all work out fine," Mercuri smiled. "You and Bear aren't there yet. It's still all about sex, right?"

Pope didn't bother to waste a glare on Mercuri and decided a warning would suffice. "Remember what I said about this not being the day to tease me?" He managed a grin when Mercuri responded with a laugh.

"I'm in love with her, Mercuri." Pope loosed a laugh of his own. "Hell, have you ever heard me say anything so stupid?"

"Actually I have," Mercuri chided and then raised a hand. "But that isn't stupid." He settled back as Pope listed all his reasons to the contrary.

"...and we've only known each other less than a minute. I don't really know her at all. She sure as hell doesn't know me-none of the things she should, anyway."

"But you know you love her."

"Like I said, stupid."

Mercuri shook his head. "Pope, I don't profess to understand love, but what I believe I've learned is that it's not about what you learn about each other's pasts, but what you learn about each other." Mercuri leaned against the wall, looking out over the room as though he weren't really seeing it.

"After I got past how goddamn gorgeous she was, it was Tee's...sadness and that haunted way she had about herself that gripped me and wouldn't let go. Then, it was that fierce love she's got for her friends. She'd throw herself in front of a bus to save them."

Pope's soft laughter hit the air. "She'd have to fight Bear for the chance. Did you know that ranch of hers sponsors a kids' week? A full week she devotes to kids from all across the state-all walks of life."

Mercuri returned to the table and listened.

"One day she has a game creator giving away all kinds of freebies," Pope raved. "Next, it's a movie day, full barbeque day...she refuses to endorse any candidate who doesn't have a robust platform for kids. She's even tougher on the locals-ones who don't do anything worth a damn." He smoothed a hand over his jaw while he walked the cozy room.

"She's tough as hell on her employees, but if they ask it, she'll arrange getaways for the ones who don't have a clue how to romance their wives," he laughed softly over the fact.

"Sounds like you know the lady pretty well," Mercuri said once his laughter had tapered. "You also know how useless it is to wait around for the right time."

"Because there *is* no right time," Pope returned without hesitation. Yes, that was a truth he was abundantly familiar with.

\*\*\*

Bear hadn't taken the time to enjoy her last visit to Pope's place on its lonely cliff overlooking the Pacific. She hadn't *taken* the time because the previous trip hadn't been for enjoyment.

The situation hadn't changed, but she had enjoyed the evening's drive much more than the last. Perhaps, it was because she'd gone ahead and accepted that it was over between her and Pope.

Had it ever really began? She wondered. Afterall, they'd only really had some pretty amazing sex. Her hand fisted where she gripped the steering wheel. Of course, she knew it was more than amazing sex. It was why she was doing her damndest to psyche herself into being okay with letting the man go.

She beat her fist to the steering wheel then and asked how the hell she'd let herself fall in love with him. Then again, she didn't suppose she'd had much choice. Men like Pope Apostolou didn't wait meekly in the shadows while a woman made up her mind about him. Men like Pope made their presence known in almost every way imaginable- in the most sensual, irresistible ways.

"Bear..." she cautioned herself, feeling the twinge of need take residence somewhere she preferred not to think about.

Men like Pope had ways that surpassed sensuality. Ways that were simply endearing-like the bone-deep love he had for his friends. Not to mention the way he carried himself-like a sleeping giant. He was a man all too aware of the power he commanded, yet confident enough to opt for gentleness over strength.

Those were the ways that opened the door to stronger emotions-ones far more powerful and longer lasting than lust. They were ways with the power to overcome the reality of a man seeing the woman he was to hold dear, being held by strangers who subjected her to all manner of things.

"You're a fucking idiot, Bear. There *is* no such power." She grumbled, clenching her fist with visions of using it on herself.

Still, those...ways of his had her tumbling happily and merrily into all the L word entailed. And it terrified her.

It terrified her so, that she was on her way to making sure her terror ended-and soon. Unclenching her fist on the wheel, she patted her hand to the hard plastic folder containing the infamous discs. They would do the trick, there was no doubting that. She'd even made sure of it by including the disc she should've already burned.

She thought back to when she'd called Tee a fool for so much as wanting to breathe a word about those recordings to Mercuri. Now, she was going one step further in supplying Pope with the complete collection. They had only given Mercuri the footage from the hotel's main entrance. What she was giving to Pope was everything Caleb Stein had passed to her that night. With the exception of LuCarolyn's, Prin's and Tee's recordings, there was an account of everyone who had been inside the hotel-on every floor, in every room.

All that data, she mused; taking the dirt road leading to Pope's. All that data and only one piece had the power to destroy the one thing she was as terrified to keep as she was to lose.

~~~

She didn't find him leaning against the towering columns lining his porch as she had upon her last visit. She hadn't expected to. He'd responded to her text that morning with one of his own, giving her instructions to just 'come on in' when she got there.

Bear parked the Jeep and hopped out. She couldn't resist taking a moment to breathe in the sea air and humble herself before the stunning view. By then, the evening sky only showed a hint of the rich, purplish pink tint it had when she began her drive.

Bear shook herself free of captivation and grabbed the folder from the seat. She made a quick sprint up the wide, front porch steps.

"Pope?" She hadn't really expected to find him waiting by the door when she pushed it open.

Bear made her way into the living room, her white canvas shoes barely made a sound when they covered the travertine floors.

"Pope?" Her call had an absent tinge as the house took her breath away once more.

Some might accuse the designer of having a proclivity for museums, but Bear found the place welcoming. A perfect spot for clearing the mind, she thought, running her fingers across the back of a midnight blue recliner among the bay of sofas in the high ceilinged room.

The place was mostly moonlit as it'd been during her last visit. The memory had Bear again shaking off a bewitched state and switching direction from the livingroom to the grand *Gone With the Wind* type staircase toward the rear of the room. The stairs seemed wider than those on the porch and were carpeted in a shade of blue. The shade wasn't quite as vivid as a certain pair of eyes, but one that reminded her of them just the same.

"Pope?!" She'd scaled the staircase and was taking the landing. Slowly, she headed toward the left corridor.

"Are you here?! If not, I'm leaving!"

"Here I am."

The deep, easy tone had Bear shrieking and whirling to find him right behind her. "Jesus!" She closed her eyes and inhaled deeply. "Could you at least breathe heavy or something to let me know you're around?"

"I didn't mean to scare you, Cub."

"Like hell," she thrust the disc folder at his chest.

Pope took it without looking at it and set it to a wide ledge along the corridor.

"So that's that," Bear posted up on her shoe soles and then moved to walk around him when he didn't budge. He caught her arm, turned her back toward the direction she'd been heading.

"I don't have time for this-"

"You'll want to make time."

"Pushy *and* a know it all."

"I try."

239

"Pope-"

"Quiet."

She cooperated. Easy, once they reached their destination. The room was surprisingly simple given the majesty the rest of the house screamed. Globe-shaped lamps on end tables sat next to the bed that looked to be the size of a lake. There was a screened fireplace to one side of the room and a powerful looking telescope to the other.

The bed took up an immense portion of the deep, brown hardwoods but it wasn't what rendered Bear speechless. She could find no words for the view from the space. She'd agree that it even outmatched the one she'd recently enjoyed in Mexico.

Talk about being humbled, she sat along the foot of the bed. "Amazing," she whispered.

Pope sighed then, tugging his gaze from Bear to the moonlit waves and shore beyond the room's retractable glass walls. They offered a sweeping vantage point.

"Sometimes, I open the place up and let the air in," he told her.

"How often is that?"

"Not often. I don't spend a lot of time out here. Until lately, I never had a good reason to."

His words jiggled her simmering unease that had Bear pushing to her feet. "Well, this is really great-"

He was there before her when she stood. "I'm in love with you." He said it simply, matter-of-factly and with unwavering certainty.

"You can't," Bear reclaimed her spot along the center edge of the bed.

Pope followed, taking a knee before her. "I can do anything and that's done, Bear. It's not changing."

"It will."

"I don't need to see them."

"Why?"

Pope grinned. Bear's expression was suspicion at its finest.

"I told you I'd find another way." He smoothed his hands along her thighs.

"You have to see them." She shook her head.

"Them, Cub? Or one in particular?"

She closed her eyes.

"Why would you want me to see that or think I'd want to?"

"So you'll know-"

"So I'll know or so I'll walk away?"

"Don't you already have that answer too?"

"I wouldn't have asked if I did," he squeezed her thigh. "Do you want me to walk away, Bear?"

She rolled her eyes, but shook her head.

"I'd like to hear you say it."

"No, but-"

He kissed her, joining her on the bed when his tongue went deep. So deep, Bear moaned suddenly, sharply in response. It was pointless to seek escape, but she tried and wrenched her mouth from his. Escaping the bed was pointless as well, given its size and Pope's.

He caught her easily when she thought to crawl away. One hand locked over a trim ankle and he dragged her back to where he wanted her. He destroyed any plans she had for a second attempt and made quick work of undoing the fastening of her denim capris.

Bear couldn't verbalize resistance, but she did fold shaking hands over his busy ones. "Wait," she managed when he yanked down the denims.

He stopped only when her shoes got in the way. Bear watched them fly in opposite directions across the room. Her capris followed soon after, joining a shoe that landed near the open doorway.

"Wait, I-" she gasped out a whimper when his thumb launched an assault on her clit, still snug beneath her panties.

"Pope please I-I didn't come-"

"You will."

Her breathless laughter escaped before she tried again. "I didn't come for this."

He stopped then, leaning back to watch her. "You're really saying no to me?" He took her hand, put it to a denim clad thigh outlined with the thick, elongated ridge of muscle.

She couldn't resist squeezing in addition to squirming in anticipation of receiving.

"I didn't think so," he murmured as though speaking to himself.

Bear bit down on her thumbnail while Pope tugged her from the scrap of lace hugging her hips. She wasn't surprised to hear them rip.

"Sorry about that."

His half-assed apology would've made her laugh had she not been choking out a gasp in reaction to being claimed by his wicked thumb. His middle finger mercilessly stimulated her clit with tormenting

241

rotations. She turned her face into one of the massive pillows lining the bed and shuddered her pleasure into the midnight blue casing.

Sensation flowed as she squeezed his thrusting finger. Greedy for more, she squeezed a breast, her nail flicking at the nipple hardened beneath her T-shirt. Pope promptly slapped away her hand and she could've sobbed when he deprived her of his touch. Suddenly, he'd scooped her up by the waist and tossed her down closer to the upper edge of the bed.

Bear heard him slam a hand against the wall and the room turned a dim gold. Her eyes adjusted to the lighting while her ears picked up on the sound of more ripping fabric. Her shirt.

Pope wanted to see her, needed to see the lithe frame in motion as it responded to his touch. He wanted his eyes to have the treat of roaming the dewy soft caramel toned skin, same as his fingers did. His fist stroked the curve of her breast and then on past her ribcage. His left dimple flashed in reaction to the smile he gave when she moved to touch herself, but thought twice about having her hands slapped away again. She eased her palms over his thighs instead. He didn't stop her when she curled her fingers over his jean fastening. Dexterously, she released the button fly that strained against the pressure put to it by his erection.

Bear was determined then to have him as nude as she was. She pushed up to free him from the denims. He wore nothing beneath them and the discovery made her mouth dry. She abandoned the jean fastening in order to relieve him of the lightweight V-neck sweater. It was easy to tug him free of the loose, finely made garment.

Pope was no help. He only followed Bear's every move with his electric gaze. Bear didn't risk eye contact, knowing full well the jolting capability of his vibrant stare would render her incapable.

She got the sweater over his head and tossed it. As he'd yet to stop her, she pushed him toward the head of the bed, urging him to take her place. Once he'd leaned against the pillows crowded there, she resumed her work with his jeans.

Pope remained notoriously unhelpful, barely moving when Bear tugged at the loose fitting denims. She managed to get them just below his perfect ass. Good enough, for it freed the part of him she most hungered for.

"Bear," he squeezed her elbow when her head lowered.

She retaliated with one dismissive swat to his wrist in route to her destination. She outlined his stunning length with the tip of her nose and then her tongue. The act weakened him instantly-visibly- against the pillows. She repeated the move, her tongue bathing the purplish veins crossing his copper-toned shaft. She took extra time at its wide crown. Her heart hammered in her ears when she took it inside her mouth. Memories of the organ's ability to stretch and penetrate, sent need dampening her thighs. Triumph chilled her skin when he grunted her name and then a lurid curse.

Her hair pampered his chest and abs until he reached out to smooth it from her face. She released the softest moans as she worked over him. The sight of her loving him like he was her favorite treat and the sound of her moaning, took Pope outside himself. His hand, useless then, fell to the tangle of covers. His hips, the only part of his body seemingly able to move, began faint feverish drives.

"Shit," he hissed when the familiar tightening took hold of his dick much too soon. He savored a few more-a little more than a few- of the sultry thrusts into her mouth.

"Fuck," the quiet roar underscored his voice then. He forced himself up, toppling Bear to her stomach in the process.

She looked up at him, her mocha gaze blazing with surprise and a touch of hurt over his treatment. It didn't take long for her to see how far gone he was.

Pope's eyes lowered to her mouth where droplets of his pre-cum glistened. For the second time that night, he was dragging her back to him and ripping out of his jeans in the process. He kicked them past bare feet he'd padded around in for most of the afternoon.

He kept Bear on her stomach, massive hands smothering her hips to position her to receive him. She cried out when he took her, the sound a cross between gasp and sob. His response to the sound was another ruthless thrust that elicited the same response.

Bear gripped the thick, navy satin comforter for purchase and met the erotic lunges with her own wicked fire. Still pumping into her, Pope leaned down to cup her chin. He turned her in for a kiss she willing gave and tasted his body on her tongue. The discovery had Pope melting over her amid his fierce claiming.

"Christ, Bear..." he breathed against her mouth moments before he withdrew to put her on her back. He wanted to see her beautiful eyes glazing and overdosed by passion when he came inside her. He drew a shapely leg up high to rest against his chest. Bear's cries were shameless and steady when he plied the back of her knee with a wet, famished suckle.

He took her with the same stretching penetrating thrusts that sent her out of her mind with pleasure. He kept her immobile with one leg at his chest while the other lay trapped to the bed thanks to his hand on her thigh.

"Pope…"

"I know, love," he understood they had both reached their limits. He was, in no way, done with her though. As it had happened in Mexico he'd uncovered a new layer of her mystery that night. For the time being, he was going to enjoy that success immensely. He covered her again, giving her some but not all of his weight even when she slid her arms around his waist in an attempt to draw him closer.

Bear shuddered into his chest when Pope erupted to coat her walls with generous splashes of his need. Pope exchanged his hold on her for one on the sheets, fearing he'd bruise her as climax had its way.

"No," she moaned when he at last relieved her of his weight.

His response was to draw her back next to him, burying his face in the lavender and talc scented crook of her neck. Relaxation was instant. Sleep visited quickly and deeply.

~~~

Bear woke, far more contentedly than she probably should have given all that had occurred the night before. At the top of that list was Pope's unexpected confession.

Unexpected? She turned her face into a pillow and winced. She'd known, hoped, suspected at least that his feelings might be heading where hers surely were. Now, she knew without a doubt. He'd said so himself.

He also said he didn't need to see the recordings. She couldn't take the coward's way out though. She'd leave them and let the chips fall. If they fell badly, then this was never meant for her in the first place.

Ordering herself to be alright with that, she carefully left the bed and quietly searched the room for her clothes. Her jeans and shoes were the only things fit to wear. She clutched them to her chest then.

As he owed her a shirt, she took the very nice sweater she'd stripped off him. She returned to the bed, instead of racing right out and kneeled next to the side he'd taken.

She watched him resting on his stomach, his face turned into a pillow. The sheet rode scandalously low on his hips, but she resisted the urge to run her fingers across his wide, muscular back. Instead, she gently toyed with the glossy, dark waves of his hair.

"I'm in love with you too," she whispered. "So much, that the fear that I'll...fuck it up is one I can't seem to conquer. I... I'm sorry," she spoke the apology into his hair and then rushed from the room to dress downstairs.

Hearing her confession and quite content then, Pope smiled into his pillow and snuggled in for a little more sleep.

# CHAPTER 22

Bear had hosted her annual shooting soiree for the past three years. The months she and her staff sank into the planning were always worth it.

Her steadfast rules for keeping the guest list to a tidy 100 attendees had proved to be far more of a challenge for the 4th annual event. There were a few complaints on that score and Bear didn't sweat it overmuch. She decided it'd be satisfying to accept any surprises that might arise if it meant the chance to unveil Senator Christopher Morrow for the phony self-serving figurehead he was.

That year's soiree dinner; the first ever held in conjunction with the shooting weekend, was also a fundraiser. Guests were encouraged to visit the giving table any time before dinner was served to give and generously to the city's and state's various independent organizations that serviced at risk youth.

As far as Bear knew, Morrow had never done anything for his home state except to ask for its vote. She was looking forward to the dinner, during which, donor's names would be announced at various intervals throughout the meal and over the remainder of the evening. Morrow's name was sure to be absent from the list.

Aside from the Senator's attendance, Bear had broke the rules to include friendlier faces to the guest list. She made her way through the crowd, mingling and making small talk. She saw Mercuri and Tee on the large dancefloor in front of the wide stage that showcased the live jazz band booked for the event. Bear watched the couple, smiling at the love and desire radiating off them like sunbeams.

"Way to go, Tee," she whispered and felt the subtle pressure of tears behind her eyes. Before the pressure grew too pronounced, she felt arms enfolding her into a tight squeeze and giving her a little shake.

"Told you this would be a good idea."

Bear shook her head, her smile gaining definition at the sound of Mike's voice near her ear.

"Yes, yes you did. So how long am I gonna have to hear you guys gloat about it?" She turned in Mike's arms to see his handsome dark face twist with a playful grimace.

Mike pretended to debate. "I'm guessing on at least a few months."

"Where's Shaun?" Bear asked once she and Mike had shared a round of healthy laughter.

"Over at the giving table, I think."

"Anybody seen Morrow over there?"

Mike shook his head. "Don't think he's gotten around to it yet according to security."

Bear's smile was serene. She had insisted her team keep a close eye on the senator. "He's got no idea about those donation announcements I'm planning for later." She gave into a playful shiver. "It's not nice to be petty, but sometimes it feels so good."

Mike and Bear were still laughing when she suddenly choked on the gesture. Mike followed the direction of her panicked, fixed stare and he grinned.

"Shaun and I asked Mr. Apostolou to drop by if he could- to see what kind of spread we put out. Maybe next year he and his friends could attend for the soiree. Think of the donations *they'd* put down." Mike gave Bear another squeeze and then headed toward Pope who he greeted with a hearty handshake and shoulder pat.

The men conversed for a few moments, giving Bear time to compose herself. It had been days since she'd seen him- left him with the discs. She was just getting used to the fact that they were done before they really began.

*Liar*, a voice hissed inside her head. Bear sized him up, completely out of costume for the black tie affair but no less devastating in dark trousers and the matching sportcoat under which he wore a cream shirt open at the collar.

How did any woman 'get used' to the idea of being done with a man like that? Not easily. No where near as easily as the way she was trying to convince herself she was.

Pope finished his chat with Mike and made his way toward Bear. She ignored the chill taking hold of her bare arms and kept her smile welcoming.

"I see you made the guest list."

Pope grinned, scanning the scene before his eyes. "You really employ a great group of guys," he said.

"Yeah and it doesn't hurt that they're all a little in love with you," Bear teased.

Pope couldn't resist then smoothing the back of his hand down her arm. "Surely they're not the only ones, Cub?"

Her gaze faltered as her breathing elevated. "Pope-"

"The discs," he injected and waited to see her panicked gaze snap back to his face. "I left the folder at the security house."

She stiffened. "Is that all you did with them?"

"That's all I did with them."

Her panic glazed over to suspicion as she searched his bright eyes with her darker ones. "But why-"

"I told you why."

She didn't want to discuss what had been said. Not there, anyway. Thankfully, Pope didn't seem to be in the mood to discuss it any further either.

"Let's dance," he said instead.

"Uh-no."

"Come on," he raked his gaze down the length of her. "You can't come to an event like this in a dress like that and not expect to claim your share of offers to the floor."

Bear cast a wary look to the floor in question.

Meanwhile, Pope let his eyes linger on the gown Bear wore. The cut flattered her leggy frame, offering glimpses of the toned limbs behind the split on either side of the floor length skirt. The bodice was a scooped neck creation that covered more than it revealed but accentuated her tempting breasts just the same.

"I um...I can't do that," Bear said.

Pope frowned. "Dance?"

"Not like that. That's Tee's and Prin's thing..."

Casually, Pope took her arm. "You only need a partner who knows how to lead."

Bear's brow quirked. "You? I suppose?"

"Damn right." He grinned devilishly when she laughed.

The couple strode right by the guest Senator Christopher Morrow had brought along as his 'plus one'.

"I knew it," the glass in Brody Alberts' hand shook almost as fiercely as his low voice.

~~~


"This is some place, huh?"

"Mmm..." Tee closed her eyes, fully content while resting back against Mercuri's chest and taking in the loveliness of the ranch after nightfall. "Sometimes I don't even come out here to see B, just to take in the atmosphere and think."

Mercuri flexed his arms just slightly about Tee's small frame. "You find yourself needing to do that often? Getting away to think?"

"Often enough," she sighed, the gesture was light.

Mercuri nodded as though fortifying himself to continue. "Guess it's a good thing you've got Bear's ranch- and then there's your apartment."

Tee opened her eyes then and turned to stare way up. "Mercuri I- I just haven't found the right people to take it, is all." Her tone was soothing in a softly endearing way. "I love you."

"I know that, Tee."

"Do you?" She tugged the lapel of his tux. "Everything's happened pretty fast for us."

"I know that too, Sprite. Just like I know you're all there is for me and that I won't rest until I know you're wearing this, along with my last name."

Bewilderment sparkled in Tee's pitch stare for just a moment. Then, her gaze was shifting to the diamond twinkling directly before her eyes. The gasp she would've uttered, was enveloped in a tiny, amazed cry.

"Mercuri-"

"Marry me." He swallowed hard and then grinned, satisfied that the question had finally taken flight. Seconds later, a touch of uncertainty intruded. "You can uh, take as much time as you need to-"

"Yes."

He frowned then, looking down at the ring as if he were having a difficult time processing the fact that he'd just gotten the one thing he'd obsessed over- the one thing he truly wanted.

"Yes?" He queried.

"Uh huh," she nodded, tears glistening in her eyes instead of bewilderment.

"Really?" he persisted.

She nodded again. "Uh-huh."

"Even if it's really soon?"

"Uh-huh."

"You're sure?"

"Uh-huh. Are you?"

"Uh-huh."

Laughter surged between them and then Mercuri was adorning Tee's finger with his ring.

"I would've gotten down on one knee," he eased the ring home, "but that'd just put us eye to eye, so…"

Tee shook her head. "Will I have to put up with these pitiful insights for the rest of my life?" she asked.

Mercuri tucked the empty ring box into his pocket and took Tee off her feet. "For the rest of your life? Uh-huh." He promised before taking her mouth in the sweetest kiss.

***

Bear arrived in her room exhausted, but satisfied that her first soiree dinner party could be counted a success. She couldn't decide which part of the evening had been more satisfying. Perhaps it was having all the guests attend and give generously-all except the distinguished Senator Morrow.

While the man's lack of generosity wasn't satisfying, his embarrassment was. This was especially true for Bear when the donations announcements began to roll out.

Yes, the night was an enjoyable one. Most enjoyable was when Mercuri and Tee pulled her aside to share news of their engagement. Bear was, of course, thrilled that Mercuri had finally found his courage-even more delighted that he'd decided to propose to Tee there at her place.

The only thing that came relatively close to competing with the feeling brought on by her friends' news, was the fact that the discs were secure inside the safe in her home office. A member of security brought them to her shortly after the gates closed behind the last departing guest.

Bear quickly tucked them away before she called it a night and adjourned to her bedroom. She made the journey alone.

Pope had decided not to stay. He'd said something about friends coming into town later that night. He'd also seemed to have made the decision not to mention their very emotional scene from the night before. His only 'mention' of it had been to tell her he'd find another way when he returned the discs. They'd enjoyed the night, even took time to celebrate Mercuri and Tee with a champagne toast. Pope left shortly after.

Now, in the quiet privacy of her bedroom, Bear had to ponder what was to come next. Pope said he didn't need the discs, but how could he not? He said he'd find another way, but what better way was there than to scour those recordings for evidence that would lend insight to what happened that night… and why.

The coward in her savored the contentment brought by knowing the discs were back in the safe. The realist in her warned that this was far from over.

She took a long shower where she'd washed her hair free of the product sculpting the elaborate coiffure she'd worn than night. Eager to pour herself into sleep, she debated on whether to wear a PJ bottom to bed. She sent a longing look to Pope's sweater slung across an oversized scoop chair in the corner.

She shook her head, resisting the urge. She'd slept in the thing for the past two nights. It swallowed her, made her feel like she was in his arms all night. Tempted then, Bear was making her way to the chair when a thud seemed to shake the framework of the two-level suite. Frowning, she moved barefoot from the room and went to stand at the ledge overlooking the lounge and kitchen nook.

She was convincing herself that the sound was a truck door slamming in the distance, when it sounded again. The 'thud' then was more like a boom that actually rattled the door to the corridor leading down to the private entrance enclosure.

A third boom, that one seeming to rattle the door on its hinges, had her bolting back inside her room and going to the gun safe- one of three she kept. Fingerprint scan unlocked a steel door fashioned beneath a trick drawer in the bedside table.

There, encased in springy black foam was a gleaming handgun and two full clips. With expert efficiency, Bear checked the barrel and chamber before she pushed one of the clips home and scrambled up from the floor. In seconds, she'd sprinted down the stairway and made it to the door. Silently, she cursed that there was no privacy screen. Following a brief, quiet prayer, she whipped open the door and gave the corridor a quick scan with the gun barrel aimed toward the ceiling. The area was clear.

She moved stealthily. Aside from her door, there was only one other. It led to the stairwell. Bear had a clear line of sight but that didn't make her feel much better. The booming sound had been too intense not to have come from inside the enclosure.

"Calm Bear," she told herself while approaching the stairwell entrance. After another quick prayer she opened the door.

"Stop!" Surprise, had her firing way too soon and missing.

"Shit! Fuck, Bear!" She'd walked in on one man hunched over another. Her call had stopped him from delivering another blow to the man who appeared to be writhing on the cement steps.

The intruder retaliated with gunfire of his own. His aim was far better than Bear's, but still off the mark and hit the door frame inches from her head. Bear recovered from the missed shot and fired again, that time hitting a stair mere centimeters from the gunman's foot. The perpetrator ran and Bear gave chase. Running past the man lying on the steps, she pursued her prey down the flights leading to the enclosure's outer door.

The man turned and tried his luck with another shot- that one deflecting off the steel railing of the case. That shot sent sparks flying, but the display didn't hinder Bear's pursuit. She took point on the top step of the final landing and fired just as the man whipped open the outer door. He responded with an enraged bellow when her bullet tore through his shoulder. Bear didn't take time to celebrate the blood splatter high along the doorframe. She aimed for a higher target along the door, fired and set off the red lights she knew triggered the alarm all over the ranch.

Then, Bear continued her hunt. Her prey moved well for a wounded man. She raced past the enclosure door and found no trace of him. The fact had her responding with an enraged bellow of her own. Then; whispering a curse, she raced back up the stairs having remembered the injured man there.

She covered the steps at enviable speed and practically tripped over her feet when she saw the man lying on his side, his back to her. His hair was matted with a garish black smear. The color of his hair made the substance hard to determine.

Bear knew it was blood, but the realization wasn't what had her staring motionless at the prone figure. It was his hair. His fuzzy cap of auburn curls.

"No." The word filtered out on a breath followed by the sound of the gun clicking against the cement step when her legs gave and she sank to her knees.

"No, no, no, no…" she smoothed her hands along the man's back, his tuxedo jacket grew blurred in her watering gaze. Shakily, she pressed her fingers along his neck to feel for a pulse. She found one-albeit weak and thready. It was enough to have her heart pounding in relief and gratitude.

"Shaun? Shaun, baby it's Bear. Honey? Honey can you hear me?"

His voice was even weaker than his pulse when he murmured something in response. Gently, Bear eased around to look into his face and pressed tender kisses to his cheek when she was leaning over him.

"Bea...th-the-"

"Shh…" she put another tender kiss to his cheek. "Don't talk, Hon. Shh...they'll be here any second to fix you up." She tried not to weigh the odds of that being possible given the amount of blood darkening the concrete.

"The-wan…"

"Honey shh...please, please Shaun…" Her voice was thick with the emotion filling her throat.

"They want…" his words were garbled but more recognizable then.

"Shaun…" Bear feared some sort of delirium might be settling in, a consequence of his injuries. She pressed her face into his neck, unmindful of his blood wetting her hair.

"They...want ba-bag…"

"Shaun…" Bear moved, hunching closer as she was becoming more terrified to let go of him.

"Bag…"

"Okay Shaun, okay…" she put a kiss to his neck. "Just keep talking then…keep talking, Sweetie. Stay with me…"

"Ba…Bea…bag…"

"Stay with me. They know we're here, Shaun. They're coming Honey. Shaun? Shaun?" He'd grown silent, but the thready pulse was still there when she felt for it.

"Bear?! Bear girl, answer us goddammit!"

"Up here, Flow!" She recognized the voice of her security chief. Smile wavering, she turned her watery eyes back to Shaun.

"They're here, Shaun. They're here. Stay with me. Stay…"

The sounds of boots and artillery drowned her voice as it all echoed in the enclosure. Seconds later, Bear and Shaun were enveloped by bodies in tactical gear. Shock commanded the expressions of each man, but they quickly dismissed emotion to focus on getting to the bottom of what had just occurred.

The onsite security made way for the medical team to enter. Bear felt hands on her arms, at her waist and was lifted from where she'd curled around Shaun. Her vitals were checked, but it was all a blur for Bear. She could only look on as the medical team worked on Shaun.

"My fault," she murmured too low for anyone to hear.

"My fault," she said again in the same indecipherable tone. She experienced a wave of dizziness and then her vision seemed to cloud before everything went black.

~~~

An hour later, Shaun Oates was pronounced dead.

# PART III

*Either conquer the night, or become one of its conquests*
*Abigail Biddinger*

# CHAPTER 23

The large, rear table near the back of Luden's Wines and Spirits grabbed loads of attention that evening. Of course, it wasn't exactly the table grabbing the attention that evening, but the three men who had camped out there for the better part of 2 hours.

Josh Luden adored his bar patrons, but knew his revenue was always sure to exceed expectations when he got a visit from the three who patronized his establishment that night. It took a lot to satisfy appetites that size.

Rutger Eliades and Slayte Miltiades arrived in San Francisco that evening with plans to descend on Mercuri's place. It was the usual manner of things whenever they came to town. Mercuri and Tee were expecting them so there would be no surprises. Only no one could've foreseen that night as the one where Mercuri would ask the woman he loved to marry him. As a result of Tee's acceptance, the unexpected guests decided new arrangements were in order. Rut and Slay opted for suites in town and joined Pope for drinks to celebrate Mercuri's new found happiness.

"The son of a bitch did it," Slayte's violet eyes twinkled with a mix of disbelief and approval.

"The son of a bitch did it," Pope lifted his beer mug in toast.

"Mercuri and Tee," Rutger tapped his mug to Slayte's and Pope's.

Slayte broke into rich laughter then. "I can't believe that scumbag is about to be someone's husband."

"Not just someone, a real angel." Rutger said.

"Damn right," Pope tapped mugs with his friends again before they each drank deeply and dissolved into more laughter.

Laughter from the threesome seemed to carry over every square inch of the 3-story pub. The sounds and the men responsible for them, consistently stole the attention of many women. Not to mention the men who were more than a little peeved that their dates couldn't resist peeking around to get a load of the jovial (and sexy) giants livening the bar with their good moods.

~~~

"You guys are gonna have to excuse me but it's gonna take a while for this to settle in," Slayte was telling his friends a while later.

"You're not the only one," Rutger mused, shaking his head. "What were the odds of any of us taking vows?"

"Too infinitesimal to count."

"Amen," Rutger and Slayte said to Pope's words.

"Patch came close," Pope studied his nearly empty mug. "Sheriff back in Vermont said he and his girl had gotten pretty close before…"

There was no need to complete the thought. A somber wave crept in as the guys remembered their lost friend.

"Merc's a lucky guy," Rutger finished off his beer and signalled their server with 3 raised fingers to indicate a refill on the enormous pitchers they'd emptied.

"Damn straight he is," Slayte reared back in his chair and raked all ten fingers through his loose curls. "Talk about long odds. I mean, what're the chances of finding a girl like Tee, fighting through all the shit she had beating down on her and coming out to a beautiful life on the other side?"

"Now *that's* infinitesimal," Rutger declared just as the server arrived with 3 foaming pitchers.

"Caleb Stein says all that shit was part of a set up," Pope shared once the servers had exchanged the empty mugs and pitchers for chilled refills.

"Stein? When'd you see him?" Rutger asked.

"He um...came to Bear's ranch." Pope readied himself for a slew of questions.

"Bear Arms?" Rutger's tone was awe-filled.

"Ah jeez," Slayte reached for his mug. Rutger's shooting weekend fantasy was well known.

"It's cool, Slay. Rut knows I've already been there a few times." Pope took his mug as well.

Slayte's gaze sharpened as he took in Rutger's smug expression. "You've been seeing her?" His voice was akin to a quiet growl.

Rutger chuckled into his mug. "He's been doin' a little more than that."

"Son of a bitch," Slayte practically snarled then. "And we haven't gotten so much as an intro." He shifted a deadly look to Rutger. "Or am I wrong about that too?"

"No." Some of Rutger's smugness faded. His provocatively set whiskey browns narrowed then as well. "No Slay, you're not wrong. What gives, Po? I'd say we've been pretty patient."

"You've also been pretty gone," Pope laughed and leaned over to top off his beer. "I can't help it if I live closer to where the angels are."

When Rutger and Slayte only continued to stare mutinously, Pope caved. "I'll see what I can do, alright? Now can I get to telling you about Stein?"

A lengthy moment passed before Rutger and Slayte shrugged. Neither looked too happy. Pope decided to take what he could get. It didn't take long to share that Caleb had pretty compelling evidence to suggest Tee and her friends didn't kill all the men in that room that night. Attention riveted then, Rutger and Slayte listened while Pope recalled what Caleb said about members of The Ten suffering gunshot wounds from a gun other than the one Caleb took from Bear at the scene.

"Motherfuck," Slayte sighed.

"Yeah," Pope downed half his fourth mug of the night.

"So what now?" Rutger asked.

"Now, is figuring out what Brody and Jake are up to." Pope said.

"And Cale's sure they're in on it?" Slayte asked.

Pope shrugged. "Pretty sure. We all know they weren't happy playing second to anyone-including their dads. We also know how greedy they are."

Slayte hissed his curse that time. "So it's not enough that they made our mothers take their wonder drug with its psychotic tendencies, they've gotta shovel it into more unsuspecting women." He grimaced. "And now there's you in the driver's seat," he added.

Rutger rested his elbows to the table and rubbed at the crop of dense curls adorning his head. "So how do we prove all this? Much less figure out what the fuck they're up to?"

"Caleb talked about finding out who else was in the room with them." Pope chimed in.

"Which means having to see those discs," Rutger grunted laughter. "We can't ask 'em that, Po."

Pope was shaking his head. "I already gave them back to her."

Slayte traded a quick look with Rutger. "Gave them back to her?"

Pope recapped again, sharing that Bear had given him the discs and then his chat with Mercuri that had only solidified the plan he'd already settled on which was not to look at them.

"And don't ask me what my next move is because I haven't got a clue."

"You're in love with her, aren't you?" Slayte watched Pope drag his hands through his hair.

"Very much." Pope's confession came without hesitation.

Slayte gave a decisive nod. Meanwhile Rutger placed his mug to the table with exaggerated force.

"So we don't leave until we figure a way that doesn't involve looking at those discs." He said.

Slayte grinned his approval. "Do you think it's a good idea to keep the beer coming?" he asked.

Rutger spread his hands defensively. "Beer helps me think."

The roaring laughter resumed.

"Po? You good with sticking around?" Slayte asked.

"Sounds good to me if-"

"Po?" Slayte watched his friend stand and rise from the table so suddenly, the mugs and pitchers teetered.

Rutger and Slayte followed Pope to the counter where he called for the bartender to turn up the volume on the TV. It was no use given how loud the establishment was. There was little need for sound, when the caption beneath the gates of a well known ranch, said it all.

'Real World Shooting At Bear Arms'.

\*\*\*

It took the guys a while longer to leave Luden's Wines and Spirits than it otherwise would have with Rutger and Slayte almost coming to blows with Pope for possession of the keys to his truck.

In spite of all the beer they'd consumed, it wasn't nearly enough to give them a buzz. Still, it was clear to Pope's friends that he was in no shape to drive. The trio eventually set out and were approaching the turnoff to the ranch 30 minutes later.

"Judging from the activity, it's gonna take us another fifteen minutes to get past the gates." Rutger announced from the driver's seat.

The guys studied the blur of lights amid a whirlwind of bodies. There was the occasional bleat of a siren when an authorized vehicle zoomed past.

"What the hell happened out here?" Slayte's baritone brogue loomed from the rear seat.

"Get this thing up front," Pope's voice harbored its usual roar at a much higher volume that time.

"You got it," Rutger gunned the engine and put expert driving skills into play as he angled around the many news vans lining the road. There were also a fair amount of spectators all eager to catch a glimpse of the action.

Rutger soon had the truck wedged between the iron entrance fence and a police cruiser that was within a few feet of the security booth. "Best it's gonna get," he said.

Pope clapped Rutger's shoulder and bolted from the cab. Rutger and Slayte were right at his heels.

~~~

Rutger was instructed to drive the truck on over to the house once security had gotten wind of Pope's arrival. The guys were cleared and soon entering the hive of activity that was the lower level of Bear's home.

In that span of time, they'd chatted with enough people to piece together an accurate enough account of what had happened. Pope's expression was a grim one as he shook hands and offered his sympathies to members of Bear's staff who he recognized.

Though disheartened by Shaun's death, Pope's electric gaze lost none of its intensity as it scanned the room for Bear. He dismissed the flash of slicing anger which surprised him when he saw her with Mike Hough. They shared one of the chaise sectionals on the long L-shaped sofa. Bear was huddled into a ball and curled tight against Mike's side, her head on his shoulder while he rubbed her back. Her face was blank, her features unresponsive in a way that had Pope closing the distance between them in the gap of a few seconds.

Mike gave a brisk nod and took Pope's hand with his free one for a rapid shake.

"I'm sorry, Mike. Shaun was a good man."

"The best," Mike's voice broke a little on the last word and he gave another fast nod. "I don't think any of us are believing it yet."

Pope was settling to the sofa on the side closest to Bear. He reached out to smooth a lock of hair tangled at her shoulder.

"Did you hear...how it happened?" Mike asked.

A muscle danced feverishly along Pope's jaw. "Fucker was on her doorstep."

"Literally." Mike confirmed. "If it hadn't been for Shaun..." he gathered Bear closer. "She hasn't said a thing since we...lost him. We got her to change clothes, take some tea...she won't let the doc close to give her anything to help her sleep. The cops are still taking statements, but they've been done with her for a while. They've roped off where...it happened, but the rest of the house is open-she doesn't have to be here. She pitches a bloody fit though if we even suggest her going up to bed." He shook his head. "It's weird seeing her like this-things are weird enough."

Pope knelt close to Bear, gave her hair another tug. "Hey beautiful? It's your know it all."

She remained lifeless against Mike.

"Cub? Come on, honey. Don't give me the silent treatment. I'll only have to bully you out of it. What do you say we go upstairs?" He watched her grip tighten on Mike's shirt.

"Come with me?" He pressed. "I promise I won't leave you there. Cub? Please?" He traded a look with Mike when she raised her head.

261

The reaction was enough for both men. Mike shifted, relinquishing his hold on his boss to the man at their side.

"It's alright, babe," Pope soothed when she turned her face into his neck.

The room silenced as Pope got to his feet with Bear in his arms. Onlookers watched with hope and uncertainty flooding their eyes. Over the last few hours, many of them had watched their boss experience more blows than she'd been dealt during the entire time Bear Arms had been in existence.

The group uttered a collective, yet inaudible sigh of relief when Bear allowed her large companion to carry her without argument.

Bear curled around Pope like a vine the moment he eased down to the bed with her in tow. He smiled, realizing she was dressed in a familiar sweater and he approved of the way his clothing dwarfed her. He wouldn't leave her that night and had already told Rutger and Slayte to take the truck back to their hotel in San Francisco. Not surprising, his friends refused to go.

It was no problem. Bear's housestaff had already been clued into who they were. Head housekeeper Jean Kearney had already squared away guest rooms for them.

In Bear's room, the covers were already turned down. Pope reclined on top of them, but had gotten Bear comfortable beneath. She unwrapped herself and allowed him a few moments to get her situated. Then, she was entwining herself about him as if terrified to let go for too long.

"Get some sleep, babe." He put a kiss to the top of her head.

Bear shook her head like a cranky child and tightened her clutch on Pope's shirt.

"You need your rest, Cub."

Again, she shook her head.

"How 'bout we take a nap together?" He bartered.

Bear shook her head a third time. "It's my fault," she said.

The admission was soft, but to Pope it sounded as if it'd come through a blow horn. Effortlessly, he freed her death grip on his shirt and snared her wrists when she would've opposed the move. He squeezed until her eyes met his. He noted they were dry. She hadn't cried. Steel vault around a marshmallow, he thought. They'd handle that display of emotion later.

"There are plenty of folks at fault here, Cub. You're not one of them. Quiet." He said when she opened her mouth for dispute.

"Your security could be labeled among those folks," his features drew into a scowl. "How the hell did someone get a gun with live ammo out here?"

"That buck stops with me," her voice was quiet, hollow and heartbreaking. "If I'd listened to you-"

"What? Tell you how to run your business?"

"You made good points about the weak spots in my security and I crapped all over them."

Again, muscle performed its fierce dance along Pope's jaw. "You're making me angry, Bear."

"Get in line. I'm past angry-Shaun's dead because I was too busy trying to show I knew what was best. Three times and I still haven't learned…"

Pope noticed her hands were starting to shake-badly. Forgetting his anger and the questions sparked by her words, he tugged her close. She was shuddering terribly and he considered locating the doctor.

"Breathe, Honey," he said instead. "I'm here. I'm here, Cub so make the most of it. This is your only night to wallow in pity. Do you hear me?" He felt a measure of hope at her faint nod against his shoulder.

He rocked her, steady at first and then more slowly. She continued to nod, but he understood it was more of a soother than a mechanical response. His fierce features softened with the realization that she was putting herself to sleep.

Just shy of 10 minutes, he felt her go limp against him and knew she'd achieved her mission. Gently, he tucked her in. He didn't forget his promise to remain and kept her snug next to him the entire night.

# CHAPTER 24

Just before dawn, Bear began to fidget. The ranch's on-site physician had visited an hour earlier and left Pope with something to give her should she need help staying asleep. When she began to thrash in the covers and murmur incoherently, Pope added the single dose, odorless, tasteless sleep inducer to a glass of water and made her drink.

Five minutes later, she was sleeping deeply. Pope figured it couldn't hurt to conk out for a few as well. He managed another 30 minutes of shuteye before he was jarred awake by the insistent gyrations from the vibrating mobile in his hip pocket.

He'd missed the call by the time he'd pulled the phone free of his jeans. The caller didn't leave a voicemail, but a followup text.

'*Security wing when you can get away, R'*

~~~

"How long have you two been up?" Pope asked when he met his friends 20 minutes later.

Slayte wore his trademark devilish grin. "It's easy to get out of bed at the crack of dawn when there's nothing lovely keeping you there."

"Amen to that," Rutger sighed and caused his friends to chuckle.

As the die-hard early bird of the group, Rutger was known to rise before dawn for a day of hunting whether or not a woman shared his bed.

"What's up?" Pope asked.

"How's Bear?" Rutger countered, his gaze steady, unreadable.

"Sleeping," Pope worked the bridge of his nose. "They gave her something. She should be out for another few hours."

"How are *you* doin'?" Slayte asked and watched his friend resort to his telling habit of raking back his hair when he was frustrated.

"She's blaming herself."

"Figures she would. She'll get over it, Po." Rutger promised. "Especially once they catch whoever's to blame."

"It's natural she'd want to lay all this at her own feet it being one of her employees and all," Slayte added. "Given how devastated they all looked last night, I can tell they're a close knit bunch."

"Yeah...that they are," Pope's voice harbored uncharacteristic weariness.

The men headed further down a wide corridor of chrome and fiberglass. The Bear Arms security wing was the most remote building on the compound. A lonely building of red brick, inside, the rectangular structure was state of the art.

Slayte whistled as they took the corridor labeled communications. Though much of the long hallway was sealed behind what was most likely one way glass, there were a few spots that offered deeper glimpses into the facility. Slayte had noticed a wall of screens that provided coverage of the current activity across all areas of the ranch.

"Jesus, this woman's no joke," Slayte breathed.

"Amen," Rutger's tone was hushed. "Pulling something like this was an idiot's move."

Pope only half listened, his mind was on Bear again. She was deep into blaming herself for Shaun's death. Three times, she'd said. It was easy to guess that Shaun's death and the situation 6 years ago involving her friends, held two of those spots, but what was the third time? The maid Cynda Duncan came to mind, but he didn't think that was it.

What of her mysteries were still left to uncover? Would she share them? Would her guilt; misplaced as it was, cause her to retreat? Cause him to lose her? To hell with that, Pope bristled eyes going flat as he brooded and followed along behind his friends.

He'd waited too long to find her. Beauty and stunning body aside, she was an amazing woman-far from the ordinary. If he let her go...he bristled again, hands flexing when he wanted to draw fists.

Until he came along, she'd successfully avoided letting a man get too close. Men wouldn't stop trying-they never did with women like Berrill Clayton. There would be one, he knew. One, determined enough to fight past her barriers and claim her for his own. That was a certainty if he let her go. That was something he had no intention of doing.

Rutger glanced back and saw his friend lagging behind. "You okay?"

Pope nodded. "Just drained."

"Well we've got the thing for that!"

The guys noticed a tall, dark, older man with a wide, muscular build standing along the corridor leading into the communications sanctum. He offered a hand to Slayte who was first to approach.

"Nate Flownell-Security Chief. Everybody calls me Flow. We've got hot coffee waiting if you like."

Rutger shook hands with Flow. He and Slayte declined the coffee as did Pope when Flow moved in to clap a hand over his shoulder.

"How's Bear?" Flow asked.

"Sleeping with the help of some really good drugs."

The man nodded over Pope's report. "This is gonna stay with her a long time. Shaun was family. We're all sick with grief... and rage and our fair share of guilt. This is the last place something like this should've happened." Deeper interest flared in Flow's hazel eyes then. "My men say you guys saw something on the feed that might help us catch this shitstain."

Pope looked on while Slayte and Rutger nodded. "You two *have* been up a while."

"We thought you'd want to see this," Rutger said and turned back to Flow. "We appreciate your men letting us see the footage," he said.

Flow waved a hand. "Shaun vouched for Mr. Apostolou- good enough for us. Any friend of Shaun's..." He stopped to rub at the tension gathered near the bridge of his nose.

Pope squeezed Flow's shoulder. "He was a good man."

"Damn right he was," Flow tilted his head. "Let's go on back."

The communications wing was a hub of sight and sound. A long wide wall supported the array of screens broadcasting the ranch. A sunken bank of cubicles faced it, each outfitted with computer terminals manned by uniformed operators.

Slayte whistled yet again. "Impressive."

"Not impressive enough," Flow brooded.

"Don't beat yourself up too much," Rutger advised. "These folks are trained to evade and they're as unpredictable as they are ruthless."

"These people," Pope didn't need a response. He picked up his pace behind Flownell who led the way to a large corner space in back of the command center.

Inside, Flownell went to a desk that occupied half the length of a far wall. There, he reached for a remote-one of three along the desk's edge. He activated the remote, bringing to life a wall screen across the room.

The feed was from the party. The click of another button grayed out the majority of the color to enhance a single figure. "We've already sent copies of this to the cops, but we can use all the help we can get i.d.-ing the shits responsible for this." Flow said.

"Son of a bitch," Pope breathed, moving closer to the screen while Flow switched the feed to the cameras at the ranch entrance.

"Guy got in as a plus one. Who was he?"

"Brody Alberts." Pope didn't look away from the screen.

"Looks like he got in with the guy ahead of him," Rutger raised an index toward the screen, then turned to Flownell. "Your men said we should see you when we asked if they recognized him."

Before Flow could respond, another voice provided the answer. "That's Senator Christopher Morrow." Mike Hough supplied.

~~~

Over the next half hour, Mike and Flow filled the guys in on the spiteful history between their boss and the state senator. Rutger and Slayte were riveted while Pope tuned in and out. He'd heard much of the story from Bear already.

Besides, there was no 'paying attention' when his thoughts were fixed on Brody. He'd been so close to doing it so many times, so close to letting the rage take him, shape him.

The situation with Brody-the legitimate son-hadn't helped. Legitimate or not, it hadn't stopped Brody's constant attacks when they were kids. They hadn't grown up under the same roof and yet, the man had always been threatened by him. What Pope had learned during his conversation with Gerrick Ferguson gave him a lot more understanding as to what fueled Brody's hatred. Pope felt his jaw tighten as memories surged of how he'd withstood it all. He'd allowed Brody's name calling, ridicule and even the insults to his mother to roll off his back.

He was done now. After all those long years, Brody had finally drawn a line in the sand that could not be erased.

Pope registered the sound of Rutger's voice. He was laying out a profile of the GAN and Brody Alberts in particular. The question on everyone's tongues was the same. Unfortunately, no one had any guesses as to why the California senator had shown up with a Memphis billionaire as his date.

"What's important for you to know is they will be back," Pope gave the warning from the long sofa he shared with Slayte.

"I'm sure what happened to Shaun wasn't part of the plan or that Alberts was expecting to find me there," Pope scanned the wall screen that was divided into 4 smaller screens. One segment showed Brody looking on as Pope whisked Bear off for their dance.

"I've known Brody long enough to know he's a coward," Pope continued. "But's he's easily distracted by the element of surprise. It makes him erratic. He's usually with partners who are more at ease with handling the uh...wet work-'scuse the expression.

Killing Shaun wasn't part of the plan. It was Brody acting out. You can be sure they'll be back for whatever brought them out here in the first place."

Rutger and Slayte traded curious looks, but Pope didn't bother explaining his strange phrasing.

"They'll approach by stealth," Pope told Mike and Flow instead. "They'll come in waves. That was probably the plan all along. They were most likely here on some kind of recon mission, getting the lay of the land-testing for strengths weaknesses. Security being so high around here is probably why they didn't try smuggling in additional eyes save Alberts' and Morrow's.

Losing Shaun has you all on edge, but what happened may give you time to prevent a second attack," Pope theorized. "They'll expect security to be even tighter now. They've got to know you've caught 'em on camera."

"Pope's right," Slayte chimed in. "This Morrow is probably under a rock somewhere tryin' to cover his ass."

"Same with Brody," Pope continued. "He's been in the system since he was in college-his dad didn't use his contacts to wipe out that blemish, thought it'd teach his son to be a little more careful when he broke the law. His DNA has to be over every inch of the crime scene."

"Not to mention him being caught on camera in the stairwell committing the crime," Rutger noted.

Pope nodded. "He knows he'll be hunted. The GAN doesn't have quite the shielding power it once did."

"So you're suggesting we tighten up our forces and wait to be attacked again?" Flownell huffed out a laugh. "Sorry fellas, but I ain't one for sittin' around doin' nothin'". He tugged back the cap he wore and scratched at a tuft of curly salt and pepper hair. "We know who the filth is, let's go get it." He decided.

"You're right, Flow." Pope leaned forward on the sofa. "You'll get Brody, maybe the Senator but that still leaves his whole foul network who'll claim it had no idea about the boss flying off the deep end. In short, they'll be back for whatever brought Alberts out here in the first place. It's important to them. Taking time to shore up your defences isn't idle work, Flow. These people are more desperate now but that makes them even more dangerous."

"What do you suggest?" Mike asked.

"Give me time. I can't tell you how much. I want Brody Alberts dead- not sitting in a suite at his private club on house arrest awaiting trial that may never come. The GAN may not have the shielding power it once did, but it's still got lots of low friends in high places. Using completely...legal means to get him may not work to your benefit." Pope cautioned. "Give me this time. You won't regret it."

Mike shared a look with Flow and then they were looking to Pope with nods of acceptance.

~~~

"*Whatever* they're after?" Slayte queried once they were leaving the security complex. "What'd you mean? We know it's those discs. Did you just not want to tell them that?"

Pope slowed his steps along the gravel drive and stroked his jaw. "I'm not so sure that's it anymore and I can't lock in on *why* I'm not sure."

Rutger and Slayte understood. They both knew Pope had an eerie sixth sense of perception. They'd known him long enough to have seen him utilize the ability with striking results.

"You think Brody and this senator had some beef with Bear outside of the discs?" Rutger tried to prod his friend.

"No," Pope shook his head without hesitation. "No whatever it is has to do with the discs, but not in the way we're thinking. Something about what Caleb said…" he moved on, murmuring to himself.

"About there being a coup inside the GAN?" Slayte was next to prod.

"Maybe...maybe…" Pope didn't sound convinced.

"Give it a rest, huh?" Rutger clapped Pope's shoulder. "Your brain has got to be pretty shredded after you spent most of the night looking over Bear."

"Yeah...yeah…" Pope worked muscles bunched at his nape, his thoughts immediately settling on the idea of her curled in bed. At once, he was tugged by the need to be there with her.

"Say, we're gonna beat it, head back to the hotel," Rutger decided.

"Don't check out yet, alright? Stick around town for a while, okay?"

"Way ahead of you there," Slayte said.

"Get some sleep," Rutger urged. "Give us a call when that head of yours clears."

Pope gave a weak grin. "You so sure that's gonna happen?"

"Damn sure," Rutger added a sly wink.

The men parted ways. Pope headed back toward the walking route that would take him back to the house. He wished he shared Rutger's certainty. Just then, he was sure of one thing. The next time he saw Brody Alberts, one of them would not walk away from the confrontation alive.

\*\*\*

Bear was still asleep when Pope returned, but he knew it wouldn't be long before she woke. She'd kicked off the covers and he could tell by the disarray of pillows that she'd been tossing.

He went to the side of the bed where she hung perilously close to the edge. Gently, he situated her to a safer spot and went to tug the

270

covers back into place. Instead, his touch lingered above the toned dark line of her bare leg. The ultramarine of his gaze seemed to blaze more vividly as it followed the curve of the limb. Moments later, his fingers were adding touch to sight, skimming her silken skin.

He took to the edge of the bed. By then, he was already cupping the back of her thigh. Squeezing intermittently, his touch roamed higher toward the curve of her bottom. Next, it was his mouth and then the tip of his nose making contact with the spot. Lush waves of ebony slid forward when his head dipped and tilted as he worked over her, nibbling, kissing and inhaling the soothing lavender and talc scent from her skin.

She wore only his sweater and a scrap of red lace boyshorts beneath. She sighed, turned on her back as he hunched over her, pushing up his sweater's hem. He tasted her with greater intensity. He was covering her hips with his hands and preparing to take his mouth lower when she called to him in the midst of her thinning sleep.

"Pope...I love you..."

And there *he* was preparing to rip off her panties when she'd just suffered a crushing loss. Quietly cursing, he righted the sweater and eased away. He tucked her back beneath the covers, but chose to rest atop them. He didn't trust himself at all not to make a second attempt at taking advantage of her. Resting a hand to her hip, he waited for sleep to visit.

Bear took his hand, drew it between her breasts and sighed reassuredly. Pope put a kiss to her ear.

"I love you too," he said.

~~~

She was awake when his eyes next opened. At first, Pope was hesitant to touch her and then he reached out to let his knuckles brush her spine.

"It's not a dream, is it?"

"No sweet. I'm afraid, it's not." Pope followed the trail he charted down her back. He watched her begin to shove back the covers. "Where're you going?"

"Have to find out who did this. Why."

Pope pushed up on the bed where he'd rested well for two hours atop the covers. He was pleased to see her making the effort, but knew she'd be back to blaming herself once the culprits identities were revealed. Besides, it was best she heard it from him.

271

"Babe-"

"No Pope." Her voice was soft but the decision sounded firm. "I know you don't want me blaming myself, but I do and will until I find out who had nerve enough to come here and take-"

Pope watched her force herself to continue.

"And take one of my people," she scooted for the edge of the bed and found herself restrained a second later when Pope pulled her back to his side.

Bear's eyes blazed mocha fire while she braced in his hold. Pope turned her to face him and waited patiently for her struggles to cease.

"Quiet," he soothed when she opened her mouth to blast him. "We already know who's responsible," he felt her tense frame loosen in his hold. "Flow let me check out the security feed. You had one of my former associates from the GAN at your dinner last night." He saw awareness flash in her eyes and didn't like the way it settled.

"His name was Brody Alberts. He came as your Senator Morrow's plus one."

Bear's expression cooled almost as suddenly as it had heated. "Christopher Morrow." She wilted then and would have slumped back to the headboard had Pope not been holding her.

"Bear?" He squeezed her arms, adding a tiny shake in the process.

"All this time denying the prick and I let him walk right in. I wanted to prove my point-"

"Bear-"

"Wanted to shame him in front of the people whose approval he wants most," her mouth twisted into a wry smile. "He showed me, huh?"

Pope squeezed her tighter, gave another shake in the process and seemed pleased when she gasped at the pressure.

"Have I got your attention now?" He didn't take offense when she refused to answer. "I really don't think Alberts carried out his plan because your senator got his feelings hurt."

"Alberts." Awareness returned to her dark eyes. "You told me Nathan Alberts was your father."

Pope released her then. The surge of his rage would've had him crushing her as the bitter truth hit home. "Brody's my half brother-something he hates and has spent a lifetime making sure I knew how much."

"You said your fath-Alberts left you everything? Was what happened to Shaun a retaliation for that?"

Pope gave a quick shake of his head. "I don't think so. I think Brody and your senator were looking for something."

Bear didn't need any time to puzzle that out. "The discs? But why? Everyone on them is dead."

"Not everyone- and no, not you, Tee, Prin or Lu." He assured when panic welled in her stare. "There were lots of other people in the hotel that night. Lots of people who could have a hard time explaining an association with the GAN."

"Morrow."

Pope let Bear sit back against the headboard when she slumped that time. He joined her there, turning to face her.

"There's somethin' else going on here," he said. "Something we haven't tapped into yet. Don't ask me what." He cautioned when she seemed ready to do precisely that. "Just know that I think it goes beyond those discs."

"But they're involved," Bear probed.

"Not highly, I'm sure of that."

"Sure or positive?"

He shook his head. "I can't confirm that, Babe."

"Could something on those discs help you figure out what's going on?"

"I don't need to see them, Cub."

"But seeing them might explain what's going on? Why they came here. Why together. What would've been in this for Brody Alberts?"

"You." Rage twisted his gut in reaction to the response and he left the bed to walk it off.

"Security caught Brody watching us when we danced. Didn't take much to see how that ate at him. I don't think what happened was precisely about you and your friends but you did help set certain things in motion."

"He saw us together?" Bear had latched onto that one fact above all of Pope's other insights. She drew her knees up to her chin and rocked herself. "My fault-my fault just like I said…"

"Hell," Pope interjected the curse along with a hand shoved through his hair. "Cub, I swear-"

273

"You should look at them," Bear was the one interjecting then. "The discs? You know you should," she insisted. "If it gets you a clue in all this, then what's the harm?"

"Are you serious, Bear? The harm is to you."

"Only if you see something you can't accept."

Her words gave him pause. "Something *I* can't accept?" Obscenely long lashes seemed to flutter when he shook his head and grinned. Returning to the bed, he treated his knuckles to another graze across her skin, cruising her arms and lingering at her collarbone.

"Honey I've killed people-many with my own hands," he studied his fingers stroking the vulnerable base of her throat. "How could I not accept you when I've done that?"

"Women are different when it comes to acceptance...understanding," she gave a cold smirk. "Most men can't even handle knowing there's an ex-boyfriend somewhere. Let alone...that."

Pope shook his head, the grin defining to send his dimple flashing. "You aren't gonna let up about this until I see the damn thing, are you?"

Bear let her expression serve as response and confirmation.

"I don't handle rage well, Bear. When Mercuri had his idea to leave the GAN, I thought he was crazy but I prayed it would work. It did and I've spent every day since, buying up as much of the world as I could in hopes that it'd help me forget who I was- who I once had to be."

"Has it?" Bear knew if he said yes, she'd ask him how long it'd taken. It had been six years for her, her ranch was a bonafide success and still...

"No," he said. "The place in Cabo? It's mine. I asked Mercuri and Tee not to tell you, didn't think you'd come if you knew. It, nor any of the other properties I own, have made me forget. I don't believe such a thing's possible. All we can do is try like hell not to let the past dictate the present. I still have trouble with the past."

"Yeah..." Bear looked to her lap, studied her twiddling thumbs. "I wish I could go back to the past-just a few weeks back. Shaun would be here. I'd get my head out of my ass obsessing over that cottage and tighten security around my own back door the way you suggested-"

"Cub-"

"I'll make you a deal," she took a wad of his shirt in her fist. "I'll drop the argument over my disc if you at least check out the recordings from the cameras outside the suite. We can't afford not to make sure they don't tell us anything."

"And if they don't?"

"Then you look at mine. See if it at least gives us anything on who else was in that room. If your boy, Brody trusted them enough to kill The Ten, maybe he trusted them enough to tell them what he was up to with Morrow."

Pope uncurled Bear's fingers from his shirt, kept his eyes on them. "And what about us?"

Bear watched his hand on hers. "Guess we'll see how well we do with not letting the past dictate the future."

# CHAPTER 25

Thurston McCambridge, Dr. Mac to everyone at Bear Arms, came by to see his patient later that morning.

Following their talk about the discs, Pope had bullied Bear into eating some broth. By the time he'd gotten the soup into her system, the doctor had arrived.

Pope celebrated the man's visit. Not only because he was worried over Bear's lack lustre eating and sleeping, but because it overshadowed further discussion about the discs. They'd reached an agreement which he didn't at all agree with.

Pope had made himself scarce shortly after the doctor's arrival and headed out to his place for fresh clothes. He returned in time to find head housekeeper Jean Kearney leaving the suite through the main door that opened into the house. He waved when he saw the woman heading down the corridor.

"Dr. Mac leave already?" Pope asked.

"Fifteen minutes ago," Jean appeared stressed. "The man made the mistake of telling our girl about that sleeping tonic he had you give her."

"Mmm...and was she pissed enough to get her ass back to work?"

"If only!" Jean laughed and nodded approvingly. Her animated expression sobered all too quickly. "At least she was willing to brush her teeth and trade sitting in bed for sitting in the tub. I'll leave it up to you to get her out." Again, Jean sighed. "It's strange seeing her this way-rare for her to spend this much time in the house during the day and *not* be working. She's very close with her three girlfriends though, maybe-"

"Already contacted them," Pope gave his own encouraging sigh. "They'll be out to take over in a few days."

"Thank God," Jean raised her hands and then clasped them at the waist of her smock. "I pray they can get her to grieve-it's obvious she hasn't cried over our Shaun yet."

"Yeah." Pope looked toward the bedroom door.

"It's also obvious that you two have become quite close."

While Jean eyed him consideringly, Pope experienced an uncharacteristic loss of words. Jean burst into another round of laughter.

"Don't be embarrassed, Sweetie. We're like a little soap opera town around here. Not much is kept secret for long 'specially when it's seven feet of tall, dark and handsome."

"Not quite seven feet," Pope grinned.

"But tall, dark and handsome just the same. Girls on the house staff are all a little jealous of Miss Bear."

Pope looked playfully dismayed. "You're gonna hurt my feelings if you tell me you don't feel the same."

The older woman laughed with a sparkle in her emerald stare that made her even more of a beauty than she was. "You can rest assured, Honey. I'd be mighty jealous of our little Bear if I wasn't so happy for her." With that, she patted Pope's arm and left him at the door.

Pope was still grinning when he stepped inside the suite and shut the door. As reported, Bear was in the deep foam-filled tub. He didn't much care for finding her ensconced in candlelight while it was barely past one in the afternoon, but at least she'd made a move from the bed. He'd *try* not to complain.

He knocked on the doorframe and saw her give a start at finding him there. She recovered quickly.

"Have you finished watching the discs?"

Pope dismissed the agitation her question sent lancing through him. "No," he managed to keep the answer soft. "We just talked about

277

this a few hours ago, remember? Besides I'm assuming they're locked away somewhere."

"The safe in the office down from the livingroom. The combination is in the top drawer of the nightstand out there."

Pope's frown was brought on by surprise instead of agitation then. He sat on the wide base of black granite surrounding the tub where flat plates held gleaming candles. "Just like that?" He queried.

Bear shook her head slightly. "Like what?"

"The combination to your safe. Not something to give over lightly, Cub."

"Why not? I love you."

All he wanted was to celebrate the moment by making love to her for the rest of the day in that tub. He decided instead to forfeit pleasure for a deeper purpose.

"Prove it, then," he said. "Step outside this room, come downstairs and give them to me yourself."

Bear scooted to the base of the tub. "I'm not exactly dressed for downstairs."

Pope brushed at a lock of hair that hung outside the messy ball atop her head and clung damp at her clavicle. "I can wait," he said.

"And I can think of something better than waiting."

"Cub-"

"Please?" She pushed to her knees and took his mouth with a hungry, desperate thrust of her tongue.

The contact was Pope's undoing and he took Bear soaking wet from the tub to have her straddle his lap. The kiss went beyond lusty. It was breathtakingly erotic as each tongue battled for possession of the mouth it invaded.

Pope could barely think with her sleek and limber in his hands. Raising up from the base of the tub, he put Bear on her back. A thick, merlot colored rug made an ample pallet.

Her legs had but a moment to lock around his waist before he was tugging her thighs, spreading them as he kissed his way down her body. With heated stops along the way, he paid homage to her breasts cupping them to be nibbled and sucked and bathed with wet generous strokes from his tongue.

The irresistible lavender and talc fragrance was clearly something she bathed in. The scent of it on her wet body took his desire for her over a sheer cliff while he nibbled and sucked his way lower.

Bear tunnelled her fingers through his gossamer locks and arched her back when his tongue plundered her navel. She pushed his head lower, frowned when he resisted.

"Don't stop," she gasped and gasped again when he took her wrists and pressed them flat near her head.

"I promised you a night to pity yourself. Now you're trying to weasel out another twenty four hours?"

"Pope-"

"Shaun wouldn't want this," he watched her flinch as though he'd threatened to hit her, but he wouldn't relent.

"What the fuck do you think he was doing in that stairwell but tryin' to keep that cocksucker away from you-to keep you alive. He led the bastard there instead of through the house because he knew there'd be no access unless you were expecting it. You're fine with wasting away in this room? Just know he died for nothing if you do." He left her naked and trembling on the floor, hoping his words would have her jumping up to lay him flat with words of her own.

She didn't stir.

Pope went back to the tub. He spit out the candles and slammed a fist to the knob that drained the water. "Bath time's over," the savage timber came through clear in his voice then. He stormed past her and out of the room.

Bear took her time getting to her feet. When she did, it was to slip back into Pope's sweater. She returned to the bed where she took the dose of the sleeping aid left by Dr. Mac. She looked to the door leading down to the lower level of the suite and then crawled beneath the covers. Patiently, she waited for the medicine to help her lose consciousness.

***

*2 Days Later~*

Suffering defeat was a foreign issue for Pope. One such as he, rarely had to. Suffering defeat however was exactly what he'd been forced to do when he'd gone into Bear's room after their-his-blow up in her bathroom. He hadn't tried to rouse her then, there was no need once he'd spotted the empty medicine vial and half finished glass of water on the nightstand.

279

He'd put a kiss to the top of her head and then found the safe combination in the top drawer of the stand. From there, he went to do what he'd tried to avoid.

For Pope, wasting time was a foreign concept as well. That's exactly what he felt he was doing though, following his first viewing of five of the thirty-odd discs. Two days later and he'd practically completed the viewing. It wasn't difficult considering he'd taken to nodding off in the suite's lounge area once he'd come up from viewing the discs down in Bear's office.

All the good it had done him. Nothing earth shattering had popped up on the recordings aside from the distinguished senator, that is. Christopher Morrow clearly knew his dear brother and Jake Grodins. The discs caught Morrow, Brody and Jake in several conversations, during the infamous night 6 years prior.

It was a shame the rooms weren't wired for sound, Pope thought. What was more of a shame was that Brody and Jake hadn't made their way up to The Ten's suite in time to meet whomever went to the party packing a pistol, he mused.

The twosome did make one visit to the suite however, but left within a few minutes-not enough time for them to be part of the night's entertainment. If they had, to hell with finding out *why* they were in cahoots with Morrow-they would both be dead. He have no reservations then.

Pope wondered if that was why he was so unwilling to see that disc of Bear's. Of course her fears that whatever he'd see would change things, were totally baseless. Regardless of the pain in the ass that Brody had always been, he'd never wanted the man dead before. He'd also never been able to grasp the logic of such reasoning but there it was.

A knock to the half opened door to the viewing room inside Bear's offices, had Pope looking up. He smiled in approval and gratitude when he saw Rutger. Pope waved the man in and his smile turned curious when he saw no trace of Slayte.

"We stopped by to see Merc. Slay's gonna wait around on him to finish up some meetings. They'll drive over together."

Pope laughed over Rutger's explanation. "Thought Mercuri would still be huddled off somewhere with Tee."

"That'd probably be the case if she was in town. Merc says she had some business trip. She didn't want to leave after hearing about what happened here, but it couldn't be helped."

"That's right," Pope recalled Mercuri telling him the same when he'd called days earlier to see if Tee could get the other girls together to come over and draw Bear out of her funk.        Tee was out of town, as was Prin. Lu had just wrapped up an at home meeting with her staff. She was leaving the gym when Pope called her cell. He'd gotten a text a short while ago letting him know she was in route. During the call, she'd told him they all knew Bear was in good hands with him. Other than calling with condolences and to check in on their friend, LuCarolyn, Prin and Tee had decided to wait a while before descending on their girl. While Pope appreciated knowing he had the approval of the people Bear loved most, he was more than a little impatient to have them come take over.

"Any luck?" Rutger gave a slight nod to the wall screen at the front of the rectangular room.

"Not a lick, aside from proving that almost everybody in that hotel had some perverted sexual tastes and that prick Morrow definitely knows our old associates."

Rutger took one of the wide swivel chairs down from the one Pope occupied on the long aisle. The room was fashioned like a mini theater. "What do you know about this guy Morrow?" He asked.

"Not much, aside from what Flow and Mike told us. Truth is, I haven't looked into it any further than checking out these fuckers," he threw a hand toward the discs littering a squat round table near the front of the aisle bank.

"Is Bear still out of it?"

Pope confirmed the query with a tight smile.

"Still blaming herself?"

"I don't think she'll ever *not* blame herself for this and that's not hard to understand. There're things in my life I'll always blame myself for, but she doesn't deserve this. She's too good a person to be blaming herself for this or anything else."

Rutger's eyes blazed with something close to amazement. "She's really got you hooked, doesn't she?"

"She really does."

"Well then," Rutger reached into the front pocket of the navy shirt he wore over a gray tee. "Let's find out a little about our old associates' newest friend."

Pope swirled his chair to take in the sight of the man with a phone. Amazement struck Pope as his eyes sparkled devilishly. "This can't be Rutger Ulysses Eliades with a smart phone?"

Rutger didn't look away from the phone screen. "I told you never to use my middle name unless you wanted to die. Besides, Ben said I should get in touch with my technological side," he referred to his Chief of Security, Ben Weiss.

"I didn't know you had a technological side," Pope remarked through a lazy chuckle.

"Let's see…" Rutger ignored the dig and began to read from his phone.

"Christopher Morrow, thirty-six, California native and senator of his home state. Inspired by his mentor the late Senator Thomas Doyle-"

Rutger's whiskey browns collided with Pope's marine blues. Both men got to their feet simultaneously and with the same fluid grace.

"Inspired by his mentor, the late Senator Thomas Doyle," Rutger continued. "Morrow made a bid for Doyle's revered post following the senseless killing of the beloved senator."

"Beloved senator who held a secret board post for a crime syndicate." Pope finished.

"If it was a hit, was the payoff Doyle's senate seat or his seat with The Ten?"

"Neither's worth killing for," Pope said to Rutger's speculation.

"True," Rutger smoothed a hand across his whisker darkened jaw. "But there's more power with The Ten."

"A post he wouldn't have gotten without a senator's label and that's not even a guarantee," Pope took Rutger's phone and read ahead. "The guy was a nobody before six years ago-an aide for Doyle."

"Who knows the favored sons in a crime organization?" Rutger breathed an incredulous laugh. "How'd *that* happen? Did they all grow up together or something?"

"It'd have to be more than that for Brody and Jake to carry out a hit for the bastard." Pope continued to scroll the screen. "They'd have to be getting one helluva payoff."

"Does it say the guy came from money?"

"No, but I'm guessing that's a negative. Brody and Jake wouldn't have needed to carry out a hit for money."

"Power on the other hand," Rutger considered. "But what kind of power would a senator's aide have? And how is it no one in the GAN put this connection together?"

"No reason to," Pope still viewed the screen. "No one would've been paying attention to those chats that night with all the…entertainment floating around that place. They wouldn't have a disc to scour-wouldn't have thought to."

"You think this Morrow blackmailed Brody and Jake into it?"

Pope shook his head. "Guy like that? No way. But he had something they wanted and it must've been damn good."

Pope's phone buzzed and he handed over Rutger's to pull his own from a front jean pocket. His expression softened when he read the faceplate and turned away from Rutger to take the call.

"Ms. Young-" his greeting was interrupted and he began to laugh. "LuCarolyn."

Rutger abandoned his phone then too, shoving the device into his back pocket. A scowl took possession of his arresting features as the tone of Pope's conversation with LuCarolyn Young adopted a sickeningly sweet element.

"...I appreciate whatever you can do," Pope was saying. "... No, nothing's changed," he laughed again, but the sound carried less humor and more distress then. "...yeah...yeah, Lu I hope you can."

There was more soft laughter that had Rutger bristling. Lowering his head, he focused on clenching his fists and not reaching out to snatch the phone. Thankfully, the call was ending.

Pope's satisfied smile faded when he saw Rutger's mutinous glare directed his way. "What?"

"Pretty chummy." Rutger flicked a glance to the phone.

"She's Bear's best friend. What'd you want me to do?"

"Introduce us."

"Seriously? With ev-"

"You owe me more than you could ever repay, but I'll start with collecting on the very helpful info I just uncovered."

Pope shook his head, though his azure eyes sparkled a little more humorously. "You do realize I could've found that had I taken the time to Google the little shit's name?"

"Could've is a long way from did," Rutger was shameless in his persistence.

Pope gave into a burst of laughter and relished the sensation. "It's either hunting or fucking with you, isn't it?"

"Don't try to change the subject."

Pope's laughter was a lengthy and full bodied roar then. He clapped Rutger's back. "You're right. Listen, LuCarolyn's on her way up to Bear's room now. If you can give her about ten minutes to try with Bear, I'll get you your introduction."

Rutger spread his hands, satisfied. "All I ask," he said.

*** 

"Bear?" LuCarolyn's voice was hushed when she cleared the doorway to the bedroom and found her friend almost totally hidden beneath the covers.

Puffing out her cheeks, LuCarolyn drew up her hair and twisted the coarse locks into a high ponytail while she continued on toward the bed. Toeing off her sneakers, LuCarolyn pulled away the plum jacket she'd worn over a gray workout unitard. Quietly, she climbed atop the bed and crawled to the head. She eased the covers down from Bear's face, pleased the woman hadn't burrowed herself in too snugly.

"B?" LuCarolyn murmured, letting a kiss linger to Bear's forehead.

Bear didn't stir until LuCarolyn reached beneath the covers to tickle her. Her heart lifted when she saw the woman smile in her sleep.

"B...?" That time, LuCarolyn received a sleepy murmur in reply. She tried again, putting another kiss to Bear's forehead and got more than she bargained for. Bear not only murmured, but rolled to her side and took LuCarolyn's hand with her.

"Ms. Clayton...? I'm the wrong friend for this...Bear." LuCarolyn spoke firmly when her hand was in imminent danger of becoming scandalously wedged between Bear's breasts.

Bear gave a little grunt and then turned to her back, still clutching LuCarolyn's hand. One eye opened to a slit and Bear groaned upon realizing who shared her bed.

"Girl, bye," Bear drawled, turning back onto her side.

"No can do, hot stuff," LuCarolyn cuddled close again. "I'm out here at your man's request. Once you're out of bed, I'm gonna kick your ass for keeping *that* news to yourself."

"Mmm...he's a friend of Mercuri's...Tee and Prin know..."

LuCarolyn's honey-toned gaze began to blaze. "Yeah, that skinny ass is definitely due for a kickin'-"

"Wait." Bear had become more lucid. She forced her eyes open and frowned up at LuCarolyn. "You talked to Pope?"

"Only by phone and if he looks as good as he sounds-"

"He looks better than he sounds," a naughty chord filtered Bear's still sleepy tone.

LuCarolyn seemed to swoon and snuggled her head into one of the pillows. "So? What's it like having something that sounds that good in your ear all night?"

Bear wakened further. Trace amounts of regret took shape in the deep mocha of her eyes. "I'm afraid I might forget soon. He's been sleeping downstairs for the past few nights." She gave a pitiful half-shrug. "Pissed with me," she added.

"Hell B, can you blame the man?" LuCarolyn braced on her elbow. "It's goin' on a week. Shaun's memorial is in a few days. Your soiree starts soon after. You can't hide out here forever."

"Don't you think I know that, Lu?" Bear huddled deeper inside the covers then. "When I-when I'm here this-none of this seems real. I can believe none of it's happened-that Shaun's just downstairs in the office with Mike or off somewhere, running an errand."

She sent a quietly brooding look to LuCarolyn. "I don't expect you to get it. You don't get close to your staff."

"Hey?!" LuCarolyn took offense. "That doesn't mean I don't care about them. It sure doesn't mean they'd want me living in denial of their deaths or looking like death, cooped up in bed." She fixed Bear with a brooding look of her own. "I'll bet you haven't even let Jean in to change these sheets, have you?"

Bear's response was to tuck in deeper.

"Alright..." LuCarolyn's trademark slyness took shape on her expression. "Listen, I promised Pope I'd get you out of this bed. Not only will I do *that*, I'm gonna do Pope *and* Jean a favor and change these sheets while you've got your stinking butt in the shower."

"My butt doesn't stink."

"Doesn't matter. It'll be in the shower within minutes of me unleashing my secret weapon."

The words clearly held special, horrific meaning to Bear for she groaned and tried to hide her head beneath the covers. LuCarolyn wasn't having it and, with one vicious yank, drew the comforter and top sheet from Bear.

"Hmm..." LuCarolyn eyed her friend's attire. "This is nice," she smoothed the sweater between thumb and forefinger and smiled coyly. "Is it Pope's?"

"Lu-"

285

"Damn he's a big son of a bitch-"

"Out!"

"You first." LuCarolyn countered the order.

Looking miserable, Bear turned her face into a pillow.

"Okay…" LuCarolyn left the bed and began to hum.

Bear pulled a pillow over her face and groaned again.

~~~

"What the hell?"

Pope and Rutger slowed their steps within seconds of entering the lower level of the bedroom suite. The air had suddenly come alive to the sounds of Diana Ross' "I'm Coming Out".

The guys traded amused and curious looks before following the music up the staircase. When they arrived in the doorway, curious amusement made way for pure male shock and thorough approval.

Bear, obviously not quite ready to relinquish her bed, maintained her prone position in the center of the mattress. LuCarolyn straddled her friend and merrily sang away while using a pillow to slap Bear's face and chest to the beat of the music. If Bear succeeded in snagging the pillow and throwing it blindly, LuCarolyn merely chose another and continued the slaps.

"Rutger Eliades, LuCarolyn Young," Pope gave soft words of introduction and patted Rutger's back when he acknowledged the tease with barely a tilt of his head.

Chuckling, Pope cast another intrigued look toward the dark beauties atop the bed and then he left Rutger to occupy the doorway alone.

Gaze fixed on LuCarolyn, Rutger was as pleased by her playful demeanor as he was by her centerfold quality curves outlined beneath a unitard. Hunting and fucking. Pope had accused him of only ever having those two activities on the brain. His friend would be surprised to learn that hunting had only occupied a scant portion of his thoughts since he'd discovered the existence of LuCarolyn Young.

LuCarolyn had tired of pillow slapping Bear in time to the music. She got to her feet and began to treat the bed like a trampoline until Bear began to frantically slap at her legs.

"Alright goddammit! Stop! I'm up!"

LuCarolyn wasn't taking any chances and continued jumping until Bear wrenched herself from the covers and stomped into the bathroom.

Laughing, LuCarolyn shut off the music and toppled to the middle of the bed where she lay on her stomach. "If I don't hear that shower running in one minute, I'm coming in there and we'll take one together!"

The shower started 3 seconds later.

Pleased, LuCarolyn pushed off the bed and went to root around in the closet where she knew Bear kept fresh linens. She worked efficiently for a few minutes, never noticing the man watching her from the front of the room.

By then, Rutger was resting his imposing form against the doorframe, arms folded across his very broad chest while his stirring whiskey toned stare was filled with intent. It remained so, even when he felt the hard thump between his shoulder blades. Pope.

"Intimidated?" Pope grinned at the look he got in response to his quiet query and then he moved on into the room.

LuCarolyn was finishing up with the bed when she heard a single knock echo. The pillow she held, slipped from a suddenly weakened limb and she studied the man who approached. *Oh Bear, you are so getting your ass kicked for keeping this news to yourself*, she silently threatened. The man's smile brought to life a blindingly radiant blue gaze as he took her hand and gave his name.

"Pope Apostolou."

"Lu," she forced out the syllable. "LuCarolyn Young. Everybody calls me Lu um, Bear's in the shower."

"Thanks Lu," Pope's words were soft but healthy with gratitude.

Pope shifted then and LuCarolyn saw the man who joined him. She wasn't sure how she'd missed him given his size-same height as Pope but more...massive. It was his face that forced the gasp from her mouth, though. Aesthetically perfect with knife edged bones and seductively chiseled angles, set beneath a cap of dark close cut curls. It was a magnificent face and a familiar one. Pope was drawing her between him and the man who was seriously impeding her ability to think.

"Lu, this is my friend Rutger Eliades. Rut, LuCarolyn Young."

"Nice to meet you," her voice was mere decibels above a whisper as Pope put her hand into his friend's.

"Same," Rutger squeezed her limp fingers.

LuCarolyn wondered if she looked as ready to faint as she felt. She commanded herself to focus on something other than the jarring intensity of his features or his voice which was deep as a cavern.

The still running shower did the trick and she turned to Pope.

"I'm gonna get going, but everyone should be back in town by the end of the week-we'll all be over to see her then."

"Sounds good," Pope took her free hand and squeezed it to his chest. "Thanks Lu."

Feeling decidedly subdued by the men dwarfing her, LuCarolyn could only nod her response. Cooly, she eased her hands from their smothering holds and hurried from the room.

Rutger watched her flee.

"Aren't you going after her? Convince her to let you in her bed?"

"She already wants that." Rutger's response was flat with certainty. His eyes remained on the door.

Pope laughed. "Intimidated yet confident. I like it," he squeezed Rutger's shoulder and headed off to find Bear.

Rutger's gaze remained fixed on the door. Yes, LuCarolyn Young wanted him in her bed, he could see that easily enough, but it was the rest of what he saw that told him to wait. Beneath the wanting was realization... and shame.

Just then, she was adjusting to the fact of who he was and what he knew. That was exactly what he wanted her to do. When the time came and it *would* come- he wanted there to be no misunderstandings. No deceptions. He wanted LuCarolyn Young full and well goddamn aware of who she was being claimed by.

# CHAPTER 26

$P$ope checked on Bear in the shower, but chose not to intrude when he found her there. Of course the idea of her in bed was enough to keep a permanent smile on his face. The thought of her in bed and depressed however, had waged a war on his patience and his concern.

If he could have returned Shaun Oates to her to see that fierce light return to her eyes, he would have. As that feat was beyond him, he was willing to resort to any *possible* device to draw her from despair. LuCarolyn Young proved to be the right choice.

LuCarolyn and Rutger for that manner, were long gone by the time Pope returned to the suite's lower level. He made a pitstop in the kitchen nook, decided to treat himself to a beer before going back up to check in on Bear.

He was halfway through the bottle when he heard her on the top stair. Instead of calling out to her, he waited.

~~~

Bear left the shower with plans to kick LuCarolyn out of her room, lock the door and climb back beneath the covers. Storming out of

289

the bath to find the space empty, left her with nowhere to spend her bolstered attitude. The bed was freshly made and she smirked over LuCarolyn keeping that promise as well.

The room door was open and she wondered if LuCarolyn had left or if Pope was still there...she finished towelling off and lotioning. The plan was still to pour herself back into bed. Still, she bypassed Pope's comfy sweater and opened the drawer containing her leisure wear. She selected a plain T-shirt dress and moved to the door instead of the bed. Slow steps on bare feet took her to the ledge overlooking the lounge area.

She seemed to be alone and the fact encouraged her to move on toward the stairs. Her eyes locked on the door at the rear of the lounge. Her stride gained momentum once she cleared the bottom stair.

~~~

Pope decided to wait until she'd taken a seat in the lounge before he made his presence known. When she bypassed the living area, he frowned though his expression cleared when he realized where she was headed.

As though she were afraid to touch it, she outlined the back door knob with the tips of her fingers. Seconds passed and then she laid her hand flat on the door, following the move by resting her forehead against the surface. She let out a quick breath when her hand closed over the knob, turned and the door opened just a crack. Instead of crossing the threshold, Pope watched her continue to rest her head against the door as if waiting to see whether courage or cowardice would show up.

He could only imagine the war that must've been waging inside her mind. He'd only wanted her out of bed and not allowing despair or defeat to claim her. He would've never tried to persuade, let alone bully her into returning to the scene of that crime. Yet, there she was, working to conquer what had to terrify her.

She continued to lean on the door and Pope decided she'd tried hard enough. He was moving out from the nook when she left the door and disappeared into the corridor beyond. For Pope, another inner debate ensued-whether to let her be or give her the support he thought she could use.

Deciding that support was best, he followed her to the stairwell where she'd taken position on the top step. It was a short distance from where the police tape still sectioned off the area. He didn't think she'd sensed his presence behind her while she sat looking down on the spot where Shaun Oates' blood was spilled almost a week prior. He didn't want to intrude on her grief, but he didn't want her to feel as though she were alone. He was opening his mouth to speak, when she beat him to it.

"He can't be gone, Pope. It-it's not time for him to be gone. I'm not ready..."

"I know, Babe." Pope went to join her on the step.

"I don't...I don't know if he understood how much he meant to me."

"He did. He did." Pope squeezed the back of her neck, bared where her hair was tugged into a messy ball. Gently, he worked his fingers against the muscles tensed there.

"I hardly told him. I hardly tell him *or* Mike."

"They know, Sweet. They know. Shaun knew it."

She cried then. The emotion came on softly at first-spiking her lashes while moisture pooled her eyes. The sobs built and released on a wave of heartbreaking sound that shook her slender frame.

Pope gave her time to spend the emotion, massaging her neck and using the contact to rock her slowly. When her sobs drew into dry shudders, he pulled her close to settle into his lap. He kept her there for a long while, steadily rocking her as the shudders began to subside.

When the cleansing seemed to have depleted her, Pope stood and carried her back to bed.

***

Shaun Oates hailed from a huge Irish family. His siblings had already arranged for his body to be shipped back to Dublin where funeral arrangements had been made so that the majority of the relatives could attend.

For the large clan there in California, a wake had been organized at a well-known pub near The Bay. Given the suddenness and circumstances of Shaun's death, Pope wasn't sure if he should've expected the kind of Irish wakes he'd been in the midst of following the passings of other associates.

Those uncertainties proved unnecessary he discovered when he and Bear arrived for the send off that had begun that evening at dusk. While no small amount of tears were shed, laughter, revelry and gregarious stories were in high supply. It appeared that Bear knew a great many of Shaun's kin.

Pope had to remind himself more than once that this was an occasion meant to ease sorrows. Therefore, he resisted the urge to tug Bear free of all the lingering squeezes and mouth to mouth kisses she received from Shaun's brothers, uncles and cousins who were in heavy attendance that night.

The occasion seemed to be revving into an all night affair. A good thing, since much of the Bear Arms staff began to pour in long after the boss' arrival. Pope and Bear said their goodbyes and left shortly after hour three got underway.

They drove around for awhile not really heading anywhere in particular. They'd taken one of the ranch Jeeps and; with the evening being quite mild, enjoyed the breeze barreling into the vehicle to ruffle their clothes and hair.

They weren't in any hurry to head indoors. Pope took them up the coast, glancing toward Bear at brief intervals. Her head rested against the seat back while her hair flew fiercely about her oval face. Pope moved his hand from the gear shift to smooth it across her thigh. When he reached for her hand, she accepted the contact, squeezing his inside both hers.

~~~

They wound up in Pacifica and Pope waited for Bear to question his choice of destination. She didn't.

When he put the Jeep in park, she didn't take the steps up to the front door. Instead, she went to the front of the 4wheel drive and leaned against the hood. Pope joined her there and they remained so, for well over ten minutes enjoying the starry sky.

"Where does that go?" She pointed to a railing cutting a path through a perfectly trimmed hedge a few feet away.

"Leads down to the beach."

She moved toward it. Pope let her put a little distance between them before he followed. The dress she'd selected for the wake was a simple, ankle-length number. Its blouse styled bodice flowed into a long, billowing skirt. Bear paid no mind to the sand collecting along her hem once she'd cleared the steps and strode toward the shore. She stopped some feet away from the foaming edge and took a seat.

"Quite a sky you've got here Mr. A," she commended when he dropped down next to her.

Pope reclined in his spot, as unmindful of his clothes as Bear when he set his elbows behind him in the sand.

"It'll do, I guess. It's not in the league with Cabo or that place of your grandparents, I'd bet."

Bear was silent for a time. "I lost them like I lost Shaun-violently." Her tone was a soft one that somehow carried over the dull roar of crashing waves.

The moon beamed strongly that night and Pope could make out the somber set of her features doused in its silver glow. "I'm sorry," he said.

She shook her head. "It was a long time ago and it wasn't sudden like with Shaun. It *happened* suddenly, but I saw it coming-saw it coming for a long time."

"You don't have to talk about it, Cub."

"Yeah I do, I...you need to understand why-why I'm afraid."

He pushed up slowly. "Afraid of what?"

"This. Us. That I won't be able to keep you."

He made no move to console her or to tell her she was wrong. He understood that she didn't need that then.

"I was named for my grandparents. Bert and Merrill." She gave him a sideways glance then. "Don't laugh."

"I wouldn't dream of it." Soft, adoring lines set his expression. "They sound like great people."

"They were. They raised me better than my own mother."

Pope nodded, recalling the story she'd shared when they were in Mexico.

"They were together all their lives. Can you believe that? To be with someone for as long as you can remember?"

"Sounds like a beautiful thing."

"It was...but beautiful things can have ugly sides too, you know?"

"What happened?"

"I told you my grandfather was old school. Women were to be seen. *Loved*, but quiet. Silent as far as giving opinions went."

"Must've been hard for you?" Pope nudged her shoulder.

Bear nudged him back, accepting the dig. "It really wasn't, considering I was a kid who respected her elders. Anyway... my life was damn near perfect, no need to argue over sharing opinions. My mother was out of our hair-no more arguments in the dead of night and being terrified that she'd drag me off somewhere. When she left, my life was exactly how I wanted it. I'd do anything to protect it."

"What happened, Bear?"

"I told you what a great place they had? Well, other people thought so too. Thought so, so much, they were willing to fight very dirty to get it. Things started going wrong. Property tax payments got lost. Produce shipments from the farm never made it to their destinations. My granddad fought them for a long time, but he really didn't know who *they* were...unless *they* were defined as racist inbred pricks."

"Got it."

"No offence."

"None taken. For the record, I'm not racist or inbred, though there has been the occasional woman who's seen fit to call me a prick."

"The nerve."

"I'll say."

Bear laughed, appreciating the stress relieving reprieve. Too soon, her features was sobering.

"My granddad saw white folks he'd called friends for years, retreat to the sidelines. It all came down to money, you see? Hope that the inbred pricks might win and break off a piece of my grandad's land for them."

"So the inbred pricks were rich, huh?"

"Mmm...but not as rich as the farmers two counties over- a family of black farmers. My granddad knew them well. They were very successful, very incorporated. They were willing to give him all the help he needed. From money to security."

"What was the problem, then?"

"Problem was, *I'd* sought them out. Well...my grandmother was the one who went to him with the idea. I knew he'd never accept it from me, but my grandmother was willing to hear the plan." Bear shook her head and smiled sourly.

"My grandfather said, the day he needed to be bailed out by his wife was the day he stopped being a man. Can you believe that?"

"I can, actually." Pope responded without hesitation, shrugged when Bear snapped her head around in surprise.

"You said it yourself," he went on. "Women were to be seen, loved and quiet, but you forget one-protected. Having the women in his life come to *his* rescue was unacceptable."

"Worse than being killed?"

"For some men, yes."

"For you?"

"I don't know. I *don't*, Cub." He stressed when she drew back in surprise. "It would honestly depend on the situation," he frowned as he watched her. "Is that why you're afraid we won't make it?"

"They fought. Bad…" Bear began her response. "I'd never heard it so bad. Not even with my mom. Yelling...and granddad threw things. He didn't hit my gran-angry as he was...a lesser man would have...My gran let it go. She said granddad knew what was best and he was all she'd ever known. She said she wouldn't lose her marriage over land and it was *that* simple for her. She lost her life over pride."

Bear made a woeful sound deep in her throat. "I didn't have a marriage to protect. I called those farmers, told them we'd take their security. I didn't think granddad could deny it, then. Not if they drove right up to the front door."

"But he did."

"Yeah and with both barrels. Literally. Held them off with a double barrelled shotgun." She smiled over the memory, but the gesture didn't hold very long.

"He was so pissed with me," she removed her wedge heeled wrap sandals and burrowed her toes in the sand. Leaning forward, she rested her chin on her knees.

Pope followed Bear's lead, removing his shoes and socks. He didn't exhibit half as much concern as Bear and merely tossed the items aside as though he hadn't a care for where they landed.

"I was the one yelling then," she said. "I'd never done that- not even when I was small. Not-not ever. I called him a foolish old man who loved his pride more than his wife. I left with the farmers' security guards and when I went back two days later, they were dead."

She stood as Pope reached for her, barely evading his grasp. "They ruled it a robbery, even though nothing was missing-said it must've been a drifter looking for drugs and he killed them when he couldn't find any. Two days-" emotion choked her and she bowed her head until composure resumed.

"I never had the chance to say I was sorry. Had I...been there-"

295

"You would've been dead too," Pope stood then, took Bear's forearms and made her face him. "You were a kid."

She hung her head again. "Maybe that's why they never came before. I was a kid. Had I been there-"

"You can't still believe that?"

Bear straightened, stiffening in his hold. "What I believe is that I never wanted a love like what my grandparents had-one I'd ever be so blindly committed to that I'd put my life in its hands. The bank took the farm. I ran and kept running 'til I met Lu. Then, Tee and Prin...we all found jobs one summer working for the huge furniture outfit Prin's parents own in Virginia," her smile was faint but warm.

"Those were good times and then...there was Vegas and I've spent the last six years *believing* love would never happen-making sure it'd never happen by being as tough as...hard as I could and now here you are and I...I'm so in love with you and I can see myself falling as blind in love with you as my gran did with my granddad and it scares the shit out of me."

"Dammit, Bear don't you think I'm scared too?" Pope gave her a slight shake. In the moonlight, he could detect the surprise on her face when she looked at him.

"Love is the last thing I ever wanted. It may not have even been the last thing. I doubt it ever even made the list," he grinned slyly yet with agitation. "Love made losing it hurt too much. When I met-*saw* you, all I wanted was you in my bed. I was sure I'd want you for more than one night, but not because of love. You see I made sure love would never happen to me either. You're not the only one who lost a love that can't be replaced."

"She must've been incredible," Bear could hear the sorrow etched richly in his voice.

"She was...beyond that," he gave a quiet laugh. "This time I'm gonna have to ask *you* not to laugh. It was my mother."

"Pope, I-" Sorrow held her expression then. "I'm so sorry I-for your loss, but here I am griping about mine and yours-"

"Shh...no. No, Cub."

"You said you were taken from her."

"Yeah...the people who took me were part of my father's organization. My mother...she was part of my father's organization. He brought her here from Greece to be...his."

The meaning was clear. Bear took a step back, laboring to study his darkly haunting features captured in the moon's glow. "What happened to her?" She asked.

"I don't know for sure, but I have a good idea. I never saw her again. Losing her that way...I never wanted to feel that again so...while women were always in season, love wasn't." He smiled over the dig for barely half a second.

"I reserved love for my friends and no one else," his smile made room for the fierce grimace that slashed his face and ignited his dimple. "Then we lost our friend, Patch. He was like a brother to the rest of us. We were all better for knowing him. Losing him was hard and senseless and could've made me turn my back on friends who were the only family I had."

He moved closer, taking Bear's hands. "Losing Patch had just the opposite effect and I realized love wasn't about what you lost when it was gone, but what you gained for having it." His eyes remained on Bear's hands. "Can you tell me that the *fear* of losing what we've had in the short time we've known each other means more to you than what we actually have?" He dropped her hands and stepped back. The weight of what he was about to say-what he so didn't want to say-crested over him like a massive wave.

"If your fears mean more to you, then I'll walk away."

"No," looking stricken, Bear went to tug his hand into hers. "I don't want that."

Pope didn't look reassured. "You don't want me to go, but my leaving doesn't mean as much as protecting your fears does?"

She sighed, finally accepting the full weight of his argument. "I won't tell you that today or tomorrow or maybe not even next week but one day...one day those fears could get the better of me I-I don't want to lie to you about that."

"So I guess it comes down to the fact that we've got both fears to conquer." He said. "Are you okay with being apart until we do that? Or would you mind handling *one day* when it gets here?" His hand tightened on hers. "It's been way too long since I've kissed you and I much rather be taking care of that right now. The idea of anything taking you from me makes me mad enough to kill and anything includes my fear," he said. "Surely you're tough enough not to be dictated to by your fear, Bear?"

297

She considered the point he made and then tilted her head at a playful angle. "You drive a hard bargain," she sighed.

"Hard? Yes. But irresistible too, right?"

She laughed, the sound carrying gaily over the night breeze. "Irresistible too." She agreed.

"May I have my kiss now, Bear?"

He asked sweetly and she puckered, tilting back her head in expectation of a gesture to parallel his tone. Instead, she was taken off her feet, her mouth plundered seconds later by deep, repetitive lunges of his talented tongue. He rendered her breathless in moments and gave her no chance to recover. Heat became an impenetrable force that repelled the strong, cool breeze Bear had enjoyed for the better part of the night. He inflamed every inch of her skin with velvety soft lips that cruised with expert skill and left her limp yet aroused in his embrace.

"Pope," she panted, barely able to pronounce his name. She was so overcome by the pleasure erupting from his sensual brutalization of her earlobe. The harsh, wet suckles underscored hungry moans stirring low in his throat and sent her heart flailing against her ribcage.

"So how private is the beach of yours?" she asked.

# CHAPTER 27

He preferred to show her rather than tell her. Concern had Bear's heart thudding instead of flailing at her ribcage when Pope set her down and she felt his hands moving to the bodice of her dress. Memory flashed as she recalled the fate her clothes suffered during her last visit there.

Quickly, she covered the hands that were fully prepared to wreak destruction on the frock.

"Let me," she suggested.

Obliging the request, Pope stepped back to watch her with eyes that were hooded and hungry.

Bear was careful with her clothing while Pope gripped his shirt collar. One long tug sent the garment up and over his head. Bear's dress fell soundlessly to the sand and left her in a lacy, black pushup and matching panties. She'd eased down the straps and was reaching to undo the back hooks.

Pope felt he'd waited long enough. Bear shrieked when her feet left the ground. Pope knelt, cradling her effortlessly above the sand as he dragged over his discarded shirt to lay her on. The waves seemed to crash about them with an enhanced ferocity. It was as though nature perceived the sensual tumult at work between the couple trading heated kisses and hushed words of needy approval.

Bear had already half heaved out of her bra. With the straps lowered, Pope had only to hook a finger beneath the cups to free her of its confines. The hooks were still in place however. It made no difference to Pope who gave a single sadistic yank that tore them free of their superior stitching.

Bear's annoyed cry, stoked his grin. "Sorry," he said.

"Liar," she hissed.

Pope's chuckles trailed off into soundlessness as he devoured a newly exposed breast. Arching instinctively, Bear's moans vied for space against the gasps inside her throat. Pope nourished himself at the nipple he sucked deep into his mouth. His touch was feather soft, while he stroked her hips and sides. His big hands intermittently cupped and squeezed as he worked on one breast before switching to its mate.

Bear threaded shaking fingers through Pope's hair, gloriously splayed in rich, dark ribbons across her chest. Another layer of sensation emerged when she felt his fist at her center. Already in dire need of him there, she began to grind against the insistent nudging, hungry for whatever release it might bring.

Pope freed himself, kicking free of trousers and boxers. He claimed her fast, sparking a mutual groan between them as contact was made. For Bear, the contact was intensified by the delicious width of his shaft when it stretched her walls with an almost painful sweetness.

"Bear," Pope shuddered, squeezing his eyes shut as sensation slammed. She was almost unbearably tight, yet molded beautifully to the length and thickness of his shaft clutched in the fist of her inner muscles.

The waves had not ceased their insatiable pounding. Pope and Bear drew closer to the water. Writhing and twisting, they took extreme delight in the friction roused by the consistent advance and retreat of fevered strokes. Bear had taken care to keep her dress and shoes a safe distance from the water that grabbed Pope's shirt and dragged it into riotous depths.

Next, the surf made its play for Pope and Bear. It sluiced over, under and between their bodies like a third lover come to join them. Bear trembled as powerfully from the force of the claiming waves as she did from Pope's exquisite possession of her body.

He took her slow, with strokes that spanned long, carnal moments in time. He abandoned her breasts in order to study her reaction to what he put her through. Bear was too far gone by satisfaction to care about what her expression revealed. She curled her fingers into her soaked hair and met his steady patient thrusts with her own languid sways.

She wanted to sob when he filled her with his tongue and used it to duel with the water that pulsed for supremacy inside her sex. For Pope, the seawater enhanced her addictive flavor. He could've fed off her forever but his cock was demanding and wanted more of what it selfishly considered its own. He wouldn't argue the logic there and stole a few additional moments to devour her.

Bear felt almost completely limp yet fully capable of taking delight in the pleasure that ruthlessly pummeled. She didn't argue when Pope deprived her of his mouth. She was too depleted to form the necessary words. Depletion had nothing on arousal when he flipped her to her stomach and subjected her to more filling strokes. He cursed obscenely and in sheer approval. Bear pounded the wet sand in appreciation as she took her pleasure.

Once more exercising his strength, Pope used an arm to support Bear. He kept her back to his chest, her torso just above the water. He cradled her breast, thumb flicking at the firm wet nipple. His other hand, hidden beneath the waves, cupped her mound to work her clit with strong circular rubs.

Despite the force of the water, Pope was sensitive enough to feel her coming hard on his still rigid shaft. The force of it snapped the remaining tie he'd used to bind his need. He erupted, coating her walls with the proof of all he'd held back, having forbid himself to touch her while she'd been grieving the heaviest.

The strongest climatic waves began to ebb, leaving them both speechless and weak. Not surprising, it was Pope who recovered his strength the fastest. He dropped a stream of slow, wet kisses across her back and withdrew from her body, semi-erect and already firming for more of the pleasure only she could provide.

He reached for her dress which was soaked but not yet seized by the loud waves. Pope slung the garment over his shoulder and hooked the straps of her sandals over a thumb. He took Bear up from the sand in a show of shameless ease. He bent his head, his tongue teasing apart her lips to ply her with a slow, sweet kiss. Bear whimpered and eagerly participated as Pope carried them toward the house on its lonely cliff.

~~~

"Stop staring and drink up so we can go to bed," Pope's order was playfully gruff when he found Bear watching him.

Inside the house, he'd wrapped her in a fleece blanket of soothing heather brown. He'd put water on for tea and even gotten her settled on his den floor in front of the enormous brick hearth where he built a fire. Soon, a vibrant blaze filled the room with warmth and muted golden light.

"Stop staring? Seriously?" Bear wondered how the hell he expected her to focus on drinking tea. He joined her on the floor and rested back against the base of a massive easy chair that flanked the sofa where she relaxed.

While Pope had given Bear a blanket to warm herself in, he seemed content with using the warmth from the fire...and nothing else. No way could any woman-hell, Bear thought-any*one* with eyes focus on anything other than the picture of rugged, nude physicality he portrayed.

"It's impressive how the cold doesn't bother you," she said in an attempt to dismiss the more basic reasons for her stare. Smiling coyly, she snuggled into the blanket to ward off the ocean's chill that still lingered in her bones.

"Supernatural body temp," she mused, "ability to get by on little sleep...I'd love to sample your vitamins."

"Hmph," Pope's easy expression took on a harsh edge in the firelight's glare. "No, Bear. No you wouldn't."

Something in his voice, a stonier undertone to its natural animal chord, had her holding the heated mug a little tighter. "Did I say something wrong?"

"No, Cub," he gave her the benefit of a brief haunted look. "I told you why my mother-why my and my friends' mothers were brought here?" He waited for her nod.

"They were more than entertainment for them..."

Bear scooted to her knees when he trailed off. When she would've moved closer, Pope raised a hand to prevent it.

"I need you to hear this part-this part more than the rest." Again, he waited for her nod.

"When they got pregnant with us, they uh-our fathers' organization, gave them a *vitamin*," he sent her a meaningful look.

"A supplement the organization wanted to mass produce, but not as a drug. As a drug it would've required strict testing-stringent trials to ensure its safety. As a dietary supplement-"

"Oversight rests with its creators," Bear guessed.

Pope's smile carried grim satisfaction. "They weren't willing to share the formula so they held back on pushing it through. They never gave up on looking for a way to make it happen, though. In the meantime, they found other ways to make it work for them. My friends and I-many others like us-were bred to be weapons, soldiers for hire. Some never even knew their mothers and were taken straight from the womb, raised...I don't know where, until they were old enough for the military schools we all went to around nine or ten."

"Were there ever any girls?" Bear's voice was quiet and hesitant.

Pope was looking into the fire. "Only ever boys as far as I know-they wanted *specimens* who; in their twisted opinions, were mentally and physically superior."

"Did this...supplement guarantee boys?"

"I don't know that either. Any girls would've stayed with their mothers, kept elsewhere or-"

Bear's gasp, halted the chilling reply. Her hands went to her mouth as her eyes widened in understanding. Long seconds passed before she tried her voice again.

"So this...supplement guaranteed kids who were smarter, stronger, bigger..." she scanned the nearly impossible perfection of his face and physique. "Sounds like every man's dream child. Should've been a piece of cake to get it approved. Why all the secrecy? Aside from the fact that they were breeding..."

"Killers," Pope finished.

She winced. "Sorry."

His expression softened. "Never apologize for telling the truth, Cub. There was a nasty side effect to this wonder drug, but in the GAN's eyes even that had its uses. In the eyes of anyone ethical, it would've been seen as an abomination. Some of the offspring showed psychotic tendencies after a few years. It was a tendency the GAN exploited or suppressed depending on how strongly it carried in the individual."

"I see."

"Sweetness..." Pope graced Bear with a pitying smile. "I'm afraid you don't," he looked back into the fire.

"In the past, I've gone out of my way not to leave behind any...traces of myself. I haven't done that at all with you. I don't think I ever wanted to. I haven't been careful with you and I can't say I'm sorry about it."

"I told you I'm on the pill," Bear forced herself not to obsess over how weak the argument suddenly sounded.

Pope was looking as though he could read her expression. "I should've told you all this but I only recently found out the whole story. By the time that happened...I was hooked on you -on sex with you- on what we might share beyond that. At the time, I didn't want you to know what you'd be taking on- what you could *potentially* be taking on with me."

She blinked, gave a slight shake of her head. "At the time? What-what's changed?"

"What's changed, babe is I don't want to lose you over another omission, especially if there's a chance you could one day..." he let his gaze drift down below her waist.

Bear moved to her knees again, scooting close until she was straddling his lap to wrap them both in her blanket. "What was that you said about one day?" She kissed his cheek. "Let's deal with it when it gets here."

Pope took her hands when she would've touched his face, sandwiched them between his own. "Baby, I think 'one day' is already here. Honey, I've killed people-more than a few- way more and not all of them were from behind a rifle scope miles away, but up close and personal with my own two hands." He let go of hers suddenly as if not wanting them in contact with his own.

"It takes a level of madness to do that, don't you think?"

"You wouldn't hurt me that way, Pope."

Her certainty made him smile, albeit sadly. "I tell myself and my friends that all the time- that we aren't those guys anymore, but knowing this about myself Bear it um...scares me." He sighed over the admission as though the confession were some great achievement.

"It makes me wonder if the nastiest parts of the guy I was are just laying in wait. I don't deal too well with fear, Cub. Actually I never had to deal with it 'til I met you."

His smile sent a not entirely unpleasant chill up her spine.

He shrugged. "That fear's been building since I discovered all this-that I'm not done with it, with the rage or what follows it."

"You wouldn't hurt me," Bear persisted.

"No. I wouldn't." His confirmation was immediate. "But there are all kinds of ways to hurt someone without ever putting your hands on them and somehow I don't think you'd enjoy sleeping with a murderer."

"You do realize I've had- *still* have similar feelings?" Her query held a challenging edge. "My past? What I've done in it-and don't say it's not the same," she ordered when he seemed primed to do just that.

"Sometimes I think my business is a testament to how unfinished I am with the past. I think I surround myself with things that kill because I'm either still terrified by that night, because I need the security or because I now crave being surrounding by things that take lives."

Pope shook his head then but the gesture was more in amusement than denial. "We're a pair, huh?"

"A dangerous pair," Bear's lovely dark face was a picture of slyness. "We are who we are. Sexy, huh?"

Pope shrugged as if to consider her point. "Guess it's not so bad if you look at it like that."

"See?" She shoved his chest. "And that guy you're so concerned about?" She held his face then. "I don't know him-never met him. He's long gone. You aren't that guy anymore."

"You might have to remind me of that. Often. Getting me to buy it may not be easy," he forewarned.

She shrugged off the caution. "I can handle whatever I have to take from the likes of you."

"Is that right?" His expression grew more animated and he tickled her waist.

Bear dissolved into a fit of giggles, hair falling into her eyes as she pounded his chest in an earnest plea for him to stop. Laughter still had her in its grips when Pope caught her waist and sheathed her sex over his in one fluidly erotic glide.

"You were saying?" The animal roughness of his voice was like a balm when he murmured the words at her ear.

Bear could scarcely moan.

"Sorry? I didn't catch that." Pope suckled her earlobe while commanding her moves on his thick rigid length.

At first, Bear was incapable of doing any more than taking it. Her forehead rested on his shoulder while her emotions ricocheted from amusement to desire. Her inner muscles seized, drawing rich sensation as well as an approving curse from Pope. The satisfied torment in his words made Bear feel triumphant and soon she was taking charge of the moment. Lifting and settling herself with innate sensuality, she savored his build, the girth that stretched her to the point of delightful discomfort.

Pope exchanged his hold at her waist to weigh her breasts in his palms. It was Bear uttering approving curses against the sensation of being tweaked and rubbed. He abandoned one breast and her sad moan silenced when he cuffed her neck to tempt her mouth with a kiss.

It was a gentle act, with a sweetness that was almost the exact opposite of the sinful rocking of their hips. The moment touched on many levels-from the most carnal to the most meaningful.

The truths that rested between them, open for display and consideration, brought security to the foundation building beneath the range of their emotions. The robust fire crackling in the hearth; filling the space with golden heat, was the only thing to rival the intensity of what they shared.

# CHAPTER 28

The next day, Bear put in her first full slate of work. As preparations for the soiree were practically done and had counted for much of her workload, the day was relatively easy to take on. That was until a reminder flashed across the bottom of her monitor.

"Dammit to fuck!" She kicked out into the space beneath her desk and closed her eyes.

To anyone who had missed the outburst, it would've looked as though Bear were a picture of calm. If one overlooked the clenched fist raised just above her desk, that is.

Pope; who had overheard the outburst clearly from the viewing room in back of the home office, came to look in on her. He was a portrait of casual amusement. One heavy, sleek brow lifted as he leaned on the doorframe.

"That's a good one," he teased, arms folded over a worn Pearl Jam T-shirt. "Mind if I use it?"

"Bite me."

"Tell me where."

Bear laughed, but the gesture ended on a groan. "It's this damn CBM dinner tomorrow night. The California Business Magazine's annual entrepreneurial dinner," she explained in response to his blank look.

"That's right," he gave a nod. "You're their cover girl. Hope you're not thinking of backing out."

"Not just thinking of it," she grumbled.

"Am I gonna have to bully you, Cub?" His voice held no trace of casual amusement then.

"Pope, I can't go to that thing. Not with all I have going on- and it's got nothing to do with Shaun." Her smile was sad, but hope stirred given she was able to say his name without wanting to cry. "There's all this soiree stuff-"

"But you're done with that."

"Damn you and don't you have business of your own to oversee? Aren't the architects coming to look at the cottage today?"

Bear had already talked with the firm that would transform her recreation house into a full service security hub and guest lounge. She knew Pope was curious about what it would involve and had asked if he'd served as point man for the project. While he was in town, anyway...

There hadn't been much discussion about living statuses pertaining to their relationship. It was still a long distance arrangement for the most part. Pope had houses all over the world. While Bear wouldn't dream of clipping his wings, she hoped he'd feel at home enough to stay with her.

Pope was smiling a knowing smile that verified he saw through her argument and that it was a weak one. "None of that means you can't go to this dinner and be adored."

"I don't need to be adored."

"But you've worked hard for it," he countered. "My guess is there aren't many women who make the cover of that magazine."

"No...no there aren't," acknowledging the sudden tension in her neck, Bear rubbed at the spot and groaned. "And I can count the black women who've made it on one hand-all four of us."

"Well then," Pope pushed off the doorframe. "Only question now is what are you gonna wear?"

"There's actually another question after that. What are *you* gonna wear to enjoy all this adoration with me?" She sighed and had the express pleasure of watching him be thoroughly surprised.

***

***Memphis, Tennessee~***

"You were goddamn lucky and goddamn stupid."

Brody rolled his eyes but didn't turn away from the bar where he prepared his Scotch. "Goin' for a record on how many times you can tell me that J?"

"Hmm…" Jake seemed to consider the idea. "Guess I could. Had I known you'd come back with us in a more fucked up situation than what we already have, I'd have gone with you-"

"And all that would've done was to have us *both* laid up with shoulder injuries."

Jake grimaced. "And you were never *laid up*. That thing's just a flesh wound- one that's got you in a world of trouble."

"May as well be laid up," Brody grumbled. "Been on virtual house arrest since I got back."

"You should be glad you made it back at all. If they'd caught you-"

"But they didn't."

"But they did catch your face."

"We don't know that," Brody's words contradicted his expression.

His face and later his name had been splashed across network and social media since the hunt for him began following the release of Bear Arms' security footage. The footage hadn't been enough to agitate his nerves. They hadn't positively identified him and he had never actually met Bear Clayton before that night.

His hackles didn't start to rise until word leaked of the blood trail he'd left behind. That would send the hounds after him with lightning speed and it did.

Thankfully, the GAN still pulled some weight. It wasn't hard for him to locate resources to patch up his wound and provide him with transport back east. A good thing, as his *date* to the Bear Arms' party hadn't stuck around. The esteemed Senator Morrow left shortly after identifying Bear Clayton's two, trusty assistants. Later

Brody...encouraged Shaun Oates to give him a tour of the grounds. The cameras were enough to give him pause, but not nearly enough to douse the anger that ate at him.

"You would've understood had you been there, J." Brody downed the Scotch, grateful for its burn.

"So explain it to me, then." Vague explanations of the event nearly two weeks prior were all Jake had been able to get out of his friend.

"He was there. They both were."

Brody's words only got a raised brow from Jake.

Brody needed another drink before continuing. "Pope and Mercuri were there."

Jake stiffened, adding a couple of inches to his height. "Did you see Rutger?" He asked.

Brody shook his head. "Just Pope and Mercuri having a high ol time with their black whores. From the looks of it, I'd say they two assholes are in love."

Jake snorted. "You mean lust. Have you see those girls? Looks and bodies-all of 'em. If Rutger and Slayte haven't had a taste yet, they will soon."

"It's not lust." Brody regarded his empty glass. "I know what lust looks like. It's the way my old man looked at his picture of that bastard's slut mother." He went to slosh more liquor into his glass and drank it fast in hopes of wiping out the image of Nathan Alberts perched on his desk, clutching the framed picture of Ariadna Apostolou.

His father thought no one knew of the picture, but Brody had. More than that, he knew what it had meant to the man.

"He looked at my mother with love," Brody swore it, though he wasn't altogether sure. He'd never been altogether sure.

"Seeing Pope with her, Mercuri with her friend...love, happiness...power...Pope waltzed in and took-was given," Brody confessed with a distinct bite to his words.

"He was given everything-power he doesn't give a fuck about, a looker who probably sucks his dick like a champ every night...I didn't mean for things to go so far that night, Jake but I was mad enough to kill. I still am. You were right all along. We should go in and wipe them out. Had I killed Pope before my father kicked his own bucket, maybe I'd be sitting in the driver's seat right now."

310

"Well the point is moot now, isn't it?" Jake shrugged. "Unless you really think Pope doesn't want it all."

"What difference does it make now?" Brody swatted a hand. "He spat in the face of everything my dad wanted to give him, begged him to take and he got it anyway."

"Do you think he'd give it to you?"

"Not in a million."

"But if he did?"

"What the hell are you sayin', Jake? Now you *want* us to develop a wait and see attitude?"

"Has its benefits."

"I don't care- I want Pope dead."

"They'll suspect you."

"I don't care I...I promised Denny, Jake," Brody paced the living room. "I went to his grave and promised I'd make Pope pay for what he did. Hell, I'm finished anyway. How long before they come knocking to drag me away?"

"We've fought against worst, Bro."

"And what about the attacks we can't see coming? You forget our enemies aren't just *outside* the GAN, Jake."

Jake knew that all too well. What had him most concerned was Brody's attitude. He needed his friend back on his game. If it meant ridding the world of at least one of the fuckers responsible for upsetting all their carefully laid plans, so be it. Even if nothing else came of it, he'd have the satisfaction of knowing Rutger was suffering the harsh blow of losing another one of the few people in life that he did care about.

\*\*\*

California Business Magazine's Entrepreneur's Dinner was an annual event that never failed to turn out the best, brightest, most consistent and worthy contributors to the state's economy. The event was a mix of California's business, athletic and artistic communities.

The publication's year-end photo spread always drew shameful amounts of speculation as to who would grace its coveted pages. Who would grace its cover, drew a whole other level of speculation entirely. That it had been Bear Clayton was no real surprise. Many of the most respected members of the California business community knew it would only be a matter of time, given her record number of features inside its pages.

Also believed to have played a role, was the fact that CBM's lead photographer was rumored to have a major crush on the gun ranch owner. Bear's occurrence or recurrence on the magazine's pages was said to be a result of it all. At any rate, no one could deny Bear's merits for the cover position.

The only question had been when the time would come. Why it hadn't happened sooner, was no real surprise. Bear was, after all, a *woman* in business- a male dominated business at that. That she was a black woman was the icing on the cake or; as some mused, the final nail in the coffin.

Whatever the reason for the delay, Bear could no longer be denied all she had justly earned. Several would be on hand to celebrate individual achievements, though it was understood that Bear would be the darling of the event.

She would look the part as well. The question of what to wear, settled when Pope asked if he could make the selection for her. Bear humored him by allowing it. She was sure he'd choose something from her vast and rarely worn collection of evening wear. She was already prepared to sweetly reject his choice, when he presented a gown that surpassed captivating and hadn't emerged from the bowels of her wardrobe.

The dress was a creation of black satin over a powder pink underskirt and bodice that accentuated the dewy caramel tone of her skin. The fitted bodice tapered into a full bell shaped skirt that just touched the floor and allowed the rounded toes of black satin slippers to peek out beneath. The off shoulder cut left one tight sleeve cinched at her wrist while her other arm was beautifully bare.

"It's too much," she was breathless as her eyes roamed the wide bed where the dress lay in the gargantuan box it'd arrived in.

Pope simply gathered her back against him as he also studied the gown. "Nothing's too much for you," he said.

Apparently that went for Bear's request for him to join her as well. Pope arrived to pick her up promptly at 7pm. It took Bear at least a minute to make it down from the last two steps in the living room when she saw him.

Pope Apostolou in everyday wear was a mouthwatering vision. In black tie, with his wavy onyx mane pulled into a low tail that enhanced his striking features, he was beyond remarkable. The embodiment of all his heritage implied when one conjured images of Greek gods and their ethereal beauty.

Head housekeeper Jean Kearney had opened the door to Pope with a sound that had merged the lines between shock and...desire. It hadn't taken long for word of the man's arrival to spread to the other women in the house. By the time Bear got downstairs, she and her date had collected a small following to see them off for their evening.

"Coming?" Pope said as though totally unaware of the aura he exuded to every woman in the room.

"You didn't have to go to all this trouble," Bear said once they'd made it from the house and the front door had closed behind them.

"Now you tell me," Pope sent a pointed look across the drive where a thoroughly over the top Hummer Limo waited.

Bear's laughter was the perfect start to their night.

~~~

The dinner was given at a local art gallery/museum. Bear drew all the interest that the year-end CBM cover feature was expected to grab. Yet, it was the man escorting her that took the 'interest' into the exosphere.

If Bear was concerned that all the attention might be too much for Pope, the sensation wore off within the first 15 minutes of their arrival. She'd already known him to be a natural charmer and he proved it with the ease in which he handled members of the press and anyone else who got a moment of his time.

Pope didn't mind the attention he drew. It was the attention Bear stirred that had him eager to see the end of the event. He didn't have an issue with the press vying for her attention, or her colleagues ...her female colleagues. Those of the male variety however...While it was clear that she was well liked and one of the guys, the dress she wore that night distinctly labeled her as anything but.

Of course, it was just as he'd intended. He'd wanted to make her feel like a princess and he'd succeeded, but forgot about lurking toads. He couldn't blame the poor sons of bitches. Hadn't he been shamelessly vying for her attention not so long ago?

Swallowing the pettiness of jealousy, Pope retreated to the hall that had been reserved for the cover display. There, all CBM covers for the past year were featured. Specially showcased in her own alcove, was Bear.

Pope spent the next half hour in virtual heaven taking his time to enjoy the life sized layout. The feature caught Bear in candid shots with her team and in more stylish poses in full glamour. He'd already heard from one of her female colleagues that the photographer had crush on her. The same apparently went for the man's camera. The shots were incredible. *She* was incredible. She was the woman he loved.

The phrase came to mind with such ease, such suddenness, such truth. While it had in fact been sudden, there was no doubting. He'd spent a lifetime courting death and destruction. Now, somehow God had seen fit to bring the sweeter things into his life. He wasn't about to squander the blessing by wasting time debating whether or not to accept it.

"Speaking of wasting time," he murmured figuring he'd given the lurking toads time enough to fawn over the belle of the ball.

He returned to the main hall and felt his patience again threatening to snap. The two he found towering over her were way too close for his liking and it was that thought that made him stop and grin at himself.

He wasn't going to waste time pondering the suddenness of his love for her. He sure as hell wasn't going to waste time flying into fits over every man who drooled over her. He'd be flying into fits constantly if that were the case. Better to be in a constant state of patting himself on the back for being smart enough to claim the gift he didn't at all deserve.

Satisfied and still grinning at himself, Pope closed the distance from the laughing threesome ahead. He was within a few feet when recognition dawned.

The happy light in Bear's eyes, amplified by several watts when Pope stepped between his friends to punish their backs with twin slaps.

Rutger and Slayte rolled their eyes in perfect unison. They were equally devastating in evening attire as well. Along with Pope, the three drew more than their fair share of attention-female and male alike.

Bear stood as rapt with disbelief as anyone else. She could easily imagine the stir the four of them-Mercuri included-must've caused when they were out together.

"Rutger I'm sorry Lu couldn't be here," Bear continued the explanations she'd been giving before Pope approached. "She had some last minute upset with a project. Tee was supposed to be here too but she's still away on her trip so Lu's gonna have a small dinner at her place next week-kind of a celebration for my thing and Tee and Mercuri's engagement too. You're welcomed to be there. You both are." She moved her smile from Rutger to Slayte.

"Prin should be back then too," she said. It'd been obvious when the men had first approached that they were quite interested in her friends. Bear had enjoyed a secret smile. Obviously, she wasn't the only one of her friends who'd been keeping secrets.

"I'm gonna find out about dinner. I'm starving," she sent Pope a wink and then squeezed Rutger's and Slayte's forearms. "It was nice to meet you guys."

Pope watched his friends bend low to put their kiss to Bear's cheek. He waited until she made her way into the crowd before he jostled the men from behind as he moved between them.

"What the hell?" Pope spread his hands in confusion.

Slayte tugged his jacket cuff and traded a shrug with Rutger. "We came to show our support," he said.

"Bullshit," Pope decided.

"So I guess you forgot the Mercuri Fleets board is invited every year?"

"And every year, you two toss your invites into the garbage," Pope returned his own reminder.

Slayte waved a hand, knowing he'd been bested. "Alright, alright. Hell Po, we paid for our mischief, okay?"

"Exactly. Her friends aren't even here," Rutger brooded.

*Lurking toads*, Pope silently noted and then chose to extend a measure of pity to his friends. "Some event, huh?"

"I'll say." Slayte agreed as something serious flooded his stirring violet eyes. "She's somethin' else, Po."

"Absolutely," Rutger's molten stare, lingered where Bear had disappeared into the crowd. "I'm impressed," he fixed Pope with a raised brow. "A take charge woman like that, tolerating a pompous know it all like you."

Pope was the one tugging his cuffs then. "She appreciates all my qualities. Even the ones lesser men are threatened by."

Deep, exuberant laughter flowed between the friends, but it wasn't long before more unavoidable topics presented themselves.

"Making any headway with the discs?" Rutger gave a tight smile. "Course not," he answered his own question having read Pope's expression.

Slayte murmured a curse while accepting champagne from a passing server.

"They aren't showing me anything I didn't already know. Since I'm no longer in the market for wasting time, I'll move on with what I've got."

"Which is?" Rutger queried.

"The GAN can't weather much more bad press. They'll sacrifice Brody quick. If we can depend on Grodins to go along with what I've got planned, it won't be long before Jake follows his friend into the sunset."

Rutger took a step closer. "You mind telling us what you've got planned?"

"A little recipe I've been working on," Pope shrugged, his eyes level and scanning the room. "Something that'll go down a lot easier without those two leading the voices of dissention."

"But somethin's still naggin' at you, isn't it?" Slayte drained his glass while considering Pope.

Pope smiled. "Who's the know it all, now?" He teased, but his amusement didn't last long. "It's like there's something staring me right in the face. Doesn't matter if it's in those discs or not. I feel like it's something I should already know."

~~~

Dinner was a noisy, enthusiastic affair. The plates may've been $1000 per, but the high society gloss ended there. Generous cuts of steak, massive potatoes, assortments of fresh steamed and grilled veggies and more were heartily devoured without the slightest adherence to pristine table etiquette. Afterwards, the party continued. The crowd worked off the filling meal with more dancing or walking the museum's great rooms to marvel over the exquisite work lining its halls.

Pope and Bear danced off their acquired calories, though what they did couldn't exactly be classified as dancing in the normal sense. They simply embraced, barely swaying to the quietly sensual melody that floated into the room.

Bear savored the lazy decrescendo of the evening. Things were beginning to wind down and she didn't care what they did so long as Pope kept holding her. She could hear the soothing steady beat of his heart where her head rested on his chest. His strong hands roamed her back, as they gently swayed in time to the music. If this wasn't heaven it was very close, she decided.

"Pope…?"

"Mmm…?"

"When does our limo turn back into a pumpkin?"

"Cub, Cub…are you concerned about the time?"

Bear shivered in adoration of his voice softly thundering in her ear through his chest. She was reluctant to move, but did so and found reward in the sea blue fire of his fixed gaze.

"I don't think I remember what time it is," she sighed, content.

Pope nodded, tugged her earlobe and then a tendril of hair left dangling from her low chignon. "Then, my job is done," he said.

Her content smile remained, yet apprehension claimed her eyes. Briefly, she studied the room. "Are you threatened by any of this? I mean, this isn't the first time I've brought a date to this thing. I wasn't nearly as much in the spotlight as I am tonight, but I guess it was a bit much and…I mean…you aren't spooked by this, are you? By-" her brow furrowed. "By me I-I mean?"

"You?" Pope paired the lone word with a lopsided grin.

She couldn't resist smiling in response.

Pope appeared to be considering his own response. "You've left me shaking in my shoes a few times," he said. "But I wouldn't go as far as to say…*threatened*," he added a false, indignant sniff.

She laughed then, totally in love with his humor. In love with him.

"There's no shame in admitting it," she tugged his jacket lapel. "I'm at the top of the Cali business scene, you know? All these people at my feet," she offered a lazy flutter of her lashes and heard him laugh. "I'm pretty revered, you know? Powerful-"

"Mmm and multi orgasmic," his brows lifted in challenge.

"You didn't have to take it there," playful light spewed from her warm mocha stare.

His dimple flashed. "Just making my argument. It's kind of hard to be threatened when I know what you sound like when you come and that it's me you're coming for and that you come for me every time I call…"

"Pope…" Heat had consumed her desire to play. Her desire then, was to have him.

He closed his hand around her neck and propped her chin on his thumb. "You're floating around here dazzling these people in the dress I bought you and have spent the better part of the night thinking about taking you out of...threatened? No Cub, that's not the emotion I've got in mind right now."

Her eyes were wandering helplessly across his face and repeatedly settling to his mouth. He crushed it to hers and she eagerly accepted the kiss that stirred discussion and a fair amount of envy among their many admirers.

# CHAPTER 29

Bear woke with a slow, enjoyable stretch amid a fierce tangle of sheets. She was alone and naked with her dazzling dress discarded to the floor. The party was hours in the past, but her memory of it and the night as a whole remained at the surface of her thoughts.

Feeling such happiness should've had her uneasy, but there was none of that. She had no interest in debating what was to come, she only wanted to relish every minute that belonged to her. Content with the choice, she raised her head, tilting it to listen for any sign of Pope in the room. After a minute, she slid from the bed and; as the top sheets were practically on the floor anyway, wrapped one around her body and made her way downstairs. The house was still empty that time of night-er morning, making it easier to locate Pope's whereabouts.

Downstairs, the only light she found, aside from the electric candles glowing gold along the corridors, was that coming from beneath the door leading to her home office suite. Inside, she saw the telltale shifting light coming from the cracked door of the viewing room. She scratched the wood beneath her nails while pushing the door wide.

Pope occupied one of the larger swivel chairs that hugged the end of each aisle in the room. Seeing Bear, he immediately reached for the remote to shut off the screen.

"No please," she gave a slight wave. Her eyes slid back to the screen she'd already glimpsed upon peeking through the door.

"Anything?" The sheet trailed behind as she trudged to the front of the room.

Pope shook his head. "Nothing…" he regarded the remote as though still debating whether or not to stop the playback of the security feed from the infamous party night six years prior.

"I've watched all these discs once-the ones featuring your senator, way more than that and… nothing."

"You still think there's something there?" Bear's eyes didn't leave the screen.

"A fool's hope. Not even necessary," he muttered. "Brody Alberts' is as good as gone-so's your senator- especially with the contents from the feed on your security cameras from the soiree dinner putting them both at the scene."

Bear hugged herself in the sheets. "If only I'd looked at them before...least I would've known how little Morrow could be trusted. I could've gotten him thrown in jail-not just off my property. The fact that he's acquainted with those two proves he's into something shady, doesn't it?"

"It's not concrete," Pope glanced toward the viewing screen again. "But Morrow would have a hard time proving otherwise. Stands to reason more than a few of his constituents would run for cover if they knew."

"The crap bucket," Bear grumbled.

"Hey?" He beckoned to her with barely a wave indicating that she sit on his lap. When she was there he tried to tease her from her mood, looking down into the sheet bunched at her breasts and nibbled her ear.

Bear's smoky stare remained fixed on the screen.

"Kicking yourself won't change anything, Cub."

"I know," proof of that had her rolling her eyes. A sardonic smile curved her mouth and she breathed out a tuft of air intended to be a laugh.

"At least I finally know who to thank for bringing that horrible bag to the party."

The concern in Pope's gaze transitioned to curiosity as it shifted from Bear and back to the screen.

"...thing's heavy as Hades, even without the discs inside."

"Jesus..." Pope breathed.

Curiosity grew vibrant in Bear's eyes then too. "What?"

Pope stood, placing Bear in the spot he'd just occupied. "A few months ago we met with Enrique Roya's son, Eduardo."

"Right," Bear watched him rewind the playback of Morrow. "Mercuri told Tee. She told me, Lu and Prin."

"Roya junior told us a bag of discs was taken and that he had sources inside the GAN- those sources were Caleb and Luke. Seems they put up a loyal front to ensure they'd know if anyone was coming after you. They got cut out of the loop but knew enough. The day he came to your office, Caleb said Brody and Jake were pissed when Harris and Zubin were tapped to track down the bag. Now we've got your senator giving the same bag to Brody and Jake long before those discs were ever in it." he pointed to the time count at the bottom corner of the screen. "That's right, isn't it?"

Bear tried to nod, but only managed a shaky jerk. "I think so," she straightened suddenly, both hands going to her mouth.

Pope saw the stricken look she wore and was kneeling before her in seconds. "Babe? Honey talk to me."

"That night with Shaun..."

"It's alright, Cub," Pope rubbed her thighs through the sheet.

"He tried to talk to me. I thought he was just-just in shock and he...he said they-they wanted the bag."

"Where is it?" The animalistic chord was alive in his voice.

"The safe. The-in the very back." Her voice was all but a whisper.

Pope tugged her from the chair and out into the office. The safe was a massive iron construction behind a cabinet of dark oak. It took only a few moments to open and then Pope was searching the contents. In the depths, he saw the outline of a wide square.

"It's empty," Bear said when he tugged the bag out. She'd come to stand by the credenza running along the side of the safe.

"But heavy," Pope cupped the bag's chrome bottom, weighing it in one hand. "Why would those fools be after an empty bag?"

Bear regarded the bag with a stony countenance and tried to ward off the images it evoked.

Pope regarded the bag as well, but ran his hands over the sides and bottom as if doing so would provide the answers he sought.

"You crafty son of a bitch…" he breathed the words just before he pressed his thumb into one side of the chrome bottom.

There was a barely audible click and Bear gasped as the bottom jutted outward to reveal its velvet lined interior.

"What the hell," Bear's voice was indeed a whisper then. She moved closer to watch Pope raise a vial-one of many from the section. She watched him smooth his thumb across the labeling when he held the vial to the light and tilted it slightly.

"Is that…blood?" She asked.

Pope didn't answer but withdrew another vial, that one containing a clearer liquid. "I'll be goddamn…"

"What the hell is it?" Bear's hiss mirrored the shock in her eyes as they fixed on a flat clear plastic vial that carried a frighteningly familiar substance. "Pope?"

He shook his head. "This, Ms. Clayton, is a payment that keeps on giving."

\*\*\*

"A very elaborate-very effective form of blackmail." Mercuri's tawny stare roamed the vials of hair, nails, saliva and blood. There were 10 sets, each containing 4 vials.

Slayte snorted. "I didn't think Brody and Jake had the brainpower to put together somethin' this intelligent."

"I don't think they did," Pope chimed in. "This Senator Morrow, though…"

"All this to have a drug marketed as a vitamin," Rutger sounded incredulous.

"A vitamin that could bring in untold amounts of cash on the open market." Pope chose a seat on a sofa across the room. From there, he watched his friends gathered around Mercuri's desk in the 70th floor office of Mercuri Fleets. He'd left Bear early that morning to head into San Francisco where he'd asked the others to meet him.

"Untold cash and no oversight." Rutger's liquid brown gaze was hooded as he glared down at the vials.

"But there's only DNA here for six of the ten," Slayte noted. "These other four are from sources who were very much against the serum being available on *any* market because of the side effects."

322

"Please. With this kind of leverage they could've gotten the stuff marketed as baby oil if they wanted."

"Rut's right," Pope said. "With Morrow in his senate seat courtesy of a sympathy vote for the late Thomas Doyle, then blackmailing the GANs governing body-two of which had high ranking positions in the FDA…"

"Who also happened to be the most outspoken critics," Mercuri added.

"With all that in place, they could've done whatever they wanted." From his seat, Pope looked over at the vials again. The helpful labels identified each of the owners allowing the scenario to more quickly come together.

"Is it safe to say you've got a plan for how to use all this new found info?" Mercuri leaned against his desk and looked to Pope.

"As a matter of fact, I do," Pope wedged deeper into the sofa. He was a picture of relaxation with his legs crossed at the ankles and resting on the coffeetable.

Slay's grin harbored a wicked assurance. "You gonna tell us or just sit there lookin' like a prick?"

Pope raised his hands, but didn't move from his comfy position. "I can tell you or I can show you."

\*\*\*

*Memphis, Tennessee~*

"How sure is Sumner that this is about to go down?"

"Very sure, but it doesn't matter, they're here. I'll call you back-"

"Jake!"

"Just stay calm 'til I get there," Jake ended Brody's rebuttal and shoved the phone into his jacket pocket.

The offices of Womack, Mebane and Urnst was again the sight of more fallout from Nathan Alberts' suicide. Jake's at-office contact Cory Sumner had called that morning to say his bosses had gotten word that Pope was coming in to sign papers enacting changes to his inheritance.

Specifically, he didn't want anything of Alberts' and was ready to make the decision official. The question remained however-what *was* the decision? Lorne Grodins and several others had been specially contacted. As it was an open meeting, Jake thought it couldn't hurt to be in the midst.

Understandably, Brody couldn't attend; not that he wanted to. Brody's talent for patience and subtlety was all but gone, Jake knew. Now, the man could only think of seeing Pope Apostolou in his grave. Learning that his half brother was on his way into Womack, Mebane and Urnst was a bitter pill to swallow given the arrangements Brody and Jake had already made.

Pope arrived with the only men he considered brothers including Jake's own half brother. Jake studied his father's pride-his father's specimen. Rutger.

"Your time's coming, bastard freak." Jake seethed.

His focus redirected though when he saw Pope and the others bypassing those who had gathered. They headed in the opposite direction down the hall that dead-ended into another large conference room. The door had only been closed behind them for a minute, when Gerrick Ferguson and Lorne Grodins were tapped to join them.

~~~


Pope noticed reverence and something similar to pride in Gerrick Ferguson's searing gaze when the man shook hands with Slayte and Mercuri. He'd noticed a similar reaction from Gerrick when he and Rutger had met with him weeks earlier. Pope guessed it wasn't everyday that a scientist got to see his creations roaming the wild.

Or a father got to see his favorite son grown up in enviable fashion. Pope took note of Rutger's tight smile as he shook hands with Lorne Grodins. Pope guessed it mattered very little whether the son hated the father's guts. Pope thought of his own father then, but easily dismissed the memory.

"Thank you both for coming," Pope said to Grodins and Ferguson. "This won't take long. I'm in possession of a bag, one that was taken from The Crudup Hotel-in Las Vegas six years ago." He watched the older men trade looks.

"Funny thing about this bag is it left the hotel with four women and was filled with discs but it arrived in the hands of Senator Christopher Morrow, then Senator's Aide Morrow and it was empty or so it appeared."

"Pope I-I don't understand." Gerrick said.

"Neither do I," Grodins added.

324

A rolling of eyes commenced between Mercuri, Slayte and Rutger. They were taking seats while Pope continued his explanation.

"Only four members of The Ten were to die that night. They weren't meant to die at the hands of those girls, but someone else already planted in that room to strike quietly once the party wound down. It's why Brody and Jake made themselves scarce. If I recall, *they* were supposed to be on the other side of the door while Caleb Stein and Luke Robb manned the hall."

"But why?" Grodins moved forward. "Why'd they do it?"

Pope fixed the man with a mock look of admonishment. "Have you already forgotten your psycho inducing serum? The one you wanted to pass through as a dietary supplement?"

Grodins looked quickly to Gerrick who fixed him with an accusing and unflinching glare.

"They needed to know," Gerrick said.

"But there was no reason to-" Grodins turned back to Pope. "We were making a mint with it on the black market *and* the military."

"Yes, but the market can be fickle and the military...it could've been only a matter of time before they tried to take it out from under you." Mercuri pointed out.

"On the open market," Rutger added, "You maintain full control and an endless supply of hopeful moms and dads eager for the perfect kid." He was grim faced even when his father fixed him with a beseeching look.

"It's a magnificent product," Grodins championed with outstretched hands. "The four of you are living proof-"

"And what of the psychotics?" Slayte inserted. "Like Harris Van Deer and Grant Zubin?"

Grodins looked away.

"What would Brody and Jake hope to gain by murdering The Ten?" Gerrick asked.

"Not The Ten," Pope corrected. "Only four-the four who posed the greatest threat against getting the product past the FDA as a supplement. They'd planned to blackmail the remaining six members and four others from the GANs scientific division," he looked to Gerrick.

"Blackmailed? For-for what?" Gerrick stammered.

Rutger sighed then, looking entirely bored with the conversation. "You mean aside from drugging unsuspecting women with something that could turn their babies into monsters? Oh yeah, they planned to hold you responsible for a lot more than that."

"That empty bag showed up to the party," Pope went on. "It had a false bottom. Inside were ten sets of vials-four vials in each set. Hair, skin, nails, blood." Pope saw vague understanding slid over Grodins' and Ferguson's faces as the contents were listed.

"So, an elaborate frame, complete with DNA evidence- all so the GAN could peddle its shit the way it wanted."

"We know nothing about it!" Grodins argued Pope's summation.

Pope spared the man a dismissive look. "No, I don't think you did. This deal wasn't meant to secure yours and your partner's chairs at the head of the table, but to pull them out from beneath you."

Gerrick looked on in disbelief. "After everything we told you-you-you-you can't possible want to blackmail us to see that poison on the market?"

"Don't worry Gerrick. I don't want that. I don't want that at all."

~~~


"Effective immediately Gerrick Ferguson will serve as the chair of what will become the governing board of the Grodins Alberts Network. Dr. Ferguson, along with his colleagues Daniel Schultz, Ned McCaffrey and Hoyt Ingram will be the founding members of the new Ten."

A soft, yet steady current of conversation began to accompany Lorne Grodins' words when he addressed the crowd who filled Womack, Mebane and Urnst's main auditorium. Looks were exchanged and shock adorned more than a few faces while others carried the unmistakable look of outrage.

"Doesn't anyone get a say in this, Lorne?!" One of the outraged called out above the chorus of grumbles.

"Everyone has a say," Grodins' face was impassive.

"Since when does someone with half ownership call the shots, Pop?" Jake was next to speak out.

"Since the wishes of both parties are on one accord." Grodins' impassive expression remained.

The low grumbles gained volume then. Grodins merely raised his hands and waited for the crowd to acknowledge his silent request for calm.

"Not long ago, we lost one of our founding members," he reminded the group. "Nathan Alberts was a dear friend-my dearest friend. He-we both- had different plans for The GAN when we started it. We took the Network into places we never dreamed it could go- far beyond the modest dreams of two medical supply salesmen who had seen way too much of the world and its horrors.

Though he never said it, I know Nate always regretted that we never looked back to fulfill our original plans. I want to start making up for that now. With the help of Doctors Ferguson, Schultz, McCaffrey and Ingram, I'll keep the promise I've made to myself to honor a dear friend."

The room had gone utterly silent and remained so for several moments after Grodins completed his speech. There was no applause when the rumble of conversation returned, yet the tone of the mingled voices held a curious calm.

The calm didn't carry to all corners of the room, of course. Jake Grodins stood amid his own unhappy group. Unlike the soft grumblers, Jake maintained his silence. He studied his father near the head of the space-in his own group. The group he'd obviously chosen during the secret meeting before he'd made his damning address.

No...Jake's mouth twisted into an accepting smile. His father had chosen his 'new group' long before he'd walked into that room. Lorne Grodins had chosen the day his bastard freak of a son was born. With that thought in mind, Jake took the nearest exit out of the conference room and bolted down an empty corridor.

"It's me," he murmured into the phone once Brody answered. "My father fucked us over just like we expected. Enough of this shit, I'll be there soon."

There wasn't much left to be said and the call ended shortly after. Jake continued his stony pursuit down the hall and was about to turn into an elevator bay when he heard his name. Rutger stood on the other side of the corridor.

"Come to gloat, Rut?"

"I don't care enough to gloat, Jake. Just thought I'd help these gentlemen find you, is all."

"Jacob Grodins?" A man inquired while reaching inside the pocket on a crisp suitcoat. He presented a thin wallet which he whipped open to present an ID.

"I'm Detective Samuel Canter," the man said and half turned to the other man next to him. "This is my partner Detective Deek Prinze, We're with the Memphis P.D."

"Nice to meet you both," Jake said as Prinze presented his identification. "I've got a pressing engagement so-"

"Mr. Grodins we're hoping for just a moment-an unofficial moment." Canter explained, with the easy over rigid smile perfected by those in his line of work. Canter's partner wasn't quite so suave.

"Mr. Grodins we can wait if you rather the official way," Prinze offered. "I'm sure your lawyer's somewhere in the building."

When Jake only regarded the men in silence, Canter gave a singular nod and gestured to the three men accompanying he and his partner. "Mr. Grodins, these are detectives Rummels, Dover and Poyner of the Burlingame and San Francisco Police Departments. They've got some questions about your associate Broderick Alberts."

Bristling, Jake shifted a look to Rutger who observed him with an easy over rigid smile of his own.

"Mr. Grodins?" Canter's smile was cooly expectant.

Jake moved toward the detectives and away from the elevator bay where he'd planned to take his exit. He slowed when he neared Rutger.

"One day I'll take everything from you."

Rutger responded to the vow with the lazy roll of a massive shoulder. "Haven't you been trying to do that all our lives?"

Jake's smile was tight, yet cold. "Thing about people who *try*, is they eventually succeed."

Rutger chuckled. "But that would depend on the manner of their trying, wouldn't it?"

Jake's expression went glacial and he moved on with the detectives.

Alone, Rutger unclenched the fist he'd been aching to use.

~~~


"It's been good seeing you both," Gerrick Ferguson's searing hazel stare was alight with approval as he shook hands first with Mercuri and then with Slayte. "Don't be strangers in my neck of the woods, alright?"

Slayte spoke up while Mercuri laughed. "No offence, Sir but the farther we keep from GAN HQ, the better off we'll all be."

There was more laughter and then Gerrick was clapping Pope's shoulder. "Well done, kid and I'm not just saying that because you left me partly in the driver's seat."

Pope inclined his head. "I feel good about it. Just don't make me regret it."

"I don't intend to," Gerrick said.

Pope was scanning the room with a measuring look. "How hard do you think it'll be to convince them?"

Gerrick grimaced, but the gesture carried an easy air. "The dissenters, dissented the loudest and think that means they're in the majority. There're more here cheering today's events than you realize."

"Gerrick." Pope extended a hand to shake and then he went to catch up with his friends already making their way down the hall.

Gerrick was watching the men take their leave when Daniel Schultz came up to pat his back.

"Regardless of the mistakes," Dan said, "those are four you should be proud of."

"Oh I am, Dan." Gerrick's gaze never wavered. "I am."

# CHAPTER 30

Rutger was chuckling as he shut down his mobile. It was a sight that cast a skeptical air to Pope's expression.

"I don't know if I like seeing you so savvy with that thing," Pope watched Rutger slip the device into a charging dock setup on a low coffeetable in the cabin's living area.

The four had made a speedy departure from Memphis. Just then, they were in route to San Francisco aboard a Mercuri Fleets jet.

"Agreed," Slayte called drowsily from the sofa where he reclined with his arms pillowed behind his head. "Seriously Rut, you need to stick with what we all know, which is you bringing in firewood or heading out to the wilderness to hunt down whatever roadkill you're craving for dinner."

"Fuck you all," Rutger sighed amidst the quiet rumble of his friend's laughter.

"Any news on Jake?" Mercuri thumbed a laugh tear from his eye.

"Not much," Rutger glanced at his phone on the dock. "That's to be expected, I guess. Havin' to talk to the cops will piss him off, though. When he's pissed he makes mistakes."

"You really think he'd lead the cops anywhere besides The Marshall?" Pope referred to the private club.

"And good luck getting in there without a warrant," Slayte drawled.

"Doubtful they'd even get a warrant," Rutger added. "With half the Memphis brass being members and the rest with membership apps under review."

While his friends debated the odds of Brody's hideout at the club being infiltrated, Pope decided to give Bear a call. He'd left her the night before with no real explanation of his plans once he'd gotten to Memphis.

Truth be told, he hadn't believed his plans had a shot in hell of going over. Nevertheless, they had, and the reality of cutting that final tie with the GAN was one he hadn't quite had time to process. There was time enough for that later, he decided.

Pope mouthed a curse when Bear's voice came through over voicemail. He left a message anyway.

"Hey...we're on our way back. I'll tell you how everything went when I see you. If you can get away...we can talk at my place. I'll call when we land, I love you." He studied the phone for a few seconds after breaking the connection. The cabin's heavy silence made him wince soon after.

Rutger's sigh broke the silence. "Didn't know you were capable of such sweet talk, man."

Pope grinned. "Jealous?" He rested back in his seat, accepting that he was in for at least 20 minutes of ribbing from his friends.

"Well..." Rutger frowned as though he were pondering his response. "If Bear wasn't so sweet, I could be a little put out seeing as how you're never so nice to any of us."

The roar of laughter followed the critique.

"Hey Rut?" Mercuri called once the volume of the outburst had lowered. "Did Po ever tell you about the um...misunderstanding Bear had about you guys?"

"Merc..."

Pope's warning tone had Slayte's expression sharpening. "Spill it," he ordered.

Mercuri was all too happy to share.

*\*\*\**

Bear had already decided that the day wouldn't end without her taking a trip to Pope's place in Pacifica. He'd given her a key the day before he left for Memphis. She'd refused to preoccupy herself with thoughts of what it meant for a man to give a woman the key to his place. Well...she'd made every effort to refuse.

In the end she'd reminded herself that the man practically had carte blanche status at her place. It just made sense that he'd return the favor. That flimsy reasoning had lasted all of two minutes.

Pope Apostolou knew damn well what he wanted. Him giving her a key to his home, meant exactly what a woman *hoped* a man meant when the gesture was made: trust, commitment, future. He'd lived a lifestyle that cast a glaring light on the uncertainty of the future and the precious nature of time. Time was a thing he was unwilling to waste and Bear believed it was a way of life she was open to adopting.

It was afternoon by the time she'd arrived. The sun wouldn't be setting for hours yet, but it held the sky at an angle that beckoned a closer view. She parked her Jeep, but bypassed the front door to take the path leading down to the beach.

The breeze off the water was a smidge cool against her arms bared by the capped sleeves of the denim mini-dress she sported. Still, the view was too devastating to be ignored.

Bear was cheering her decision to head for the beach when she saw Pope's shoes coming into her line of vision five minutes later.

"You're early," she rested back on her elbows and squinted up.

"I don't know Ms. C.," Brody stooped to bring his cold gaze level with her startled one. "Looks like I'm right on time." The chill in his eyes warmed with lechery as it crawled over her breasts and arms.

Bear didn't need introductions. She'd seen the man before, standing over Shaun as he'd died.

"Now let's-" Brody didn't have time to finish his directions.

Bear dashed a fistful of sand into his face and made a mad scramble to her feet.

Brody sputtered. "Bitch!" He reached for her while using his free hand to rub at the sand clinging to his face.

Bear ran and was making headway when Brody closed the distance. He caught her ankle and yanked her to him when she fell. She fought like a wild thing, writhing and hurling more sand across her shoulders in hopes of again making contact with her assailant's eyes.

Prepared, Brody foiled her moves by dropping his considerable weight over her slight frame. Her breathing was at once labored beneath his bulk, yet she continued to writhe and gnash her teeth when the chance came to catch his skin.

They grappled in the sand until Brody snagged Bear's wrists, drawing them back to be cuffed in one hand and pressing them high and hard between her shoulder blades. Pain seared through her arms, lancing her neck with agonizing spikes. She cried out then, more angry than terrified.

"It can get worse before it gets better, Ms. C.," Brody panted in her hair while working to slow his breathing. He twisted her wrists brutally and wedged his free hand beneath her body when the pain made her shift. He cupped her breast and she stilled.

Bear felt his mouth move in her hair as he spoke.

"That's better, isn't it?"

Bear felt nauseous and released a feral sound.

"None of that now," Brody hissed. "I know how you used to make your living. I'm sure my bastard brother knows. I bet he knows very well. Bet he benefits from your expertise every night, doesn't he?" The panting returned to Brody's voice, but not as a sign of overexertion.

Bear forbid herself to move when he took his hand from her breast to cup her crotch and squeeze.

"Now or later, Ms. C?" He spoke against her bare nape then. "I'd like for Pope to see you at work, but I wouldn't mind a sample of the goods now, would you? Good girl." He added when she gave no response.

Again, he nuzzled his face into her hair and gave another lurid squeeze to her mound. "Maybe I *will* have my taste now and let my guys save up for later. They'll give my brother quite a show."

Pleased with the decision, Brody pushed to his feet. Bear took advantage of his loosened hold. She wrenched her head back full and firm and felt the connection her skull made with his palate. Stunned and livid, Brody curved his hands to his nose and pulled them away to check for blood. There was none, but the pain was tremendous.

Bear didn't stop to take stock of her handywork. She was again racing out across the sand, kicking up tufts of it in her wake. She could make out the stairway leading up to the driveway and quickened her gait while risking a look back at her attacker.

The risk proved to be her literal downfall and she slammed into what felt like a solid wall. The contact sent her sprawling into the sand- only for a few brief moments however. One of Brody's men fisted a wad of her hair and dragged her brutally to her feet.

Brody approached out of breath and enraged. His response to Bear's treachery was a punishing backhanded fist that put her on her knees and turned her world black.

***

When the guys landed, there was talk of getting together for drinks and dinner. During the flight, it had occurred to them that they'd yet to have a proper celebration for Mercuri's engagement.

It sounded like a plan. Tee was fresh in from her lengthy business trip and thoroughly exhausted. A night without her fiance would receive no argument.

Pope hadn't heard back from Bear regarding his plans for their evening at his place, so no firm arrangements had been set. Mercuri, Rutger and Slayte waited, milling around on the tarmac and in conversation with the pilots while Pope tried to reach Bear. There was no answer by the first or second ring. Pope was prepared to leave another message when the dial tones silenced.

"Cub?" He called after three or four seconds of dead air.

"Cub...? I'm afraid that doesn't at all suit this piece of dark and lovely."

Stance defining and features razoring with malicious possession, rage took its place near Pope like an old friend. Intentionally, he eased his hold on the phone knowing it was in danger of being shattered. "Where is she?" The natural animal hardness of his voice made the words nearly impossible to decipher.

Brody had no trouble making the translation. "It's a place with a damn fine view, especially from the bedroom. Listen, don't worry yourself about rushing to get here. She's just starting to uh...come around."

"You won't survive this, Brody."

Brody chuckled, low and smug. "Ah brother dear...I think you should worry if *she* will."

The line went dead. Pope barely registered slipping the phone into a front pocket of his jacket. Hands free, he clenched them, held them, took seconds he couldn't spare to urge himself to calm down and think.

Mercuri, Rutger and Slayte had waved off the pilots and were discussing dining possibilities for the evening. The sound of screeching tires and a fully revved engine surged across the tarmac. They watched a single Rover speeding away and knew at once who was behind the wheel.

"Looks like that's a 'no' on dinner, guys." Mercuri watched dust fly in the wake of Pope's exit.

***

Brows drawn close in a fierce frown, Bear labored to open her eyes. She managed a heavily lidded stare that was blurred by the sheen of tears. Laboring once more, she worked to lift her head from the pillow but hissed when the movement succeeded in sending fresh pain blooming along her neck.

It took well over five minutes for her to angle her head up and back. She was able to peer at the cords binding her wrists in elaborate twists about the head of Pope's bed.

She was still at his place, which meant her Jeep was probably still in the driveway. Probably...if she could get to it-she could get her own gun and take out the two fuckers who had the goddamn gall to put their hands on her.

At least she still had her clothes on-partly. Her dress had been ripped open-the cocksuckers, she silently raged noting the missing buttons along the front.

"Fuckers," defiantly, she resisted the discomfort when she moved her head and tested the tautness of the restraints. Both wrists were bound as were her ankles-spread eagled-of course. Her restraints disappeared over the foot of the bed, tied around the posts beneath, she guessed.

They certainly weren't taking any chances on her escape, Bear tried to hang onto the molten anger that kept her from dwelling *too much* on her terror. Again, she looked to her clothes and wondered how long it'd be before her captors tired of enjoying a peep show.

"Christ Bear, how the hell are you gonna get out of this?"

~~~

He'd have to go in empty. There would be no time to grab weapons. They'd descend the second he crossed the threshold. That is, if *they* didn't try taking him out the minute he left the car.

Pope assessed his property with a level, alert glare. Brody wouldn't come without backup. There was a Jeep parked close to the porch. He knew it was Bear's before seeing the familiar logo. Most likely, Brody and his men had found some cove to park their vehicles while they laid in wait. Chances were strong that they were already in the house and that they were in there with Bear.

He drew the Rover to a halt and began to punish the dash with stinging blows that dented the space with stunning efficiency. He crashed out of the SUV and bolted up the porch steps three at a time.

The imposing maple door opened behind a singular kick given with such force the door's lever stuck into the wall upon making contact. Under ordinary circumstances, it would be assumed that the flashy entrance was intended for show and that a trap was set. These weren't however, ordinary circumstances. Brody had taken what was his. The rage was on him, blinding him- mistakes were to be expected.

"Bear!" Pope roared, another effective method for giving away his position as if his boot through the door wasn't enough.

It didn't matter. He was ready to end this. He was ready to give Brody what he wanted if it meant saving Bear's life. He took the first floor landing and saw them emerge from the shadows along the opposing corridor.

They were sloppy, he mused but didn't acknowledge them. He was far too distraught to care or to pursue anything other than Bear's whereabouts. He chose not to react when he sensed them at his heels. He willed his fists to remain unclenched when he felt hands-two pair-closing over each of his biceps.

"Easy Po," voice one soothed close to his ear. "Let's not lose that killer temper of yours."

"Not yet anyway," voice two chimed in. "Wouldn't want you to miss the show and we've got a hell of one planned."

Pope bristled. "Where is she?"

"Calm down, dude. We're takin' you to her."

Silence loomed while the three made their way to the bedroom wing.

Pope's simmering rage bubbled into a noxious bile, when the bed came into full view. He saw Bear trussed up, her dress left open to set her on display in her underwear. Her head rested against the pillows gathered at her back.

Pope and his escorts waited for Bear to raise her head, her gaze slowly tracking the room until it rested on them. Pope knew the moment her recognition registered-despair grew in her mocha dark eyes. It lasted all of a second and, just as quickly, Pope felt the missed sensation of pride swell his chest.

Most men would've expected to see their beloved's eyes shining with tears of joy and relief. There was none of that from Bear who frowned as though she were outraged.

"Pope? What the hell? What are you doing here? Please tell me you just happened to be in the area and that bumbling oaf didn't trick you out here?"

Pope gave a dismayed shrug. "I came to save you," he watched her study him and his companions with frank distaste.

"Save me, huh? You're doing an awesome job so far."

"Ha!" Brody's laughter preceded him into the room. He clapped. "Damn Po, she's a pistol! My guys are wondering if she's as much of a firecracker in bed-we can't wait to find out."

Bear rolled her eyes while Brody's crawled over her.

"I'm afraid we're one short of a full ten, but maybe Pope will be willing to join in if we give him a good enough show, don't you think. Besides," Brody gave another quick clap. "She's been handling *you* all this time-quite a job, right Ms. C?" He sent Bear a wink followed by a curious look.

"Or maybe I'm speaking out of turn," he said. "Has he told you that part, pretty girl? That he's only about ten percent man and ninety percent...enhancement? A serum's responsible for all the perfection women fall to their knees over and fathers prefer over their natural sons."

"You envy him," discovery blazed in Bear's coffee toned eyes.

Brody snarled. "He disgusts me! Him and all the rest of the specimens like him."

"That why you joined up with Harris and Zoo?" Pope challenged.

"I didn't have a choice," Brody answered without making eye contact. "The old men forced us to work with them to recover the-" he paused, "the discs she and her friends took."

"Right, right...the discs...and I guess the old men forced you to work with Thom Doyle's aide to get the serum that disgusts you, approved as a vitamin?"

Brody froze for a moment and then a deceptively warm smile spread his mouth. "So you *have* been looking at the discs? Have you seen all of them, I wonder? I hear Ms. C and her friends are pretty talented once they get in the swing of things."

Bear remained purposefully aloof. Inside, she was seething. She didn't trust herself to look at Pope then.

Pope however was focused on Brody. "It's funny that you'd know that, considering all the partakers are dead but...oh yeah, that's right-the lone gunman you and Jake put in there to take out Thom Doyle, E.J. Maxwell, Jonas Sykes and Todd Jessup...that guy-the gunman? He walked out there under his own steam, didn't he?"

"Bastard..." Brody's expression iced over with hate.

Pope's shrug was slight given his escort's restraining holds. "Me being a bastard has been established. But you're a legitimate son. I think I prefer being labeled a bastard instead of a traitor."

Brody evidently deemed that label most unforgivable. He exploded with a crazed cry in route to Pope who he punished with a barrage of blows to his midsection. Bear cringed on the bed and tried to draw her legs up beneath her. The velvety soft cords held her fast though and burned when pulled taut.

Pope gave no indication that he felt the blows and Brody decided to lash out with his words instead.

"You dare say that to me after what you and your asshole friends did to Dennis?" His voice was hoarse as though it pained him to speak.

"Dennis?" Pope's gaze became slits of ultramarine light when he grinned. "And you dare call *my* friends assholes."

"He was our blood!"

"*Our*?" Pope made a tsking sound while shaking his head. "You can't have it both ways, man. One minute I'm a bastard, the next I'm...blood? I'm afraid I don't know what to make of that. Not when you *and* Denny always made sure I never forgot my place." It was Pope's voice that harbored the ragged hoarseness then. It was accompanied by the natural roughness that shimmered with murderous promise.

"Why would I give a fuck about him or you? Denny, his death, didn't mean any more to me than you do."

338

Brody raged again and returned to punish Pope with more of the stinging abdominal blows. Bear's lashes were spiky with tears but her eyes widened when she noticed the lack of pain in Pope's eyes. His gaze seared through his hair, which tumbled into his face like loose inky black coils.

"You'll have to do better than that, brother," trademark cockiness shone through in Pope's grin.

Brody stepped back, smirked. "Oh I can." He looked to Bear then.

She tried to put forth the same brave front that Pope had, but feared she was failing miserably.

"Tell the others to get in here!"

Brody spoke to no one in particular, but Bear saw a man she hadn't noticed before emerge along a far wall. Absently, she watched as he dug out a walkie from his dark suitcoat. Her greatest focus was still on Brody who had already stripped off his top shirt and was undoing his trouser fastening. She was so focused on Brody, that it took her some time to notice the confusion on the other side of the room. Bear only looked askance when movement registered in her peripheral. Her doubletake caught Brody's attention and he turned, staring with his mouth open.

Pope had braced himself, pouring his considerable strength into forearms he used to propel his captors towards each other. Their faces met with a subtle crunch that sent blood and tormented groans into the air.

Brody retreated from the bed, looking on in helpless fascination as he waved a hand toward the thug who'd been calling in reinforcements. The thug appeared as stupefied as his boss.

"Dave!"

Brody's yell, jerked the man from his devastation. He dropped the walkie and began a slow shuffle forward.

Bear wasn't surprised by the man's hesitation. Not at all, given the savage intent radiating from his opponent across the room. Pope stood, hunched, arms bowed out. He was braced for impact-wanting it. At his feet, lay his two captors. The men were moaning, trying and failing to lift their heads.

Brody's man, 'Dave', lunged and managed to back Pope up a few feet. His success was short lived when Pope pivoted to catch him in a spoon-like hold that he soon used to trap Dave in a sleeper hold. His adversary lost lower body strength and slipped to his knees. All the while, Pope's glare-then a dense indigo-was fixed on Brody.

Bear watched, stunned as the man bolted. He paused to grab the walkie dropped by his associate who was then dozing in Pope's sleeper embrace. Brody continued his retreat, leaving through one of the room's retracting glass walls.

Pope didn't give chase. He stood to let his sleeper slide to the floor. Stepping over him, he crossed to Bear.

Horrified, Bear looked from Brody's escape route to Pope and back again. "What are you doing? Go after him!" The entire scene had taken barely 3 minutes-to Bear it had seemed like an eternity.

Pope didn't bother to glance toward the retracted wall. Instead, he entered a code along the bottom of the bed. A square drawer ejected. From it, Pope selected a short, yet grotesquely serrated blade.

"Who touched you?" His tone was chilling as he severed Bear's restraints with smooth efficiency.

She swallowed hard as relief flowed when the bonds were cut and blood began to circulate in her limbs.

"Bear?"

She shook her head. "No one, not-not like *that*. They knocked me out but I was coming back around by the time they got me up here. They only ripped my dress to entertain themselves-the fuckers." She shivered against the sensation of her muscles relaxing.

"They touched you. Who?" His voice remained quiet, but the insistence was evident.

Bear nodded. "The one who was holding you-the blond and the-the other one," she looked to the retracted wall again. "Brody." She pushed to her knees, drew her mussed hair into a ponytail. "He killed Shaun. He can't get away."

"He won't." Voice flat, Pope left the bed and went to the semi-conscious blond. Seconds later, an echoing crunch signaled the sound of a breaking neck.

Bear's stunned shriek followed. Her hands went to her mouth and then slid away as dark satisfaction took root in her smoky stare.

Pope disarmed the other men and then returned to select more weaponry from various concealed doors at the base of the bed.

"Can you walk?" He asked her.

"Damn right I can," Bear levered off the bed and stood.

From the drawers, Pope withdrew full magazines along with an assortment of handguns and knives. He laid them on the bed.

"Can you shoot?" He asked.

Bear chose one of the Glocks, checked the barrel and chamber and then inserted one of the full clips.

"All day long," she said.

# CHAPTER 31

They approached the bedroom door by stealth. They left the room under the cover of lengthening shadows. Sunset was growing near. The house was quiet with not even approaching footfalls rising in volume.

Bear and Pope kept their guns at the ready. Their grips were sure and precise in the manner of true marksmen. They swept the corridor and made their way to the grand staircase. They maintained the sweeping pattern while descending.

A shot whizzed from someplace overhead. Bear whirled, exhibiting superb agility and instincts when she returned fire and caught the gunman perched behind them on the landing. Apparently, the plan had been to draw her and Pope to the staircase and into open territory.

The idea had occurred to Pope as well. He used a perceived weaker position to defeat a stronger one. The gunman fell to his death while he and Bear made for the bottom of the staircase where they engaged four other shooters in the process.

Pope took out two on the far end of the livingroom that was ablaze with the late afternoon light. A shot impacted above Bear's head to lodge in the newel post where she crouched. The gunman went for another shot, but found himself on the receiving end of Pope's aim. A bullet beneath the arm and one to his side, was the man's downfall.

Pope came to stand over the downed shooter and then looked to Bear poised to fire.

"Thanks," she panted.

Pope lifted his chin to acknowledge her gratitude. "You okay?" he asked.

"Yeah I-Pope!" Bear fired when he sidestepped her aim and ducked.

The shooter held his position in the doorway. For a moment, Bear wondered if she'd hit him. Then, the man buckled at the knees and he staggered back into the foyer.

Bear looked to Pope as he pushed to his feet. "Jeez, how many are there?"

"By my count, eight." Pope exchanged his empty clip for a full one. "Brody makes nine," he said.

Bear frowned. "How do you know that's all?"

"Going by Brody's count. In the bedroom, he said they were one short...of a full ten."

Bear could only cringe at the lurid reference.

Pope shaved the distance to Bear and helped her to her feet. "Stay close to me. When I get you to my car, you'll see the keys under the floormat. I want you to drive and don't look back."

Bear snatched her arm from his hold. "What do you mean, get *me* to the car?"

"I need to stay, Bear."

"Why? Brody's long gone-" She clipped her response when Pope began to shake his head.

"He may be too much of a coward to fight me straight on, but he won't leave 'til he knows I'm dead." He dragged Bear to the door before she could lash out against his logic.

By the time they passed the threshold, she'd returned to warrior mode, sweeping her gun across the porch while descending the wide steps.

"Come with me," she pleaded as they made for the black SUV just down from her Jeep.

"I have to do this." He wouldn't look her way. "I need you to go now, Bear."

"Pope-"

"Go!"

He roared the word and her blood froze, rendering her immobile. Regret softened the savagery in his eyes, then. Fisting a wad of her open dress, Pope pulled Bear to her toes. His kiss was both passionate and punishing. Then, he was taking her waist and one-arming her into the Rover. He slammed the driver's side door and Bear heard his voice muted through the window, but no less savage. Again, he was ordering her to go.

Terror-stricken, her face dampened by tears, Bear did as she was told.

Pope waited, keeping an alert eye out for Brody. He slapped the hood when the engine sparked and he waved Bear off with a fierce swat of his hand.

Bear gunned the engine, sending the SUV rocketing down the lonely road. She weaved across the road, sparing little attention to the rules of driving. Her eyes were glued to the rear view where she could just make out Pope racing toward the stairway leading down to the beach.

She gave a fleeting glance toward the road, shrieked and just about collided with a hulking black truck in her path. She hit the brakes and sat idling along the shoulder where she'd veered off.

The truck rolled up alongside Bear seconds later. Mercuri, Slayte and Rutger stormed out. Rutger wrenched open the driver's side door while Mercuri leaned in to pull Bear out from behind the wheel. Slayte had already lowered the truck's tailgate where Mercuri placed Bear and waited.

"Bear? Honey can you hear me?" Mercuri rubbed both her hands briskly between his.

Bear took only a few seconds to register her change in circumstance and another few for discovery to dawn at the sight of the three men eclipsing her line of sight. She gripped Mercuri's shirt, nails sinking deep.

"He's there, back-back there with a man-Brody, his men they…" she started to ramble, spilling everything that happened from the time she met Brody on the beach to Pope going after him seconds earlier.

Rutger removed the denim shirt he wore over a long sleeved tee. He passed it to Bear. The guys turned away to give her time to replace her ruined dress. Rutger's shirt fell well below her knees.

Slayte and Rutger settled into the front of the truck. Mercuri kept Bear in back with him. By then, her energetic explanations had melded into nervous mewlings. By the time they'd returned to the house, her nerves had been replaced by angry anxiety.

Bear fought to race out, before Mercuri, and Rutger when they left the truck, but Slayte caught her easily. He kept her close while propelling her forward. She saw they were headed in the direction she'd seen Pope take and didn't argue. They all stopped at the top of the stairway. There was no need to venture further to find Pope. He was on the beach. So was Brody Alberts. Brody held a gun to his side. Pope appeared unarmed.

"Slay?" Mercuri's tone was easy and without so much as a waver. "Hold onto her." He said.

"Yep." Slayte; already with a hand on Bear's arm, drew her back against him. He kept her secure in a spooning hold.

Mercuri slanted a look to Rutger who un-holstered the gun at his side and took aim.

Bear observed, eyes huge as she regarded the man's casually lethal stance. She held her breath. Slayte's hold felt crushing but she savored the reassurance it gave.

~~~

"Still afraid to face me without backup, aren't you?" Pope looked to the gun at Brody's side, another was tucked at his waist.

"Always the soldier, huh Pope?"

"No. I just really want to kick your ass."

"Never satisfied, are you? You've been kicking my ass for years-taking away the man who was like a brother to me, taking away the man who was supposed to be a father to me-to *me*!"

"You do realize the man had his own mind? I was born a weapon, Brody. Do you really think your father would've approved of me had my mother not agreed to-or was forced to-take his invention? Had that invention not turned me into what he hoped? His love for me was conditional. You had it because you were his-naturally-pure. Your father came from nothing-made the GAN from nothing-no enhancements, physical or otherwise. You came from that, Brody and you pissed on it."

"Shut your mouth," Brody's fingers flexed on the butt of his gun.

345

"You think he hated you because you weren't me? He hated you because you weren't him."

Brody's movements were swift. He aimed and a shot rang out across the beach. A howl followed as Brody stumbled and fell, clutching his calf where the bullet tore through his pant leg.

Pope scanned the direction of the shot's origin. He was making out Rutger and the others just as the air exploded with a second shot. Brody had reached for the gun at his waist...and used it on himself.

Mercuri and Rutger broke into a run, followed swiftly by Slayte and Bear who flung herself against Pope when she reached him.

"You don't listen worth a damn, you know that?" Pope's words were fierce against her hair.

Bear didn't care and only held on tighter.

"Little idiot," Pope drew her up higher.

Bear turned her face into his neck, breathed him in. "It wasn't my fault," she shuddered.

"She's right, Po," Mercuri said. "We met her on the road, made her come with us."

Pope nodded. "Thanks, man."

Rutger approached then. "I only meant to disarm him."

Pope reached out to squeeze his friend's shoulder. "Looks like that's what you did."

Rutger looked back to Brody Alberts' lifeless form, his clothes, hair and face doused by sticky sand. Pope squeezed Rutger's shoulder again.

"One of us was going to end up dead today and I'm fucking elated it wasn't me." Pope sighed.

Mutual grinning turned into quiet chuckling. Rutger nodded and then moved on to join Mercuri and Slayte who were heading back toward the house and the sound of sirens in the distance.

Pope set Bear to her feet and she immediately turned to study Brody Alberts lying a few feet away.

"Hey?" Pope didn't wait for a response, but took Bear with him in the opposite direction. He didn't want to spend any more time there than necessary but he knew the authorities would require some kind of explanation.

They walked a ways down the beach in silence and then Pope was pulling Bear down to sit with him in the sand. He drew her into the vee of his thighs and rocked her against him for several minutes. The quiet roar of the waves soothed and reset a better mood.

"I'm sorry, Cub. This thing...between me and Brody it's been stirring up for years. I'm sorry you got caught in it. Even sorrier you had to see me..."

Bear turned when he didn't finish the thought. She didn't need him to.

Pope didn't look at her, but kept his gaze narrowed. Blue slits emitted a fierce fire fixed on the endless sea. "I almost believed I was done taking lives, but I knew. I always knew that part of me was still there waiting...like something...dormant but ready to spring into action any time."

Bear scooted to her knees, grazed his jaw beneath her nails until his eyes met hers. "I'm sorry to hear you questioning yourself. You don't deserve that."

His smile was quick. "We are who we are, remember?"

"But we can't live our lives being defined by the past. I'm sorry you had to go back to a dark part of it, but I'm damn glad you were here today."

Tears made her eyes sparkle and Pope put a hard kiss to her mouth before setting his forehead to hers. "And I'd do it again in a goddamn minute."

"I'm still sorry about this." Bear glanced back in the direction they'd come. "He was your brother," she said.

"My brothers are there," Pope nodded to where Mercuri, Slayte and Rutger were leading a few plain clothes detectives toward Brody. "They're my family. All I ever needed. All I ever thought I'd want."

He gave Bear a little tug and she saw in his eyes what he hadn't put into words. "Are you saying you're in the mood for more family?"

"Well..." Pope gave an exaggerated shrug. "Mercuri's giving me a sister. I figure the time might come when he'll expect me to give him one back."

"Mmm..." Bear relaxed against his raised knee. "You do realize some sisters can be hard to handle?"

"Yeah," he winced playfully. "I'm getting an education on that."

"Oh? And how's that going?"

He cringed then. "Hard to tell. My teacher's pretty hard to figure out."

"So she's tough?"

347

"She thinks she is."

"A challenge?"

"Oh yeah."

"She sounds great."

"She's excellent." Pope eased Bear closer, awed by her richly colored eyes and the way they enhanced her delicate loveliness.

"I love her a lot," he spoke with a reverence, strongly mingled with certainty.

Bear drew her fingers through his hair. "And she loves you too." She smiled as the locks were wind-whipped about his face.

They resisted the kiss they very much wanted to share. Instead, they came together in a fierce hug and lost track of how long their embrace held.

***

### Soiree Weekend~One Week Later

Bear smiled, content as the radio station resumed its promised 50 minutes of commercial-free soft jazz. Though she adored the music, it was the news that she found especially enjoyable.

The Brody Alberts matter was viewed as one of the swiftest open and shut cases on record. Brody's death had been ruled a suicide. Rutger shooting Brody had been ruled self-defense given he'd arrived to find the man aiming a gun at his unarmed friend.

Pope's and Bear's involvement in the deaths was seen as self-defense as well. As the broadcast stated, officials currently believe that Brody Alberts' murder of Shaun Oates was part of a strong arm ploy to bring Bear Arms under the control of his floundering crime syndicate's west coast operations.

*...It is believed at this time, Brody Alberts tracked successful California businesswoman Berrill Clayton to the home of her rumored love interest Pope Apostolou. Alberts tried to abduct Ms. Clayton in an attempt to recover security footage that not only put him at the scene of the Oates murder, but shows Alberts himself committing the crime. In a bizarre twist, California Senator Christopher Morrow is being questioned regarding his involvement with the deceased. Alberts was the senator's plus one at a recent event for the Bear Arms soiree weekend. We will continue to follow this unfolding and fascinating story.*

Life was good, Bear thought, relaxing back on the Jeep's windshield while she took in the view of the night sky. She'd given her opening soiree weekend remarks which were; at first, more solemn given the recent loss she and her people still grieved. Encouragement infused her speech though when she charged her guests with the task of making that weekend the best on record in remembrance of one of her most dedicated people. Following pulsing applause, Bear made small talk for a short while before taking her leave.

She heard a distant engine and smiled when she saw Pope's truck. He parked at an angle next to her Jeep and doused the lights. Instead of leaving the cab, he angled out to gaze at Bear from across the roof.

"My flatbed's a lot more comfortable for what you're doing," he said.

"Well I'm only looking at the sky, you know?"

Pope shrugged. "For now."

"I've got guests, Mr. Apostolou. They expect me to handle myself accordingly."

"Speaking as a guest, I can say you're damn right about that."

"Hmm…" Bear's expression was playful and curious. "I don't think you qualify as a guest anymore."

"How do you figure?" Pope left the truck then.

"Well Rutger's got free admission to the ranch for life. So...your gesture, sweet as it was, is unnecessary."

"But surely it still grants me *some* compensation?" He stood in front of her before the Jeep's hood and tugged her to the edge.

"What have you got in mind?" She asked.

"I'll tell you once you're in my flatbed."

Bear linked her arms about his neck as he carried her the short distance to his truck. "So there's talking involved in addition to my star gazing?"

"Oh yeah Ms. C., there's sure to be talking…"

Bear laughed while Pope placed her on the folds of the down comforters that lined the flatbed. She sobered when she focused on his expression. He looked as though he'd never seen her before. His fingertips stroked her brow and the curve of her cheekbone.

"I love you," they declared at once and laughed once their words hit the air.

349

The evening's star gazing was postponed until much, much later.

Dear Reader,

I hope you've enjoyed this second installment in the Sleeping Giants series. Thanks so very much for taking a chance on this storyline that really hit me out of nowhere. I've had the best time creating this tale of danger, intrigue and of course romance. While there is no shortage of villains in this wicked brew, I hope that the spice and steam between Pope and Bear added that touch of sensuality that I, as a reader, look for in the romantic suspense stories I enjoy.

This story was a treat to write, but also a step into new territory as it allowed me to pen a series title that could stand on its own. If you haven't read book one in the series *Intoxicated*, I encourage you to do so.

There are more giants to come and I do hope you'll be on board for the ride.

Email me with your thoughts or post a review.

Very Sincerely,
Ally Fleming aka AlTonya Washington
altonya@lovealtonya.com
www.allyfleming.weebly.com

## "CONQUERED" CAST OF CHARACTERS
*(In Alphabetical Order)*

### <u>A</u>

**Brody Alberts**- Son of Nathan Alberts
**Dennis Alberts**- Cousin of Brody Alberts
**Nathan Alberts**- Co Founder of the GAN
**Pope Apostolou**- Hero of "Conquered"

### <u>C</u>

**Berrill Clayton**- Heroine of "Conquered"
**Edgar Cooper**- Senator

### <u>D</u>

**Thomas Doyle**-Senator (Deceased)

### <u>E</u>

**Rutger Eliades**- Best Friend of Pope Apostolou

### <u>F</u>

**Gerrick Ferguson**- GAN Chief Medical Officer

### <u>G</u>

**The GAN**- Grodins Alberts Network
**Jake Grodins**- Lorne Grodin's Son
**Lorne Grodins**- Co Founder of The GAN

### <u>H</u>

**Prin Holland**- Best Friend of Berrill Clayton
**Mike Hough**- Bear Arms Assistant to Berrill Clayton

### <u>I</u>

**Hoyt Ingram**- Member GAN Science Team

# <u>K</u>

**Jean Kearney-** Bear's Head Housekeeper

# <u>L</u>

**Rich Lehman-** Senator Morrow's Campaign Team Member

# <u>M</u>

**Edmund 'Ned' McCaffrey-** Member GAN Science Team
**Thurston McCambridge-** Doctor for Bear Arms
**Claude Mebane-** Partner Womack, Mebane Urnst Attorneys
**Slayte Miltiades-** Best Friend of Pope Apostolou
**Christopher Morrow-** Senator

# <u>N</u>

**Mercuri Nikolaides-** Best Friend of Pope Apostolou

# <u>O</u>

**Shaun Oates-** Bear Arms Assistant to Berrill Clayton

# <u>P</u>

**Dorinda Patterson-** Brothel Owner

# <u>R</u>

**Luke Robb-** Member of the GAN
**Eduardo Roya-** Son of Enrique Roya
**Enrique Roya-** Personal Pimp to the GAN

# <u>S</u>

**Daniel Schultz-** GAN Medical Team Member
**Etienne 'Tee' Shaw-** Best Friend of Berrill Clayton
**Caleb Stein-** Member of the GAN

# <u>T</u>

**The Ten-** GAN's Governing Board

## U

**Walter Urnst-** Partner Womack, Mebane Urnst Attorneys

## V

**Harris Van Deer-** Member of the GAN

## W

**Irwin Womack-** Partner Womack, Mebane Urnst Attorneys

## Y

**LuCarolyn Young-** Best Friend of Berrill Clayton

## Z

**Grant Zubin-** Member of the GAN

*An AlTonya Exclusive*

www.ingramcontent.com/pod-product-compliance
Lightning Source LLC
Chambersburg PA
CBHW030403180626
46812CB00005B/1909